ENGAGED IN SIN

SHARON PAGE

1 3 5 7 9 10 8 6 4 2

First published in the US in 2011 by Bantam Dell,
A Division of Random House, Inc.

Published digitally in the UK in 2011 by *Rouge*,
an imprint of Ebury Publishing
A Random House Group Company
This edition published in 2012 by *Rouge*,
an imprint of Ebury Publishing
A Random House Group Company

The Random House Group Limited Reg. No. 954009

Addresses for companies within the Random House Group can be found at www.randomhouse.co.uk

A CIP catalogue record for this book is available from the British Library

The Random House Group Limited supports The Forest Stewardship Council (FSC®), the leading international forest certification organisation. Our books carrying the FSC label are printed on FSC® certified paper. FSC is the only forest certification scheme endorsed by the leading environmental organisations, including Greenpeace. Our paper procurement policy can be found at:
www.randomhouse.co.uk/environment

Printed and bound in Great Britain by Clays Ltd, St Ives PLC

ISBN 9780091950323

ACKNOWLEDGMENTS

Sometimes writing a book is a process that involves an author traveling down a few wrong paths before finding the right direction and the perfect way to tell the story. I'd like to thank the people who were there for me during the ups and downs of the writing process.

Thank you so much to my editor, Shauna Summers, for ensuring that this book became the best it could possibly be, and for always being enthusiastic and supportive.

A huge thank-you to my agent, Jessica Faust, for being there at all times, even through more than a few "frazzled author" emails.

Much gratitude to my critique partners for guidance, brainstorming sessions, moral support, and baked goods.

Thank you as always to my wonderfully supportive husband, and to my children, who have been so patient during those times when Mommy has a deadline.

And, especially, thank you to my readers. You make it all worthwhile.

Chapter One

August 1815

The first time she'd tried to sell her body outside the Drury Lane theatre, Anne Beddington approached a handsome black-haired gentleman, without knowing who he truly was.

He had been gentle and kind. And young—perhaps only a few years her senior. Twenty-one to her seventeen, she guessed. He smiled patiently at her even as he refused her offer. Somehow he'd known at once that she was a virgin, that she had never prostituted herself before. He pressed a couple of coins into her shaking hands, then he tipped up her chin to look at her.

She'd never gazed directly into a gentleman's eyes. He had violet irises—a color so unearthly it gave him a fey air—and thick black lashes. One look and she was bewitched.

"Angel, this is not a thing you want to do," he'd said grimly. "You are an innocent and are pretty despite all that grime. Take the money and use it to go home to your family."

He assumed she'd left her country family and run away to London, or that she had come to Town to find work, as so many girls had to do. Nothing could have been further from the truth for her.

She had clutched the coins in her palm—two gold sovereigns—embarrassed to be given his charity when she'd been quite prepared to earn her money, but she had swallowed her pride, lifted the hems of her threadbare skirts, and scurried back to her mother's bedside.

The money had not lasted long. Her mother had needed so much laudanum for her pain. Eventually Anne had been forced to do what the gentleman had warned her not to.

Now, five years later, she was about to do the very thing she had failed to do that first night outside the theatre. She was going to convince the Duke of March to bed her.

This time she was not in London. And this time the duke was her captive quarry. She stood in his study in his hunting box—a manor house in Leicestershire—with her hand still on the door handle. He was sprawled out in front of her on the carpet, more than six feet of brawny, tanned, *naked* male. His long legs were splayed apart, his bare buttocks relaxed. His black hair fell in a mess of waves to his shoulders. An empty brandy decanter lay by his outstretched hand.

He appeared to be dead to the world.

Anne's heart tripped in her chest. *Was* he only unconscious? With his chest squashed against the rug and his mouth turned away from her, she couldn't tell if he was breathing.

If he had polished off an entire decanter of brandy, could he have drunk himself to death? She didn't know. In the slums she'd seen men drink quite a bit, but could a man stomach that much?

She glanced to the study door. For privacy, she had closed it behind her. Should she summon the odd, terrifying butler who had met her at the door? The stooped man had a hump on his back, tufts of yellow-gray hair at his ears, and a large gap where his front teeth should have been. He'd tried to shoo her away. She had been firm, though he'd cackled in the most revolting way when she informed him she was a gift from the Earl of Ashton and must see the duke at once.

She really did not wish to deal with the butler again.

Lifting her hems, Anne hurried to the naked duke and crouched beside him. Her body cast a shadow over his face, but she could see scars on his cheek above the haze of thick black stubble. His lips were full and soft. They appeared completely motionless.

Her throat dried. She bent close and felt his breath whisper over her cheek. Then he gave a low, rasping snore, and Anne choked on a relieved giggle.

Should she shake him awake? She had been a whore for so long it meant nothing to touch a masculine body, but she didn't know quite what to do with an unconscious duke who had no idea she'd invaded his home.

Would summoning help end with her tossed out on her rump? What if the butler suspected she'd knocked the duke over the head? She shivered. The room was damp and chilly even though it was late August. Drawing off her gloves, she brushed her fingertips over the bronzed shoulder in front of her. His skin was cool. A silk throw lay across a wing chair. She plucked it up. The chill of his skin made her feel cold; it made her shiver once more, just for him.

Gently, she arranged the blanket over his smooth, muscled back. She tugged it down to his slim waist, to cover his hips, buttocks, and legs. His bottom proved tighter, rounder, than any she'd ever seen, his legs long and powerfully built.

Any woman would quiver, faced with such male beauty, but she knew there was fear beneath the tremble of her shoulders. A man this strong could easily hurt her.

He had been kind to her once, so long ago, but she now intended to lie her way into his bed.

First she had to wake him. She gently touched his forehead to brush back his hair. A thick lock had fallen into his eye—

His hand shot out and clamped onto her wrist. A scream flew out into the room. Hers.

The duke moved so fast, she couldn't think. He pushed her down to the floor. His big hands pinned her shoulders and he was braced over her, his legs on either side of her hips. His knees pressed into her skirts. She stared up into his eyes. Still violet and every bit as astonishing as they'd been five years before.

"Your Grace." Her voice was barely a croak. "Your Grace, I—I did not mean you any harm. I am the woman the Earl of Ashton sent." The lie dropped off her lips. She prayed he believed it. Lord Ashton had no idea she'd overheard his conversation when he had been trying to coax another woman to come to the duke—her friend Kat, who already had a protector.

The duke's heart pounded against her breasts. His gaze still focused over her head. His eyes didn't look injured at all. It was only because he didn't focus on her that she could tell he was blind. Everyone in England knew the hero of war, the Duke of March, had miraculously survived a bayonet wound to the head that should have killed him, but he had lost his sight. A deep scar disappeared into his hair.

"Hell," the duke muttered. His head dropped, then he rolled off her, landing hard on his side on the floor. "Ashton sent you? You are the whore he thought would heal me with pleasure?"

Anne flinched. She still did at the word *whore*. Even though she had been one for a very long time. He spoke with such a dismissive tone, her stomach churned.

"Yes," she said, trying to sound confident. As saucy as a paid ladybird should.

"Didn't Treadwell frighten you away?"

"He made an admirable attempt, but I was insistent. After all, I had direction from Lord Ashton to see you. I do not understand why you would engage such an odd creature as your butler. Do you wish to frighten callers away?"

"Yes, angel, I do."

Anne struggled to sit up and her corset jabbed into her, below her breasts. She hissed in pain.

The duke reached for her. She took his hand and he pulled her upright.

"I'm sorry I leapt on you, my dear. But why in Hades did you creep up on me without announcing yourself?"

"Your butler directed me to your study, then left me to my own devices. I entered alone and found you asleep."

"Passed out, you mean." The lashes dropped. He stroked the stubble on his chin—more of a beard than simply stubble. He must not have shaved for many days. "Don't ever do it again. I could have killed you."

"Killed me?" she squeaked.

"Yes, angel," he snapped. "I could have wrapped my hands around your pretty neck and broken it before I came to my senses. It's a souvenir from the war: When I'm not expecting someone to touch me, I sometimes think the person is trying to kill me."

A shudder tumbled down her back. "Well, I am not." What had she gotten into? Could he really have killed her and then, when it was far too late, discovered she was no danger to him at all? Should she run from him now, before he hurt her?

She almost snorted at her own cowardly foolishness. Where would she go? Back to London to face the noose? Surely she had nothing to fear around him if she was careful.

"Angel, just what kind of whore are you?" The duke had cocked his head, obviously focusing intently on her words. "You sound as ladylike as my sisters. I haven't heard such a cut-glass accent out of the most cultured of London's courtesans."

Of course she sounded ladylike. She had been raised as a lady until she and her mother had fled from their home. It was her speech that had distinguished her at Madame Sin's brothel. She'd been called "the little duchess."

His eyes narrowed; his expression was cold, and suspicion laced his voice. "This isn't some sort of plan to push me into the leg irons of matrimony, is it?"

"Of course not," she gasped. "I am very much a courtesan, I assure you." She might have an ulterior motive, but it certainly wasn't *marriage*. "If you want me to be a lady, I will play one, Your Grace. If you want me to be the boldest, brassiest siren who ever climbed on top of you, I'll do that too." Her cheeks flamed as she spoke—even after years of being exactly what she claimed to be. He couldn't see it, thank heaven, but what on earth was *wrong* with her?

She saw his bare chest rise on a long, sharp breath. Apparently she'd said something that he liked to hear. But when he let out all that air in a whoosh, he groaned.

"Ashton had no right to engage your services, my dear."

She froze. "P-pardon, Your Grace?"

"Ashton thinks a good fuck is all I need. He's wrong."

Wrong? Raw panic flared. Then she remembered what she'd overheard the Earl of Ashton tell Kat when he had pleaded with her friend to come and service the duke. "Lord Ashton worries because you are . . . hiding here, Your Grace. That was how he put it. He thought you should have some pleasure. That it would make you . . . feel better," she ended lamely.

"Angel, I can't even see you. You could be the most voluptuous beauty in England for all I know. Not seeing you is only frustrating me."

Unfortunately, she was not the most voluptuous woman in the country. Fear was coursing through her, making her ice cold. She had known she was not the courtesan Lord Ashton wished to hire, but she'd thought the duke at least *wanted* a courtesan. She hadn't anticipated he would be as unwilling now as he'd been outside the theatre. She didn't know what to do. At Madame Sin's, she'd never had to work to coax a man into bed. She hadn't had many clients. Madame had kept her exclusively for valued customers, had charged the earth for her. The men had willingly paid the exorbitant price, because they wanted her.

"He's very concerned for you, Your Grace." Her nerves jangled like bells, but she managed to drop her voice to a purr. "He only wanted you to be pleased. I'm very good." She stroked her fingers along his arm. Along the largest bulge of muscle she'd ever touched. He was correct: If he wanted to, he could hurt her badly. Once more, fear rippled through her veins, but she forced herself to speak. "We could do it in the dark. Then it wouldn't matter that you can't see me."

"It will always matter that I can't see, angel."

He grasped her hand, gently this time, and lifted her fingers from his skin. He didn't even want her to touch him. Groaning, he leaned back, his broad shoulders falling against the side of a chair. There was such a look of emptiness on his face. "You've wasted your journey."

"Please." She had to become this man's mistress. *That* would not happen if she did not get into his bed. She scuttled across the floor until her breasts pressed against his muscular arm and her words brushed across his ear, which was mostly hidden under his long, unkempt black hair. "Won't you let me pleasure you?"

He took a harsh breath. "God . . . you do have a lovely voice, angel. I grant you that."

Her voice was tempting him. He could not see her, but he could hear her. That and touch were the only weapons she had. She lowered her voice to a husky whisper. "Thank you."

"But it's not enough." He moved away from her so they no longer touched.

She refused to let hope sputter out, but why wouldn't he yield? A man didn't need sight to make love. Any number of gentlemen preferred the dark.

"You can travel in my carriage to the staging inn at Welby, my dear. My man will purchase your ticket to London and see you safely onto the coach."

Harsh laughter fell from her lips before she could stop it.

Safety and London did not belong in the same thought for her. She could not go. Instead, she had to take desperate action. Even if she had to leap upon him. Or take him into her mouth and drive him so mad with desire he couldn't resist. Surely once they were joined, he would forget his lack of sight and think only about pleasure—

Abruptly, he grasped the side of the chair, hoisted his long, powerful body with one swift motion, and landed gracefully on his bare feet.

He towered above her. Gazing upward, she felt her jaw drop. Despite spending the last five years first as a viscount's mistress and then a lowly prostitute, she hadn't seen many men completely naked. Certainly none with broad chests and abdomens formed solidly of muscle. None as lean, roughly hewn, and beautiful as the duke.

A strange, long-forgotten yearning fluttered deep inside her.

Fool. This was business. Best dealt with unemotionally.

The duke went to take a step but swayed slightly on his feet. He let out a ripe curse and clapped his hands to his temples. "Bloody head. I should hack it off with an ax for all the use it is to me now."

Anne supposed he meant he was suffering the aftereffects of too much brandy, but there was so much bitterness in his voice. The Duke of March was troubled and angry. She understood why the Earl of Ashton had pleaded with Kat to help his friend. Good sense told her to agree with the duke—how could sex make up for being injured in battle and losing his sight? But she had to believe in it and convince him of it, or she would have to return to London with nothing and probably end up hanged.

She needed a different approach.

She clambered awkwardly to her feet, but at least the duke could not see that. Hesitantly, she touched his elbow. Perhaps because she did it lightly, it didn't disturb him. He didn't move away.

"I came all the way to make love to you, and that is exactly what I intend to do, Your Grace. The earl said you hadn't been with a woman for ages. Months. Why deny yourself the release you must need?"

Her dress was one of Kat's old ones, but still too fashionable for her to reach the fastenings herself. A few tugs and she managed to push the bodice down. Gathering courage, Anne clasped his hand and placed his palm over the upper curve of her left breast.

She gasped at the contact. At a sudden, surprising jolt that made her breasts ache. It must be the fear roiling through her that made the simple touch so intense—she had never felt anything like that before. A shock of sensation rushed through her as his hand slipped under her bodice and shift, and the calluses on his palm scratched across her bare nipple.

"It is just sex," she whispered. "Surely you must want to have sex."

But instead of cupping her breast, he dragged his hand away, then raked it through his hair. He looked as though he'd accidentally stuck his fingers in the fire.

She had to try harder.

His lips parted, and she knew he was about to command that she go. She surged forward and did the one thing she hadn't done for years and years. Arching up on tiptoe, she kissed him.

She hooked her arms around his neck. She felt the strong, corded muscles of his throat, unyielding against her arms. He tasted tart—of brandy. His lips were hot and firm and stayed closed against her assault. She pressed her tongue to the tight seam of them, but he wouldn't let her inside. Instead, he moved his face back, breaking their kiss.

Refusing to give up, she wriggled against him until there wasn't a breath of air between them. Then she felt it—felt his shaft lift and stiffen against her skirts. It was hard and long, pressing against her belly. A surge of victory took her. She had done it. She'd made him want her.

Breathless, she slid her hand from his shoulder, across the curls of hair on his chest, following the line of the soft downy hair to his navel, then lower. To take him in her hand and caress him.

"Stop," he growled.

She did. But she kept her fingertips against the firm, warm skin of his lower abdomen. He didn't move her hand. It must mean his resolve to send her away was weakening.

Suddenly, idiotically, she felt *guilty*. It seemed wrong, this calculated seduction she must carry out. Normally, her encounters were straightforward. Madame's brothel had rules, of course. Any gentleman who purchased her knew exactly what she was willing—and allowed—to do. If he desired something different, he must go to another girl. She'd never had to be a seductress and entice a man to do what *he* didn't want.

The duke hadn't wanted her five years ago either. But she had to win now: Her life depended on her success.

She teasingly stroked the hard ridge of his nude hip. "I want to pleasure you. Nothing more than that."

"And payment," he pointed out drily.

"Of course I have to earn a living," she said simply. "But you must need sex, after so long."

"I attacked you, you damned stupid girl. Didn't that frighten you, or don't you have the wit to understand what I am?"

"You are a wounded man—"

"Hell." The duke grasped her arms and pushed her away. He took a brisk step back. His hip banged the arm of the settee, but he did not even flinch. "Do you know what wounded animals do, or haven't you encountered a beast like me in Town? We bite. We just might kill."

"You didn't really hurt me, though." No, she knew what it was like to be truly beaten and wounded. If she clamped her teeth together, pain still shot through her bruised jaw. Her face was still sore from her madam's slaps. Her chest and back bore faded purplish-yellow bruises from the punches inflicted by Madame Sin's brute of a bodyguard. Her only saving grace was that the duke could not see how battered she was.

Every twinge of pain from those bruises was a reminder she was facing death. Whether it came at his hands, the hands of the law, or from starvation, what difference did it make? He was, in fact, her best hope for survival.

She forced her voice to lower an octave. "How would you like to have sex, Your Grace? Perhaps hard and fast, with a big explosive climax at the end? Or slow and sensual? You could spend an hour or two lazily thrusting your hard cock into me."

"Damn . . . damn. Damn." His breathing was ragged. It was obvious, when she let her gaze slide below his waist, what her suggestions and his imagination were doing to him.

"All right." He bit the words off.

She couldn't quite believe her ears. "You want to do it?"

"Yes. I suspect it's the only way I will get rid of you." His mouth quirked up for an instant, then dropped into a grim line.

Anne steeled herself for the next step. She licked her dry lips and pushed her gown lower to expose her breasts, which sat high, perched on the shelf of her stays. She tugged down her filmy shift to completely uncover them. Feigning bold confidence, she asked, "How would you prefer it, Your Grace? You can have anything you want."

"I'm enjoying your search," she whispered.

His tongue stroked across her nipple, pushing it in. It popped out after the hot, wet sweep of pressure, and it was plumper, harder, and almost throbbing with sensation. Her knees were rapidly turning to jelly. Anne clasped the prominent bones of the duke's hips to stay on her feet.

She had never felt so . . . unstable, so light-headed and strange when a man did things to her body before penetration. In the brothel, she was *always* in control with a gentleman; she always played her part to perfection. It had kept her from being punished by Madame. She *must* be in charge of her wits now.

To prove she was in command, that she was not going to give in to nerves or the unusual dizzy feeling in her head, she gave a sultry moan. One of her best.

The duke fondled her derrière and licked her nipple with the tip of his tongue. She felt the oddest . . . warm, aching feeling low in her belly. With a pang of sadness, she saw that the duke kept his eyes closed. Was it so he wouldn't be reminded he was blind while he touched her?

A soft moan slipped out from between her lips. One she hadn't planned. One that was *real*. It was too squeaky, not sultry at all.

His Grace stopped for breath. "If I am going to make love to you, I would like to know your name, angel."

Anne. It sounded so dull. Anyway, her name had been given to the Bow Street Runners, who had been called in after Madame's death. She had to give the duke a false name. A *new* name—a brand-new one for a whole new life. "Cerise," she murmured. It had been the color Madame had chosen for her, a scandalous scarlet. Now she must act like the sort of bold jade who would willingly wear a red silk gown and shove her bosom at a man to get his attention.

"Lovely," he whispered in return, then he opened his mouth wide and took quite a bit of her left breast into his mouth. She wasn't sure whether her name or her nipple was lovely.

He suckled hard. It was too much, the sensations too strong. She'd planned to be bold. Instead, she went stiff and tense. This wasn't pleasure anymore, but she closed her eyes and fought to endure. She mustn't stop him and risk ruining the moment. She couldn't displease him.

The duke sucked fiercely with his eyes closed, long ebony lashes pressed to his cheeks.

He freed her breast and she swayed with relief—until he moved to her right one. His large hand slid beneath the curve to cup her gently, and he fondled her lovingly. She knew he wanted to hear he was pleasing her. She parted her lips and let out another planned moan, the perfect one for this moment—breathy and filled with surprise, as though he was giving her ecstasy she'd never known before. And, in truth, this caress was . . . nice.

His Grace rewarded her with a raw chuckle. "Like it?"

"Oh, yes." She wanted him to think everything he did was perfect. Moisture glistened on both her pink areolas. Her lace-trimmed bodice was crushed between their stomachs, her corset digging into her. "Do you want me to undress?"

"There's no need." He cocked his head. "Are the drapes drawn? Is the room dark?"

"Yes." For the first time, she really looked at his study. His house had surprised her when she'd arrived by horse and cart from the village inn. It was a large manor house, symmetrical and solid, surrounded by lawns and woods. It was very similar to the house she had lived in during her childhood, the house she deliberately did not think of now.

This house seemed far too modest and simple for a

duke. The study, however, was filled with beautiful things. A globe stood by the draped windows, beautifully fashioned and lettered, set upon a stand decorated with gilt. Enormous paintings of horses covered the walls. All the chairs were leather club chairs, inviting and comfortable. Books were everywhere: on shelves, stacked upon tables, even piled on the seats of the chairs.

This was a gentleman's room and one that looked well loved. Yet it seemed so tremendously sad that it was filled with things the duke could no longer see.

"I want to take you from behind," he said bluntly. "At my desk."

Whatever he desired she must grant. It was not quite what she'd imagined for their first time together, but she did not dare contradict.

"All right." Anne took both his hands. She lifted one and sucked suggestively on his index finger as she backed to the large gleaming desk that stood along one wall. This way she could lead him without wounding his pride. When her bottom reached the smooth, polished wood, she stopped. He reached around her and felt the curved edge of the desk.

"Turn around," he said, with the curtness that lust often brought to a man's voice. Many girls in the brothel found roughness exciting. They liked lust-driven men. Anne never had before, but now she felt a flood of relief. His harsh tone proved she had gotten exactly what she wanted. The Duke of March now had to have her.

"Of course, Your Grace," she purred. She braced her hands on his desk and he drew up her skirts. The weight of the silk skimmed over her legs. She pulled the mass of fabric in front of her, bunching it between her stomach and the desk edge. His hands ran up her bare thighs. She closed her eyes. And moaned, as she knew she must, as his fingertips reached her private place.

"God, you are so hot," he murmured. "Soft as silk."

She expected him to thrust in hastily and steeled her body for a swift invasion. But he cupped her with his hand and he kissed the back of her neck, nuzzling her skin. A tremor raced down her spine—a little quiver of pleasure. This was not quite right. Why did he not want to be inside her? Was he not ready enough? At Madame Sin's, men had rarely touched her; after all, they had paid generously for her to be willing and ready without any need for foreplay on their part.

Anne arched her back and wriggled her bottom, brushing it across the duke's hard shaft. The motion drew a hoarse groan from him. She looked over her shoulder. He was panting. Deep lines bracketed his tight mouth. He was obviously aroused, but apparently he needed more.

She swayed her hips, swinging her rump across him, but he grasped her hips and stopped her.

"No, love. Not yet." He reached between her thighs once more and gently played with her. No man had ever stroked her so slowly, manipulated her with such care.

She gave a gentle sigh. She did like this touch . . .

But then his finger found her sensitive nub and rubbed there.

Every inch of her body tensed. He rubbed harder, assuming she would like it. The sensations were more powerful than those from her nipples, too strong for her to bear. At least he could not see how she winced and shut her eyes, how she had to fight not to protest. She played her part, giving him a crescendo of throaty groans, making them louder as his fingers opened her.

Then he slid inside. Deep, deep inside.

She had the fleeting feeling she always did—that it was so strange something this intimate could feel so . . . distant. Then she remembered what she must do. She had to be a *courtesan,* not just a vessel for his release. She must please him. Delight him. Tempt him.

He was behind her, his groin pressed to her bottom. She felt full, uncomfortably so, but she whispered, "Oh, yes. *Yes.*"

The duke began to thrust. Slow, deep thrusts. She arched back against him, filling the room with her moans.

He reached around and stroked her breast. That startled her, making her stumble in her rhythm. Then he did what she expected—he grasped her hips, held her steady, and plunged into her. Good. Now she knew exactly what to do.

Her moans rose to screams. "Oh, God," she cried. "Oh, goodness." She pushed violently back against him, crying out as though in sheer ecstasy. She listened to his breathing. When he was panting hard, obviously growing close to release, she wailed, "I'm coming." She knew how to display an orgasm, but could all her writhing impress the duke, when he could not see it? All he could do was feel her bottom thrashing against him.

He thrust harder. Faster.

Then he growled, low and deep. His hips drove forward and collided with her bare rump. His body rocked back and forth, climaxing inside her.

"Oh, my," she gasped.

He collapsed against her, braced on his arms. "That was lovely, angel."

Thank heaven he had liked it.

He straightened, withdrawing. Her inner thighs were sticky. She'd forgotten she could not tend to herself and clean up at his house. At least she didn't have to worry about his seed—she had put a vinegar-soaked sponge within, a trick she'd learned at Madame's.

He stroked her hip softly. "I will have some water fetched, my dear."

"That is very considerate, Your Grace." She suddenly realized how unprepared for this she was. She wanted to be his mistress, but she had no idea what to do. Kat, who *was* London's most desired courtesan, had told her a mistress must cater to her protector's every whim and make him feel like a king both in bed and out. But Anne hadn't asked how to actually do that. Her gaze landed on rumpled blue silk lying on a chair, near where she had found him passed out. "Would you like me to fetch your robe?"

His lip lifted in a rueful smile. "Thank you, love."

When she brought it back, she helped him into it, but just that meaningless bit of aid made his face darken. He tied the belt and paused thoughtfully. "Tell me why you speak so well for a prostitute, Cerise. Where do you come from?"

"I am the most sought-after incognita in London, I will have you know," she said airily. Incognitas were mistresses who spoke and behaved like ladies. "Do you think the earl would have engaged anyone but the best and most desired courtesan in London to please you?"

"Honestly, love, I would have thought Ashton would keep the best and most desired courtesan for himself and send someone else for me."

"Then that was his mistake."

The duke laughed. "You have distracted me for a while, love, and for that I thank you." He lifted her hand and softly kissed her fingers. His mouth lingered. Her heart lifted.

"I can distract you more, Your Grace."

"You have done enough, Cerise. I am sure Ashton will pay you well."

He was dismissing her again. She panicked. "There is so much more I could do for you—"

"I want to be left alone. It was pleasurable. But our time together has come to an end." He sighed. "I don't even know what time of day it is. I assume it is nighttime. That you arrived in the evening?"

"Y-yes. At half-past eight." Suddenly Anne realized he had been already passed out with an empty brandy decanter at such an early hour.

"Tonight you should stay at the inn in Welby. Take a meal there. My man will ensure you receive excellent service. A mention of my name and you will be well treated."

It was a kindness, but her teeth tore at her lower lip. There had to be something she could do to convince him to let her stay. She could not give up so easily.

"Ring the bellpull, love," he commanded.

She didn't move. He could not see. He could not find the rope himself and have her sent away.

"Do not displease me now." His voice was deep and smooth, but there was iciness creeping into it. If she annoyed him, she would ruin her chances of seducing him into keeping her. If she did as he asked, she would be in his carriage in mere minutes.

"You will have to go, Cerise."

It was a final command, issued by a gentleman who had sent soldiers into battle. But terror put words on her lips. "I cannot, Your Grace. I can't return to London."

Perhaps her tone made his head jerk up. "Why not?"

Oh, goodness, what was she doing? Telling the truth, like an utter fool. But she dared not tell him all of it—he would have his servants drag her to the nearest magistrate. No one there would believe her. No one would take the word of a whore. Not one who had been forced to hit her madam with a poker to save the life of an innocent girl and was now considered guilty of murder. She hadn't meant to do it. She had only wanted to stop her vicious madam from shooting a fourteen-year-old girl. She had meant to hit the pistol from the woman's hand. But she had killed Madame, and she would be convicted of murder and swing for it.

"I—I lied to you, Your Grace," she said shakily. "I'm

not a courtesan. I was employed in a brothel and I escaped. If I return to London, I do not doubt the madam of the brothel will find me. Or send a footpad to murder me, as an example to the other girls." Heavens, how easy it was to lie. When one's life depended on it.

"Angel, I doubt she would kill you. I doubt she would be so concerned—"

"She *would*." But Madame could not anymore. The woman was dead, and the lurid tale of her death was in the news sheets. Perhaps the duke had not yet received the London news or had it read to him. But even if he knew nothing about Madame's murder, he might hear about it soon. Was she mad to tell him she'd run away from a brothel? Wouldn't he naturally reach the conclusion she was the whore suspected of murder?

She swallowed hard. If he didn't already know, maybe she could prevent him from finding out. She might be safe as long as he hadn't heard the story. "Please, Your Grace. Please let me stay and pleasure you as Lord Ashton wished. You cannot see them, but I—I still have bruises on me from my madam's beatings." She must be truly desperate to have told him she was damaged, but she took his hand and touched her waist, her low back, her shoulders. "There. I'm bruised in all those places." Then she held her breath.

Her heart almost dissolved in pure relief as he held out his hand. "Come here, Cerise."

Surely he wouldn't be so gentle if he thought her a killer. Still, she quivered as she went.

With gentlemanly aplomb, he lifted her hand to his lips. He couldn't know about Madame's murder. How could he and brush such a soft kiss to her fingers?

"You can spend the night," he growled. "Tomorrow I'll decide what to do with you."

Chapter Three

SOMETHING EXPLODED RIGHT in front of him, and Devon Audley, the Duke of March, did what any soldier with sense would do—he launched himself at the ground.

His hands and chin hit soft carpeting. Instant recognition hit him harder than the floor. He wasn't on a battlefield, the sound hadn't been cannon fire, and the French army wasn't firing on him. He couldn't see anything but a blue-gray void, yet he knew he'd just leapt to the floor of his hallway in front of a servant—a servant who must have dropped something.

Devon tried to slow his breathing, tried to relax the instinctive hammering of his heart.

"Yer Grace! A thousand apologies. Clumsy oaf that I am, I dropped me tray and the brandy snifter landed on the floor. No worries though—it was the empty one."

The apology came in Treadwell's roughly accented voice. A hurried shuffling moved toward him from down the hall. Devon recognized his butler's limping footsteps. Treadwell had a deformed right leg, and his foot dragged along the floor. Devon used to assume walking was a torture for the man, but the butler bore his affliction with surprisingly good cheer.

Hell, Treadwell would try to help him up, and the man was in no shape for that. Devon grabbed his walking stick and levered to his feet. He jumped up as gracefully as he could. No doubt he'd done this enough times that his butler was accustomed to his mad behavior, but it didn't make it any less humiliating. By now Treadwell must be convinced he was completely out of his wits.

"Well," Treadwell said amiably, "I was coming to tell ye that yer supper's prepared. I took the liberty of having it served in the dining room. Is the . . . yer guest going to join ye for the meal, then, Yer Grace?"

His guest. Devon groped his way to the wall and splayed his hand on it. He had to touch something to orient himself, though he had no idea how far down the hall he was. Damn Ashton and his daft idea that sex was the answer to every man's problems. Maybe it worked for Ashton, given the fact that Tristan de Gray, Fifth Earl of Ashton, was an even more notorious and frequent visitor to London's brothels than Devon had ever been.

Sex without sight hadn't done what Tris had hoped. Devon couldn't forget he was blind. He could smell the pretty rose perfume his *guest* wore, and he could cup her rounded bottom and pert breasts, but he would never forget he couldn't see any of those delights. Still, he had to admit she intrigued him. She was so determined to get into his bed. Where had Tris found her?

She claimed she had escaped from a brothel, so where would Tris have encountered her? She didn't speak like the sort of light-skirts he used to find in whorehouses. There was something surprisingly sweet and innocent about her and her desperate enthusiasm to entice him. Even her attempts to be brash had been . . . endearing. Could she really think a madam would be willing to hunt her down? In his experience, madams were hard, astute businesswomen. Would one have a girl killed to keep the others in line? But Cerise was genuinely frightened—he'd heard the truth of that in her voice. There had to be more to her story than she'd told him. . . .

Hell. He had to send her away and stop thinking about her. He'd told Tris not to send a woman. He could have killed her, the poor foolish chit, as easily as he'd warned her he could. Already he'd snapped his valet's wrists when the man had done nothing more than remove his coat. Watson, the valet, had quit on the spot and run from the house.

He was going mad. "Battle madness," one of the war surgeons had called it as he was recovering in a field hospital. At that time, he'd mocked the idea—he was blind, not insane. How could any man not savor peace once war was over? Now he knew. He couldn't forget the war. It wouldn't leave him alone. And he had no intention of making her suffer for it.

"Yer Grace?"

Devon cocked his head in the direction of Treadwell's voice. "No, she will not be joining me for supper. Have a tray prepared with her meal and taken to the bedchamber she will be using. Send a bottle of good sherry as well. Give her one of my robes for her use."

"Are ye certain she'll be needing one, Yer Grace? Shouldn't ye be keeping her . . . busy?"

"Treadwell, bloody hell." First his friend, now his servant.

"Beg yer pardon, Yer Grace, but Lord Ashton told me as how he's worried about ye and the way yer keeping yerself locked away in the house, and I happen to say I agree. It's not healthy for a young gent such as yerself."

"Thank you for your opinion," Devon growled. "I

wasn't aware the dispensation of unwanted advice was on your list of duties."

He'd never been the kind of duke to glower at his servants. It would be impossible to do so now. Hard to strike fear with a ducal glare when one couldn't even look in the correct direction.

"It's not me place to speak, Yer Grace. Yer grandfather would have had me horsewhipped if I talked to him like this. But yer not like yer grandfather, the old duke, Yer Grace. A right tyrant he was, and he would brook no talk from anyone."

True, he was nothing like his grandfather, a fact that had annoyed that man a great deal. Nor was he like his father. He was somewhere in between the libertine tyrant his grandfather had been and the kind, scholarly sense of responsibility that had characterized his father.

"Meself and the others—we know ye've been a grand master, and all of us are worried about ye. Now, if ye want to send me to the stables, ye can do so, but I've had me say."

Treadwell had given sixty years of service to Devon's family, beginning as a boot boy to his grandfather. A man who had to spend his childhood as a servant with an old man's foot resting on his arse deserved some sort of perquisites in his later years. Letting him speak was the one the old servant seemed to enjoy the most. "Treadwell, you won't be whipped."

"Well, now, Yer Grace, I should fetch ye for yer meal."

"I don't need to be fetched. I do not need to be led to the dining room like a dog on a leash."

"'Course not, Yer Grace. But let me say one more thing before I leave ye. That girl is a comely lass. Very pretty indeed."

He didn't need to know. For a start, he could not see her, so what did it matter if she was a beauty? But curiosity hammered at him. Relentless curiosity. "All right, what does she look like exactly?"

"She's got lovely silky hair in me favorite shade, Yer Grace. Titian, I think it's called. Green eyes too. Not a light green, like emeralds, but dark as ivy leaves. A lass that lovely is not going to like having to spend her night alone."

He was left stunned by Treadwell's description but got his wits back and gruffly said, "It's not a matter of what she likes. It's for her own good."

Anne paced the bedchamber—the *duke's* bedchamber. He had ensured her every comfort. A fire crackled in the hearth, warding off the chill of the rainy August night. Candles glowed around the room, the golden light falling on gilt and polished wood. The duke had sent a footman with a robe, one of his own. It was made of soft dark-green velvet, wrapped almost twice around her, and trailed on the floor.

The same footman had brought sherry and a delicate crystal glass. Another had brought supper. Her heart had dropped to her toes as the servant, his face impassive, placed a large platter on a table by the fire and lifted the silver cover to reveal a gold-rimmed plate heaped with roast beef, boiled potatoes, and vegetables.

She'd hoped—*expected*—the duke would summon her for supper.

Then she'd received the news that had truly whipped the carpet out from beneath her feet. Since returning to this house two weeks before, the footman had told her, the duke always slept in his study. He did not make use of his bedchamber at all.

The servant then relayed the rest of the duke's crushing message. She would be spending her night undisturbed and she was not to trouble herself by going to him. *His Grace would prefer to be alone,* the servant had intoned without expression, *until morning.*

Anne walked the length of the room again, her robe dragging behind. Appetizing scents still filled the air from her meal, but she couldn't eat. Not with a stomach clenched in panic. In the morning, the duke would decide "what to do with her." Tonight was her last chance to convince him to keep her.

The only way she could do that involved his bed. She had to do something to him—something carnal—he wouldn't be able to resist. Something he wouldn't be able to live without once he'd experienced it.

But she had made love to the Duke of March with enthusiasm and abandon, and it appeared the earth had not moved for him. He had not begged her to stay.

How could she get another chance at seduction? He didn't want her near him.

She nibbled at her thumbnail. For the first time since she'd decided to seduce the duke, penned a quick note of explanation to Kat, then used all her remaining money to hire a carriage, Anne was beginning to question her plan.

The Duke of March was a notoriously experienced man. She was a very ordinary woman. She wasn't a stunning beauty. Her appeal in Madame's brothel had been her demure ladylike looks, her blond hair, her proper demeanor and speech. At twenty-two, she still looked like the kind of young woman who should be dancing at Almack's, yet she had been available, for a price, for almost any sin a gentleman desired. Now she was too thin, since she'd been barely able to eat for days, and a henna dye had transformed her once-admired golden hair to a brassy red.

A little voice whispered deep in her head. *You simply weren't* enough. Was she just not very enticing? Or was it possible the duke had sensed she was not feeling anything, even though she'd given a good performance of moans and ecstasy? Kat had told her it was not much different to be a mistress than a prostitute, but now Anne was not so sure.

Fiercely, she shook her head. She could not give in to doubt. If she did, she was going to end up hanged. She *had* to be enough, and the next time they made love she would try much harder to entice, dazzle, and enthrall him. . . .

She would have to ignore the duke's command. She had one last throw of the dice. He might toss her out on her backside tonight for disobedience, but she had to *try*.

Anne strode to the door and opened it. She stepped out, ready to march to the study, when she heard a loud sound, like a cry of pain.

Was she imagining things? Had someone really shouted? She waited. No other sound came. No rushing footsteps. No voices. If someone needed help, no one was racing to provide it.

Then it came again: a deep, hoarse shout. It had definitely come from the first floor of the house. It was most decidedly a masculine sound. It must be the duke. But why weren't his servants hurrying to help him? What was wrong?

It took several seconds for her wits to work. This was her *opportunity*. Whether it was the duke or not, she could say she believed it was, then of course she had to run to him and ensure he was all right. It gave her the perfect excuse to invade his study.

Goodness, what if he was truly hurt? He might have drunk more brandy. He might be foxed out of his wits. She'd heard of drunken men who fell into their fireplaces and set themselves on fire. He could be in danger.

Anne gathered up the voluminous hems of her robe and ran for the stairs.

* * *

Warm hands clamped on his arms. Devon's eyes shot open, but he stared up into darkness. Cannon fire had surrounded him seconds before; now there was eerie silence. He couldn't mistake the weight pressing on his biceps. Someone was pinning him down.

He threw all his strength against the soldier holding him. A desperate gurgle of shock came in answer. He had the advantage for a few seconds before the next thing securing him to the ground proved to be a bayonet. In one swift movement, he gripped his attacker by the arms and jerked the man up.

His brain registered the slender arms, the surprisingly light weight. *Boy,* his mind screamed at him, guilt rising like bile, but then a voice cried, "Stop!"

A panicked voice. A feminine one. "Stop, Your Grace! Please stop. You are hurting me." Her terror cut through the void, sliced through the panic and the deafening pounding of his heart.

Christ. It was Cerise's lush and lovely voice. It whisked away the fog in his head, shattered his confusion. He wasn't on a battlefield; he was lying on his settee in his study. The hands touching him had been hers and not those of someone holding him down to kill him.

On a desperate groan, he released her. He sank back onto the cushions.

"What is wrong, Your Grace?"

Devon sucked in more heavy breaths, trying to slow his heartbeat. "It was just a bad dream," he managed. Sweat coated him, cooling now that he wasn't thrashing around in his sleep. A chill washed over his bare chest.

Her soft hand stroked his cheek. She coasted her fingertips over him tenderly. "I know something about nightmares," she murmured gently.

He lifted her hand from his face. Fumbling, he reached

for the back of the chair to hoist himself up, but something planted itself on his chest. The surprise of it kept him down, and a warm weight settled across his thighs. He guessed she was straddling him. And he tensed.

"Are you certain you don't want to sleep in your own bed?" she whispered. "I would hate to cause you trouble and discomfort, Your Grace."

Trouble and discomfort. It brought a dry laugh up from the depths of his throat, one that scratched like glass on the way out. "The reason I'm not in that bed has nothing to do with you, love, so you might as well go back there. I'm not in the mood for more lovemaking tonight."

"I can get you into the mood."

"No." She didn't deserve to have her windpipe crushed because he was out of his mind.

Her weight moved, sliding lightly back down his thighs. He knew her bottom was skimming over his legs. "Go to bed, love," he growled. "I'm accustomed to the nightmares. I get them almost every night."

"Every night? Heavens."

He hoped he had shocked her into giving up, but she whispered seductively, "I could tire you out with a climax so you could have a good night's sleep."

His robe twitched open over his hips. A blast of cool night air rushed over his groin.

He had to stop her, but a warm, wet pressure ran down his sleeping cock. Sensation shot through him. He couldn't see, couldn't be sure, but he thought she was running her tongue along his shaft. His head dropped back as the pleasure of it speared him. The soft heat of her tongue caressed his flesh, swirled over the head. Suddenly his cock went hard, proving his words wrong. His body wanted this. Yearned for this.

"Mmmm." Cerise gave a moan of approval, then his shaft was engulfed in warm heat. In her mouth.

He closed his eyes. He did it so he wouldn't remember he could see nothing but a blue-gray nothingness, but instantly he had a vision of the wild black eyes of a terrified boy soldier and a rifle aimed to blow a man's head off—

She suckled, and the suction of her hot lips jerked him off the battlefield, back into the present. Back to his study, where he was sprawled on the daybed and she was lavishing her tongue all over his rigid cock. She was remarkable. Of their own accord, his hips began to rock up, seeking to push him deeper into the welcoming wet heat of her mouth and her delectable sucking.

"God, angel," he groaned. "It's good."

"Thank mmm." Her words came out muffled and he had to laugh—a raw bite of a laugh. She had him smoldering, close to bursting into flame.

Tentatively, he reached down until his hand collided with silky softness. The long mass of her hair. It spilled over his abdomen. With so much pleasure coming from a few inches below, he hadn't noticed the sweet, tickling sensation.

He ran his hand lower, until he found a silken curve that had to be her cheek. Gently, he eased her away, and the sensation of sliding past her velvety lips almost made him explode. "Ride me," he growled. "Ride me hard and fast until you pound everything out of my head."

She giggled. He was straining to hear everything, so he detected the demure notes in her light, lovely laugh. The way it was shy rather than bold. She was such an unusual prostitute, with her pretty voice, her proper speech, and her uncertainty.

Then she wrapped her hand around his shaft and he couldn't think about anything but the way she held him, the tug as she lifted him upright, the first touch to her silky heat.

He arched his hips up, needing to thrust deep. Her bottom smacked his thighs as she came down, and he rocked up into her, lifting her high, joining them as tightly as he could.

He'd begged Cerise to ride him, but he didn't give her a chance. He did the work. Lifting her to bury his cock to the hilt worked his muscles to the limit. Thrusting made sweat roll down his forehead and coat his chest. He had to do this. Had to thrust like a madman. And know only the sheer delight of sliding his erection deep inside her, of feeling her walls hug him tight, the delicious friction as he withdrew.

It was heaven. Heaven for a man who'd earned a place in hell for what he'd done.

Devon laughed as the weight of her bottom jiggled up and down on his spread legs, as she gasped and moaned and cried out. Cerise was a noisy lover. Her shrieks and squeals must be echoing all over the house.

He loved hearing them. He couldn't remember the bursts of cannon fire and rifle shot when she squealed and wailed and shouted, "Oh, goodness!"

Her hands smacked against his chest as she braced herself. Sweet as her voice might be, she rode him with hard, punishing strokes as though she knew, without words, exactly what he needed.

But he wanted to watch her bosom bounce and her hips move as he rocked her. He hungered to see her face contort with agony as he thrust. Wanted to know the color of her beautifully soft hair. See her eyes as she found pleasure too.

He yearned to see her, damn it. Hell, how he did.

Frustration boiled in him. He shut his eyes and made love to her even harder than before. He should be gentler; he should slow down, yet she gripped his shoulders and pounded on him.

"Yes, Your Grace," she cried. "I like it hard."

Then her hands—it had to be her hands—ran down his thighs and she gripped his bottom. His John Thomas swelled and grew bigger, stiffer, ready to burst. Devon tipped back his head and howled to the heavens above. He wished he could make love to her for the rest of his life. So he never had to think or remember again.

He wanted to please her. He had to hold on. Fight to last, fight for control so he could make her scream for him in ecstasy.

"Cerise, love, what do you need?" he rasped. "I won't last."

"This!" she cried. Then she gasped, "Oh, Your Grace!" She gave a long, agonized moan, bouncing wildly on top of him.

Her lushly erotic scream ripped through him, and he lost control. His arse lurched up from the sofa and he drove hard into her. His body went rigid as his orgasm roared through him, spun through every nerve, took every ounce of his strength. His muscles seemed to turn to fluid. Every thought left him. There was nothing but pleasure and the pulsing of his body as the almost endless climax pummeled him.

Devon flopped back onto the settee beneath her, a ragged laugh rising from his chest. Deep inside, his heart hammered.

Cerise collapsed on him, gasping too. Her breasts, warm and damp, crushed to his chest. The earthy scent of her surrounded him, as if enclosing them in a world built solely of pleasure. He wrapped his arms around her, cradling her tighter than he'd ever embraced a woman before.

"Are you sleepy, Your Grace?" she murmured, her voice throaty after all her screams. "Or do you want another bout?"

"All right, love. Another round." He rocked gently into her. It would take time to get aroused again. He shut his eyes and stroked her, letting his fingers see her where his eyes could not. *Much better this way.* She had the perfect back, long and slender, with a sweet dip at the bottom. He took care as he caressed her, remembering how she had described her bruises. He cupped the flare of her curvy bottom. She had a delectable rump. Lightly, he ran his fingers over her rounded derrière, savoring her hot, silky skin, and she giggled in her pretty, endearing way.

She possessed a lot of hair, and it fell over his chest and shoulders like a silken throw. He gathered a mass of it in his hand, moved it so it fell over his face and he could breathe in the scent of it. He was hard again. Ready to pound into her. Ready to make her burst—

The vision came so quickly and slammed into his head so hard, he was amazed it didn't knock him off the chair. He was back on a smoke-strewn, deafening battlefield. An enormous weight pinned his legs—the flank of his dying horse. Through a gap in the dark ash and struggling bodies, he saw the boy. A French lad. Ragged uniform. The boy had lifted a rifle, and his skinny body was jerking with tension as he got ready to shoot one of Devon's men. Before Devon knew it, his pistol was in his hand.

A split-second choice. Shoot a soldier who was little more than a child or let a good man die—a man who'd left his wife and child to go to war.

He'd had to make the choice. That damnable, haunting, inhuman choice—

Cerise shifted on him.

He couldn't do it. He couldn't make love. Not now. He grasped her arms and hauled her off him, and she squeaked with surprise and fear as he dropped her down hard on his thighs. She scrambled forward, but he tightened his hold on her wrists so she couldn't move.

"You—you're hurting me."

"It's not going to work. Nothing you do will make the demons go away. You need to get off me and go upstairs, back to bed."

"Demons?" she whispered huskily. "What demons, Your Grace?"

"Go away, angel."

"The nightmares? Is that what you mean? You could tell me about them. I want to help you." Her voice was purring temptation. The silly git wanted him to unburden his soul. To her.

"No."

"Please, Your Grace, I am yours to help you in every way I can." She ran her hands over his chest, down his abdomen, to his privates. She stroked him there. "I'm going to fondle you until you tell me."

She thought she could tease him into some kind of sanity. Like Ashton, she thought all it would take was a bit of conversation and some fucking. "You have no idea, love. I've seen men torn apart by cannonballs and bullets."

She gasped, and he knew it was in horror. But she wasn't going to stop, was she, until he frightened her away?

"Even that's enough to flood your mind with grisly images, isn't it? You do not need to hear any more. Once you've seen things like that, you can't make them go away. I can no longer see the back of my hand, but the color of human blood? Unforgettable." He needed a drink. Needed to be alone. Right now he didn't want to have to talk. He sure as hell didn't want to hold anyone. He lifted her off his thighs, intending to plant her on the floor, but when he let her go, he heard her gasp in shock, heard her fall to the floor.

"You need to get away from me," he barked, furious with himself. "Go up to your room."

"I should stay. In case you have another nightmare—"

"And you'll try to wake me? Put your pretty neck in my reach? What if I strangle you? Or start beating you to death because I'm out of my wits?"

"Y-you won't."

But she wasn't sure, was she? He wasn't bloody well sure. "I've hurt people, Cerise. Don't you remember how I grabbed you and threw you to the floor when you first came here, because you touched me? And what kind of a touch was it?"

"What do you mean?"

"I mean what did you do to me that made me leap up and slam you onto the ground?"

"I—I brushed your hair out of your eyes."

"Exactly. It was an inconsequential touch, but it set me off like a flame reaching a keg of gunpowder. I'm mad. The war, the battles, the blindness, the killing and the grief—I wasn't strong enough to let it all just glance off me. I'm no war hero—all throughout the damned thing, I was filled with pain and fury and grief and doubts. A hero is a man who is filled with confidence, who takes action and doesn't waste time on remorse. He doesn't hide in the blasted dark. He gets a damned grip on himself. But I can't. I've gone out of my wits, and I'm going madder by the day. I'm not getting better, I'm getting worse. That's why I have Treadwell to scare people away."

"You are drinking too much," she said firmly. "That is probably why you are getting worse. If you were to stop drinking—"

"I like drinking," he snapped. What was wrong with the chit? Didn't she recognize the need to get away from him and stop arguing?

"But it doesn't help—"

"It helps me. And I intend to do a fair bit of drinking

right now. So you need to get out of this room and leave me alone. For the rest of the night, you will stay in that bedchamber. You will not come out until I summon you."

Devon expected to hear her footsteps patter across the floor. If there ever was a cue for a woman to hasten out of a room, this was it. But, no, the stubborn wench was not moving.

"Go," he roared. "Get out *now*."

He should have felt satisfaction as her feet slapped against the floorboards, then the door slammed—obviously behind her as she left. Instead, he now needed a drink because he felt like a blackguard. *War hero*. His bark of laughter rang in the room. What a blasted joke that was.

Chapter Four

WHEN SHE WOKE, Anne dazedly thought she was at home again. At Longsworth.

Rain drummed against the windowpanes with the patter of an excited heartbeat. A window had been left slightly open, and the room was filled with country smells she remembered: the crisp, cool scent of early morning, the rich aroma of wet hay, the nose-tickling perfume of meadows as wildflowers went to seed.

Dazedly, she rubbed her eyes. A forest-green silk canopy soared above her head. It was so very much like the one that had been over her father's bed. Once when she was very little and playing hide-and-seek with her nurse, she'd hidden beneath Father's bed. The hiding place had proved to be too good, hours had passed, and she'd fallen asleep there, sending the whole house into an uproar—

Sitting up abruptly, Anne kicked back the heavy counterpane and the silky sheets. She shook her head, shook away memories that made her throat ache and brought longing up in an engulfing wave.

She would *not* think about the past. That part of her life was over. The young girl who had lived in that house was gone and might as well be dead. And, depending on the duke's decision, she might truly die, convicted for a crime she'd been forced to commit to save a child's life, hanged even though she had acted to protect and Madame had been the one willing to kill.

No. She would not let it happen. To survive, she'd had to do so many sinful things. She would *not* give up now.

The rug was warm and cozy beneath her bare feet, but the cool, damp morning air penetrated her filmy shift and nipped at her bare skin. Shivering, she crossed to her dress, which she had draped over a chair of polished oak and green velvet. Her corset lay in a heap on the seat. She left it there and pulled on the gown.

Bother dresses. This was one of the gowns Kat had given Anne after she, and the three girls she'd rescued, sought refuge at Kat's house. It was a low-cut creation of scarlet silk, and her friend had given it to her with a wave of her hand, claiming it was now a whole Season out of fashion and no longer of use. Anne didn't believe that. Kat was being kind and generous, just as she'd been so very, very good to let Anne hide in her home and ask her friends to help the girls. Anne had known she couldn't stay—Kat could be arrested for harboring her. Then the Earl of Ashton had come. Anne had hidden behind the parlor door while the fair-haired earl had begged Kat to help the duke, who was Kat's friend. Ashton had pleaded with her to give March sex to help him heal, as he'd put it. Kat refused, but Anne believed she had the perfect solution. She would go—she would leave Kat and keep her friend from trouble, and she would save herself.

The gown gaped at her breasts. It was fashionable enough that it hung on her without proper underpinnings. There was no way she could lace her corset by herself, nor could she fasten the back of the dress. And she had left Kat's in such haste she had no other clothing except her cloak, bonnet, and gloves.

Someone knocked lightly on her door, and the most delectable scents wafted through from the other side. Anne let the dress fall in defeat and dragged on the borrowed robe. "Come in." She prayed it was a lady's maid—someone who could help her dress.

But when the door swung wide, a footman backed in—the same wide-eyed young man who'd relayed the duke's message the night before. He carried a tray laden with dishes. Steam coiled into the air in front of him. "Your Grace insisted this be sent up, miss. And he"—the young man blushed beneath his powdered wig—"requests that you eat heartily."

Before he sent her back to London, His Grace meant.

The last thing she could face was food. She waved the tray away. "I can't accept it. I've trespassed on his kindness long enough."

The footman looked stricken. "His Grace will be angry if I don't deliver this as I'm supposed to. I don't want him displeased with me."

The lad appeared to be absolutely terrified. Why? The duke had fought her last night, but that was during a dream. The rest of the time he was controlled, cool, and gentle. Far kinder than she deserved, given she was telling him a pack of lies. Though he had mentioned he threw chairs . . .

One thing she realized: The duke must be awake if he'd arranged for her breakfast. "Where is the duke? In his study? Or is he eating in a dining room?"

"I think His Grace is in the library, miss."

The library? It seemed . . . odd, since he could not read, but perhaps it was a pleasant room. "I will need a maid to help me with my clothing."

The lad vehemently shook his head. A poppy-red blush flooded his cheeks again. "His Grace used to have parties—naughty ones—here. So no women servants, His Grace said. He has me mum and me sisters come once a week for cleaning and dusting. And His Grace wishes to see you after your breakfast. When you finish, miss, if you ring for me, I'll take you to him. He told me to say he wants to ask you some questions."

He bowed and she waved him out. She could have slammed two of the silver lids together in frustration. She had no way of getting dressed.

What sort of questions did the duke want to ask? Fear roiled in her stomach. Did he not believe her story? It shouldn't be a surprise—her tale was weak and filled with holes. Last night he'd been obviously suspicious. After all, he was right—a London madam would hardly spare a thought for a whore like her. There would be a dozen more innocents who could be plucked off the streets to replace her. Surely, though, he couldn't know about Madame Sin's murder. He wouldn't have let her stay if he suspected she was the object of Bow Street's hunt.

Her plan had been as filled with holes as her story. She'd believed that, because he was hiding here in the country, she could keep her identity a secret and become his mistress. How could she have hoped to do that forever?

Remember, Anne, it doesn't have to be forever. Young handsome dukes probably didn't keep mistresses for longer than a few months. By then, from gifts he gave her, from the allowance he would provide, she would have enough money to escape.

She glanced toward the window. A long drop to the ground, but dense woods ringed the lawns beyond the house. She could easily disappear in there. She could try to run now. . . .

But even if she did manage to avoid the Runners, how far could she get with no money? She'd used all her blunt to send three young girls from Madame's brothel back to their homes and then to hire the carriage that had brought her here. The only way to truly escape was to leave the country, but she couldn't afford passage on a ship.

Perhaps the only thing she had left was honesty. She should tell the duke everything.

Yes, tell him about her confrontation with Madame Sin and what had happened when Madame was going to shoot one of the three virgins Anne was trying to rescue. She would have to tell him Bow Street wanted to arrest her and admit that the Earl of Ashton had not paid her to come to him. Perhaps once he heard the truth, *all* of it, the duke would believe her. He would believe she did not deserve to die for saving a girl's life. He would—

Anne almost laughed aloud at her foolishness. A duke would not help her. Would he care that she'd acted to defend herself and the girls? Or would he condemn her for being a murderess and believe she should hang, regardless of the circumstances?

"Damnation, why do this? Why torment yourself by touching books you'll never read again?"

Devon groaned. He didn't have an answer. And wasn't talking aloud to himself another sign he was losing his mind?

His fingers closed around a book and he pulled it off the shelf. He felt the leather binding, the smooth gilt of the title. But he couldn't distinguish the letters by touch. It was all he had left—his senses of touch, smell, his hearing. So far he'd decided it was a fallacy that his other senses would grow better. He didn't think they had improved. They were just all he could use.

He breathed in the different smells: the mustiness of old books, the rich scent of leather bindings on the new ones, the tickle of the dust that clung to unreachable corners. His friends thought he'd taken the house solely to hold wild orgies, but he had liked to spend many of his evenings here reading. He'd stocked the shelves with thousands of books. Books his father never would have imagined he possessed. His father thought he spent all his time gaming, drinking, and skirt-chasing—and it was true he had spent most of his life doing that. Then, to everyone's amazement, he had fallen in love. With Lady Rosalind Marchant. He had plummeted into it so hard and so fast it felt as if the world had rocked beneath his feet.

Rosalind had died before he went to war. His father died while he was in battle. He would never have the chance to talk to his father again. Never have the chance to apologize for the last argument they'd had—when he announced he'd bought his commission, and his father told him it was a damned stupid and selfish thing for the heir to a dukedom to do.

Devon launched the book toward the long table that stood in the center of the large library. Glass exploded. Right in the middle of his void, and he knew what he'd done. Misjudged, lost track of exactly what direction he was facing, and threw the book out the window.

"Your Grace, I—I brought you this letter. It came for you." Hurried footsteps crossed the floor toward him. The servant sounded like a young lad—a terrified one.

"Who is it from?" Devon asked, but he knew the answer even before he heard the lad's frightened stammer. Who else would write to him?

"H-Her Grace, Your Grace. Uh . . . the Duchess of March."

Why did his mother continually send him letters when she knew he couldn't read them?

Of course he knew why. How else was she to communicate with him when he wouldn't go home? He couldn't go home, no matter how much he wanted to. Not when he could explode without warning and hurt someone he loved. He was too damned dangerous.

The letters might make his gut clench with guilt, but they let him know his mother and his sisters were well and safe. "You'll have to read it, lad. What does it say?"

"I—I don't know how to read, Your Grace," the young servant said with a surprised tone, as though the boy thought he was cracked for asking.

His valet had read the other letters to him. But with Watson gone, there was no one left in the house who could read.

"Perhaps it's time you learned," he muttered. He stepped forward, his hand outstretched. He had no damned idea why. It was instinct to move toward the letter, wherever the hell it was, and his shin smashed into something sharp and hard.

"Christ bloody Jesus," he roared. Pain shot up his leg. First the book, now this. He couldn't manage to get around in his own blasted house. He reached out and his hand slammed against smooth wood. He grasped it. It proved to be a small octagonal table. A useless piece of decorative furniture. In one swift motion, he hefted it into the air.

Seconds later the table exploded, hitting the floor with a thunderous crash. It made a skidding sound across the wooden planks. The satisfying *crack* of splintering wood echoed through the vaulted room. The footman yelped.

"Have that thing chopped into kindling," he barked. "Now."

"Y-yes, Your Grace."

Feet scuttled across the floor. The lad puffed, wood scraped. Devon groped his way to the fireplace mantel. He wrapped his right hand around the edge of it. Now he knew where he was. He would stay here so he would not look like a helpless idiot again—

"Do you wish to break anything else?"

The feminine voice made him jerk around. It was his would-be courtesan. The woman who had hauled him out of a nightmare last night, whom he had almost hit in return. She had been in his house only a dozen hours, but he already knew the nuances of her voice. Sultry and purring when she was trying to seduce him, melodic and light when she laughed, and sometimes, like now, as crisp as unripe apples and surprisingly authoritative. Indeed, she was like no prostitute he'd ever encountered before. What had she been before the brothel?

"Could I help?" she added. "I've always wondered what it would be like to throw something just for the sake of breaking it."

"Break whatever you like," he growled. "I'd never know the difference anyway."

Anne's heart lurched.

She regretted her sharp words. She should have been sympathetic rather than sarcastic. Her reaction had been instinctive—she hated the explosive and senseless violence men used. Her cousin Sebastian had used it to make her and her mother cower after he had inherited their home. Brutes used it in London stews to make women terrified and obedient. Madame Sin's bodyguard, Mick Taylor, a former pugilist, had used it to keep Madame's whores in line.

But now, when she saw how grim and pained the duke looked, Anne ached with compassion. He had simply thrown on trousers and a shirt—the tails of the wrinkled white linen trailed over his taut buttocks. His dark hair reached his shoulders. The thick stubble covering his jaw yesterday seemed to have grown more overnight. It looked like an unkempt beard this morning.

She remembered the beautiful gentleman with the dazzling violet eyes who had given her two gold sovereigns to spare her from selling her body. How different this man looked. The careless grin was gone. He looked so . . . ravaged.

Anne knew what she'd felt when she'd lost her mother, in that moment when she'd realized she had finally lost everything and everyone she'd ever loved. Anger. Horror. Despair. A pain so deep she had sat on the floor of their filthy room for two days, unwilling to move. Had the duke felt that kind of grief when he'd opened his eyes on a battlefield to sudden blindness?

She wanted to go to him. She wanted to slide her arms around his waist, press her lips to his wrinkled linen shirt, and trail kisses over his broad chest. If there was ever a man who looked as though he needed a woman's loving embrace, it was the Duke of March.

She crossed the room, rounding a long table and a row of straight-back chairs. But when she reached the other end of the mantelpiece, a mere six feet from him, she stopped. It was mad. Yesterday she had touched his naked body intimately; now she stood awkwardly with her hands fisted. She yearned to touch him, but would it be welcomed? Softly, she said, "I don't believe you truly care so little for your house and your belongings."

He didn't turn toward her. His thick lashes shielded his eyes. "Sorry, love."

"I saw you collide with the table. It must have hurt you considerably. It frustrated you and you lashed out." She suspected she sounded as her mother used to, when they had lived at Longsworth. Firm, sensible, very matter-of-fact. "I assure you I can nimbly get out of your way if necessary."

His dark brow quirked. This time he cocked his head toward her. "You've seen me at my worst—I leapt upon you, I grabbed you by your wrists, and now you've witnessed the way I throw furniture across the room. This is why you cannot stay here, love. It's impossible. I told you I would decide what to do with you and I have. I won't be responsible for harming you."

"I don't understand why you are so certain you will."

"Angel, I know what I'm capable of. I know what I've done. You cannot stay. My carriage will take you as far as you want to go. If you want, I'll pay for your services and you can use that money to go wherever you want."

How much would he give her for a few tuppings? For one moment she considered it . . . then rejected it. It wouldn't be enough. She would have the chance to eventually escape only if she could coerce him to give her the kind of allowance and gifts a mistress received.

"I wish . . ." She wished there was some way to help him. To stop his nightmares. To help him cope with his blindness. When Grandpapa had lost his sight, it had been gradual, over years. Even then, he had been delighted when she would walk with him and describe the gardens and grounds of—of her home. And Grandpapa had loved to have her read to him.

Of course, her grandfather had not been tortured by horrible dreams or prone to fits of rage. He had been an elderly gentleman who loved country life, not a young duke in the prime of his life who had been a notoriously wild rake in London.

She gnawed at her finger. She hadn't wanted to think of the past, and she'd thought it had nothing to do with her now. But perhaps it did. Would the duke like the same simple things that had so pleased her grandfather? Would they help him heal? Was it not worth a try?

"What if I could help you in other ways?" Anne whispered. She spied the rectangle of white gripped in his right hand. "I can begin by reading your letter to you, Your Grace."

Before Devon could say a word, the letter was plucked from his fingers.

He reached out to retrieve it, but to no avail. "You can read?"

"Of course," Cerise said briskly, sounding much more like a governess than a saucy courtesan. "It is from the—the Duchess of March." There came a soft crinkling of paper. Her voice faltered as she asked, "Do you have a wife, Your Grace?"

He had turned to the mantelpiece, his hands braced on the crisp edge of the marble. "No, angel. I have a mother."

"Thank heaven."

"It is a relief to you to learn I have a mother?" He had to admit, he was a fortunate man where his mother was concerned. She had been loving, gentle, and had finally lost her temper with him only when he'd dumped himself into scandal over another man's fiancée.

"I just mean I would have felt terrible, having been your lover, if you'd had a wife."

Her genuine relief and the gentle way she spoke told him she would have been plagued with guilt—a sensation he was familiar with. It surprised him, though. "Angel, explain how you could be so softhearted after working in a brothel."

"I—I did not have many clients. I was very exclusive." Now she spoke in a fast, nervous tone. "I always assumed they came to me because they weren't yet married."

Her naïveté astonished him. How had she stayed so ingenuous?

"Certainly I never asked any of my . . . clients about themselves," she whispered. "They obviously did not want to have conversations of that sort."

That brought a wry laugh to Devon's lips.

* * *

Anne shivered as the duke gave a low chuckle. She didn't believe she had revealed anything dangerous, but she had to take more care. She could not let him find out who she truly was. Distracting him was her best plan.

"Wait, Your Grace, I must open the letter."

On a small escritoire positioned in front of one of the floor-to-ceiling windows, she'd spotted a letter opener. As Anne snapped it up, she couldn't help but look outside. Beyond the library lay a half-circle terrace of smooth flagstones, edged by a stone balustrade. Other terraces lined the sides of the building. Raindrops ran down the glass, and the rainy day deepened the green of the neat grass and lush, ordered gardens. Color still bloomed despite the approach of fall, flowers of gold and scarlet.

It was lovely. It was so much like Longsworth.

With shaky fingers, she slit the seal with the opener, then set it down—it was heavy, silver, and decorated with two exquisite and surely priceless sapphires. How easy it would be to take this. She could sell it for a fortune.

No. She couldn't. Her mother had clung to pride, to propriety, even as she slipped down one rung after another, first working as a seamstress, then once, only once, letting a man buy the night. But to steal—that was to fall from the ladder completely and drop into hell.

Anne opened the crisply folded pages. There were two, and the letter was dated two days before. Clearing her throat, she began to read aloud. "*'My dearest son . . .'*" Goodness, just that brought a little tug deep in her throat. She swallowed hard and continued.

> *"It seems there is no emotion you have not brought forth in me, Devon. For three years, I've known worry and fear, praying you stayed safe during war.*

Then frustration when you sent missives to tell us you would not come home yet and would make no plans to visit. I cannot think of you without knowing love, hope, and happiness, without smiling at memories of you as the stubborn, clever boy I adored.

"But now, dear boy, you have been giving me a grand lesson in despair.

"You cannot possibly believe we will think less of you or be disturbed by your injuries. We will do everything we can to take care of you. We long to have you close again. I have been yearning to embrace you for three years, and I am almost at the limit of my endurance.

"You must come home. It is as simple as that. You were a commanding officer in battle, and a fine one, from all accounts. A grand hero. As your mother, I have decided I shall issue you a few commands."

Anne had to stop. To catch her breath. To let the words sink in. This was a private letter. Should she go on? But if she did not read it to him, who would? She bit her lip, then read . . .

"All of your sisters are here, including Charlotte and her twins, now two and a half years old. Both your niece and nephew are eager to meet their uncle, of whom they have heard so many stories. Charlotte is enceinte once more. Caroline, who is visiting without her husband, is expecting her first child and rapidly approaching her time. They worry about you, as do Win and Lizzie, and I worry about the strain this has placed upon them all.

"Lord Ashton wrote to tell us you are well yet still stubbornly hiding at your hunting box. My dear boy, this cannot be helping you. It would be far better for

you to be with family. Your family, which has grown by leaps and bounds since you left England, longs to see you.

"You need love, Devon. From your family, and my dearest hope is that you will soon find love with a bride. A life filled with love would ease your troubles. I am sure of it.

"Come home to us and we will help you find a wonderful wife. You must find love, Devon, my dear, for love is the most precious thing. It heals. It gives happiness.

"What you need, my dear son, is a wife who loves you dearly—"

"Stop," he barked.

The words were blurry and Anne blinked two tears away. She lifted her head. The duke had bit out the word. His mother had poured her heart onto the page, was pleading with him, and he had snapped as though he was irritated. She eyed him fiercely. "Your mother yearns to see you. She's missed you. For heaven's sake, why would you not go and see your family?"

"I *can't* see my family."

"You won't go because you are blind? But they won't care about that." She thought of her mother, who had been ashamed when she became ill—ashamed she had fallen so low in the world, ashamed she could not take care of her daughter. All Anne had wanted was for Mama to be well. Nothing else had mattered. "They simply want *you*."

"I thought Ashton paid you to service me," he snapped, "not lecture me."

It struck her like a slap, but he was right. She had forgotten herself. "I'm sorry. I won't use my tongue for anything but your pleasure, Your Grace."

He groaned. "Damnation. Even when you're obedient, you make me feel the blackguard."

She should stop, but she simply couldn't. "I must say one more thing. Your mother is correct. You shouldn't stay here. You do deserve to find happiness."

"That's more than one thing. And I won't marry anyone when I can't see."

"Surely there are more important things than a woman's appearance—"

"I am not going to marry anyone when I have to be led around my own home like a dog on a leash." He glowered. "I won't have a wife turn into a trembling bag of nerves like most of the servants in the house have become because they are so afraid of me. Do you think I want to fall in love with a woman, then sentence her to life with a lunatic who can't control his rages, who sometimes crawls around on his belly because he imagines cannons are firing at him? I won't take a bride when I could have a nightmare and accidentally strangle her in our bed."

"I don't believe you can't be healed."

"Angel, admit defeat. I appreciate your pretty voice and your exquisite body, but I've made my decision—you're to go home, where you will be safe."

Not safe, but absolutely broke and with no hope. "I have no money left, Your Grace." She had not meant to reveal as much, but she was desperate.

"What of the payment Ashton promised?"

She'd forgotten that, because, of course, it didn't exist. Lord Ashton had no idea she was here. "Lord Ashton won't pay me now. Not if you've rejected me."

"I'm not rejecting you. I have no choice but to send you away."

"I wish to do what Lord Ashton asked of me. But what I really wish, Your Grace, is to prove to you I would make an excellent mistress."

Before she could argue further, her belly rumbled, then made the most embarrassing growl.

His brow lifted. "Did you eat any of the breakfast tray I sent?"

"No, Your Grace. I wanted to speak with you, and I was too nervous to eat."

He sighed. "Well, angel, you must have some breakfast."

There, she had done it.

Breakfast had arrived almost instantly after Anne tugged on the bellpull and the duke gave instructions to his nervous footman. After that, the duke had carefully avoided addressing her bold request. She had very little hope he would let her prove she could become his mistress, but at least he had not given her an outright refusal.

In the brothel, she'd learned all about waiting. Waiting for her next client. Waiting to escape. She'd never been patient when she was young. Whenever she had to wait, she was always frustrated and thoroughly unladylike—tapping her feet, pacing in circles, wringing her hands as though she wouldn't survive.

That was how she felt as three footmen had brought enormous trays, a carafe of coffee, gilt-rimmed plates, and silver utensils.

She jumped up to pour coffee for the duke. "What do you wish on your plate, Your Grace?"

He waved away the idea of food. Apparently the ham, sausages, bread, and kippers were intended for her. She put the coffee cup in his hand, and he gruffly said, "Eat, love. Your poor stomach sounded hungry."

It was true but embarrassing. Kat had tried to feed her, but even at Kat's home she'd been too nervous to eat. The sight of food, the wonderful smells wafting from the dishes, made her jaws ache in anticipation. She tentatively took a mouthful. The instant the sweet and savory taste of the ham registered on her tongue, her hunger exploded. The duke stayed quiet and still, and she looked up to realize he was listening to her eat. To ensure she *was* eating, she suspected.

Finally she set down her knife and fork and picked up her coffee. Accidentally, she made an unladylike slurp. It brought a smile to the duke's beautiful mouth.

"All right, Cerise, how can I help you? If you believe Ashton won't pay you, I am willing to give you a gift. Something to help you until you find another lover in Town. With money, you should be safe from your madam—"

"No!" she cried, far too vehemently, for his brows arched in surprise.

She swallowed hard. It was not only that she could not go back to London. The truth was, she didn't want to search for *another* protector. She liked the duke. He was far more gentle and kind than any man she'd known, other than Father and Grandpapa. "I don't want to accept charity, Your Grace. I propose a straightforward arrangement."

"I can't take a mistress, love. As delightful as you are, the idea is impossible."

"But I liked . . . giving you pleasure." Even as she said the words, she knew it wouldn't work.

"Angel, I don't want to send you back to London to danger. But I want the truth from you. I think that's the best way to start. Tell me everything."

"What sort of everything do you want?" she hedged.

He made a low growl in his throat. "What brothel did you work for? What's the name of your madam? And what exactly did you do to make her determined to kill you? It couldn't be simply because you escaped, love. Did you steal from her?"

"No!" Heavens, wouldn't her life have been much easier if she could have turned to stealing?

"Then what was your crime, love?"

Murder. She couldn't tell him that. "I didn't steal from her. I just escaped."

"For her to pursue you, she would have to want something from you. Or want revenge."

He might not be able to see, but he was astute and intelligent, and she was gasping with panic, trying to come up with a plausible story. Not the truth—not the fact that she had discovered that Madame Sin had kidnapped three young girls and was going to auction off their innocence. The thought of those frightened girls had snapped something inside Anne. She had found the room where they were held prisoner and had picked the lock. . . .

She couldn't tell the duke any of this. She had no idea how many details had made their way into the news sheets. But she had to give him a reason for her flight that he would believe. "My madam kept us like prisoners."

"Prisoners? You mean you were not allowed outside?"

She heard the skepticism in his voice. "No, not ever. My madam thought we would run away. She kept us locked up until we understood there was no real escape."

The duke scrubbed a hand over his jaw. "I was kept prisoner at one point by the French. A singularly unpleasant experience. You have my sympathies. But that's not all, is it?"

Warring emotions burst in her. A flood of warmth and hope at his gentle tone. And deeper, colder fear. "It is. W-when I escaped, I proved it was possible. Obviously other girls might follow. Our madam would lose her control. Her power."

How Madame had relished the power she held over them all. Anne remembered the madam's smirk of triumph as Mick Taylor, Madame's bodyguard, dragged Anne and the girls into the brothel's private offices. Madame had threatened that Anne would be given to the clients who enjoyed whipping their women and causing pain. She had slapped the youngest, then threatened the eldest, Violet, warning that she would be sent to the most brutal clients too. Anne had pulled the frightened girls to her skirts, determined not to let them go. Madame had calmly drawn a pistol and pointed it at Violet's head. *Let them go, Anne, you stupid fool,* she'd said, *or I will shoot that one between the eyes.*

Next thing Anne knew, the poker was in her hand, and she'd swung it with a roar of fury at the pistol. Madame lurched back and stumbled, and the poker slammed into her head—

"Cerise?" The duke set his coffee cup down carefully.

She took a deep breath. "I know my madam is capable of killing me, and I can only ask that you believe me. My madam doesn't like to be thwarted. It would be nothing for her to pay a man to hunt me down and kill me."

"Where do you come from, angel, with your lovely voice and your lady's accent? How did you end up in a brothel?"

Oh, these were treacherous questions. The news sheets had used her "little duchess" nickname. She had to take care. She must distance herself from her past. "I lived in London's stews, but I was born in the country. My mother was widowed and became a . . . a housekeeper. Then she lost her position and she brought me to Town to find work. I was very young, but I'd learned how to speak well." This was all a fabrication.

"Did she end up in a brothel, angel, and bring you with her?"

"No, she worked as a seamstress. Eventually she died and I ended up in the brothel—I had nowhere else to go." That was the truth.

Five years ago, a few nights after she had approached the duke outside the theatre, she had run out of money and had to go back to Drury Lane. She had approached another man, who turned out to be Viscount Rutley. Rutley hadn't been as noble as the duke. He'd said he wanted her as his mistress. She had believed him—he gave her an allowance, enough money to pay for her mother's laudanum. Then after only a few weeks, Rutley had grown bored with her. But instead of giving her a settlement, he'd handed her over to Madame to settle his unpaid accounts.

"I'm sorry."

She jerked her head up. She didn't want him to pity her. Was there a way she could stop him from asking more questions and convince him to keep her?

"Let me try to help you," she said impetuously. "I saw how frustrated you became when you walked across the library and hit your shin on that table. My grandfather was blind, and I know the things he did to cope with it. Perhaps those things could help you—"

"Angel, I don't need help. The only way I can be 'healed' is to get my sight back and, as delightful and intriguing as you are, you can't do that for me."

"Once, my grandfather told me he believed his blindness was actually a gift."

"Then your grandfather was a madman." He reached for his coffee, and she could see he was going to knock over the cup. She lunged and snatched it up before he could. If he did something like that now, she would never win him over. And she had to. Thinking of Madame's death was like the prick of a blade. She had to make haste to survive.

"Perhaps I could show you why he felt that way, Your

Grace. I know I can't give you back your sight—I wish I could—but I do believe I can make you happy. I know you used to love to game and wager. Why don't you make a wager with me? I believe I can help make you into the man you were before you were blind. I know I can! I have weapons you can't even imagine."

"A wager?" He leaned back in his chair, his brow arched dubiously, but at least she had captured his attention. And distracted him from his previous questions.

She knew she'd thrown down a gauntlet, and she had to win. But where to begin?

The duke scratched along his jaw, his fingers stroking through his uneven beard.

Of course! She had been in the care of starchy and efficient nurses and no-nonsense governesses until she was fifteen—until her father's death. What did her nurses do when she came home with a dirty face and unkempt hair? Firm hands would propel her to the claw-foot tub, where she was deposited into the water, then scrubbed thoroughly. She knew from living in the stews how hard it was to escape unhappiness if you couldn't escape being dirty and disheveled.

That was where she would begin. She would clean him up.

Chapter Five

"You're asking me to let you go for my throat with a razor?"

"I want to *shave* you." With her hands on the duke's lower back, Anne propelled him to a stool in front of his mahogany dresser. Nerves made her take charge and act swiftly. His shaving kit was laid out upon a towel, apparently left by his valet. She'd instructed a footman to bring a basin of water. "You are sorely in need of a good shave. Now, please sit down, Your Grace."

"Angel, this is not a good idea."

"It is. You're scratching at that mess of stubble again. You would feel better with it gone."

"I do not know about this," he said warily. "I don't like the idea of you touching my throat with a blade."

"Nonsense, I shall take great care," she promised. She hoped she was not hammering nails in her coffin by arguing with him. As he had observed, she was supposed to be paid to do as he asked, not to speak her mind.

Kat, who had been lover to many peers, had explained exactly what a mistress was supposed to do. Avoiding arguments had been quite close to the top of the list. It appeared a clever mistress had skills beyond the bedroom. A successful one knew how to flatter her protector, how to make him feel like a god among men. Herding him into his dressing room like a clucking nanny was *not* the best way to flatter him.

Bother. But she had to do this—sex hadn't worked, so she must do something else to make her appear so valuable and indispensable he would not dream of sending her away. "I certainly wouldn't hurt you deliberately," she said. "And I've"—the lie slipped out with dreadful ease—"done this many times before. I think this would be very . . . erotic."

"Indeed." He grinned for a moment, but then his mouth straightened into a serious line, his eyes haunted. "I am worried about how I will react to the pressure of the razor on my neck."

Heavens, she'd not thought of that. "All you must do is remember that I am shaving you, that there is no danger, that you aren't in battle; instead, you are here in your dressing room. Just remember you are completely safe."

"All right, angel, I'm willing to try. But I wish this didn't involve a sharp blade."

His humor touched her heart, and she prayed she could do this. She had never shaved a man in her life, and she'd had only a few glimpses of her father's valet shaving him. She would have to be careful and try very hard not to cut the duke's throat.

While she was finishing her breakfast, the duke had gone to one of the enormous library windows. He had tapped his way there with his walking stick, then he'd laid both his bare palms against the panes and rested his head on the cool, damp glass.

It was a posture of such longing and pain. Suddenly she'd understood. The duke *wanted* to go home. What kept him away from his estate and his family was fear. She had no home to go to. If she had one, she now knew she would slay any dragon to reach it, she would take any risk to go to it. But would she hurt someone else? That was what he feared he might do.

This was about more than her safety, her escape. She truly wanted to help him. And right now she had to shave him without cutting his throat. Gathering her courage, she faced his dressing table. The footman had delivered two bowls—one to dip the blade in, the second for rinsing his face. Steam coiled off each one.

Grandpapa would ask her to speak, so he would know where she was. She touched the duke's cheek gently and said, "I am going to lather you now."

With trust she didn't deserve, he tipped back his head. He rested his fists on his thighs.

She swallowed hard as she took his shaving soap and rubbed it along his taut neck. His muscles tensed beneath her touch. He shut his eyes and breathed slowly. Obviously he was executing intense control of himself. She stepped up to him from behind. "I am going to touch the razor to you now."

Suddenly he lifted his arm, and Anne gasped in horror. She had been moving the blade forward. She'd almost sliced his forearm.

"No. I can't do this, love," he said grimly.

"You can trust me," she said nervously. He had agreed to let her stay because she'd wagered him she could help him heal. They hadn't yet set a value on the bet, but if he could not let her do this, wouldn't it be proof she must go?

"Angel, I cannot trust anyone. It's the sorry truth." He held out his hand. "I can shave myself. I did it in camps often enough without the aid of a mirror. This is something I should still be able to do."

She hesitated, then gave in. Taking great care, she put the handle of the razor against his palm. His long fingers curled around it and she noticed the numerous scars crisscrossing the back of his hand. She remembered the soft scrape of his callused palm on her breasts and the way it made her skin tingle. He was a duke, but he no longer had a gentleman's hands.

With the razor in hand, he tipped his head back and ran the sharp edge along his throat with a smooth, firm stroke. Lather piled up on the blade. He reached out, found one of the basins, and dipped the metal into the water, swishing to clean it. Another stroke took off more of the white foam and left a second trail of smooth skin beside the first.

Anne watched, rather breathless. It seemed so intimate to do this, to watch him shave. More intimate than it had felt to make love to him.

He removed all the stubble from his neck, then attended to his cheeks and jaw. She marveled at the ease with which he negotiated the dip at his chin, the curves of his lips, the high planes of his cheekbones. Of course, he'd done this for about a decade of his life. She knew, from all the stories in London about his heroics, that he was six-and-twenty.

He gave the blade a slosh in the basin, then laid it down. He rinsed his face from the other basin, which he found with his hand, then patted his skin with a towel. "Is there a bottle of witch hazel on my dresser?"

She put it in his hand. He poured some in his palm, rubbed his hands together, slapped it to his face and throat. The gentle bite of the astringent filled the air. He winced, and she saw droplets of blood on his skin at the exact moment he put his fingers against them.

"Not as skilled as I thought," he muttered grimly. "Perhaps I should have let you do it."

She prayed that meant he was recognizing there was reason to keep her. Tentatively, she touched his cheek. "It is so smooth now. It feels like velvet."

He laughed. "It's not as soft as yours." Then his smile faded. "Funny, I haven't really touched you yet, have I?"

She remembered where he had touched her. Foolishly, she blushed. "You have."

"Not to truly explore you. The first time I felt my own face was a week ago. I didn't want to know how badly it had been cut up."

Her heart gave a swift leap as she thought of him running his hands over his face to discover if he had been scarred. "There is nothing wrong with your face," she assured him. "You are an astoundingly handsome man, Your Grace."

"Come here. Let me touch your face. Let me know what you look like."

Her grandfather used to ask to do that. To touch and explore her face. She took the duke's hand and lifted it to her cheek.

Gently he stroked the curve with his fingertips. It brought forth memories of her grandfather cupping her face, fanning his fingers over her cheeks. Grandpapa would tell her how pretty she'd become, what a lovely lady she was going to be. Even though *everyone* had despaired of her ever behaving like a polite and proper lady, Grandpapa did not. He used to whisper to her that the hoydens made the most interesting ladies. How ironic it was that she had never gotten a chance to be a lady.

She pushed that thought away, locked it deep inside.

"You have beautiful skin," the duke murmured. His fingers coasted down to her jaw and found her lips. Little explosions of sensation burst as his fingers lightly traced her mouth.

She'd never been touched like this. So slowly. With such care. She couldn't tense at such a beautiful caress. The way the duke touched was so slow and sensual, it made her knees tremble.

"I am not a ravishing beauty." She might as well be truthful about this. "Nor am I a particularly voluptuous woman—though I suppose you have guessed that already. I don't want you to be disappointed."

Perhaps she shouldn't have encouraged him to explore. Ashton had wanted Kat to be the duke's lover, and Kat was an exotic beauty with ebony curls, full lips, almond-shaped eyes, and high cheekbones. If that was the type of woman Lord Ashton believed the duke desired, she couldn't begin to compete with that.

She was somewhat pretty. But her nose was too long, her eyelashes too fair, her chin too sharp. Men had liked her in the brothel because she had a fragile look to her, even though, when she'd been young and behaving like a hoyden instead of a proper young lady, fragile was the last word that would describe her.

The duke brushed her eyebrows with his fingertips. He lightly touched her eyelids—heavens, they were very sensitive. He cupped her face. His eyes did not meet hers, but he said quietly, "Your skin is smooth as a new peach. Your lips feel lusciously plump. I noticed you have an intriguing bump at the end of your nose. I am hardly disappointed. You feel lovely."

"Th-thank you."

He touched one of her loose tendrils of hair, winding it lightly around his finger before releasing it. "What color is your hair?"

"Bl—" She checked herself. Her hair wasn't blond any longer, not after the dye. "Red."

"'Titian' was how my butler described it. He described your eyes as dark green, like ivy."

She started at that. Never had she thought of the dark color of her eyes in that way, yet it was very accurate. "I wouldn't have thought your butler to be so . . ."

"Poetic?" he suggested.

"Yes." Anne had never expected the odd-looking servant to have such awareness. "I suspect you don't employ him only to keep people away. I think—I think he worries about you."

"He does. Too much so. Makes him poke his nose in my business." The duke's fingers trailed down her neck. That was the only place his fingertips caressed, but her skin everywhere seemed aware of his touch. He stroked the base of her throat, where her pulse thudded. He found the velvet lapels of her robe, drew them apart with both hands.

"Take it off," he directed.

She did so, pushing it off her shoulders, letting it fall.

But when she stood in front of him, in her shift, he asked, "Why are you doing this? Reading letters to me. Trying to clean me up. Why not simply take the money I offer and find a better protector? Why are you so determined to convince me to let you stay? This can't be about avoiding your former madam."

"I *am* afraid of my madam, and I'm afraid of poverty. I want to be a duke's mistress." Words spilled out of her. She was so afraid of telling him the truth, of just letting it fall out, that she began to babble. She'd had no idea a secret would sit so heavily in her heart and would want so desperately to get out.

She couldn't confide in him. It was insane to be tempted. "I know of no other way for a woman like me to find independence and freedom. I want my own house, clothes, food, and the knowledge that someday I shall be in charge of my own life. And I—I like you, Your Grace."

He tipped his head back, shutting his eyes. "You *like* me? I'm blind, half mad, and, according to you, an unkempt mess. You have very questionable taste."

"I did not mean you are a mess! Only that your beard was."

He laughed, and her thundering heart slowed a bit.

"Now that the scruffy beard is gone and my face is smooth, angel, there's something I'd like to do to please you."

It must be a good sign he was thinking of sex again, but she could not imagine what he wanted to do that required a smooth face. And she told him so.

"You don't know?" His voice deepened to a richly sinful rumble. "Angel, you must."

"No, I've no idea."

"This is something you'll enjoy very much. All women do." His lips curved in a dazzling grin. "I think there's a stool somewhere. Bring it here and sit down. Then open your legs."

She obeyed. She had no idea what he wanted to do. Not knowing made her nervous.

"There," she said awkwardly when she was ready. Her silky shift was bunched up at her waist, and she perched on the stool, close to its edge.

Guided by the sound of that one word, he lowered to his knees in front of her. He tilted his head to the side. "You must know now, love."

"I don't."

He reached out, felt for her knees, and clasped them when he found them. "This I can do without sight. This I can be very good at without sight." Determination glinted in his violet eyes. With his shirt open at his throat, his hair a wild tangle of black, and his feet bare, he looked like a pirate. At this moment, he didn't look like a man who had given up caring and he didn't look haunted. He looked like a man bent on proving a point.

Then he said, "I want to please you." And doubt slammed into her.

Each time they'd been together, she had moaned and cried out and had made him believe he'd pleasured her. Hadn't she?

She never felt actual pleasure. For some reason, it wasn't possible for her. She never felt anything at all while making love. But she gave the best performances she could.

Had the duke guessed her shouts and wild thrashing were an act? Since she'd never had a climax, she didn't know what a woman really experienced. She'd cobbled her act together based on tales told by other women in Madame's brothel.

The duke eased her legs even wider apart, until she felt the tug on her inner thighs. She sat on the small stool, both hands wrapped around the edge of it, her spine rigid. He wouldn't want to do anything bad, she was certain, but she couldn't stop apprehension from welling up inside.

He leaned forward and kissed her inner thigh.

It *tickled*. Nothing had prepared her for such a sensation. His smooth cheek stroked her skin, teasing her madly. She gasped as he nipped the inside of her leg. Then he nibbled and licked his way to the nest of blond curls between her thighs, and she shrieked in surprise.

What on earth was he doing? Did he know where he was kissing her? He couldn't see, after all. Had he meant to place a kiss somewhere else? Her breasts, perhaps. Should she direct him?

"Uh, Your Grace, your . . . your mouth is almost at my . . . my private place." Then, as she stumbled over the words, she saw her horrible mistake. Of course he knew what he was doing. She could breathe in her own intimate scent, and his lips had brushed the crisp curls nestled there. She had brought up his blindness. He stopped and rested his chin on her thigh.

She ran her tongue around suddenly dry lips.

But he didn't look angry. He cocked his head in an engaging way, his dark hair drifting over his brow, his eyes so brilliant they were the vivid color of amethysts.

"You really have no idea what I am doing? No gentleman has ever done this to you?"

She shook her head vigorously. "Not ever, Your Grace."

"Men are a sorry lot, aren't we, sweet?"

She frowned. She didn't know what he meant and she had no answer. The question sounded very treacherous—as though any answer could begin an argument.

He tickled her pubic hair, making her giggle nervously. "You're quiet for a change, Cerise. I meant that men want their own release and do not give enough attention to their partners."

"You do," she argued.

He laughed. "I intend to. I intend to give you pleasure with my mouth, while I enjoy the taste of you."

She lost her breath. "I—I had no idea such a thing was done."

"You did the same for me last night, angel."

"I am supposed to do things you like."

"And not expect anything in return." His expression became serious, which worried her, but before she could say a word to reassure him she was quite happy, he whispered, "Tell me if you like it." Then he bent and flicked his tongue at the very top of her sex, above the plump lips, to the small nub that screamed with sensation when it was touched.

Anne almost jumped off the stool. She never touched there—it was too much. She was as rigid as a rock now, enduring the way he ran his tongue over her most sensitive place. *Oh, God.* It was so powerful. It left her dizzy. It made her whimper for mercy. He flicked his tongue over it and she cried out. He took the taut little bump between his lips gently, and she melted a bit with relief—then he suckled on it. She screamed.

He paused, releasing her. He blew a soft breath, and

even that made her scuttle back on the stool. "Relax, love. It will be good."

Relax. She tried, she truly did. But as soon as he licked her again, she tensed and drove her fingers hard against the unyielding wooden seat.

He expected this to be pleasurable for her. It wasn't, it wouldn't be, but she couldn't let him know that. He would expect enthusiastic moans. Perhaps a climax, too, at the appropriate time.

But with him flicking his tongue over that place, she couldn't think. She couldn't even make sounds that sounded arousing and not like a choking goose.

It was so intense. She wanted him to stop. She wanted to grasp his head and pull his mouth away. Her feet were curled almost into balls, her hands in tight fists. The feelings were too much. They made her clench every muscle tight to bear them. She didn't want this. But she didn't dare tell him.

He stopped, and she almost gave a sob of relief before she choked it back.

"What's wrong, angel? I can feel how tense you are. Would you like it gentler?"

"Wh-whatever you desire, Your Grace."

"Cerise, you can tell me what pleases you best."

"Your Grace, I'm supposed to please you. I will do whatever you want."

"Dear God," he muttered. "Cerise, I don't want that if you aren't enjoying yourself. Would you like me to be more gentle?"

"There was nothing wrong with what you did, Your Grace," she breathed nervously.

He nipped her inner thigh. It stunned her. "What do you want?" he growled.

"I—I don't know." It was the truth. She wanted independence and freedom and security. She wanted hope for a future, a good one with a house and food and safety. But in this—in making love—there wasn't anything she wanted.

"More gently, then." He blew a warm stream of air over her sensitive nub. He nibbled her with just his lips. It was the lightest, softest, most teasing brush of his full, firm mouth.

She quivered. It was . . . not so terrifying, not so intense. She slumped back on the stool, her back braced against his dressing table. Almost nice. Truly, it was almost quite nice.

Her legs weakly flopped wider apart. As he licked her gently and teasingly, she felt as if she'd downed three glasses of sherry in a row and her head was filled with ribbons, not brains.

She had to gather her wits. She was always in control. Her future might depend on her giving the grandest exhibition of her life. Yet all she could do was make incoherent whimpers.

His Grace moved down and he licked the astonishingly sensitive bridge of flesh between her wet, aching private place and the entrance to her bottom. Anne almost toppled over, taking the stool with her. It lurched precariously. Even though he couldn't see, he caught her.

"Touch yourself for me, love," he growled. "Show me how you like it."

She blushed but moved her hand over her thigh. Touch . . . herself? She'd never done that when with a man. Nervously, she stroked her curls. They were sticky and damp from her juices, from his mouth. Her pulsing little bump was slick and wet, and she gently brushed her fingertip over it. His fingers touched her wrist, slid down to her hand, and rested gently there.

He was feeling her as she explored herself. She gave an embarrassed giggle and stopped moving her hand.

"Tell me," he whispered hoarsely, "what you do to pleasure yourself."

"I don't. I'm not supposed to." Oh, she felt miserable. She'd done this only once and she'd stopped because it wasn't proper. She might have been a hoyden in many ways, but she'd been too afraid to be sinful and naughty. After she went to the brothel, she'd wanted only to sleep and not have nightmares when she was alone in her bed.

"You're not supposed to? Angel, you're a courtesan."

Even though she'd hinted at what life had been like in the brothel, he didn't understand. What she let men do to her had been to ensure she didn't starve, didn't freeze to death on the streets. It had been for survival alone.

"Try for me, angel. There's nothing wrong with it."

"It's sinful." Goodness, she did sound ridiculous to her own ears.

"You said you would do everything I asked to please me," he teased. "It would please me to explore you together." With his hand over hers, he made her fingers rub faster. She had to close her eyes. She saw bursts of bright lights against velvet black.

"You like it fast, do you?"

She nodded. She was a wretched mess at this, clumsy, inexperienced, unknowing. But he was determined she would enjoy it. The stool rocked beneath her as she moved with their fierce strokes. He must want her to reach climax this way. And the sooner she did, the sooner this would be done. In fact, now would be the perfect time. He was breathing hard with anticipation and he'd shut his eyes tight, his long, thick lashes brushing his cheeks. Sometimes men did that when they were very aroused and close to orgasm.

She let out a loud cry. "Oh! Oh! It's too much! I'm going to come."

He lowered his head to her sex at once. He slid his

tongue into her passage, while she mercilessly sawed her fingers back and forth over her sensitive place.

She threw everything into the act. First, she thrashed on the stool, bucking her hips. Then she clutched his head, threading her fingers into his silky hair. She had to appear to be out of her wits with ecstasy. She lifted her bottom, pushed her hips against his mouth, and squealed all the while. No matter how much she bounced, he kept his mouth on her, teasing her with his tongue.

She moved too vigorously and tipped to the side. Beneath her, the stool rocked and started to fall. She cried out in shock, but the duke grasped her hips and they both tumbled to the floor. She landed on top of him, her privates against his mouth. He held her bottom so he could continue to lick and nuzzle her.

But she didn't want this anymore. She *must* pleasure him.

She drew his hands away, moved down swiftly so he could not stop her. In her haste, she was clumsy with the fastenings of his trousers. Her hand trembled as she took hold of his hard shaft, and she was so nervous she jerked his erection up rather roughly. At least she didn't hurt him—he merely groaned lustily as she took him inside. Thank heaven, now she knew what to do. And as she bounced up and down, he rasped, "Yes, angel."

She braced her hands on his shoulders while he thrust up into her as hard and powerfully as he had last night. When he came, he shut his eyes tight, slammed his head back on the rug, and his hips arched up beneath her, driving him deep.

Relief left Anne giddy. He must have enjoyed it.

She had obviously enjoyed it.

Dragging in long, deep breaths, Devon shifted his hips to slide out and lowered himself slowly against Cerise's hot, dewy body. He felt her heart pound against his. His body felt lazy and heavy from his pleasure. Also from relief.

He'd pleased her. He could do this without sight and still with considerable skill, apparently. The first times he'd made love to her, he'd ached for his sight. He'd wanted to see her climax. It had frustrated him, given his pleasure an edge of anger. Anger he'd tried to keep locked inside.

This time, he'd thought only of her pleasure. His whole world had been her: the taste of her, earthy and ripe, the silky feel of her nether lips, the crisp tickle of her pubic hair, and her lovely, frantic moans. He hadn't thought about war or loss. All he'd thought about was Cerise.

He'd felt her tension at first. She'd been almost fearful as he knelt between her legs and suckled her. What had happened to her? He wanted to know, but he didn't want to remind her of hellish things she'd been through. He just wanted to soothe her. Then she'd begun to respond. From the sound of her cries, she must have enjoyed herself a great deal.

He kissed her breasts. "Thank you, angel," he said softly. "For the shave." But what in blazes was he going to do? He had barely slept last night—he'd forced himself to stay awake so he wouldn't dream. He needed to force her to go, but right now, all he wanted to do was wrap his arms around her and sleep.

He couldn't do it. He couldn't risk having a nightmare and hurting her. He was sure that when he was in the depths of sleep, the feel of her body against him would set him off, just as he'd confused her touch for that of a soldier trying to kill him.

"I'm not quite finished," she murmured, underneath him. "All that lovely hair of yours needs a trim."

* * *

He was supposed to be pushing people away. For their own good. That had been the direction he'd given to Treadwell and the handful of other servants he kept here.

Yet Devon sat on the stool with his back to his dressing table while Cerise washed his hair. She had forced him to sit, then had tipped his head over the basin while she soaked his hair with handfuls of water.

Now she massaged soap into it. He groaned, shut his eyes, and savored the firm, circular caresses of her fingers.

He had fought against battalions of French soldiers—at Waterloo, they had faced more than seventy thousand men—yet this slip of a woman was bustling him around his dressing room with more capability for direction than his vice general had shown.

It was amazing how good a woman's hands felt on his scalp. How good *her* hands felt. She wasn't trying to make this sensual. She rubbed his head too hard for that to be her plan, and she massaged every spot—his temples, behind his ears, along the nape of his neck.

He could hear rain thrumming against the windows, rattling the panes.

"Tip your head back farther, please, Your Grace." She rinsed his hair, using her hand as a barrier to keep the soapy water off his face. He jerked instinctively as the warm water sluiced over his head, and rivulets ran down into his eyes.

"Please keep still," she admonished. "Or I will end up splashing your face by mistake."

"Yes, dear," he murmured obediently.

Her hands twisted his hair behind him, gathering it up, squeezing the excess water from it. She let it go, and it fell wetly against his neck. Vigorously, she rubbed his head with a towel.

He almost laughed. She definitely wasn't trying to artfully seduce him. She tugged his hair as she patted it between the towel, dabbed up the water that dribbled from his hairline. Then she laid the towel around his shoulders.

Suddenly his hair was yanked as though she were trying to scalp him. He tried to jolt away.

"I am sorry, but I must get the comb through." Suspicion, not apology, laced her tone. "When was the last time you took a comb to your hair?"

"Before Watson left. It must be at least a week ago."

She clicked her tongue. "It is very wrong to let yourself go to seed like this."

She spoke to him like a governess with a recalcitrant charge. He wanted to fill in details of the vague story of her past she'd given him. She did not behave like a girl who had spent much of her life in London's stews. "Why didn't your grandfather help you after your father died? Why didn't he take you in?"

"He had died by then. And we had no other family. My mother and I truly had nowhere else to go." Her voice trembled, and she sounded as though she did not wish to speak of it.

Then cold brushed against his neck, and he jerked away again. "What is that?"

"The scissors, Your Grace." She tipped his head and he felt the comb run through his hair, pulling it straight, then he heard the first swift snip of the blades. She worked around his head, telling him everything she was going to do, directing his head this way and that while she trimmed his hair.

"Angel, in London, did you have much call to shave your clients and trim their hair?"

She paused, and he felt pieces of hair feather past his

cheek. "No," she said slowly. "Do gentlemen ask for such things?" She sounded utterly innocent and surprised.

"Then why did you think of doing this, love?"

"I thought it would make you feel better," she said. "I know a mistress is supposed to do things such as warming brandies and . . . and pleasuring a man with her mouth. But this, I thought, was what you needed." She stroked the comb through his hair, caressing his scalp. "Do you feel more like yourself?"

She was right. He did feel more like himself without the itching beard and the dirty, unkempt hair. A light *clunk* told him she'd set down the scissors. And he was certain he'd heard a blush in her tone when she'd said *pleasuring a man with her mouth*. Amazing she had stayed so ingenuous.

"I wondered if you would want to come with me," she said. "For a walk outside."

That he hadn't expected. "Outside? It's raining, love. Even I know that. I can hear it."

"I know. I'm asking you to go outside because it *is* raining. I think it will help you. Come with me and find out."

Chapter Six

THE DUKE WOULD not let her outside until she assured him she was properly dressed for a cool and rainy afternoon. Rather than struggle with her gown, Anne borrowed one of his shirts and a pair of his breeches. After that, an elderly footman had helped her don a hooded cloak. The duke wore an open many-tiered greatcoat to keep off the rain, and tall, immaculately polished boots. Since arriving yesterday, she had not seen him with anything but bare feet. Yet his boots had been kept in readiness, as though he was about to attend a *ton* ball.

He looked stunning and intimidating when fully dressed. His beaver hat added a foot to his already impressive height. She was accustomed to his nakedness or seeing him with his shirt free of his trousers. Her throat dried when she saw how impeccable and ducal he could look.

"Wait for one moment," she advised him, and her voice trembled a bit. She stepped from the library to the terrace. It smelled crisp, fresh, and she couldn't help but exclaim, "It's lovely!"

On the threshold, the duke waited. “Angel, it sounds like it’s teeming down.”

“It is. That is what makes it so perfect.”

Anne crossed to the stone balustrade that ringed the flagstone terrace. She leaned forward until her head was beyond the cover of the balcony above. Closing her eyes, she tipped up her face and let the rain hit her cheeks. She stuck out her tongue and tasted a few cool drops.

She breathed in the rich, earthy scent of mud and wet grass. From the forest, she could smell the dankness of rain-soaked leaves and rotting wood. Some would curl their noses, but she loved the smell. Memories of Longsworth rose like an ocean swell. She couldn’t stop them.

“Angel,” the duke said quietly, “are you perhaps as mad as I am?”

She spun to face him. Perhaps he was right. Perhaps she *was* mad. She could not think of anyone else who would drag a reluctant duke into a downpour. He would certainly think her deranged if this idea didn’t work. He would want to be rid of her at once.

Biting her lip, she hurried back to him. She placed his hand in the crook of her arm and led him to the edge of the terrace. He frowned as the breeze blew rain into his face and almost sent his beaver hat tumbling off his head. He caught it by instinct and replaced it. Then he licked droplets from his full lips with a sweep of his tongue.

“Are you sure about this, Cerise, my dear? We’re going to get soaked.”

“Yes, I’m certain.” Though in truth she wasn’t.

Lights glowed from some rooms of his house, warding off the afternoon gloom. With her hand clasped over his, Anne found the steps leading down from the terrace. Their boots crunched on the gravel path at the bottom at the same time. She led him a few yards from the house. “Stop and listen, Your Grace.”

He frowned. He tipped back his head. Just as she had done, he caught drops on his tongue. Then he pulled off his hat, letting the rain fall on his black hair. It didn't take long before his thick, silky, newly trimmed hair gleamed like jet with wetness. Water dripped from his lips.

Anne caught her breath. Her hair was plastered to her face, her wet cloak sagged around her, and she suspected she looked like a drowned rat.

The Duke of March looked magnificent wet.

She truly looked at him for what he was—not only a duke with the wealth and power to save her and give her freedom but a man, a gorgeous one. She stared at his unusual lilac-purple eyes and his sensual, full-lipped mouth, and she saw the way the water droplets clung to his cheeks and aristocratic nose as though reluctant to let go. Heat washed across her face. Her bosom seemed to swell and tighten beneath his sandalwood-scented linen shirt.

She had never felt this with any one of her clients. Not this desire to keep watching a man just for the pleasure of it.

The duke's fingertips coasted down her arm and he clasped her hand, threading his fingers with hers. His hand was warm and strong, his fingers big but elegant. He had touched her most intimate place, but this—standing in the rain, holding his hand—felt unique and special.

The duke had trusted her enough to do what she'd asked, even though he had doubts. What man had ever done that for her? "Tell me what you hear," she urged.

He cocked his head. "I can hear the rain striking the ground."

She had to explain more. "Listen to the sound of the rain on the leaves close to us—those are the roses. Can you hear the way the rain sounds when it lands on the grass? Is it softer than the patter of the rain striking the gravel of the path?"

His dark brows drew together. "The clattering sound—is that rain hitting the window?"

Anne closed her eyes to experience it as he did. She tried to follow the sound, then opened her eyes. She was facing the house. "Yes, it is."

"The drumming sound, as though it's hitting something hard—what is that?" he asked.

"It might be the sound of rain on the path. Or the stone fountain. We are only half a dozen feet from the fountain."

"All right. I think I can distinguish the sound of the raindrops on the water in the basin."

Carefully, she described everything that surrounded them and how far they stood from each item, but then His Grace began to stroke her wet bare palm with his thumb and she stumbled over her words. That simple touch was so electric. She'd never had her hand caressed like this before.

"It's beautiful," he said huskily. "It's like a magical sheet has been thrown over everything that was invisible to me. When I had sight, I could assess the world around me in an instant, but now that I'm blind, I wouldn't know if a tree was stretching over my head, or if I was under a ceiling, or if there was nothing above but sky. The rain changes that."

It was what she'd hoped he would discover, but the way he described it made her throat ache.

"How did you know this?" he asked.

"My grandfather used to like to walk in the rain. He told me he loved the sound of it on the leaves, loved the way it drummed on the roof of the house and spattered against the windows. Rain brought everything to life for him. You told me about the void that your mind fills in with battle memories, and I thought this might help you."

He stayed silent, and she could tell he wasn't straining to listen to the rain anymore.

"My grandfather used to ask me to walk with him when it rained. Everyone thought he was mad to go out in a downpour, and my father worried about my health when I went out, but I didn't mind. Wet clothes and hair can be dried. My grandfather was so delighted when I took him, and I loved it too. I loved the smell of the lawns and gardens."

He tipped her chin up. His long lashes shielded his eyes, and droplets of rain hung on them like small diamonds. "I've had to fight in the rain," he said, "but I never thought my blindness would force me to *walk* in a downpour to know where my house stands or what is above my head."

Oh, no. Irony was thick in his tone. Perhaps her idea *had* been idiotic—

Then his large hands cradled her chin and his lips lowered to hers. For one moment she was mesmerized by the small glimpse of violet in his eyes. Suddenly his lashes dipped the rest of the way, and Anne gasped as his mouth came to hers. He kissed her sweetly. Her heart beat so fast she feared it would burst. She had never dreamed he would kiss her like this. He made love so fiercely, yet this . . . this was the most tender caress she'd ever known.

Last night she'd kissed him in the hopes of seducing him. He'd rejected the kiss, and after that, she hadn't tried. She'd never dreamed the gentle touch of his mouth to hers would root her to the ground, would make all sound vanish, rain disappear, time cease. She'd thought the stroke of his thumb over her palm was electric—this was like being struck by lightning. This was dazzling. Heat washed over her. Dizzying heat, as if she had walked too close to a raging fire. She was . . . *steaming*, even in the cold rain.

His kiss deepened. His arms tightened around her, pulling her so close that her breasts crushed to his chest and she could barely draw breath. She'd never been held like this. She twined her arms around his neck to hold him, in case he changed his mind. Men rarely kissed, she knew that. They always wanted to move on to sex. Eventually the duke would want to stop. She didn't want to let him—

He stopped. Anne's heart dropped to her toes, until she realized he still held her. He wasn't letting go, and his ragged breaths mingled with hers. "Thank you," he growled, and his mouth slanted over hers once more.

Once more, she melted. The sensuality of this—the lush eroticism of it—made her feel like chocolate bubbling in a pot. She closed her eyes and threw herself into it with all her heart. And when she made a sound of pleasure, his tongue slid into her mouth.

At once she understood. He wanted to hear her respond before he gave her more, before he took the kiss deeper into an intoxicating place she didn't know existed.

She moaned again, and this time his tongue tangled with hers in response. He groaned in pleasure into her mouth. In the shimmer of fireworks that flashed behind her closed lids and thundered in her heart, she knew one thing. This wasn't a hasty mashing of lips before he got to business. He *wanted* to keep kissing her.

She ran her fingers up into his wet hair. She'd done an excellent job—it was so smooth and clean and smelled wonderfully of sandalwood soap, and she felt a foolish burst of pride. In that heady moment, Anne answered his tempting play by sliding her tongue into his mouth.

Lovely. Hot. Erotic. She loved tasting him so intimately, tasting the fresh bite of his tooth powder, the delectable heat of his mouth.

His hand stroked down and clutched her bottom through her cloak. He pulled her closer. Instinctively, she lifted her leg, wrapped it around his hip. Now she was utterly off balance, and if he moved or let her go, she'd fall. Yet she didn't care.

She wanted to kiss him forever. Here. Outside. With the rain streaming down on top of them. She wanted to kiss him until the gray daylight faded away and nighttime fell upon them. Until the rain stopped and the sun rose again. Until summer turned to fall.

He drew back and she surged forward, wanting more. This time, though, he didn't bow his head to her and seek her mouth again. He cradled her to his chest and pressed his lips to her hair.

How could just a kiss do this? Leave her hands shaking, her legs trembling, and her heart spinning like a top in her chest?

It should be frightening—she'd touched him in the most intimate ways possible, but she'd never felt more weak and quivery than she did now. She desperately tried to force her dazed mind to think back over the last few minutes. Had she moaned for him enough? Kissed him as passionately as she should? Had she pleased him? Had she shown him she could be a skillful mistress?

Anne had to make herself care, but she simply couldn't. She couldn't care less about her performance. All she could think about was how it *felt*. She was sagging against him, and her lips were tingling.

"Look up, love," he murmured.

She did, and he kissed her cheek. Her nose. She couldn't help but giggle. Then he found her lips again and kissed her once more.

An entirely different kiss to add to her new repertoire of kisses. He kept his lips wide, forcing her to open her mouth just as much. It was almost shocking to kiss him with her mouth so wide. It was wet and messy, delicious and naughty. Their tongues dueled. And when he broke the kiss, he was breathing every bit as harshly. It didn't matter if she could kiss with skill. He wanted this. She did too. Here, now, it was all that mattered.

Devon closed his eyes and buried his face into Cerise's wet, thick hair. She smelled fresh, like the aftermath of a summer storm. She had given him something he never believed he would have again: a sense of what was around him. He could hear the patter of rain on the leaves of the roses. On the terrace flagstones, the rain made a sharper sound. It spattered against the glass, plinked down from the roof, and drummed against the house.

She was a unique and remarkable woman. What other courtesan would have cared to help him? He'd kept mistresses—each and every one had liked him quite a bit but had loved his wealth more. What woman of his acquaintance would stand in a downpour so he could listen to the rain? Just to say thank you hadn't seemed enough. So he'd kissed her.

She kissed him like no other woman ever had. She'd kissed him the way she made love—all boundless enthusiasm, as though she was throwing every bit of herself into the sheer joy of it and holding nothing back. Despite being captured into a brothel, she apparently delighted in sex. He'd never had any woman be so open. So artless. So surprisingly sweet.

And when he kissed her, everything around him had vanished. The sounds of the rain, the feel of it. All he could hear were her breathy moans against his mouth. Her little whimpers and groans and squeaks. All he'd felt was her warm body in his arms, her heart pounding against him. His world, which had suddenly become much larger in scope, had instantly narrowed down to just Cerise.

Even though she was as drenched as he was, she'd kissed him as though there was no rain, as though they had no fears or problems and nothing existed but this one moment.

He cupped her face. He tried to conjure a picture of her from what he felt. An oval face, and wet curls stuck to her soft cheeks. A pointy chin. He imagined masses of auburn waves pouring around a delicate face. He fancied that her unusual dark-green eyes were large and pretty. But when he tried to imagine her expression, he was lost. Sometimes she was wickedly seductive, and he could envision her face sparkling with wicked desire. Then she would be patient and efficient, and he pictured a serious expression. He just couldn't get a proper image of her. It frustrated him.

Then something clicked inside his head. "You couldn't have been very young when you left the country for London. I had the impression you'd done so when you were a child. And you speak as though this country estate was your own."

"Oh. I wasn't *very* young," she said in a low voice. "For I did tell you about walking with my grandfather. I didn't mean to give you the wrong impression. It wasn't my house, of course, but I loved it very much. My grandfather worked at the house too. He—he was head gardener. He helped my mother find employment there."

She sounded so desperate to please him, and it made his heart lurch. He did remember she'd said she was young, but regardless of the details she'd had a hell of a past—ending up a prisoner in a brothel. She fascinated him. Could he make her his mistress? She'd seen him at almost his worst and it hadn't frightened her away.

She'd told him she could avoid him if she had to. Did he dare keep her?

"You're wet," Devon murmured finally. "This cloak isn't keeping off the rain, is it? It feels heavy—it's soaking the water up."

Reassurance was on the tip of Anne's tongue. She could barely even feel the rain. She was all jumbled up—nervous about her mistake, dizzy from his kisses. But the cloak was suddenly whisked off her, dropped on the ground. The duke draped his greatcoat around her shoulders. Thunder rumbled, and before she could say, *Goodness, a storm has come up on us,* lightning flashed. It was as though the fork of light split the sky open and let out all the water at once. Sheets of rain swept over them. The torrent came so hard Anne could barely see through it.

But instead of running for cover, they both reacted in the same way. They stood frozen in surprise. It took only moments before the pelting water soaked through the duke's white shirt.

Anne stepped back and tugged at his hand. "Oh, no. You are drenched."

Wet linen stuck to his wide chest and arms. Where fabric touched flesh, it had become almost invisible, revealing his muscles, his skin, tanned to a rich coppery-brown. Heavens, he was going to catch his death outside and it would be her fault.

She heard the creak of a door. "Yer Grace, are you out here?" It was Treadwell.

"Indeed I am," the duke shouted.

"Are ye—are ye all right?"

"Never better," the duke called back, and Anne put her hand to her mouth to hold in a giggle.

"But, Yer Grace . . . ye're out in the rain."

"And you fear that means I'm fit for Bedlam," the duke replied. "In this case, I'm not."

With a start, she realized what she'd done. The duke feared he was going mad. She had made it look as though he was. "It was my idea," she called out. "I wished to walk outside in the fresh air, and His Grace very gallantly accompanied me. I will bring him indoors now."

"Uh . . . of course, then, miss." The door closed with a rattle.

"Now he knows to attribute the madness correctly," she said. "To me."

"Angel, you aren't mad." The duke pressed his forehead to hers. "Thank you for this. Thank you for being so patient with me. I've been a fool, haven't I?"

"No," she managed to say, perplexed. "Of course you haven't."

"I understand what you've been trying to do. You are trying to show me I'm a fool for hiding from my blindness. I already know that, but I don't know how to learn to cope with it, how to live with it. I need you, Cerise. You could help me. Please, love—stay with me."

She'd done it. He wanted to keep her. "I will stay as long as you want, Your Grace."

Chapter Seven

WHERE WAS ANNE? Damnation, he was tired of this.

Sebastian Beddington, Viscount Norbrook, ignored the presence of the strapping doorman. He strode past the brute into a foyer that stank of heavy perfume; it was papered a noxious red and was filled with pitiful faux Chinese ornamentation. The garish colors turned his stomach, and Sebastian seethed with frustration. He had planned never to return to this disgusting brothel, but he had no choice. For nearly a week, his private investigators had scoured the Whitechapel stews, searching for his cousin Anne. He'd spent a great deal of blunt on those damned men, yet they had given him no results.

He had believed she must be in hiding close to this whorehouse, the place she had run from five days before. How far could she get with no money, no friends, no resources? He'd been so certain he would find her quickly that he had joined the search himself.

It was foul. He had prowled down dirty lanes that reeked of horse dung. He had searched drafty taverns that stank of urine and sweat. In those wretchedly seedy places, he had been forced to consort with drunken, gap-toothed whores to ask them questions. Each one had instantly assessed his well-tailored clothing, his aristocratic bearing, and had fawned all over him, blowing their rank breath in his face, leaving their revolting smells imprinted on his clothing. And each and every one had cheated him. He'd handed over too many coins to too many tarts for information that had proved to be nothing more than lies.

In his present state of fury, Sebastian knew he might murder the next whore who promised to give him a lead to Anne and rooked him instead.

"Can I 'elp you, gov'nor?"

Sebastian whirled on the servant who had pursued him to the threshold of the salon. The footman tried to look menacing, with his beefy arms crossed over a barrel chest. A swift slice from the blade secreted in Sebastian's walking stick would cut this idiot down to size.

"I assume there is a new madam here in place of the murdered Madame Sin. Tell the woman Lord Norbrook expects her to receive him. At once."

The doorman lifted a brow, obviously preparing to give some excuse. Sebastian moved instantly. Grasping the man by the throat, he used the advantage of surprise to shove his heavier opponent against the wall. A painting of a nude rattled beside the servant's stunned face. Pleasure surged at the man's fear as Sebastian barked, "At once! Do you understand?"

All the bulky doorman could manage was a strangled sound, his coarse face turning red. Sebastian released his hold and the servant straightened his clothes, then hared away up the stairs.

Several gentlemen in the salon, and the large-bosomed whores fawning over them, had noticed the disturbance. They gawked and peered. He turned his back on them, pacing at the base of the stairs.

How this disgusted him. Having to come to a place such as this. And still, after what he'd endured, he did not have Anne. A thoroughly annoying thought struck him, as it did each day. His cousin could be dead by now and he would never know it.

He had to get her back.

It had taken him years to trace her to this brothel. Then that witch of a madam had kept Anne from him, had extorted an enormous fee from him before she would hand over the girl. And, when he finally thought it was over, he'd learned the bitch didn't have Anne at all.

Now the woman was dead and of no use to him.

It had taken him so long to find Anne the first time because he had never dreamed she would turn to whoring in her desperation. He'd assumed her mother would have tried to secure a more decent occupation. Anne's mother, Millicent, had still been a lovely woman when she'd fled from his house. She could have done much better than she had.

She'd had no right to run away and take Anne with her. He had offered them protection, comfort, and a home. He had even decided to condescend to marry Anne.

Instead, Millicent had chosen to take her daughter away from him. As if *he* was not good enough. Stupid bitch. Now Anne was a whore. Ruined. It made his lip curl. It made him want to vomit. This entire disgusting brothel brought bile into his throat. Yet where had Anne hidden so cleverly this time that he and a half dozen hired men could not find her?

The stairs creaked. Expecting the new madam—no doubt a henna-haired jade with big breasts and garish jewels—Sebastian jerked his gaze up. Instead, he saw a bald, muscular man dressed in a gentleman's clothes, with a starched collar that grazed his cheeks, a foul waistcoat of scarlet stripes, and a poorly tailored dark-blue coat. Not quite as bulky as the doorman he had dispatched, but obviously a bruiser with a rough background. It would be tiresome to have to slay this ox, but if it had to be done, he would do so. Anything to find Anne.

The beast in gentleman's attire reached the last step and swept a bow. When he straightened, he wore a smug grin. "Lord Norbrook? Madame Sin told me you were looking for Anne Beddington."

"Who are you?" he asked coldly.

"Name's Mick Taylor. I worked as bodyguard to Madame when she was alive."

"You were apparently unsatisfactory in your capacity. Do not waste my time."

Taylor reddened angrily, but he kept a convivial smile on his rough-featured face. "I was doing what I was told when Madame was killed—I was out searching for Anne Beddington and the three whores she stole. If you're still looking for Annie, I can help you find her."

The duke had agreed she could stay but he would not join her for dinner. The young footman brought Anne the news when he came to take her to the dining room.

She sagged in front of the vanity, where she had been trying to pin up her hair in a becoming way. The rain had turned it into a mass of untamable waves. "Why am I to go to the dining room if His Grace will not join me?"

The young servant was reflected in the mirror. A familiar flush rushed over the boy's face. "His Grace said it would be more pleasant for you to eat there. He hasn't scrimped on the food either, miss. I saw that for myself belowstairs."

Anne hesitated. This afternoon, after they had come

inside from the storm, she took a hot bath and changed into her gown. One of the duke's footmen brought his sister to the house to act as her lady's maid, at the duke's command. Then Anne guided the duke around his house. Two footmen had trailed after them at her request.

Using what she remembered of changes her mother had made to Longsworth to suit her grandfather, she ordered the rearrangement of the duke's furniture to ease his passage through his rooms. It had hurt to think again of the past, to remember her grandfather's kindness, her father's gruff affection, her mother's soft and all-embracing love. But she didn't have any choice. She must not make another mistake, though, if the duke asked about her past.

His refusal to dine with her bothered her. He was willing to learn to cope with his blindness. Even if his blindness made it difficult for him to manage his meals, how could he think she would condemn him? Why would he not let her help him?

Men were proud. Even Papa, who had been the best of gentlemen, had his moments of stubborn pride. Her cousin Sebastian, who had inherited the title and house after Papa's death, was brittle and cold, as well as cruel and arrogant. The type of man who would terrify a young girl to get what he wanted. Who nurtured grievances and who lashed out at anyone who crossed him, whether the slight was real or imagined. All her clients had been proud men who treated her like an object to be bought, used, ultimately discarded.

She pushed that dismal thought aside. That was the past. She was now a duke's mistress. More than that, she was the mistress of a kind, wonderful man who deserved to be made happy.

"What is your name?" she asked the footman.

"Beckett, miss."

"All right, Beckett. I shall do as His Grace asks."

The dining room proved to be enormous, lit by two fires. The table was set for just her, the silver gleaming, the crystal glittering in the light of three chandeliers. A battalion of footmen marched in, carrying enough food to feed an army, but Anne could barely eat enough to fill one plate.

As she slowly chewed and forced each mouthful down, Beckett kept launching away from the wall to fill her wineglass, and she sipped more than she should. To quell her nerves. Tonight she would make love to the duke as his mistress.

Did she do anything differently now? Should she be more familiar with him? Or less? She knew she should think of some wonderful carnal activity to surprise him. That was what a good mistress should do. But it was hard to think of such things with Beckett and the other footmen standing against the wall.

She knew what she wanted to do. She wanted to kiss the duke again. Kiss him as she had in the rain, and do it for hours. But even if she began by touching her lips to his and playing with his tongue, it wouldn't last all night. She knew he would want more.

What did the Duke of March expect of a mistress? What was the naughtiest thing he might ask for? She hoped it wasn't too frightening.

She set down her wineglass. Beckett sprang away from the wall, hurried to her, and bowed. "Now that you're finished, miss, His Grace wishes you to come to the study."

Anne pushed back from the table. "There is to be no brandy in that study tonight, Beckett, do you understand?"

The lad's face paled for a change. "His Grace won't be pleased."

"His Grace can come to me with his annoyance."

Beckett's sandy eyebrows shot up. He muttered something, and when she firmly asked him to repeat it, he flushed scarlet again. "His Grace used to have lots of women here, and they had lots of demands. Hot chocolate in gold-rimmed cups. Plates of cakes. Rose petals in their baths. We were supposed to treat them like duchesses. But none ever gave an order that went against His Grace's wishes."

Lots of women. Anne had no idea why it irked her so much to think of the duke entertaining other women here. Especially when she was his mistress, and she knew many women had come before her. Had he kissed other women the way he'd kissed her?

Be sensible, Anne. This is a transaction of business. Think!

"I am different from other women who have been here," she crisply told Beckett. *I am probably more desperate. And, ironically, I probably have much more to lose if I annoy him.* But she could not let him spend his nights in a chair in his study, drinking nightmares away. She'd seen women in the stews who lived for gin. Eventually it destroyed them.

"I intend to do things that are for the duke's own good," she said.

Scalding hot coffee hit his finger. Devon flinched, ground his teeth, but kept pouring. He had to stick his finger in the blasted cup to ensure he didn't overfill it.

"Goodness! Let me do that, Your Grace."

It was Cerise. Her skirts swished. She was striding toward him like a governess who'd caught him scribbling upon the wall. Or like his mother when she would seek him out to admonish him for his excessive card playing or the fact he'd stayed in his bed until late afternoon, suffering from a blazing hangover.

"Thank you, angel, but I don't need help. I am learning

to cope. Learning how to do all the things I once took for granted." Hades, why did she have to see him do this?

She'd given him something good in the rain this afternoon, but the passing hours had made him realize he wanted more than to create ways to survive with his blindness. He still wanted to see again. He knew he had to let go, but he damned well couldn't.

"By pouring hot coffee over your hand?" she asked briskly. "I don't want you to suffer needlessly when I could simply help you."

"I suppose it does hurt. But then, there are women who would tell you I don't mind a bit of pain along with my pleasure."

"Oh."

He heard her surprise, though she'd tried to smother it. He'd shocked and scared her. And he didn't know why he'd done it. Sighing, he said, "Angel, I made you an offer to be my mistress. Agreements must be made."

"Agreements?" She sounded astonished.

Speaking to her without seeing her was damnably awkward. "Yes, love. You require a contract. We have to negotiate your reward for all the hard work you will have to do. When I lease a house for you, you will be given its use for the duration of the lease. You will be given a settlement if I choose to end our arrangement. That sort of thing."

Dead silence. Devon stuck his finger in his coffee again, for no reason other than to locate his cup. He swallowed half of the bitter brew. Finally, because she wasn't saying a word, he added, "It's to protect you, angel."

"I know," she said. "I know a clever mistress should make a contract. But I have no idea what to ask for. Do we barter, Your Grace? Do you try to whittle down my demands while I try to elevate your offers?"

Her voice was flat and cold. There was nothing like

business to make sex a damnably awkward thing. Most courtesans were hardened to it and presented an army of solicitors to negotiate their contracts. But Cerise appeared as naïve about this as she had about kisses. It touched his heart. It made him want to hold her. Comfort her. Caress her until her nerves vanished. He swung around on the chair, toward her voice, spread his legs, and patted his thigh. "Come and sit on my lap, love."

"While we negotiate?"

"I'm willing to take the chance you will put me at a disadvantage."

"How—oh! You mean I could wriggle on your lap and manipulate your desire while we discuss the fine details."

Hades, but she sounded unhappy. "You'll be best protected this way, Cerise. You are free to wriggle all you wish. I want you, and I'm willing to be generous to keep you."

She gave a halting giggle. "I'm sorry. You are *already* being very generous."

At least he could tell her voice had softened, as if she was no longer hurt, or cold, or nervous. "Not as much as I'd like to be, angel. If we were in London, you would have *carte blanche* at various modistes. I would have sealed our arrangement with a gift of some pretty jewels. You would be decorating your town house tomorrow and admiring your new carriage."

He leaned back in his chair. "I must admit, I've never negotiated a lady's terms while making love to her," he said thoughtfully. "Would you like to see how generous I would be then? I'm intrigued to discover what you would ask for when you think I'm completely at your command."

Why did her belly feel so unsettled and her heart so tight? Anne couldn't understand what was wrong. This was what she had wanted, and the duke was being honorable. He was ensuring she took care of herself.

She was foolish to argue with him. What startled her was how vulnerable he looked. He had gone into battle and survived, but now he appeared uncertain. If she did not rein in her foolish emotions and use her wits, she was going to ruin everything.

Lifting her hems, she settled on his lap. He closed his eyes and made a murmuring sound of approval. He reached for the fastenings of his trousers, though she had no idea how he would remove them with her on top of him.

"Perhaps we shouldn't." She made her voice a sultry purr. "Truly, I wouldn't want to take advantage of you, Your Grace."

He laughed. Thank goodness for that. He moved his hands, leaving his falls closed, and wrapped his arms around her waist. "Here is what I propose, love." He proceeded to set out an arrangement that would encompass the next year. It rolled off his tongue with ease, as though he'd done it a thousand times, but she refused to think of that.

He promised to acquire a house for her. One in the country or, if they returned to London, a town house there. For one year—unless they chose to part ways earlier—she would be safe, she would have a roof over her head and a considerable amount of independence.

"Satisfactory, love?" he asked at the end. "There will be jewels too."

Satisfactory? "Yes," she whispered. He had just laid heaven out for her on a silver platter. She could have the life she used to dream of when she'd lived in poverty, when she'd been trapped in the brothel. If only her circumstances were different; if only she wasn't suspected of murder. She could not risk staying with His Grace for a year. He'd promised her an allowance—as soon as she acquired enough money to buy passage on a ship and begin a new life, she would have to escape England.

She should be happy. Soon she would be safe. She would be free. "It is . . . more than I could have hoped for."

"Angel." His expression grew serious. "Never underestimate your value. You are a delightful lover and a charming companion."

She swallowed hard and flushed with shame. She would have to escape long before the end of their contract. The duke had no idea she had agreed to terms she could not meet.

Unless she told him the truth and he believed her. She would be safe if he believed her, if Bow Street accepted her innocence. She turned on his lap. He had been generous, and surely he must expect her to behave like an adoring mistress in return.

But, first, she could tell him the truth. . . .

Anne bit her lip. No, it was too early to try. What if he thought her guilty without question? What if he chose to turn her over to the local magistrate? She had no way to *prove* her innocence.

The duke slid his hands up and cradled her breasts in her gown. They were his to do with as he pleased, of course. He had just paid very handsomely for them.

It was a stupid thought. This was what she *wanted*.

In the brothel, she'd learned not to feel anything at all. She must not let emotions get the best of her now. "Thank you," she whispered. But her voice wobbled, and tears welled in her eyes. She threw everything she could into the role of bold courtesan, for it would keep her from doing something foolish. Such as bursting into tears or spilling the truth.

She cupped his face. His mouth curved into a smile, one that brought deep lines to frame his lips. Heavens, he was beautiful, but though he smiled at her, he wasn't looking at her. That made her heart ache for him. One tear disobeyed, leapt free, and rolled down her cheek.

What was wrong with her? She hadn't let herself feel emotions for so long. She couldn't seem to stop them from flooding her now.

Control, Anne! She cradled his handsome face and kissed him hard. She tried every wonderful maneuver he had bestowed on her in the rain. Coaxing his lips open, she plunged her tongue inside, tasting the heat of his mouth, the bitter flavor of his coffee. She thrust and parried her tongue with his and daringly tried to make love to him with just her mouth.

The kiss scorched her from lips to toes. But she knew he would expect a more erotic thank-you than this. She slid off his lap and lowered to her knees beside him.

"Angel, where are you going?" he asked in confusion, but she gave him his answer without words. She undid the falls of his trousers.

The duke took a sharp breath. He wore nothing beneath. And he was very aroused.

She bent and gave a kiss to his erection. He jolted up beneath her lips. Fancifully, it seemed to her that the taut head of his member was straining to kiss her back. She closed her eyes and set about pleasuring him.

But try as she might, she could not bring him to release. She worked, changing her position, her motions, and though he groaned and rocked beneath her, he didn't climax. Heavens, why wouldn't he? What had she done wrong?

He let his head fall back against the top of the tall chair, sucking in deep breaths. "Lovely, angel, but I have something else in mind. Have you ever made love on a swing?"

Chapter Eight

"THIS IS NOT like any swing I've ever been on before," Anne said, then blushed acutely as the duke exploded with laughter. Perhaps she did sound oddly . . . prim for a courtesan. But it was the truth. The swing was a shocking thing, since it was supposed to be for lovemaking and he had it permanently attached in the master bedchamber of his *home*.

No, of course this wasn't his home. This was his hunting box, used for his wild parties. And she was supposed to behave like an adventurous mistress.

He had climbed on the bed, had slid away a panel in the canopy, and a bundle of white silken cords had tumbled down. The ropes were fastened in some mysterious way to the wooden structure above them. As he untangled them, she could see the swing had a woven sling, made up of the cords. He gave it a push when he was done, and it made lazy passes over the bed.

"Are you sure this thing is not dangerous?"

His chuckle rumbled through the shadows. A candle sat upon a dressing table and cast a guinea-gold light on him. "No, love. Perfectly safe. Or so I've heard. I had it installed a long time ago, long before I went to war."

His smile vanished as he swung the ropes again thoughtfully. "I've never used it."

"Why not?" He looked troubled and she wished to know why.

"I had decided to take a bride, and that meant no more mistresses. No more orgies, no more courtesans at the hunting box."

"Because you planned to marry?"

"When a man loses his heart, there is no other woman he wants in his bed," he said simply.

She might be naïve, but she believed him. Yet what had happened? Why had he not married, if he had fallen in love? Kat had told her never to ask awkward questions of a protector, certainly not questions about love, and never to pry. A gentleman wished a mistress who always agreed with him, who soothed his worries instead of provoking them.

But what lady with sense would not marry *this* man if he'd fallen in love with her?

The duke got on his knees on the bed, holding the swing steady. He was nude, wearing nothing but a wide, lusty smile. On him, nakedness was very alluring.

She used to be a hoyden; she used to climb trees, walk along the slippery railings of bridges, daringly ride bareback. Years in the brothel had sapped her strength and made her soft. Could she do this? Get on that precarious thing and make love to him without hurting them both?

"I'll help you up," he offered. He wore such a look of hopeful anticipation, she knew she must try. He held her hand, as a gallant knight would, but getting her onto the seat involved much squealing, the heart-dipping fear she would fall off, and his gentle, desire-roughened laughter.

She must be making a dreadful mess of this. This must be a fantasy for him. She knew erotic fantasies were tremendously important to men. If she kept squealing with shock and almost falling off, she was going to ruin it—

"Up you go," he rasped, and her bare bottom landed on the silky rope seat. It dropped with her weight, and the ropes followed the curve of her rump. They were surprisingly soft, the touch of them unexpectedly exciting.

Her feet brushed the bed and she carefully pushed off. The instant she took flight, swinging beside him, she had to bite her lip. This was what it was like to be wild, young, and carefree.

The duke stretched out beneath her, and she forgot to breathe. The swing dipped so low, her quim brushed his stomach. Her privates were scandalously exposed by the holes in the seat.

He caught her hips. Desire turned his expression harsh. "Take me inside you, angel. Swing on me. Be as daring as you want."

"All right." Cupped in the swing, she reached down, almost toppled off. "Eek!"

"Cerise?"

"I am all right." She wriggled back on. She felt more herring than daring—a fish caught in a net. "You'll have to . . . um . . . hold yourself. I can't reach."

"Ah, not quite that well endowed, am I?"

"Oh, yes!" she cried, afraid she'd made a mistake. "You are very much so, but my hand cannot reach unless—" Then she saw the teasing twinkle. He wrapped his right hand around the hilt of his erection and held the astonishing length straight up. He slid into her, filling her. Goodness, it was true—it was a thrilling sensation to have him inside, to be floating on top of him, barely touching him except where his thick shaft was buried deep in her. It was so new and different, she could not take her mind somewhere else. She didn't want to. She'd wanted to do this for his delight, but she actually liked it too.

He pushed gently, making her swing on him. Agony

contorted his delectably handsome face. "I wish I could see you. I want to see you sway. See my cock inside you. Hell, I want to see your face as I pleasure you."

She didn't want this to remind him of loss. "I wish I could see you, but I have my eyes shut."

The silence left her breathless . . . then he laughed gently. He pushed the swing, twirled her, swayed her from side to side. Sensations exploded inside her—so much so, she almost let go of the ropes. Then she opened her eyes and saw herself in the large looking glass.

A wild creature floated on the white silk swing, one with loose, tumbling hair. With flushed breasts and pink cheeks. The curves of her derrière squeezed between the mesh pattern of the seat.

"Oh, goodness. I look scandalous," she gasped. Forgetting. Hastily she added, "I mean, I look a mess and, well, a bit silly caught in the swing. You are not missing much."

"Don't say that." He stopped the swing. She ached for the pleasure of rocking on him, but he wouldn't let her. "I cannot see you, but I know you are beautiful. In every way."

It was so sweet, it made her throat tight. She was supposed to be saucy, not teary. "Let us swing, Your Grace," she said, trying to sound bold, "and soar to a climax."

He swung her back and forth, her legs and derrière flying atop him. Pleasurable tension grew inside her. The ache intensified. The need for more . . . to move harder . . .

Anne wriggled in the seat, for it made her swing the perfect amount. It made her most sensitive place rub against his shaft. Unexpected pleasure slammed into her. Then he touched her there, on her clit, and stroked her as she glided along him. She had to close her eyes again. She gripped the ropes so hard, her nails broke strands.

This time she didn't want to simply endure his touch,

she yearned to enjoy it. How did she do that? She tried to think of nothing but how he felt inside her. She shut her eyes and rocked on him. Desperate. Determined. But the more she tried, the more she felt the pleasure slipping away. She opened her eyes wide, drinking in how beautiful he was, how erotic and wicked this was, how perfect . . .

It was too late. She just *couldn't*. She had to pretend, as she always did. Frustration hit her so hard she could have screamed. But whatever she did, she couldn't disappoint him. "Your Grace!" she cried. She made her quim pulse around his shaft, squeezing him tight. She moaned and wailed as though in the grip of shattering ecstasy. He gripped her hips to plunge up into her. He roared his orgasm, the harshness of the sound stunning. He arched up into her, while his body bucked, his eyes closed, and he cried out her name.

He fell back, his chest heaving. His member softened and slid out of her on a wash of hot fluid. He held out his arms. "Come to me. I can't see you to help you."

She clasped his hands. "That doesn't matter. This is all I need." He supported her as she put her bare feet on the bed and struggled off the swing. She lost her balance and tumbled on top of him, but he only laughed. "My adventurous Cerise," he whispered.

Her heart made a giddy little trip at his words, pushing away her disappointment with herself. He rolled them over so they lay on their sides, facing each other. He kissed her, gently and lovingly. "Thank you," he murmured. He took a long, ragged breath. "That was . . . unbelievable. Angel, would you tell me what it looked like?"

Perhaps giggles were not the best response for that. She thought of what she'd looked like on the swing, how awkward she'd felt but how sensual and thrilling it had been. And how much she had liked hearing him laugh—she realized she'd never heard a man laugh while making love. "Well, you looked exactly as you always do, devilishly handsome, rather like a Grecian statue come to life, except for your magnificent erection, which was sticking up. I looked like I had been scooped up in a net—"

His booming laugh stopped her. Suddenly he slid his fingers into her underarms. "Teasing me, are you? I can do the same to you."

"Your Grace—" He tickled her! She couldn't help but laugh. Then she couldn't stop, because he wouldn't stop tickling. Her face was burning hot—it must be red from all her helpless giggles. Hardly the look of a skilled, enigmatic courtesan, but she didn't care. She couldn't care. She felt buoyant with pleasure, the kind of wonderful delight she hadn't felt for a long, long time. When was the last time she'd laughed like this? She couldn't remember. For years she hadn't had any reason to laugh. But she was giddy with mirth now. It spilled out no matter how much she tried to make it stop.

Finally he withdrew his fingers and she gasped for breath. "I never took you for a giggler, angel," he whispered. He levered up onto his arm, facing her. "I haven't laughed so much in longer than I can remember."

It would be wonderful if the laughter did not have to end. And the way to stay joyful would be to make love again, wouldn't it? He began to get up, but she wrapped her arms around him so he couldn't leave the bed. "When you are ready for more," she asked, "is it possible to make love with you on the swing, Your Grace?"

This time his brows shot up, almost vanishing into his black hair. "That sounds dangerous from my point of view, love. Why don't we try it together? With you on top, of course."

* * *

He'd sensed Cerise's tension when she rode on top of him on the swing. Devon felt it again as she straddled him while he settled on the rope seat. His hands bumped hers where she gripped the rope, clutching it tight. Hades, her knuckles must be bone-white.

Was she just scared of the swing?

She lowered on him so her silky, hot quim pressed to his rigid, naked cock. Pure pleasure rushed through him. But he still felt her tension. He'd noticed the same stiffness in her when he first performed oral sex upon her. He thought he'd pleasured her enough to make her relax—she'd certainly shouted loudly when she came. On the swing, she'd laughed for him. She must have enjoyed it.

Why, then, was she so tense? What did she fear?

He remembered how she had taken his fingers and traced bruises on her back. Of course she was afraid. She had been in a brothel, and she claimed her madam had beaten her. Was she afraid he might use his fists on her? Realization hit him hard. He'd warned her he could hurt her, told her he could inflict worse damage than her madam. Of course she was terrified of him. She must have been afraid each time they'd made love.

"Don't be afraid, angel," he murmured. He sucked in a sharp breath as her fingers slid around his shaft. He was hard as a brick. "I won't hurt you."

"I know." With her hand wrapped around the pulsating hilt of his rod, she stroked him against her, teasing him with the heat of her moist cunny. "I know you won't." She took him inside her, and he struggled to think against the onslaught of fire and need that flooded him.

Pump into her, pleasure her, his body insisted. But he didn't want to take his own pleasure while she was perched so stiffly on him. He struggled for control. "What are you scared of, love? You were tense on the swing. And as brittle as ice the time I kissed your lovely quim."

"I—oh, I'm not tense."

"Angel, you are. I can feel it. Since I can't see you, I have to focus on everything else." He ran his hands along her forearms. "They are locked with tension." He caressed the back of her neck. "Your muscles are as tight as knots."

"I don't have my balance on the swing. That's all."

He wanted to believe that was all, wanted to ease her fears, make her come. He loved the crescendo of her cries when she found her pleasure. He was determined to give her every bit of the ecstasy she gave him. "Hold me then, and let us swing," he said gruffly.

He gave a gentle kick and they coasted back. She squealed on top of him. They swung forward, and his cock followed the arc, sliding deep inside her. Hell, the sheer heavenly joy of it shot through his brain. But she was still stiff. *Relax, Cerise. Come on, angel. Enjoy it.* Dimly, he realized he was begging out loud for her to do so.

Then she moaned. A moan as dark as chocolate, as deep as his thrusts felt, as hoarse as he knew his voice sounded. With each pass of the swing, she cried, "Oh! *Oooh!*"

But now he could hear it: the forced quality in her voice. She groaned, and her voice dropped to a sultry purr guaranteed to drive a man mad as she gasped, "I'm coming! Oh, Your *Grace*." But even though she was wailing through a climax, she was still like a board on top of him. She was screaming with pleasure—but was she feeling any of it? He felt his arousal slipping away. He focused on Cerise, on every throaty wail and breathy gasp. He slid his hands between them and touched her quim. She wasn't wet. Not lushly slick, the way she would be if she came. Had she made all that noise even though she hadn't liked it? Had she been giving him a performance?

He asked, wondering if he really wanted the answer, "Angel, did you like it?"

Then he knew—no matter what she said, he had to know. Making love should not be only about him getting serviced. He wanted her to enjoy it too. It wouldn't be pleasure for him if he thought she was going through the motions, unhappy, uncomfortable, scared. "Is it good, Cerise? Am I good?" Hell, was she too afraid of him?

"Your Grace, you are wonderful. Of course it is good. You make me come so many times."

He heard the fear in her tone. "No, I don't, angel, do I?" Was it because he was blind? Or had he lost some of his technique? It had been a long time since he'd made love. He hadn't done it since he lost Rosalind and went to war.

"You *do,*" she insisted, and she sounded almost desperate. "Let me prove it, Your Grace."

"You don't have to prove anything, Cerise. I just want to give you pleasure."

How had he known? What had she done wrong?

Anne froze on the duke's lap. The women in the brothel had insisted every man loved a good performance. Men, they claimed, always wanted to think they were superb lovers—so they readily believed a woman's screams and moans. But the duke had guessed hers weren't real. He'd said he felt her tension. Heavens, had he been *that* perceptive of her during sex?

It was so ironic. She *had* enjoyed it. She was *not* afraid of him. She had been so very close to pleasure, but an orgasm would not happen for her. And now he feared she hadn't liked it at all. "You do give me pleasure," she insisted. How could she convince him? He sounded . . . hurt. The whole point of being his mistress was to keep him content in bed.

"Is it because I'm blind?"

The question confused her so much, she muttered, "Is what—" before she stopped herself. "You are so very good. Everything you do to me is wonderful. It is *perfect.*" If her performances had not been enough, what could she do now? Why should it matter whether she came or not? "You are the most perfect lover ever, Your Grace. And all I want to do is give you pleasure."

In the silence, her heart thundered. She had told him the truth—he was wonderful at lovemaking and she truly did want to delight him. Finally he groaned. "All right, my dear. Then let us share pleasure together. Perhaps this time on the bed?"

Anne snuggled sleepily against the duke's chest.

Goodness, had they really spent two whole days making love? That night, after he questioned her about her orgasms, they'd indulged in three more sexual bouts. She was certain the duke now believed she was climaxing. She suspected he *wanted* to believe it, as the other women at Madame's had said. The frustrating thing: She simply could not come. Perhaps it was the way she was. Or it was because of her past. She loved to make love with the duke, but she could not find the ultimate pleasure from it. And she must keep that a secret.

They'd stopped lovemaking only long enough for the meals that were served to them in the bedroom. She'd quickly learned why the duke had not wanted anyone to witness him dine. He was still learning how to cope with eating food he could not see.

Using a trick from her grandfather, she had shown him how to arrange his plate in a pattern that suited him: his meat at three o'clock, his potato at nine, his vegetables at twelve. Quietly, she instructed Treadwell to teach the footman to serve His Grace this way. They must arrange his food in the same way at each meal and discreetly explain each dish they served onto his plate.

"Angel, I think we're going to have to get out of bed." Grinning, the duke stroked her loose, disheveled hair. It was a delightful caress.

"Mmm. Do we have to?"

He laughed. "It is time to change the bedding, love. Crisp, clean sheets will be a treat."

"That would be lovely." Then, daringly, she asked, "Perhaps you would share them with me all night?"

She knew he didn't sleep in the bed with her. He waited until he thought she was asleep, then he went to an adjoining bedroom. He would close the door, likely so she would not hear him cry out with nightmares or know he paced for most of the night.

But she had heard all those things, and each time she heard him shout, she'd gone to him. No matter how much he thrashed, she would sit at his bedside and soothe him. He must have been exhausted from their lovemaking, because he didn't wake when she touched him. Each time, she was able to coax him back to sleep.

She knew Beckett had not listened to her: He brought brandy to that room. For two days she had watered it down when the duke slept. Little by little, so no one would notice.

He didn't answer her, so she asked again, "Would you try sleeping with me, Your Grace?"

He sighed. "Angel, why would you want to take the risk? There's no need for us to sleep together. We can have sex and then I'll leave you to your rest." He wrapped one of her tangled locks around his finger. "It works perfectly. Even my mother and father, who were devoted to each other, didn't share a bed. My father always insisted part of the continuing excitement was to go to my mother's room and rap on the door and hope she was equally randy."

She had to giggle at that. It was true: Married couples did not share beds. Why was she so determined to coerce him to sleep with her? It would prove to him he was healing, and she was certain he was. But she feared if he had a nightmare and hit her, he would take that as proof he was going mad.

He wasn't mad. After the past couple of days with him, Anne was equally certain of that.

He patted her bottom and lifted her off him, gently letting her sprawl on the tousled sheets beside him. "I've ordered the carriage to take you into the village. There's a dressmaker and a milliner's. Choose as many clothes as you wish. The seamstress is to complete them immediately. Write a note with those instructions and I'll sign it."

"You wish me to buy clothing?"

"It occurred to me you have nothing but that robe of mine and the dress you came in. I can't keep you here and force you to stay in the same dress day after day."

"For two days you have kept me out of it."

"Remember our contract. I'm failing in my duties as protector." He spoke lightly, but his mouth was grim. "If we were in London, you would have rushed out to the most fashionable modiste in Town first thing in the morning after I made my offer."

Would she have? The truth: She would not have done so. She wouldn't have thought of it so quickly. For years, she hadn't been able to dream of buying a gown. But as his mistress, she would shame him if she was not fashionable. Ironically, she would embarrass him if she did not lavishly spend his money. She was relieved, though, that he seemed to have forgotten her tension.

"Would you wish to accompany me on my excursion?" she asked. "Your Grace, Treadwell told me that the afternoon we walked in the rain was the only time you'd left the house in two weeks." Surely it would help him to not be indoors all the time.

"Apparently I ran out into the woods one night, when I dreamed I was in battle. I ended up in the stream and almost drowned. Since that foray onto my grounds went so well, I decided to defer another attempt."

Heavens, no wonder he wouldn't leave the house. "Come with me now. It would be lovely to walk together."

"No, angel. Go yourself and take some of my servants. Buy anything you wish. I won't be able to see it, but I want you to be pleased."

The ducal carriage rattled down the high street of the village of Welby, which lay four miles from the duke's house. Anne peered out the window. Sunlight darted from behind gray clouds, dappling the row of narrow shops. Children stopped in the street, then raced behind the carriage. Tradesmen came to their doorsteps. Ladies hurriedly adjusted their daughters' apparel.

This village was so like Banbury, near her home of Longsworth, and Anne struggled to forget the reminders of a life she'd lived long ago. She'd vowed she would think only of selective things of that time—things she could use to help the duke.

But the smell of the bakeshop made her think of walking in to the one in her village, with a penny in her hand. The stretch of green commons reminded her of village fêtes, and Maypoles, and scampering over the grass despite the fact she was usually wearing a pristine white muslin dress. Then Father had died suddenly of an attack of the heart, and before she had recovered from the shock of losing her father, Sebastian had come. He was the viscount. And he still had wanted her. He wanted to marry her.

Ever since Anne was eight years of age, Sebastian had shown a great interest in her when he visited Longsworth. He began to kiss her—not cousinlike pecks but horribly wet kisses on her lips. Whenever he found her alone, he would touch her on her chest or her bottom, or he would slip his hand beneath her skirts and stroke her legs. Even now, thinking about it made her shudder. It made her feel so bad, so wrong and guilty and sick in her stomach.

She and her mother had been in Sebastian's power. Mama had agreed she was not to marry Sebastian. She was only *fifteen*. But one night he'd come into her bedroom. He said if he took her innocence, she would have to marry him. She'd frozen at first as he climbed on top of her. Then she'd been so horrified at the thought of marrying him, she managed to slither out from under him while he fumbled with his clothing. Desperately, she grabbed for a weapon. Her fingers closed on the lip of her chamber pot. When he leapt at her to haul her back onto the bed, she threw it at him.

Her mother had come, along with servants—the housekeeper, maids, footmen. All summoned by her shriek, which had been more in anger than terror. Then she had seen her cousin's face and she had truly gone ice cold with fear. Red-faced, with bulging eyes, he had looked as if he wanted to kill her. That very night, Mama gathered a few of their things, loyal servants prepared a carriage, and they ran away. They had nowhere to go. Her mother's family was estranged from them, because her grandpapa—her mother's father—had married an unsuitable woman. Her grandmother had been a former opera dancer who once performed on the stage. Her mother had said they could not go to any of her family—

none of her mother's relatives would help them. So they had gone to London. Despite their poverty, despite the long, arduous hours her mother worked, Mama had tried to make Anne feel as surrounded by love as she had been when growing up at Longsworth. . . .

By the time she reached the narrow shop front with fabrics displayed in the window, which stood right beside the milliner's, Anne has discovered that a heart could feel unbearably small and tight yet full to bursting at the same time.

A footman helped her down from the carriage. She pushed open the door to the dressmaker's, and a tiny bell gave a melodic tinkle.

The modiste hurried forward, a tape draped around her neck. The woman had gray-streaked brown hair swept up in a chignon and wore a well-made, tasteful day dress. Anne had brushed and pinned up her hair and wore her cloak over her gown, but it was a scandalous gown for the middle of the day, and it looked worse for wear. There were two women in the shop. Anne's heart sank. Respectable ladies, of course. Members of the country gentry.

She explained her purpose—and the fact that the Duke of March would pay for her purchases.

The dressmaker's brows rose sharply. "I see. I am grateful for His Grace's condescension, but . . ." Her voice was awkward, brittle. The woman glanced toward the two ladies, one thin and dark, the other stout and fair. Lowering her tones, she murmured, "This is a respectable establishment, miss. I dare not offend the sensibilities of the gentlewomen of this village."

The ladies gazed coldly at Anne. The thin one whispered to the stout one behind her gloved hand. The blonde's mouth opened in a large O. No doubt the thin one had said the word that scandalized all respectable ladies. *Whore.* Anne would be less despised if she carried the plague.

She knew she could tip up her nose and use the duke's name to demand service. But courage fled. She turned on her heel and raced out of the shop. The bell gave a tinkle, the door snapped shut behind her, and the impassive footman promptly opened the carriage door as though it was customary for the duke's mistresses to run from shops.

Stupidly, Anne buried her face in her hands as the carriage rumbled off. What did it matter if she wasn't respectable? What did it matter if Bow Street wanted to hang her? She *wasn't* bad. She had saved those three innocent girls from the brothel. And she might just survive. Survival was all that mattered.

It seemed the carriage reached the duke's home far more quickly than it had taken to get to the village. A groom was leading a horse away from the front steps. Anne's heart dropped. Could it be a Bow Street Runner? She must stop *panicking*. It could just be a friend of the duke's. . . .

It could be Lord Ashton! After Kat had refused his offer to service the duke, he would have continued to search for another woman. What if he'd come to tell the duke he'd found someone? The duke would know her story was a lie.

Anne forced her feet to move toward the front door. Treadwell met her and took her cloak. By now she was accustomed to his odd appearance, and she'd noticed his eyes normally held a merry twinkle. At this moment, though, he looked gravely serious.

"Does the duke have a visitor?" How normal her voice sounded. Astonishing, when her heart pounded so hard.

"Aye, miss. An investigator from London. Name of Mr. Wynter. Used to be a Bow Street Runner, I hear."

* * *

Lord Norbrook was a haunted man.

In his bedchamber, Sebastian blearily faced his reflection in his looking glass. As usual, his dress was faultless—sheer elegance in the style of Beau Brummell. Yet inside he seethed with frustration and his head thudded from the effects of too much port. Last night, he'd dreamed of having Anne in his bed. He'd dreamed of her the way she used to be at Longsworth. He wanted her so much. And he hated her. Hated, hated, hated her.

How could she have refused him? He shook his head, even though it made his brain slosh painfully in his skull. She could no longer be the lovely little angel she had once been. She would be dirty now. When she'd been young, she had been so precious. So pure.

He wanted so much to touch her. He could not forget how beautiful she was as a young woman, when her hair had first been put up. He was haunted by the memory of tendrils of gold coiled against her smooth neck and the pretty push of youthful breasts against her bodice. But how could he caress those delightful breasts now, knowing she was no longer untouched?

Before his looking glass, Sebastian adjusted his expression, as though he was putting on a mask. Now he appeared as a viscount should, not like a man suffering lust for an ungrateful chit who did not deserve his desire.

Each step brought a slice of pain through his skull—and it was Anne's fault he'd had to drink so much, tormented with erotic memories of her girlish beauty—but he went down to his drawing room to greet his guest. The elderly lady, Anne's maternal great-grandmother, rose from her seat as he entered. Her hair was silver, rubies glittered at her neck, and silk swathed her slim form. Her face was drawn with worry. "Have you found her?"

"Not yet, my dear Lady Julia." Feigning gentlemanly concern for the trembling old lady, Sebastian hastened to her side. "But it will not be long. I have spared no expense in the search."

Pained dark-green eyes peered at him, yet this woman's sorrow only irritated him. She knew nothing of what real torment was. She thought he would find Anne, then she would reconcile with her great-grandchild, and all would be happy. She had no idea that Anne was now ruined. She had no idea how greatly he was suffering—both hungering for Anne and hating her.

"I fear she is dead, Norbrook," Lady Julia whispered. "I wanted to make amends to her, but I fear I am too late."

"No, you must have faith." Sebastian clasped the old lady's hand and drew her to sit on the settee. "I am certain Anne is alive." Yes, he was certain of that. He wasn't so certain Mick Taylor could find her, as the brute had promised.

"I have no other family, Norbrook." Lady Julia clutched his arm. "My son, Anne's grandfather, is dead. My two daughters are gone, and they died childless. I have two titled wastrel sons-in-law. They expect I will leave my wealth to them. I will not. I despise them. I have made Anne my sole heir."

He'd heard the tale a dozen times before and the only part that interested him was Lady Julia's assurance that she had made Anne her heiress. She had disowned Anne's grandfather—her son—over his marriage to an opera dancer. She had refused to acknowledge his family—his daughter, Millicent, and his granddaughter, Anne. But once she ended up alone, the old witch had come to Longsworth to find Anne, who was the only family she had left.

"Yes, my dear lady. You will have Anne home soon." This time, Sebastian would make Anne marry him. Anne would be desperate now that she was suspected of the madam's murder, and he had to wed her. For he desperately needed money.

Those gaming hells had cheated him. He was a clever gentleman—how could he have lost so badly at a simple game of dice? But he did not dare hint that he'd been cheated. The brutes running the hells did not take kindly to such charges. However, they did want their blunt. And he had none.

Sebastian had mortgaged the estate and the income did not begin to touch his debts. When he married Anne, he could use his expectations from Lady Julia's estate for funds.

It meant marrying a tarnished, ruined woman. It meant touching Anne, when she was now revolting to him. But he had no choice.

"If only my granddaughter had not left her home." Lady Julia's shrill voice cut into his thoughts. "She would be alive and Anne would be safe. I still do not understand why she took Anne to London, Norbrook."

His head throbbed. Why did the old woman keep harping on this? "Anne's mother was having an affair with a married man," he lied smoothly. "She pursued him to London but he ended the sordid relationship. Millicent had no money and ended up in the stews. But it does not matter." Would the old crone not let it drop? It was not his fault Millicent had run away with Anne. "I will find Anne. I promise."

Anne should have done as she was told. She should have married him. Sebastian had only one consolation for having to wed her now: Once she was in his power again, he would punish her for her disobedience. That he would enjoy greatly.

Chapter Nine

HE NEEDED ACTION. He had to do something, but he was capable only of walking slowly while counting steps and swinging his walking stick to warn him of oncoming furniture.

Damn the blindness.

In his study, Devon fingered his glass of brandy. His investigator in London, Maxmillian Wynter, had brought him a report of his findings in London's stews. The former Bow Street Runner had given him an address, but his quarry—the wife and the child of Captain Tanner, a man who had been killed at Waterloo—had disappeared.

He'd already downed two glasses of brandy. The stuff had been watered down again, and he'd roared at a footman until his supply was replenished with the full-strength variety. The young footman, Beckett, had finally admitted they were diluting the stuff on the orders of Miss Cerise, as they called her belowstairs.

Two things had occurred to Devon at that moment. First: He didn't know his mistress's last name, and he couldn't read their contract to find out what she had signed on it. It was bloody embarrassing to have to ask her now, after he'd made a legal agreement with her.

And second: Since when did a duke's ladybird give commands about his liquor supply? And why in blazes were his servants paying more attention to his mistress than to their master?

"If Miss Cerise has returned from the village, fetch her for me," he barked, assuming that a servant lurked somewhere close by. "At once."

He got up and paced the same path in his study that he restlessly trudged each night. Exactly fifty steps from start to finish. He began at the settee and, when he reached the end of his count, he had to turn to avoid hitting the corner of his desk.

"Your Grace."

Cerise's voice was a breathy whisper, a lush sound that set desire on fire at once. But he heard a shaky tremble. She sounded fearful. Afraid of him because she knew she must be in trouble over the brandy? Guilt hit him. "You aren't in trouble, love," he murmured.

"Oh! You—what do you mean? I—" Her melodic quaver of a voice died away. "You had a visitor—he was an investigator from London, I believe?"

Instant panic hit him. Had she heard any of his conversation with Wynter? Devon's annoyance over his brandy vanished. His body reacted to the threat of confrontation. Every nerve went on alert, his heart ran at a gallop, his breathing came quick and light.

"Yes, he was from London." He left it at that, waiting to hear what she would say, learn what she knew or had overheard. Damn, he wanted to see her. Watch her eyes. Assess her face.

She stayed silent, and he realized it was like being in a field hospital with a shattered leg. Better to agree to the pain of the saw than hope to keep the leg and die of the spread of infection. If she knew what his business had been with Wynter, he wanted to have it out with her now. "Did you happen to overhear my conversation with him, Cerise?"

"No! Of course not! But you look grim. Pale."

"Don't I always look grim and pale, Cerise? Treadwell tells me I do."

"You don't! Over the last two days you looked happier. Your . . . color was much better."

"Flushed with exertion from making love, I expect."

"So there was no bad news . . . nothing to disturb you?"

He let her question stand between them for a while, dissecting every rise and fall of her breath. Finally he asked, "What is it you are searching for? Confirmation of something you suspect?"

"Heavens, no. What—what do you mean by that?"

He had meant confirmation of what she might have figured out if she'd listened in on Wynter and him. She sounded honestly confused. They were dancing around something, but he didn't know what. "All right, you want to know what Wynter—my investigator—and I discussed? It was nothing of import. Business in London."

"Oh." She let out a sigh of relief, one he wouldn't have heard if he hadn't been listening closely. "I wondered if you had been asking him questions about me."

"Angel, he came to bring me information I requested. How could I have asked questions about you? I'd have to do it by post, and the only person who can write a letter is you."

"You could have sent a footman with questions."

Her answer came so swiftly he knew she had been working out possibilities in her head. "What are you afraid I would learn? What are you afraid of in London? The truth this time."

"I *told* you the truth. I was afraid that if you'd sent

this man to inquire about me, he might have spoken to my madam and she might now know where I am."

With sight, he could have seen if she blushed or paled. He could see a shift of her gaze, a bite of her lip. He would know, with a lot more certainty, when she was lying. "I didn't ask Wynter to investigate you, Cerise. I saw no reason not to trust you. What do I need to know about you that you haven't told me?"

"There is nothing else you need to know about me." The sultry purr. "I missed you, Your Grace, even for just the short time I was in the village." Her dress rustled; she gave a breathy sigh. "That's much better. The bodice was squeezing me too tight."

What did that mean? Had she unfastened the buttons on her dress?

"Did you want me to come here to make love?" Her mouth lingered over those two words. *Make love.* It was as though she could perform feats of magic. Levitate his erection with two enchanted words. And something fell, with a soft *plop*.

"There. I managed to get out of my dress. But I can't undo the corset by myself. Would you care to assist me, Your Grace? I think it would be so . . . erotic to pleasure you while I am utterly naked and you are so handsomely and completely dressed."

To meet Wynter, he'd forced Treadwell to play valet and help him into a silk waistcoat, a tailcoat, and polished boots. Now she was *playing* the mistress. He could hear it in every deliberate little breathless giggle and moan. He knew an act when he heard it.

And it was working. He couldn't help it. A dozen erotic scenarios exploded in his head. He could take her from behind as she leaned against the wall. Or have her wrap her legs around him and brace her back to the wall. Or lie down on the carpet and let her ride him to oblivion.

He could imagine each scene with perfect clarity. All he had to do was give the command and she would service him in any way he wanted. Any way he needed. He could use her to pound away the guilt that sat like acid in his gut. But he had no right to do so. "No, Cerise," he growled. "Not now."

No.

Anne had gnawed her thumbnail nearly to the quick. If the duke knew about Madame's death, knew she was suspected of murder, he would have confronted her by now. He couldn't know. But he was angry. Was it because he'd guessed she was faking her orgasms? How had he done so? This morning he'd laughed with her in bed; now he didn't want to touch her.

She had been an absolute fool. His business had nothing to do with her, but her awkward questions had provoked suspicion. She'd hoped to distract him with sex; now she didn't know what to do. What if he asked more questions and drew closer to her secret? What if she clumsily gave him a clue? She *had* to seduce him.

"I can think of many ways we could make love right here," she purred.

"So can I, angel."

Did that mean she'd piqued his interest? "You look so . . . unhappy. You looked pleased over the last few days, when we made love all the time. I would like to make you smile."

"That may prove difficult, love."

"Oh, dear." She feigned dismay, but real fear gnawed inside her. "Then I shall try very hard, Your Grace." Her saucy voice rang falsely in the room.

"No," he snapped.

What could she do? She gazed at the walls, which held many paintings of horses. Perhaps a dozen beautiful works stacked one atop the other, from wainscoting to soaring ceiling. For the first time she noticed that in the middle of all the pictures of horses hung a small portrait of four young women. One was seated gracefully upon a Queen Anne chair, her hair as black as the duke's, her eyes large and the same intriguing lavender color. Her dress was a spill of ivory satin and white lace, and she wore a mischievous smile. Three young girls surrounded her, each a beauty. One was dark, and the other two had golden hair and large green eyes.

"Are all these your horses?" The question seemed inane, but the silence pressed on her like a block of lead.

"At one time or another. My father complained about the money I spent on my mounts."

"And the ladies? One looks as though she must be your sister."

"They all are. Of course, when I held wild parties here, I would cover their portraits."

"That was very noble of you."

His brow lifted in ducal hauteur. "Are you making fun of me, Cerise?"

"Of course not." Heart hammering, she moved to him. Daringly, she pressed against his chest and stroked her way up the front of his coat. She clasped his hand and coaxed it to her bosom.

He cupped her breast and bent his head to the crook of her neck. He kissed her throat, and a tumult of emotion hit Anne—hope, uncertainty, and the fear that she might reveal more than she dared. She kept her mouth shut and let him kiss and fondle her. In some way she had conquered his resistance, but she didn't quite know how.

His lips followed the arch of her throat and brushed the spot where her jaw met her neck. He flicked his tongue, setting off a deep, low throb between her legs. "Do you like this? Your heart is pounding, Cerise."

"It always does," she said swiftly, "when I am with you. And I do like it. Very much."

"I need to work off some frustration, love. What I can't decide is whether I want to make love to you or go for a ride."

"A ride?" she echoed. "Do you mean on a horse?"

His hand moved back from her breast, his lips lifted from her neck. "You assume I can't."

She could have bitten her tongue. It was her goal to help him, not remind him of everything he could not do. He was already in a belligerent mood. "No, but I was told you had not gone outside, except when we walked together."

"I haven't ridden since Waterloo." His next question surprised her. "Do you ride?"

"Yes." She spoke before she'd thought of the wisdom of a truthful answer. Surely admitting that couldn't give her secrets away. But she saw his brows lift with surprise.

"Indeed? Then ride with me."

With no riding habit, Anne borrowed the duke's shirt, coat, and trousers. They walked to the stables. She didn't need to lead him, he could follow the smell—the clean smell of horses and new hay, the ripe smell of dung.

She hadn't ridden since Longsworth. Every moment with the duke seemed to draw her deeper into memories of the home she'd lost. Once she had owned a white Arabian. She had called her mare Midnight, because her white horse was as brilliant as the bevy of stars that glittered above her house in the middle of the night.

She watched His Grace's expression. Carved stone, with his jaw clamped shut. Of course—he must be remembering what it was like to ride when he had his sight. His face looked as firmly set against memories as she imagined hers must.

The groom brought the gelding to a halt. The duke acknowledged his servant, then turned to her. "How much experience have you had in the saddle?"

She flushed, aware of the double meaning. But he appeared so serious, she knew he had not meant that at all. "Years and years ago, I rode every day. I rode whenever I could."

The duke took a step toward the nickering horse held by his groom. "That sounds like Abednigo. Give me his reins, Benson, and bring out Angelica for Miss Cerise."

Minutes ticked by—the groom must be saddling Angelica. The clop of hooves on the stone floor of the stable had Anne breathless with anticipation. She savored the thought of riding again. Soon a beautiful animal emerged, walking elegantly behind young Benson. Angelica was jet black, obviously a purely bred Arabian, and carefully groomed.

Benson held the mare's bridle. Anne mounted, swinging her leg over the horse's back, and she settled on the saddle. It might be scandalous for a lady to ride this way, but she wasn't a lady anymore, and she could ride faster astride. She yearned to give Angelica her head, to fly across fields and countryside. But she couldn't, because the duke couldn't, and she had to subdue her exhilaration. Angelica danced skittishly beneath her. They seemed to be kindred spirits, both eager to do something they loved.

Anne held her breath as Benson helped the duke mount. She watched the duke's gloved hand rest on the horse's withers and saw how gently he patted the animal. He murmured something and, as though listening to an old friend, the gelding stilled. Despite his blindness, the duke mounted smoothly.

Anne lightly spurred Angelica to walk to his side. She

didn't want to ask for the reins in front of his servant. She sidled so close to him, her thigh brushed his. He turned to her, grinning—a bigger, more dazzling smile than she'd seen in all the days she'd been here.

He pointed ahead of them to the lawns that stretched out toward the house on the left and to the edge of the woods on the right. "You explain where we're going. Point out the obstacles in the way and I'll follow your every word. I'd like to head for the south fields. There is a good track to follow."

He wanted her to talk him through it, not lead him? Could she do this well enough so he would not get hurt? She had to try. "Then we'll go there, Your Grace."

It had been so long since she'd ridden, the saddle slapped her bottom mercilessly at first. Angelica snorted her disgust. Anne knew she must describe things to the duke, but she couldn't stop watching him carefully. Then she began to stare. At the way lines bracketed his sensual mouth, at the length of his curling eyelashes. She adored his cheekbones and the cleft in his chin.

"You do realize I asked you to give me directions so I could hear your lovely voice," he said.

Her heart gave a foolish flip in her chest. He was so beautiful, it would be so easy to fall in love with his face. A clever mistress didn't do that, so she directed her thoughts to guiding him.

Suddenly he called out, "Stop, love." She reined in and he tipped his face toward her. "God, this feels good. The sun beating down, having you at my side, listening to you speak."

His words—*having you at my side*—warmed her more than the sunlight. She had never ridden with a gentleman. She had never simply walked a horse along at a man's side, chatting beneath a summer sun. It was a pleasure she would gather up and lock away.

"I'm glad you were so stubborn, love. If I'd sent you

back to London, I'd never have known the pleasure of this. But now I want more."

She jerked her head up. "More? More what?"

"I want to gallop."

"No." The word snapped out before she could stop it. She accidentally jerked Angelica's reins, and the horse whinnied with indignation.

His smile disappeared. "Angel, I need to gallop."

"I can't allow that. How could I give you directions and guidance quickly enough? What if you fall? What if you break your neck?"

"Maybe I'm not afraid of that."

"What on earth do you mean?"

"I didn't survive Waterloo because I was too stubborn to die. Or too cowardly. I survived because living through battle came down to sheer luck. On that day, my luck was in. For thousands of others, it wasn't. Maybe I want to test my luck."

"Test your luck? No! For heaven's sake, you survived! Do you have any idea how precious survival is? Why would you try to kill yourself now?"

He rose up in the saddle, a wild grin on his face. "Is there still an old oak in the middle of this meadow? Is anything standing between that tree and me?"

"Only me—"

"Then let's race, angel. First one to the tree wins. You may have a head start."

"I am not going to race you, Your Grace. I—"

Before she could finish her protest, he spurred his mount's flanks. His horse shot forward, racing around her, and galloped straight for the tree. She hadn't proved a barrier at all. He must have used the sound of her voice to locate her, to go around her. Now he was riding on a tear toward the oak. He truly was willing to throw away survival for *pride*.

She wheeled Angelica around and galloped in pursuit. "You could fall! Stop this!"

Could he hear? The wind must be roaring past his ears. He appeared so intent on reaching the blasted tree first that he was oblivious to everything else. He certainly wasn't obeying *her*.

His beaver hat flew from his head and tumbled to the ground. His coal-black waves streamed back as he leaned forward, pressing low to the horse's straining neck. His taut buttocks lifted, his rock-hard thighs bulged beneath his trousers.

What was on the path? There could be anything—rocks, ruts, an animal's hole. He could be charging right into disaster. He could be *killed*.

Flicking the reins, she urged her horse faster. She had to remember how to ride and push herself to go faster than ever before to catch a man who rode like a streak of lightning. Instead of gaining, she was slipping farther behind. "Come on, Angelica. We have to stop your master from killing himself!"

But even with the mare racing flat out, with her body laid along the straining neck, Anne knew Angelica's strides were too short. She and Angelica were female—they couldn't catch up to two males driven by mad pride. Suddenly her wits clicked into place. She could shout that he'd *already* reached the blasted tree. Make him *think* he'd won, and he would stop.

She sucked in a deep breath to shout as loudly as she could. "Your Grace, you've passed the oak! You've won! The race is over!" She threw in another lie. One to make him act more quickly. "You must stop. There is a tall hedge ahead of you!"

He reined in the instant the words left her mouth. Her shout and the horse's thundering hooves must have startled a grouse—the bird exploded out of the grass in front of the duke's horse with the whirring of flapping wings. The horse reared.

The duke straightened abruptly on his saddle, pulling back on the reins, fighting for control. She could see him struggling to stay on with the strength of his powerful thighs, with a brute force that set the broad muscles of his back straining against his coat.

He brought the horse down with a thump that shook the field beneath her. Then the black gelding suddenly bowed his head, as though remorseful over his panic, and the reins went slack. The duke clawed at the air, obviously expecting the horse's neck to be in front of him.

He fell, toppling headfirst over the shoulder of his horse. His bare head hit the ground before he flipped over, to land with another earth-shaking thud on his back. His body lay still.

"Oh, my God." It was all Anne could say. Over and over, on every frantic breath. She spurred Angelica toward him, and when she was just a yard away, she swung off her mare so swiftly she fell to her knees. She scrambled up and raced to him. "Your Grace!"

He was still in the same position, and his eyes were shut. His long legs were splayed and relaxed, his arms flopped out at his sides. He was definitely unconscious. She dropped to her knees. She knew how to feel for a heartbeat. Holding her breath, she stripped off her gloves and pressed her fingertips to his throat. She had to adjust before she felt the soft thud of his heart. A regular beat, not thready and weak.

Relief struck her so hard she almost fell on him, her hands gripping his shoulders. "Wake up. Please wake up." She was afraid to hurt him—and at the same time she wanted to shake him senseless. How could he be so careless about his own life . . . ?

His eyes flickered open. "Christ . . . oh, yes, I can't see. Cerise, is that you? Where am I?"

"You are on the field," she gasped on a ragged breath. "Where you fell off your horse. I thought—I thought you'd been killed."

He grinned. "No, angel, still alive. A bit banged up and bruised, but none the worse for wear. I have to admit, flying through the air into blackness proved interesting."

Interesting. Anne had to grasp her right wrist to keep from thumping him on the chest. "I am glad you were entertained," she said tightly. "I feared you were *dead*. Perhaps it was interesting for you, but it was *horrific* for me." She scrambled back, but before she could get to her feet to stalk away, his arm wrapped around her thigh.

"I'm sorry. Don't go."

He was *sorry*. She had been so afraid he was badly hurt, that she'd . . . lost him. Tears had stung in her eyes for him—they still did, for heaven's sake.

He cocked his head, putting on his most endearing look. She could see him doing it.

"I would like to make love to you here, bathed in sunlight," he said gently. "I think it would prove spicy, with you so angry with me. Are you still willing, Cerise?"

Willing? She wanted to smack him. Or cry. Or hug him and never let him go, never let him get on a horse again. She had wanted him distracted—he certainly was, but she felt as though she was going to fall to pieces.

She was about to tell him she did not care if he found the idea of making love to her right now as spicy as curry from India, when he lifted her hand to his mouth. He brushed a warm kiss over her fingertips, then pursed his mouth around her index finger. And suckled.

She desperately tried to cling to her annoyance, but it melted away like ice in the heat. Her body followed—as he sucked each finger in turn, every inch of her went hot and quivery. "Stop this," she finally managed. "I am angry with you."

He ignored her. One swift tug of her hand and she fell on top of him. He rolled over so they lay face-to-face on the grass. Golden sunlight bathed them; wildflowers bobbed over them.

"Let me make it up to you, angel. Let me make this good for you." He kissed her slowly, sensually. But even with his hot kisses ravaging her mouth and the sun beating down on her, she could not lose the icy fear that had wrapped around her heart. She knew she shouldn't give in and let him have his way after ignoring her warnings, after putting her through hell. Even though she was his mistress and she was supposed to do as he wanted.

But she wanted to hold him, wanted to wrap herself tightly around him and savor the fact that he was safe. "All right," she whispered. "I'm willing."

Chapter Ten

PAIN SHOT UP Devon's back as he jerked off his coat and threw it on the ground. He rolled Cerise onto her back on the coat. Of course he felt a spasm of agony through his muscles—he'd almost broken his neck. He stripped off his waistcoat, tore off his cravat, hauled his shirt over his head. His boots wouldn't come off, so he had to shove his trousers down to his knees.

He needed Cerise. The word slammed through him with every beat of his heart, every pulse of blood surging to his cock. *Need. Need.* He had vowed he wouldn't use her to work out his anger or his frustration, but this was different. Adrenaline was racing through him because he was alive, and he was drunk on it. Drunk on wanting her.

He reached blindly for her legs. Followed them up to the placket of her borrowed trousers. "Open them, love. Push them down." There was no tenderness in his tone, no seduction. "I need you *now*."

He licked the smooth skin she exposed—the lovely curve of her belly. Then he slid his hands under her bottom, lifted her to his mouth, and devoured her. She'd given him spectacular performances in his bedroom over the last few days, but he knew her wild climaxes were faked.

Maybe he could no longer race a horse and know the exhilaration of riding like wild across his fields, but he could know the victory of making Cerise truly scream.

He suckled her lavishly, teased her with his tongue, and waited for her moans. But she didn't make any sound. No whimpers of surrender, no groans of agony, and no cries of ecstasy—real or otherwise. He was determined to give her pleasure. So he didn't stop.

Something strange was happening to Anne.

As soon as the duke put his mouth to her quim, she'd tensed as she always did. She had been ready to please him by feigning delight, taking care to make her act *very* convincing. But this time the lush sweeps of his tongue, the lavish suckling was . . . good. It wasn't too intense.

She relaxed all over, sinking into the heavenly scent of his coat. Her whole body was floppy, light, languorous, and she felt as if she floated above the field, lying on sunbeams.

I need you now. She couldn't speak. Or make any sound. All she could think of were those words. She seemed to be growing tighter inside, like clockworks wound to the breaking point. Her hips arched up to him, and she was pushing against his mouth. Seeking . . . something.

Her hands clawed at the ground, tearing out chunks of grass. Her toes curled. Her body went utterly rigid, her eyes shut tight. Deep inside her, everything . . . exploded. She was coming apart. So much wild, fierce ecstasy washed through her like a wind-whipped wave, she feared her heart would stop—

Stars shot in front of her closed eyes. Her climax took her; it made her body jerk and jolt, it made her eyes open wide, her head smack against the soft ground, and her brain simply cease to work. She soared as though she were flying—spinning—in graceful loops on the summer breeze. It made her heart thunder. Stole her voice with wonderment, and she could make almost no sound at all.

Dazedly, she remembered how other women in the brothel used to whisper about this. The elusive pleasure women sometimes found. It was rare and precious, they said, a jewel that dazzled more than a diamond.

She could see why. Dreamily, through half-closed eyes, Anne saw the duke move over her. His cock pointed at her, thick, obviously rigid. He didn't use his hands to position himself. He was so hard, and her pleasure had left her so wet, he easily sank inside her. Her insides still pulsed, clutching at him, trying to pull him deep.

He pressed his mouth to hers, and she tasted herself on his lips. Salty, earthy, rather ripe. She clung to him, wrapped tight around him. She sobbed with delight and shock and astonishment. How would she have known the throbbing would last so long? Leave her so spent? Make her so very sensitive that she came again after just a few of his long, slow thrusts?

One agonized little "oh" was the only sound she could manage. Her arms slipped from his neck and she fell back.

He suddenly grunted, low and hoarse. His groin collided with hers; he thrust as deep as he could. His lids and lashes covered his eyes, and he jerked helplessly above her.

She held him throughout his ravaging climax. It seemed to punish his body far more than her orgasm did to hers.

"Oh, God, angel," he groaned, and sprawled beside her, his body obviously as spent and boneless as hers. She was too weak to move to him and lay on her back, hot and sated, loose and floppy, like a sleepy kitten curled in the sun.

She could barely remember being angry with him. And surely he'd learned his lesson. Surely he would never take such a dangerous risk again.

He levered up so he was leaning over her. His lashes dipped down. "You didn't enjoy it, did you, love? You were so quiet."

Heavens, she had *never* known pleasure like that. She'd never had an orgasm before. He'd given her the very first one. "It was the most wonderful—" Abruptly, she stopped. Of course he thought she hadn't liked it. She normally shouted to the heavens when she was faking. When she really felt it, she'd barely made any sound. If she tried to explain, he would know she had been acting all the other times she had cried out for him.

Desperately, she sought an explanation that wouldn't anger or hurt him. "I was afraid someone would hear us."

"As opposed to when we are in a house filled with servants? You must be tired from spending the afternoon leading me around, humoring my demands. After we take the horses back, your duties are done for the day, angel." Quickly, he launched to his feet and tugged up his trousers.

She was certain he would change his mind, but he kept his word—for the rest of the night, she was abandoned. He stayed in his study with the door locked. At midnight she knocked and called for him, but he simply told her to go to bed.

The shouting woke her.

Anne jerked up in her bed. It must be the duke—he must be having a nightmare. Holding the hem of her robe, she ran downstairs. She reached the study as

Treadwell, with Beckett at his side, holding a candle, was fumbling to unlock the door.

"What if he gets outside again?" Beckett whispered. "Gets into the woods? Last time he ran through there, he fell into the stream and almost drowned."

"He won't get out," Treadwell snapped. "But if we don't get in there, he could hurt himself."

As if in terrifying answer, something shattered within the study. Shouts came from behind the door. Anne couldn't understand them, but they sounded authoritative, like directions barked out in the midst of a disaster.

Beckett shoved the light forward, almost setting Treadwell's hair on fire. "If we go in there when His Grace is like this, he could hurt one of us. Last time, he went at you with a knife."

"His Grace thought I was the French. I came up behind him without warning."

"He's got to be mad," Beckett muttered. "How could he think he's in battle, unless he's lost his wits?"

Treadwell's shaking fingers dropped the key. Anne snatched up the ring. "Let me."

"No, miss—" Treadwell began, but she turned the key in the lock and shoved open the door. She snatched the candlestick from Beckett and ran into the room.

"Your Grace," she called, forcing a decisive note she didn't feel into her voice. Where was he? In the absolute darkness of the room, the glow of the candle barely penetrated. It blinded her more than it helped her. She held it far out in front.

The light fell on the floor ahead of her, and what it illuminated twisted her heart. The duke was on the carpet. He was crawling toward the windows, snapping orders and directions to men who were not there. Men who, Anne realized with sickening horror, might be dead now.

I'm going madder by the day. His words squeezed her

heart. No wonder he thought so. But she refused to believe he would have to be trapped in these nightmares forever.

Holding the candle, she rushed to his side and crouched by him. Her hand closed around his shoulder and he flinched. Would he strike her? She shook him. "Wake up, Your Grace. You're having a dream. You are in your study, in England. You are perfectly safe! No one is shooting at you."

"Get down," he growled. "You'll get your head blown off."

"It's Anne, Your Grace."

"Christ, he's only a boy. He's going to shoot—" He grasped her wrist and pulled her down.

In the glow of the candle, she could see that his eyes were filled with a feral fury. She had seen this look on men in the stews—it was the look of a man who would kill anyone in his way. He shoved her flat onto the rug and moved over her, as though shielding her from danger. She set the candlestick on the floor and eased it away. She was pinned beneath him, but she said firmly, "Your Grace, it is all right. This is just a dream. It's Anne—"

Oh, God. She'd used her real name. Done it *twice*. She prayed that in his condition he wouldn't register the slip. "Your Grace, you must wake up. It's *Cerise*. You're having a nightmare. Please, Your Grace." She shook him harder.

Her shaking did nothing to him. He still looked haunted, and he seemed so lost. Could an embrace do anything when shoving his shoulders about had not? Could a kiss?

Desperately, she pressed her mouth to his. He might hit or attack her, but she must reach him. She had to try anything. She kissed him slowly, sensually caressing his mouth with hers.

He gave a low, guttural moan. His lips parted and softened against hers. To her relief, he began to return her kiss. It broke the hold of the dream, it seemed, for he suddenly pushed her back and rolled away from her. "What the—where am I? Angel, what are you doing here?"

"You were dreaming," she said quietly.

"On my hands and knees, crawling for cover?" he asked drily. He rose to a sitting position, his forearms resting on his knees. Naked.

She glanced toward the footmen. "Leave us, please." The men hesitated, until the duke growled the same words. The moment they were alone, Anne snuggled close to the duke. She wrapped her arms around him and pressed her cheek to his shoulder. "In your dream, you spoke of a boy, a boy who was going to shoot—"

"My mind plays mad tricks on me. I suppose I am mad."

"No, you aren't," she argued. "I had nightmares for weeks when I was first in the brothel."

He embraced her, drawing her to his chest. "I think you must have gone through a worse hell than I did, Cerise. We make a fine pair, don't we? Filled with visions of hell, plagued by nightmares, staying here because we both have no place else to go."

"Actually, I think we do make a good pair," she said firmly. "You've helped me. And I want to help you." She kissed him again.

He eased her away. "Not that way. Not tonight. Angel, you should go away."

"I won't. I won't leave you to endure this alone."

"Then let me hold you for a while, Cerise." But his body shook and his arms trembled against her back as he embraced her.

"Have you talked to *anyone* about the memories that haunt you?" she asked.

"No. I refuse to torture someone else by describing these things just to buy me a bit of relief. Talking about them isn't going to make it go away. There's nothing to be done. Don't speak of it."

But she hated to feel him shaking so much. She yearned to take away the blank, hunted look in his eyes. He didn't want to make love. What else could she give him to distract him? In the past, to help her grandfather, she walked with him, read to him. . . .

She slipped out of the duke's embrace. "Wait here." She hurried to the bookshelves—even though the library was filled with volumes, there were more here in his study. Books on the breeding of horses, on animal husbandry, and guides for the management of hunting lands. But at the very end of one shelf was a copy of *Sense and Sensibility*.

It seemed an odd book for a gentleman to keep in his study, but she took it out. She turned, then she saw it. The brandy decanter, lying on the floor.

Anne picked it up. There was enough in the bottom to fill a thimble, and the strong aroma of alcohol hit her. Frowning, she tipped the decanter and tasted. The brandy was full strength.

Later, she would speak to his servants. For now she wanted to give the duke some peace.

She clasped his hand and took him to the settee and sat down. "Rest your head on my lap." Gathering as much of her robe as she could, she wrapped it around him.

A smile flickered on his lips, and Anne's heart gave a pang. Then she opened the book. Clearing her throat, she started to read.

Chapter Eleven

THE SHARP RAP at the door to the bathing room didn't surprise Anne, but it did rouse her from drowsiness. She blinked and sat up, water sloshing around her. She had dozed off in the bathtub with her head propped on the curved rim.

A hand landed on the door again. Not in a knock but with a hard, angry slap. "My brandy, love. What in blazes have you done with it?"

The duke had come himself. Anne jerked up on her knees in the tub so swiftly that water splashed onto the floor. She might lose everything for this, but she knew—knew in her *heart*—she was doing the right thing. "I instructed your footmen not to give it to you anymore."

"They take orders from you, Cerise?" His voice rumbled through the closed door. "I know you were having my liquor watered down, but each night I had the stuff poured out and replaced. This time, when I insisted one of them bring a bottle to me, they all refused."

"Your Grace, I told them they must do that. It is not their fault—"

"Apparently," he barked, "they are more afraid of *you* than of me. I've never known my servants to cower like this before my mother, never mind a—" He stopped abruptly.

Never mind a tart. He did not say it. He didn't need to. It was what he meant. She stepped out of the tub and wrapped a thick white towel around her. She padded to the door, leaving a trail of wet footprints on the gleaming wood. With her hand on the key, she took a deep breath. He was furious. She was trembling, but she opened the door.

The duke was leaning on the lavish molding. He wore a white shirt with the sleeves rolled up. The tails hung out over dark trousers. He'd left his feet bare.

"It's not me they are afraid of," she said simply. "I told Treadwell it could hurt you to supply you with liquor endlessly. That's why they are not fetching your drink. It hardly helps you."

"I happen to think it does." He slumped against the frame. He didn't look like a man preparing to hit a woman. Instead, he looked like a man at the end of his rope.

"You don't need it," she insisted. "I think it makes your nightmares worse. Last night, when I read to you, you seemed happy. After, when I left you to sleep, you didn't have a nightmare, did you? You do not *need* the liquor. I could read to you each night."

"You read for hours, Cerise. Until close to dawn. I can't ask that of you each day."

"Why not? I am your mistress. It is what I am willing to do."

"You are my mistress. Not a slave. I will not make use of you like that."

With that, he pushed away from the doorframe, turned, and walked away.

She stared after him in astonishment as he strode down the corridor, swinging his walking stick ahead of his steps. He moved with so much more confidence now. In only a handful of days, he truly had changed.

Last night he had relaxed enough to fall asleep in her lap. He'd stopped her reading *Sense and Sensibility,* though, and made her read a manual on horse breeding, which would put anyone to sleep.

She was his mistress—she was supposed to be available anytime he wanted, for anything he desired. Yet he'd just told her he would not make use of her. Should she be pleased or worried?

Was she right?

Devon let one of the footmen put on his greatcoat. He could feel the weight of it dropping on his shoulders. He held out his hand for his beaver hat and drew it on ruthlessly. Once he cared about his appearance. He had no right to anymore, not when a choice he'd made had cost a good soldier his life, which meant the man's wife and child had been thrown into grief and poverty. And now they had vanished somewhere in London's slums.

He needed his liquor, but Cerise's warning kept hammering in his brain. Was the brandy hurting him more than it helped him?

He'd thought drink would dull the pain, grief, and anger. When he didn't soak his mind with liquor, his nightmares were soaked with blood and echoed with screams. Brandy turned them into vague and formless things he couldn't grasp but that still tormented him. Admittedly, it had never once given him the gift of a night's sleep.

Perhaps she *was* right.

If he couldn't escape in liquor, he had to do it another way. There was sex, but he wasn't in the mood for an activity that required him to act more like a human and less like a growling, guilt-ridden blackguard. Anyway, he sensed there was a wall between them, forged by his determination to drown his anger and guilt in drink and her equal insistence that he stop. Intriguingly, the only way to tear down the wall was for one of them to win.

Instead, he was going to ride. This time he would take more care. He couldn't throw his life away by breaking his neck.

Guilt twisted his gut hard at how close he had come to killing himself. Thousands of men had died in war. Likely all of them would trade positions with him in a heartbeat. Besides, his mother would expect him to produce an heir before accidentally killing himself—

"Yer Grace." The puffing voice was Treadwell's. "Another letter has arrived from Her Grace, yer mother. Should I give it to you or to Miss Cerise?"

"To me, damn it." It was as though Treadwell had read his mind, had known he was thinking of his family. Devon stuffed the letter in his pocket. No doubt it would be another entreaty for him to fall in love and marry. Hell.

He knew where he was. Probably.

Devon braced his hand against the rough bark of a tree, while Abednigo danced beneath him. As he soothed the horse, he tasted late afternoon in the heavy sweetness of the air, felt it in the heat of the sun beating across his face. Even blind, he knew the woods around him were drenched in the gold of the dropping sun. He would likely never see it again.

Though there was a chance he would. He'd been to specialists in London, and no doctor could tell him exactly why he was blind. They had explained that a nerve ran from behind his eyes into his brain. He'd suffered a blow to his head. The doctors believed something was pressing on the optic nerve. A knot of blood, they speculated, or a splinter of bone broken off when a young soldier's bayonet had slammed into his skull. His sight could come back, the doctors had told him, if the thing moved. But if it did move, it could also slice its way through his brain. It could kill him.

"Your Grace!"

Devon turned in the saddle toward the anxious voice that fell over him in a breathless rush. Skirts swished and boots crunched over fallen twigs. "You followed me on foot, Cerise?"

"Yes." She let out her breath in a whoosh. "In a corset, no less. I can barely breathe. Why are you out here alone?"

Holding the reins, he dismounted. "I didn't want you to run after me."

"I wanted to ensure . . ." She hesitated, and her pretty voice died away.

"I can guess what you're thinking, love. You're wondering if I know where I am but you don't want to hurt my tender feelings by asking me."

"Your Grace, I thought I'd already proved I am not very mindful of your feelings." Her tone was so wry it made him smile. Then she paused. "Do you know where you are?"

"Yes. I can smell apples. Behind me, the stream is rippling softly, not splashing noisily. Given those clues, I would say I'm in the woods, south of the apple orchard, near the path that heads down to the village. Where the stream is at its deepest."

Her silence landed on him like a slap across the head.

There was only one reason she wouldn't say anything. "All right. Where am I?"

"At the northern end of the orchard, I believe."

He'd been completely wrong. "Damnation," he muttered.

"You did excellently," she said loyally.

"I don't need false praise to make me feel better," he said grimly. "I wanted to map out my property in my thick head, and I need to get it right—"

"You lost your sight. That hardly means you have a thick head. Let us work on this together. I will describe things to you as we walk along. Where do you wish to begin?"

Her crisp tones brought out guilt with an acrid twinge in his heart. He hadn't expected her to leap so vehemently to his defense. But that was what she did, wasn't it? She insisted he wasn't mad, no matter how much evidence he gave her to the contrary. She risked injury to help him, risked his wrath to take his brandy away. Last night she had gone without sleep for hours so she could read to him, keeping him from falling into another nightmare.

Cerise was unlike any courtesan he'd ever known. Most would have run screaming. None would have worked so hard to help him. She deserved better than his bad temper.

He took a deep breath. "Angel, I apologize for my stupidity. Not about being lost, but for snapping at you. I don't deserve you, but I need you."

This time he didn't know what to make of her silence.

He coaxed her to mount Abednigo and he swung up behind her. To fit on the saddle, he lifted her so she sat on his lap. Then they explored the woods.

Her descriptions amazed him. She explained how the path meandered through the trees, giving him details of every twist and turn. She pointed out where the oldest trees stood, their bark drenched in lichen. They reached the stream again and she gasped in pleasure.

"It is so . . . mystical," she whispered. God, how he was aroused by her, by every squirm she made on his lap, by every ingenuous, luscious sound that fell from her lips.

"How is it mystical?" he asked, mainly to keep her talking.

"It makes me think of a fairy grotto, as though fey creatures must live within." She described to him how the branches of ancient willows trailed in the water, how long grass waved along the edge of the stream and patches of silvery ferns carpeted the forest floor. She told him of the rocks in the stream, smoothed by the flow, that made a natural but slippery path across. Every word she said had his heart pounding.

"I used to leap across stones like this. Once I fell in. I was in terrible trouble, for it was just before church, and I was wearing my best dress—" She stopped and went stiff against him.

Why? What had she feared she was going to reveal? He slid his hand higher, and he could feel her heart pound. "You said you grew up as a housekeeper's daughter in a house in the country, then you lived in London's stews. But your manners, your accent, the way you treat me, as if you're a woman accustomed to managing—your story doesn't ring true. You behave more like a lady than a servant."

"I—I did work as a governess for the family before we went to London. I suppose I learned to manage then. But it doesn't matter, does it? It was such a long time ago."

How nervous she sounded. "Couldn't you have become a governess again, Cerise, after your mother died?"

"I—no, I couldn't. When we were living in the stews, my mother became ill. I knew I had to earn money, but my choices were thieving or prostitution, and she made me vow I would not do either. But my mother needed laudanum for pain. A great deal of it. So I . . . I had to break that vow to get money."

This had to be the truth. She sounded as he had after battle—emotionless, almost distant.

"Was that when you went to work in the brothel?"

"Not then. It was after my mother died, as I said before. I hoped to become a gentleman's mistress. I thought that would be the best way to survive, but I ended up in the brothel instead. Yet now I have become exactly what I dreamed of becoming. And we have reached the lawns, Your Grace. I can see the house. Come, we should go in."

She didn't wish to speak any more about it. It didn't take brilliance to decipher that in her brisk tones. He understood why she would not want to think about the past, but he wanted to know more. Where was her family? Why had they not helped her? But he didn't want to push her.

"I—I hope I did a good job of describing your woods to you," she said shakily.

"You did, angel," he murmured. He wrapped his arm around her waist. His heart ached for what she'd endured. He leaned forward until he felt the tickle of wayward strands of hair, then he kissed her bare neck. "Your descriptions were so lovely, so vivid, you almost made me see it."

"Truly?" Her voice was rich, irresistible. "I am glad."

There was one more thing he needed her to do for him. Fumbling, he found the pocket of his greatcoat and drew out the letter. "Another from my mother. Would you read it?"

She hated having to lie to him. Anne glanced at the duke's face as she took the letter. His smile had vanished and the corners of his generous mouth were cranked down. He might be resisting his mother's entreaties, but she saw how much it hurt him to do so.

"'*My dearest Devon,*'" she began. Her gaze slid down the page, rapidly reading ahead. The duchess had poured all her worry for her son into the letter. Bewildered pain leapt from every word. "'*I cannot understand why you do not send any response to my letters, why you do not come home. Or why you do not at least go out into Society, so your friends could write me assurances and tell me you are healthy and well. I wish, I dearly wish, you would consider opening your heart to the idea of courting a bride. If Lady Rosalind had lived, she would have made a wonderful wife for you. She would have helped you heal. But you cannot shut yourself away from love because you have known loss. It has been three years—*'"

"That's enough, angel." He put his hand on her wrist.

She stopped, as he requested, but she hated to think of the poor woman worrying about her son. For the three years the duke was at war, the duchess must have been terrified. Anne would have been. She remembered how she had felt when her mother was slowly fading away. She eventually forgot to eat or bathe, change her clothes, or care about herself. "I could write a reply to your mother, Your Grace. You tell me what you wish to say, and I will write it and have it sent to her."

"I don't know what to say to her. You're a female. Would you be happy to get a reply that tells you I'm not going to do any of the things you want me to do? Do you think that would set her heart and mind at ease?"

"I suppose not," she had to admit. "But perhaps your mother is right. About a wife, I mean."

"Angel, I don't need a harping mistress—" To her surprise, he stopped then and smiled—a hard, bitter twist of a smile. "All right, love, you've wanted me to confide in you. On this, I will. Do you remember the book you read to me last night?"

She frowned. "*A Noble Treatise on Equine Breeding*?"

"No, the other book."

"You mean *Sense and Sensibility*."

"Yes, angel. You see, that book wasn't mine. It belonged to Lady Rosalind Marchant."

"The woman your mother mentioned in the letter. You were . . . engaged to her?"

"Not quite. I fell in love with Rosalind, I stole her away from a very good friend, and I intended to marry her. But she died of a fever before I made my proposal of marriage. I fell in love, I betrayed a good man to get her because I couldn't live without her, then I waited too long. And I lost her."

"I'm sorry."

"*Sense and Sensibility* was her favorite book. I used to watch her read it when we went on picnics. I read it myself—it was one more weapon with which to seduce her and win her away from my friend. When she fell ill and couldn't leave her bed, I bought her that copy. Her mother gave it to her, since I wasn't allowed to see her while she was ill. They would not even let me go into her room when she passed away. I barged in after she died, and that was when I got down on one knee and told her how much I loved her. I held her limp hand and poured out everything I felt, in the desperate hope she would somehow hear. Maybe I believed I could bring her back if I made her know how much I loved her. But I was too damned late. All the while, her mother was shrieking about the impropriety of it. Her father finally summoned servants to drag me out of the bedroom."

"He did? Even though you were—"

"A duke's son?"

"—so very much in love."

"I understood. They were racked with grief. They blamed me—I'd created a huge scandal by coaxing Rosalind to break her engagement to my friend. Within a month, I'd met her, tempted her away, and convinced her to jilt him. She had never been strong, and her parents believed the scandal had made her ill again. Perhaps they were right. I used to be a wild rake, but once I saw Rosalind, I didn't desire any other woman. I thought only about what I wanted. Even when she died, that was what I did—I took what *I* wanted." He breathed deeply. "The book was in her hand and I grabbed it just before they hauled me out. I wanted to keep the last thing she'd touched."

Anne's heart stuttered as his lashes lowered and a regretful smile touched his mouth.

"She used to become so absorbed in a book," he murmured, "she didn't even notice the rest of the world around her."

There was no doubt he had been deeply in love. She could see it in the way his eyes shut and he lowered his head, as though grief was weighing on him all over again. "I'm so sorry. When I read from the book, it must have reminded you of all that—oh, goodness! When you asked me to read from a horse-breeding book, it was to stop the pain of remembering, wasn't it?" She had been so determined to do what *she* thought was best. "How stupid I was not to ask you what you wanted." She had brought back all his sorrow over the woman he loved, then she'd taken away his brandy so he couldn't find any solace. "You must be furious with me."

"I'm not. It hurt at first when you started reading. I went to war right after Rosalind died. I did it so I could escape the pain. I thought with all the action and risk, I'd have no place for grief. That was a stupid mistake. When I made you stop reading *Sense and Sensibility,* I realized I'd made another mistake. I didn't want to hide anymore—I wanted to remember her."

Anne twisted in the saddle and cupped his face. His horse shifted beneath them, but the duke's arm tightened around her waist. "Perhaps I shouldn't do this," she murmured. "Push me away if you want. But I need to kiss you, Your Grace."

He pulled her to him until their lips almost touched and they shared the same swift breaths. "I loved Rosalind deeply, but no woman has ever treated me as you do, angel." He moved that one last hairbreadth and kissed her.

The kiss in the rain had been dazzling, but this one . . .

His mouth touched hers gently, so tenderly that she had to close her eyes, had to grip his shoulders to keep from melting into a puddle and sliding off the horse. She had never been kissed like this. She'd never known what it was like to want to cry over the caress of a man's mouth. Now she did. It was so wonderfully sweet she wanted to weep.

Slowly he drew back. "Read to me again tonight, love? Would you promise?"

"Of course," she whispered.

No wonder the duke wanted to hide away here. No wonder he had nightmares and drank too much brandy. Anne paced in her bedchamber—the room that should be *his* bedchamber. She ached to help him, but she didn't know what to do.

How terrible it must have been for him. He went to war to escape grief, only to end up surrounded by pain, violence, and death. He had not given himself time to mourn the woman he loved. It must haunt him now. Grief for Lady Rosalind must be in his heart, along with sorrow over his memories of war and the loss of his sight.

How could she help him overcome it? She didn't know how to stop the pain. She still felt it for her parents, for her lost home. She'd refused to even think of Longsworth.

She couldn't help but think about his mother. In her mind's eye, Anne could picture her as a silver-haired woman bent over an escritoire, writing a letter to her son, brushing at tears as some dropped to the page. She could picture an untouched tray of food and a woman consuming herself with worry. Was his mother forgoing food, forgetting sleep, as Anne had done?

She didn't know how to help the duke get over the pain of losing Lady Rosalind, but she did know what she could do for his mother. The duke would never have to know.

Two days later, as Anne finished her breakfast in the dining room, Treadwell approached. He waited respectfully, twisting his hands in front of him. She knew by now that the butler cared deeply for his master. His look of confusion instantly speared her with worry.

"Is something wrong with His Grace?" She was off her seat, ready to run.

"No, miss. Everything is . . . right with him. I came to tell ye that His Grace has not asked for brandy for the last two nights. Not before he retired for the night. Not after his dreams. I even . . . well, I was worried about him and thought a little nip couldn't hurt him. I offered to bring him some, on the quiet, so ye wouldn't find out, miss. But he turned it down."

She lifted her brow at the butler's admission, but she couldn't help but echo, "He turned it down?"

"Indeed. He told me he believed ye would not approve."

She blinked. She hadn't quite believed she could convince him to give up brandy. He'd been so obstinate. Yet somehow she had touched him, she had made him see sense, she had helped.

"His Grace also wishes ye to join him this morning. It

is his plan to make an excursion into the village, and he has asked for ye to accompany him."

Her teacup hit the saucer with a clatter. "He wishes to go into the village?"

"Aye." Treadwell grinned, his lips opening wide to reveal missing teeth. He winked. "His Grace has not been into the village once since he came here. This is a grand thing, miss. All of us—the staff—we're all very pleased."

She stood up from the table. "*I'm* very pleased," she repeated, before she followed the butler to the front foyer, where she found the duke pulling on black gloves. Already he was dressed immaculately in a tailcoat, his beaver hat perfectly placed on his head, his snow-white collar points framing his handsome face.

"Where did you wish to go, Your Grace?" she asked.

He grinned so beautifully, her heart almost fractured. "You will soon see, angel."

The duke's carriage stopped in the narrow street in front of the dressmaker's shop. Anne froze. She had never told him of her disastrous visit. "Why have we come here?"

"Treadwell informed me that no gowns have arrived for you and there have been no bills for clothes and bonnets. I assume you did not come here when I instructed you to?"

Embarrassment turned her cheeks to flame. "I did, but I could not stay. Respectable ladies were in the shop, and they guessed at once I am your mistress. The modiste was terribly nervous, but she made it clear I was making her patrons uncomfortable. So I left."

"Indeed. Well, it is my duty as your noble protector to buy you gowns, my dear. I intend to see it through."

She could guess what he wished to do, but she was not certain she had the courage to face it. "Your Grace, we will thoroughly scandalize this woman if you go in and buy clothes for me."

He would not be deterred. His footman opened the carriage door, and the duke leapt out, then helped her down the steps. He held open the door to the shop and waited. Meekly, she went in before him. At once, the dressmaker hurried forward, a chubby seamstress trailing behind her. Both women curtsied. There were two other young ladies in the shop, and they dropped their handfuls of ribbons, goggling at the duke.

"Good afternoon, Mrs. Wimple," the duke said coldly. He peered over both women's heads.

As Mrs. Wimple rose, her face was as white as her bolts of muslin. She sputtered a greeting that dripped with deference. The duke quirked his brow, this time displaying aristocratic hauteur. "This dear lady is a close friend of my family."

The modiste's shoulders trembled before his measured yet ominous tones. He was rather frightening when he spoke so quietly, like the stillness of the sky before a storm exploded.

"Yet when I sent my dear friend to you," he continued, in that deep rumble, "I believe she was not treated with the civility and deference I expected."

The modiste quaked. "Your Grace, I . . ."

Anne saw the woman flounder. The duke turned to her, knowing where she was because she had placed her hand on his steely forearm. "My dear Miss—Miss Cerise, would you be so good as to fetch me a chair? I know the fitting of a lady's gown is a long business, and I would like a seat."

Anne flushed at his stumble over her name. She should have given him a last name. It had blown his lie apart in a moment: He would not search for her name if she was truly a close family friend. However, he appeared utterly unperturbed by the slip.

The dressmaker gasped. "No! No, Cherrywell will fetch a seat." She waved frantically at the plump seamstress. "Hurry and bring a chair for His Grace. If you will follow me to the dressing rooms, Miss Cerise . . ." The woman's gaze swept over her borrowed dress, and in a low voice she said, "You will want something bold, I presume, similar to the gown you are wearing?"

Anne shuddered at the woman's false smile. She wanted to walk out, but she couldn't. She had no point to prove. She was a fallen woman and had accepted it. She knew exactly the kind of treatment to expect. Heavens, in the village of Banbury, near Longsworth, respectable ladies would cross the street if they saw a ruined woman walking on their side. As though ruination could be spread through the air.

The duke wore such a look of fierce determination, she didn't want to disobey. He settled into the seat, close enough that she could whisper in his ear. "This isn't necessary," she hissed. "You shouldn't be so angry."

"Of course I'm angry. You deserve a hell of a lot better treatment than this."

His words stunned her. She turned to Mrs. Wimple. If she must do this, she did *not* want to be stuck in the kind of garish gowns she used to wear for Madame. "I would like gowns with simple but elegant lines—" She stopped. There was a way to crack the tension. She turned an ingenuous smile on Mrs. Wimple. "I can see you have a superior sense of style. Why else would His Grace insist on your services?"

The words had an instant effect. The woman thawed, ever so slightly.

"Please use your discretion," Anne went on. "I am sure your designs will be flattering and fashionable. I have no doubt your gowns will be the talk of London, when I return there." A bold lie. She had no intention of being seen *anywhere* in London.

"Yes." The middle-aged woman thoughtfully stroked her chin. "I do believe I can envision exactly what would flatter you best."

Anne had no idea if it was true, but the woman was animated now instead of resentful. Mrs. Wimple was warming to the chance to impress the Duke of March. Before she disappeared behind the curtain to the fitting room, Anne glanced back at the duke. He waited patiently, sipping tea served to him by Cherrywell, while young seamstresses peeped at him from the workroom door. The sight made her smile. Her heart felt oddly . . . lighter. "Thank you," she whispered. He couldn't hear her, of course. Her thank-you wasn't for the clothes; it was for insisting she be treated as more than a ruined woman.

The duke looked entirely too relaxed in places that sold women's apparel.

At least, he had at the beginning. After they saw the dressmaker, they had to visit the milliner's. It was obvious he'd done this with mistresses before, though perhaps not in this village. But Anne had seen disappointment flash in his eyes when she was trying on bonnets. He'd stood abruptly, told her to buy every one in the shop rather than spend time making a decision, then swept her out the door.

Now, in the carriage, he sprawled on the seat across from her, utterly silent, as they rumbled toward his home.

She knew he was not going to lash out at her, and it hurt her to see him look so grim and tense. Was it the reminder of his blindness? Or was his unhappy expression because he was thinking of the woman he'd loved and lost? "Your Grace—"

"Angel—" He spoke at the exact moment she did. They shared a nervous laugh, then she asked, "Would you come and sit beside me?" at the same time that he said, "Come sit on my lap."

"Your lap? Why?" She was perplexed for a few seconds. Then he lifted his hips, the motion making his intent obvious.

"In the *carriage*?" she asked, astonished, for it jiggled and lightly swayed.

"Cerise, you are adorable. Yes, in the carriage."

"Can it be done?"

"Very carefully," he teased.

She moved to him, sat on his lap, and discovered he'd already opened the falls of his trousers. He bent so his lips brushed her hair. His voice came as a hoarse rasp. "Make love to me. I've discovered how much I need it. Angel, I don't think I could ever do without you."

Goodness. His words both broke her heart and set it soaring. With it pounding madly, she hitched up her skirts and climbed onto his lap. She wrapped her arms around his neck. Never had she wanted him more. "You must tell me what to do," Anne said.

"This, love," Devon growled. "Take me inside, bounce on top of me, make yourself come."

She was the only thing that could make him forget grief—grief for Rosalind, for the men who'd died in battle, for Captain Tanner, who had been lost to his family. He knew so much grief. He felt it even for the French soldiers he'd killed, their faces ingrained forever in his memory. For his father, who had died during the first year he'd been at war.

The carriage began to climb a hill, rattling slowly, and Cerise tightened her lithe arms around his neck. With just a sensual twitch of her hips, she took his erection inside. He shut his eyes, groaning at the sweet pressure and the weight of her bottom settling on his thighs. He was becoming addicted to her. More than he had ever needed brandy, he needed Cerise.

This time, he would make her come for him. On the grass, in the field, he'd thought . . . he'd imagined he was close. She had felt so relaxed, so creamy and hot around him. But she had been so quiet, he was afraid he'd hurt her and she was trying to hold in sounds of displeasure. This time he would be gentle. And make it good for her.

Balancing against the motion of the carriage, he held her slim waist and thrust inside her. He ground his molars to hang on to his control and arched his hips with deliberate slowness, in a gentle, teasing rhythm, until she whispered throatily, "Harder. Please. I want it . . . hard. And fast."

Focused so intently on her, he could hear her over the rattle of the wheels. And her wish was his command. He made love to her so vigorously that he lifted them off the seat and set the carriage bouncing on its axles.

Her lips found his and she kissed him hungrily. Greedily. Did it mean she liked it, or was she playing mistress? He didn't know, but he answered with a hot, open-mouthed kiss of his own. He couldn't see her breasts, but he felt them brush his chest as she bounced. She panted into his mouth, but she didn't make a sound. The carriage grew hotter, though, hot as wildfire. He wanted to make her explode, hungered to give her a climax that would make her howl her pleasure.

He slid his hand between their tight bodies, working by feel, and pressed his thumb to the apex of her slick, steamy cunny. She gave a shocked gasp, then a soft, melting moan.

"Yes." He panted through each wild, hard thrust. "I want to bring you to your peak. Tell me what it takes for you to get there, love. I'm yours to command."

"I—I don't know," she moaned. "This . . . this is so good. You are. You made me come when I never thought I could . . ."

Her words touched him like no other caress had. He

drove deeply into her, trying to do the exact thing she apparently liked. Then she gripped his shoulders and took him at his word. She bounced, wriggled, and found a rhythm that pleased her. The carriage echoed with her moans. A lovely feminine "Oh, oh, oh!" rang by his ear, then she jerked on top of him and gave a wonderful, earsplitting scream.

It set him off like a fuse to a cannon. He braced—for they were going downhill—and arched up, burying his cock to the very hilt, and his muscles seemed to melt like wax as he came.

"Oooh." She slumped against him. "Mmmm." She drank in fierce breaths.

He was holding his. She sounded content, honestly so, and he wanted to know her sweet sounds were real, not faked. "Did you come?" He sounded like an uncertain lad.

"Yes."

"For the first time?"

"Not quite. I—oh, I'm so sorry, but you were right. I didn't come before. But I did this time. And I did in the field, when I was so quiet and you became angry. That was my very first climax. It wasn't your fault before. It truly wasn't. I thought I would never have an orgasm."

"You aren't flattering me?"

"No! This is the *truth*. I never knew my muscles would flutter inside when I came. Or that my heart would pound so much. I never knew my nipples would grow so plump and hard at the peak of pleasure. Does that make you believe me?"

Their carriage stopped and familiar voices, those of his grooms, shouted up to his coachman. Devon stayed seated, wrapping his arms around her. "Yes. I'm glad I gave you pleasure."

"I—I am too."

Yes, hell, he was completely addicted to her.

From outside, there came a cacophony of sound. A man's shouts, loud pounding, and a rumble like the clatter of fast wheels on gravel. Devon jerked up from the seat, shifting Cerise on his lap. He turned for the window, then remembered. "Angel, you'll have to look. From the sound of hooves and the crunch of wheels, I'd guess it's a carriage. One barreling up my drive. You'll have to tell me who it is."

Anne's heart thundered in her throat as she slipped off the duke's lap and pressed her face to the window. They were indeed on the drive in front of the duke's house. Pulled by four galloping grays, an elegant white coach rattled up the drive. It stopped beside them. There was something on the door—a gilt-trimmed crest, partly obscured by dust.

Anne swallowed hard. It was a member of the aristocracy, not someone from Bow Street.

The carriage door opened and a woman stepped out—a woman wearing a blue silk pelisse and a deep-brimmed bonnet that shielded her face. The lady slowly turned to their carriage. Anne saw an oval face, very pale, and lovely features. She saw the woman hesitate and chew her lip.

"Who is it?" the duke asked.

Anne started. In her shock, she'd forgotten he was dependent on her eyes. "It's a lady with dark curls and a very beautiful face. I think she must be your sister."

Chapter Twelve

FROM THE CARRIAGE window, Anne watched the duke jump down from the steps and turn toward his sister as the tall, dark-haired beauty let out a squeal of delight. His face softened, and his arms extended toward the happy sound. Anne's heart gave a tremendous lurch in her chest. She had never seen him look so surprised or so deeply touched. In that moment, he was more darkly handsome than ever.

This was a disaster. She was a fallen woman—she should not be anywhere near his sister, who would probably be mortified to know she stood not six feet from her brother's ladybird. Shame and embarrassment rolled over her. Anne desperately tried to smooth her skirts and straighten her crumpled bodice. She had told the duke she must stay inside the carriage. It would be highly inappropriate for her to come out, even if she only lurked in the background and was not introduced to his sister. She would sit in the carriage until it drove around the house, then she'd slip in the back door.

She would gather her things. And she would have to go.

"Devon, thank heaven! Thank heaven you are alive and you are home safe!"

His sister's cry made Anne twist her head toward the window again. She saw dark-blue silk flap as the duke's sister launched herself fiercely into him. Quite a bit shorter than he, the young woman collided hard against his chest. The duke's arms shot around her and he cradled her close. His sister embraced him tightly, then gave a squeak and moved back, placing her gloved hand on her stomach.

Anne felt her eyes grow huge. His sister's hand cupped the pronounced curve, almost completely hidden by the voluminous folds of her pelisse. She was enceinte. *Very* enceinte.

Even from where she sat, Anne could see the sparkle of tears on his sister's blushing ivory cheek. Then a delicate hand in a white satin glove lifted, and the duke's sister smacked him playfully on his chest. "Why did you stay away, you awful brother?"

Guilt nipped at Anne's heart. If she had tried harder to heal him, perhaps he would have accepted the truth—he was not mad, he had no need to hide, and he should go home to his family.

Or was he hiding for a reason other than war and nightmares? Could he have refused to go because he hadn't recovered from Lady Rosalind's death and he didn't want to court a bride?

She knew she must turn away and give them privacy when his sister cried, "You appear to be exactly the same and just as healthy and hale as your mysterious friend promised us you were."

Mysterious friend? Anne's stomach dipped. Had her letter been the thing that lured his sister to come here? Surely it wouldn't have done that. She'd written it to *reassure* his family.

"Mysterious friend?" the duke asked slowly. "Who are you talking about?"

"The author of that letter, of course." His sister smiled up at him. Then she wiped tears with the back of her glove. "Goodness, you haven't even asked how I am, Devon!"

"Wait—Ashton. It must have been Ashton." He kissed the top of his sister's rose-festooned bonnet. He tipped his head back, and pain and regret flashed over his handsome features. "Of course I want to know how you are. But the truth is . . . I wanted to surprise you. I wanted to guess exactly which of my sisters you are. I was certain I could do it by the sound of your voice. I thought I wouldn't need sight to recognize you. But I do."

"You daft thing, you should have asked! It's Caroline, of course. The enormous bulge of my belly should have given it away." His sister took his hand. Smiling, she placed it over her stomach. Anne's eyes watered as she saw the duke's expression change to one of amazement, then undeniable pride and admiration. But his next words to his sister truly broke her heart.

"You are enormous, Caro. Which means you should not have been traveling to see me."

Enormous. It was the sort of teasing word a brother would bestow on a sister. Anne never had brothers and sisters, although she had learned about how dastardly a brother's teasing could be from girls in the village near Longsworth. But the sharp lines bracketing the duke's mouth revealed how worried he was.

"Well, I am tired of 'lying in.' I've had enough of lying on a chaise longue, waiting for a baby who seems determined never to arrive."

"You must be exhausted," he said. "You should sit down."

"I've been sitting for *hours*. Though that carriage jiggled all over on the road, and I had to stop at every coaching inn to use the necessary. You have no idea what a baby does to you—"

"I don't think I want to find out, Caro."

"Well, you can't find out. Not personally, I mean. Stop looking so terrified. You've been through war—you can't be afraid of me simply because I'm enceinte."

His brow quirked. "I'm not afraid. Let's get you to a seat that isn't moving. Are you hungry?"

Anne couldn't help but smile as the duke hurried through a list of questions. Did she want tea? Or biscuits? Sherry? Or perhaps some pheasant and potatoes and pie? He looked so worried for his sister, Anne thought her heart would swell to bursting just watching the two of them.

Then Caroline frowned. She touched his disheveled cravat. "I've never seen you look quite so . . . rumpled, Devon."

Heat flared again in Anne's cheeks, but the duke answered softly, "I can't see what I look like anymore, so I don't seem to care."

"You need a woman's touch," his sister declared.

"True," he replied. "There is nothing like a woman's touch to set a man to rights." At that moment, the coachman called down to ask if he should take the carriage away, and the duke shouted in answer, "Take it to the stables."

Anne knew what this meant. It was time for her to leave.

The carriage lurched into motion. She allowed herself one last look at the duke. At the clop of hooves and jingle of the traces, he jerked up his head. He followed the sound and his eyes met hers as she gazed through the window. He couldn't see her, but he didn't turn away.

Anne sank back so his sister would not see her. But faintly, obscured by the rattle of the wheels, his sister's lovely, rich voice tumbled in through the open window.

"That letter I spoke to you about. It wasn't written by the Earl of Ashton, you know."

Oh, no. The carriage slowed. The horses were turning so the duke's large black carriage could move past his sister's jauntier white one. With the softer rumble of the wheels, Anne could hear every word. And she *had* to.

"Apparently it was written to Mama by a lady friend of yours. Unsigned, but we were certain it was a woman's handwriting. Anyway, Ashton's letters are usually a scrawl. I was terribly curious to find out who this lady is. Devon, have you fallen in love?"

Anne peeped out the window in time to see the duke put his hand to his temple, as though he had just felt a sharp pain. Her head throbbed, too, as she waited for the disaster to crash down upon her.

"Oh!" His sister clapped her hand to her mouth. Her violet eyes widened, her dark lashes reaching so high that they brushed her eyebrows. "She is your *mistress,* isn't she? How utterly shocking. But if she had not written, we would have had no idea what was happening to you. We would not know how much you are suffering from the memories of war and how cleverly you are conquering your affliction."

"She wrote a letter to our mother." The duke cocked his head and said the words with infinite care, as though he was coaxing his sister to give him a denial. But of course she wouldn't—for this was exactly what Anne had done.

"Yes. But who is *she,* Devon?"

"Caro, you traveled all this way because of this letter? When you are, what—days away from the birth of your child?"

His sister had her right hand on the crook of his arm, but she waved the left one airily. "About two weeks. *Of course* I came once I knew you were staying away simply because you are being s-stubborn—" Suddenly his sister's voice wobbled and she stopped. Her look of wide-eyed innocence crumpled. She turned to Devon and pressed her head to his chest. The slender shoulders shook.

He wrapped his arms around her, but he went pale. "What is it, Caro? What's wrong?"

At that instant, the horses set off at a swift trot. The coachman must have flicked the reins. The bounce and rattle of the wheels drowned out all other sound. Anne could see the duke's hands braced on his sister's shoulders. Caroline was speaking animatedly, and the duke drank in every word, his face growing increasingly stony with every expressive sweep of his sister's hands. Then they vanished from Anne's sight as the carriage rounded the house.

"Where are you planning to go?" The duke's deep growl startled Anne, and she dropped the silver hairbrush he had let her borrow. It clattered to the glass top of the vanity. She had tried to tidy her hair swiftly and stick the pins back in—making love in the carriage had left it disheveled. Jerking her gaze from the mirror, she swiveled on the stool. He stood in the doorway, then he took a step in and closed the door. He leaned on the head of his walking stick.

"I don't know." She'd thought she would not see him again before she left. "I— Where do you wish me to go?" He was her protector—she suddenly realized if she wished that to continue, she must do as he commanded. Her hands clenched as she waited. *Not London. If I have to run with nothing but the clothes on my back, I'll do it before I go to London.* Then she thought of something else. "Or do you wish to bring an end to our contract now that your sister is here?"

This should be what she wanted: He would give her a settlement, as they'd agreed in her contract, and she could use the money to escape. It would be perfect, yet her heart felt ice cold. She would never see him again.

Fool. It has to happen sometime. Just as Kat told you—a clever mistress always remembers that someday there will be an end and she plans for it.

"No, I don't want that." His walking stick tapped against the floor as he came toward her. "My sister came all this way to meet you—the author of an unsigned letter to my mother." The closer he approached, the more his broad-shouldered, battle-hewn body seemed to loom over her.

She quickly stood. "Your sister did not come here to see me. I saw her collapse into your arms and begin to cry—" Biting her lip, she stopped. "I'm sorry, I didn't mean to eavesdrop. And I am sorry about sending a letter without telling you. You must believe my intentions were good. It bothered me that your mother was worrying about you. I have lost people I loved, and I know what it is like to be almost sick with fear. All I did was tell her you were healthy and strong. I told her in the letter I was a—a friend of one of your friends."

Waiting for his anger was terrible. She was certain it was rumbling within him. Finally he asked, "Am I anywhere near the bed?"

She blinked. "Yes, you are. Will you let me take you to it?"

"Of course, angel."

She led him by the elbow and he sat down heavily on the edge of the mattress. This was his bed, but he never used it—not to sleep in.

He lifted his head as if he knew exactly where she was. She was breathing quite hard. "My sister will have to stay. At least for the night."

"Of course she will. She is your sister."

"And any sister should know better than to flush her brother out in his bachelor quarters." He groaned. "You meant well with the letter, Cerise. But you should have told me."

"I know, and I regret it. I won't keep any more secrets from you—" Anne sank her teeth into her lip again to stop any more foolish words. Worry for him had made her speak too impulsively. She was making a promise she could never keep.

Pure anguish flashed in his eyes. "Caroline has no idea what I'm like. I couldn't bring myself to tell her about my nightmares, my battle memories, my rages. She has enough troubles of her own. But I have to tell her. She has to be warned not to approach and surprise me. She's big with child—what would happen if I hauled her to the floor? I wish you could stay, Cerise, so you can watch me, make sure I don't hurt her. But obviously that is impossible."

She knew it to be the truth, but it twisted her heart. "I know I cannot stay. I'm your mistress, and it would be a tremendous insult to your sister for me to be here. But you won't hurt her. I'm *certain* you won't."

His broad shoulders slumped. "How can you be when I'm not?"

"I happen to believe you are not mad. Surely you can recognize how much you have changed. You no longer drink brandy to blot out your memories. And when I read to you—"

"Which you cannot do if you're not here. Cerise, I don't know if I can survive a visit with my sister if I don't have you in my house to make me feel better."

How her heart leapt in her chest. Yet she couldn't stay. As he'd said, it was impossible. "Tell your sister Caroline the truth. There's no reason why you should not. In my letter, I explained that you were haunted by memories of battle, memories that made you shout out in the night and kept you from sleeping."

"So you were brutally honest?"

"Yes. I wanted your family to understand why you were staying away."

"And why do you think that is?"

"So you could protect them from yourself, obviously. Isn't that what you said to me—you wanted to send me away for my own protection? I wanted your family to know it was not their fault. In your mind, you were doing the most noble and loving thing for them that you could."

"I was doing the sensible thing," he countered, his jaw tight.

"You are not going to hurt your sister. All you must do is explain to her how you could react, and she will know to be careful."

"She shouldn't have to be careful, damn it. She's come running to me for help, and all I am is a danger to her." He made a fist and he slammed it with uncanny accuracy into the wooden bedpost. The entire canopy shuddered. Anne shuddered.

"Why did she come to you for help?" she asked. She clambered onto the bed and walked, on her knees, until she was behind his back. Gently, she massaged his shoulders. They were as hard and tense as iron, unyielding to her kneading hands.

"It is a private matter."

"Of course."

"Hell, Cerise, she asked me to promise I wouldn't repeat it."

"You have changed," she said reassuringly. "You move so confidently around the house now. And when was the last time you threw a table across a room?"

His laugh was gruff and self-effacing. "I can hardly remember. But without you here, angel, I might start tossing things again."

"If you wish, I—I could stay close by." She had no idea what to do. All she knew of mistresses was that the lucky ones lived in beautiful town houses. But that was what a courtesan did in London. Here, in the country, she was utterly at sea.

"There's an inn in the village," he said. "The Black Swan. Would you take a room there, Cerise? I want you close, to visit you. When my sister leaves, you can come back to the house."

"Is it a respectable inn?"

"Of course." She could see his reflection in the mirror—he looked affronted.

"Then would the proprietor want to let a room to me and turn a blind eye when you came for visits?" It was the truth, but she knew she had dragged it up as an excuse. The Swan was a public inn in a village on one of the most important routes of travel out of London. She knew the story of Madame's murder and of her own disappearance had been in the news sheets; the odds were high that people traveling out of London would have read of it. But would any of them recognize her with her dyed hair? Would anyone dream to connect a duke's ladybird at an inn with a London whore wanted for murder?

"He will," he said with confidence, like a man who always got what he wanted. "We will concoct a story for you. You can be an acquaintance of the family, a respectable widow traveling to visit family. The mention of my name will ensure you are not given any trouble or disrespect."

She thought of her first visit to Mrs. Wimple's, but she didn't contradict him. Surely she would be as safe there as anywhere and much safer than she would be if she went back to London without money for escape.

"What's wrong, angel?" he asked.

She swiftly massaged his shoulders to distract him. Surprisingly, he gave growls of pleasure when she gouged her fingers hard into his tight muscles. "Nothing. I was merely thinking of your sister. She looked so very happy to see you."

He groaned and let his head drop forward, and Anne remembered that he would not know how delighted his sister had looked. He would not know how his sister had lit up as she'd flung herself into his arms.

"When I held Caro, all I wanted to do was look into her face," he said. "At first I didn't even know which of my sisters she was. Then, when I knew, I wanted to see what she looked like. I tried to imagine she hadn't changed at all from the last time I saw her, three years ago. For my peace of mind, I had to think that. But I knew it couldn't be true. Obviously it isn't, since she's expecting a child."

Anne hugged his neck. "Would you want me to describe her to you now? Perhaps together we can determine how she's changed, so then you will know. The most important things will not have altered at all. She obviously loves you very much, and I can tell that you equally adore her. That's all that matters, isn't it?"

"Yes, I suppose so." The duke lifted her right hand and slowly, lovingly, kissed each of her fingers. "Angel, how am I going to survive the night when I know you won't be there to read to me after I wake up hollering? Or to make love to me, against my better judgment, and successfully push every other thought out of my head?"

She had to tease or she might give in to tears. "I thought all I had done was annoy you."

Grinning broadly, he turned and caught her around the waist. He dragged her onto his lap. But it wasn't lust burning in his eyes. It was something she couldn't quite read. "You are a highly unconventional mistress, Cerise, but I've begun to think it would be impossible to live without you."

Impossible to live without you.

How those words haunted Anne for the two days she

had spent at the inn, for she was beginning to fear she felt the same way about him. And that truly *was* impossible.

She cupped her tea with trembling hands. No one had pointed a finger at her and screamed, "Murderess," but she was living on tenterhooks, waiting for it to happen. It was proof she couldn't stay in England. How could she live the rest of her life in fear—fear that someone would recognize her and turn her in to the magistrate, fear that she would be arrested for a murder she had not meant to commit? She was still guilty, even though she had acted to save a child. The penalty for her crime would be hanging.

She set down the tea. She yearned to stay in England, and it was for the most foolish of reasons: She didn't want to leave the duke. For two days, he had not come to see her—no doubt because he did not want to leave his sister. He was finding a way to live without her. But she missed him terribly. She worried about him. She ached for him.

But she was *only* a mistress. She couldn't risk ending up hanged just to spend as much time as possible as the duke's lover. She *couldn't*. But what did it mean that she was silly enough to consider staying, even once she got enough money to run?

Swift footsteps sounded in the hallway, and Anne stiffened as they stopped in front of her door. It was madness to be afraid instantly—it could be a servant. A soft rap came, and a female voice asked, "Miss?"

Anne sagged with relief. Indeed, just a maid. "Come in," she called.

The door opened and a young maid curtsied, her eyes filled with stars. "Begging your pardon, mum, but the Duke of March wishes you to meet him in the parlor."

That made her smile. "Thank you. You may take a message back to him. I shall be down in a moment."

"Oh, he's in the tap right now, mum. All the local men

are toasting his victories in battle. His Grace is a great hero of war."

"Yes, he is." But as the girl left and Anne turned to the vanity mirror, she thought of how much he had paid for his heroics, how much they had hurt him and changed him. She quickly reviewed her gown—one of her new day dresses the duke had sent to the inn. She looked well enough. The duke had not come to her room; she wondered why. Did he want to give at least the outward appearance of respectability?

On her way to the parlor, Anne passed by the taproom. She glanced inside.

There, on a bench, sat the duke. The sight of his face and his smile made her knees wobble. She rested her hand on the doorframe, simply watching him. The way his hair fell over his brow reminded her of how carefully she had tried to cut it, working with slow diligence to ensure she didn't stick him with the scissors. The way his smile widened reminded her of how he had grinned after falling from his horse and how she'd been so worried he was dead.

Staring at him, she felt warm inside, like a hot bun that gave a burst of steam when it was pulled open. He set down his tankard and turned. He couldn't see her, but he must have sensed she was staring. She turned away and hurried to the parlor. A servant would take him a message, would bring him to her. In just a few moments, they would be together. Alone.

Oh, heavens, she was quivering with anticipation. Her heart pounded. What exactly should she *say*? She hadn't been this nervous the first time she'd tried to seduce him.

She was very much afraid of what this meant. Only a very stupid mistress fell in love. She had lost her home, her past, her parents—why would she willingly put her heart at risk again?

* * *

"I came to talk about my sister."

It was the last thing Anne expected. The duke flopped back on the settee by the parlor's fireplace and rubbed his temple as though it pounded with pain.

"Caro asked me not to tell anyone, but I've realized I'm going to lose my mind." He gave a wry grin. "Finally, after everything you've done to convince me I'm not mad, my sister is driving me insane." He tipped his head toward the rustle of her skirts, looking astonishingly helpless and undeniably appealing. "I need your help, angel. I don't know where else to turn."

"What is wrong?"

"Caro didn't come here because of your letter. She came because she was running away from home. She is nine months pregnant and she has run away."

The maid had left a tea tray. Despite her surprise at what he'd said, Anne poured a cup and pressed it to his hand. "Why did she do such a thing?"

"Only you would take that in stride and give me a cup of tea." He moved to put it aside, but she stopped him.

"Well, a sip will help, Your Grace." She stubbornly lifted the tea to his lips. Her heart gave a pang. Her mother used to say that after they ended up in the stews, as though a simple cup of tea could make up for fear and poverty.

At her command, he took a deep swallow. "Caro told me she came because, as she put it, her marriage is in tatters, her heart is broken, and she is about to bear the child of a man who no longer cares for her."

"Her husband no longer cares for her?" She blinked. "He would have to be . . . an idiot. How could he not love your sister, who absolutely glows with beauty and is about to have his *baby*?"

The duke sighed. "I don't know. I can't get a coherent

explanation from her. She told me she could not stay at her home in London a minute longer. Her husband is the Earl of Cavendish, by the way. Their marriage, like all the ones in my immediate family, was a love match."

"She would not tell you why she believes he doesn't love her anymore?"

"She thought it might be because she is now the size of a house," he answered.

"That can't be possible," she declared. "What sort of husband could be so shallow?"

He half-turned to her, his lip curved in a grim smile. "You give men more credit than we deserve. I've known gentlemen who spent the night in a brothel while their wife was at home laboring through the birth of a child."

Anne couldn't answer. Perhaps some of the gentlemen who had come to Madame's had been doing that.

"Caro left her home and went to March House. That's the ducal home in London, where my mother is living along with my two unmarried sisters, Lizzie and Win. Caro spent only two days there. Long enough to be given your letter to read—apparently every female in my family is speculating as to whom the anonymous author is."

"I am sorry about that, but it is better than having them worry about you."

His brows shot up. "Caro found she couldn't tell our mother about her troubles. She came to me because she didn't know where else to go. Since I'm a male, she thought I would understand the workings of her husband's mind. She wants me to explain why he doesn't care for her anymore and tell her how to win back his love. Since I won Rosalind's love, she thinks I should know how to do it. But there's a problem. . . ."

His features hardened, his expression grew resolute. "Since I can't get Caro to calm down long enough to tell me exactly what Cavendish did, I'm guessing he was unfaithful. He broke my sister's heart. Right now what I'd like to do is kill him. Call him out and face him at forty paces on a foggy field."

"Heavens, no!" Panic gripped her and she squeezed his arm. "You cannot do that! You could be killed. Or, if you aren't, you'll kill him. What good will that do your sister?"

"None, I agree. I could just pound some sense into his head."

Anne thought of her parents—they solved all problems by talking to each other. "Has your sister spoken to her husband? She must have confronted him over this."

"I have no idea. When she tries to explain, she either begins to cry or she gets embarrassed. *I'm* embarrassed every time we talk about this, so I can't figure out what she's trying to tell me." He groaned and dropped his head into his hands. "She married for love, had her heart broken, and I'm the last person who knows how to heal from that. My solution was to go to war, and you know how well that went." He looked up, gave a rueful, heartbreaking grin. "As best as I can tell, she wants to win the blackguard's love, while I want to beat him senseless. I'm almost at the end of my rope. She asks my opinion, then she won't listen to a word I say. She gets angry with me when I point out this is Cavendish's fault, and somehow I become the villain."

Anne smothered a smile at his exasperation.

"This is how I behaved with you, isn't it, when we were arguing about my brandy? Why were you so tenacious and determined to help me, when I really deserved a kick in the backside?"

"Because you deserved to be helped."

"I'm glad you were so stubborn, Cerise." The duke shook his head. "My sister needs a woman to confide in, but there is no one."

There was someone—Anne shook her head. Of course she could not speak to his sister. She was a fallen woman.

Besides, she knew nothing about loving husbands, and while she knew the details of her parents' happy marriage, she had no idea how to salvage an unhappy one. "I think you must let your sister calm down; you must give her time, truly listen to her, and then try to talk to her."

"I'll have to struggle through this on my own, but I don't know if I can. Charging into battle was easier than this."

"You don't have to struggle alone. You can come and talk to me whenever you need to."

"I need you now." He looked up, his eyes unmistakably hot with desire. "I've missed you for two days, angel. Go and lock the parlor door. I've hungered for the taste of you."

She wanted him, but there was the fear of causing a scandal. "Here? In the parlor?"

"It's more discreet than having you lead me up to your bedchamber." A smile curved his lips. "This time you will have to be quiet."

"Of course, Your Grace."

He cocked his head. "I want you to call me Devon, angel. Would you do that for me?"

Anne caught her breath. To use his Christian name was an intimacy she had not expected. Suddenly she realized she had never been so intimate with a man—she'd never had a gentleman reveal his doubts and worries to her. No man had ever let her glimpse his heart.

As he wrapped his strong arms around her and drew her down on the settee, she whispered, "Yes, Your—Devon."

"Good. Now ride me, angel. Do your magic."

Chapter Thirteen

IT FELT ILLICIT yet special to even *think* of Devon's Christian name, much less use it. Even Kat referred to lovers only by their titles.

Anne strode up a narrow path that led to the back of the inn—she had followed it as it carved straight borders for acres of fields, then wound through the forest, until her rumbling stomach demanded she return. She had walked for miles this morning, but no amount of beautiful views or vigorous exercise could stop her from thinking about Devon.

Her dreams used to be about freedom and independence. Now they were all about him. Over the last three days, Devon had told her a half dozen times that he missed her. Each time it both warmed her heart and gave it a sharp wrench. She had to remember it did not mean anything. She was not an innocent young lady anymore, who might take those words from a duke and spin an entire hopeful future involving matrimony and children. All protectors were fascinated with their mistresses at first, but the interest waned. If she used her wits and kept control of her heart, she could save herself.

After stamping mud from her boots on a flagstone,

Anne stepped inside the front door of the inn and took off her gloves.

"Oh, there you are, mum!" One of the maids rushed up and bobbed a hasty curtsy. "A visitor for you. Waiting upon you in the parlor."

It had to be *Devon*. Anne's heart soared, refusing to be controlled, but when she opened the parlor door she saw a rose-trimmed bonnet and ebony curls. Shock bolted her to the floor.

The duke's sister spun on her chair, revealing blushing cheeks and violet eyes. "Oh, I'm so glad you've come. I feared you would choose not to see me."

Anne blinked. Dimly, she remembered, through rising panic, that this lady was the Countess of Cavendish. "I cannot believe you have come to see me." Somehow, manners had prevailed over shock, and she realized she was rising from a deep curtsy. Goodness, was it possible the duke's sister did not know she was his mistress?

Her pulse thundered. This could hurt Devon's sister. The gossip, the sniggers. If Devon found out . . . He had agreed she should be nowhere near his sister.

Anne swiftly closed the door. "There is something you must know. I am so very sorry, but once you know who I am, you will want to leave here—"

"You're Devon's mistress. I know that. Treadwell told me Devon had a 'lady guest' in the house. Of course, my brother stuttered out some nonsensical lie, but his blush made it obvious."

"Your Ladyship, you must go. I wouldn't want to taint you."

Lady Cavendish waved her hand. "I've discovered there are some things far more important than proper behavior. Ladylike behavior might get a woman wed, but I've learned it doesn't delight a husband." She gave a surprisingly cynical laugh, one that made Anne's heart lurch; such a beautiful lady should not be jaded.

The countess tipped up her chin, showing the strong, stubborn pride Anne saw in Devon. "I believe you are the only one who can help me. You must know all about seducing gentlemen. I want you to teach me."

"I beg your pardon, Your Ladyship—"

"I desperately need to learn how to seduce my husband."

Anne must have shown her shock, for Lady Cavendish's expression suddenly crumpled. "You think I'm a fool, don't you?" Devon's sister covered her face with her hands and sobbed.

Forgetting propriety, Anne rushed over to the couch and wrapped her arm around the woman.

Anne firmly pushed the teacup and saucer into the countess's bare hands, just as she had done for Devon. "This will make you feel better." Of course it couldn't. But the countess took it with a small, grateful smile and sipped.

Anne knew she should not even be in the same room with a countess, but the woman needed help. "Does your brother know you've come here?"

"Of course not. But I'm *desperate*. It's obvious how infatuated my brother is with you. I hoped you would teach me your arts and allurements."

"Teach you," she repeated slowly, "my . . . my arts and allurements?" *Infatuated?*

"I've lost my husband's love and I can't *bear* it anymore."

Devon didn't know his sister was here. Would he be angry she was speaking to the countess now? "What did you tell the duke?"

"I did not tell him anything. He was locked in his study. Treadwell confided to me that my brother does not sleep at night and that he has nightmares. Apparently they have been worse since you left."

Anne's heart sank at that. Without her to read him to sleep or distract him with sex, he had gone backward. He hadn't admitted that to her when he'd come to visit.

"I told Treadwell I was coming to the village to shop, of course." The cup rattled in the saucer. "Perhaps I'm being foolish. Worrying about my husband's love when Devon—"

"You are not being foolish, Your Ladyship." Anne now saw the lines etched in the countess's forehead, the shadows beneath her eyes. "Your brother has nightmares about the war, and I—I was trying to help ease those for him. Or at least help him cope with them." Her cheeks were burning, because of course she was admitting she spent nights with Devon. She was the foolish one, given that his sister was married and knew what she was. But since the day she and her mother ended up in the slums, Anne had never even spoken to a respectable lady.

It occurred to her that, as a viscount's daughter, she would have been very much like the duke's sister now if Sebastian had not forced her mother and her to leave their home. Married. Perhaps expecting a child.

The countess set down her tea so swiftly, it sloshed to the saucer, then the table. She grasped Anne's hands. "Thank you for helping my brother. Treadwell told me what you have done for him. How you've helped him cope with his blindness, and how he has grown more accepting of it."

Admiration glowed in the countess's eyes. Anne squirmed, a little uncomfortable. "I do not know if I have done that much, and I suspect time is responsible for much of what—"

"Treadwell does not think so. He also admitted you wrote the letter to my mother."

Anne began to apologize, but Lady Cavendish squeezed her hands. "That letter gave my mother such relief and peace of mind. She has been so worried about Devon. She feared he was wounded far worse than she had heard, that he was more badly scarred than we had been told, or very ill, or perhaps that he had even lost his wits."

The very thing he feared was happening to him.

"After Devon went to war, our mother barely ate or slept. She became perilously thin. Your letter cheered her so much, my sisters were able to coerce her to eat, and she stopped staying in her rooms. She had spent hours alone, writing letter after letter to Devon. Most she simply crumpled up or tore to pieces and burned. What you did was a wonderful thing."

"Th-thank you." Anne's heart lurched. Suddenly she knew she had to make him go home. He *must* go to his family—

But if he did, would he allow her to stay here? Would he let her go? It didn't matter. Reuniting him with his family, easing his pain, his mother's pain—that was the most important thing.

"What is it?" Lady Cavendish stared. "You look as if you are arguing with yourself."

"It's nothing."

The genuine kindness of Lady Cavendish stunned her. A lady of the *ton* should be either horrified by her or utterly condescending. Lady Cavendish made her think of her mother, who had always been gracious, generous, kind.

"Would you be willing to help me with my husband? Or is there nothing I can do, since I'm the size of a carriage and not pretty at all anymore—"

"Rubbish!" Anne spat the word impetuously. The countess reeled back. Fumbling over her words, Anne went on, "You—you are stunningly beautiful. What gentleman could not see the sheer loveliness in a woman who is carrying his child? You absolutely glow."

The countess smiled wryly. "You must know what men are like. My husband may be pleased that he is going to have a child, and he is hoping for a son, of course. But he has desires, and he feels he can't come to my bed anymore, so he . . . I think he has gone to someone else's."

A blush washed over Lady Cavendish's face. "There's no one else I can speak to about this. Devon is the only other person who knows. And he became so angry he wanted to *fight* with my husband! I want to win my husband back—away from the clutches of that horrible widow who has snared him."

Anne tried to follow the countess's impulsive words. "A widow?"

Devon's sister nodded, her curls bouncing. Then she suddenly tensed and put her hand to her belly. Pain racked her face.

Anne got to her feet. "What's wrong? Are you all right?"

"This . . . keeps . . . happening," Lady Cavendish gasped. "My belly tightens. It goes so . . . hard." She stared ahead, looking dumbfounded and a little fearful.

Anne stroked her arm. "When I was younger"—she must not forget and accidentally say "in the slums"—"I saw several births." Her mother had even helped in some labors in the lodging houses in which they had been forced to stay. "I do remember that a woman's belly goes hard as her time comes near. One of the midwives called it 'practice.' Try to relax and breathe through it."

"Relax!" Lady Cavendish cried, smiling ruefully.

Anne had no idea how to broach this without causing worry or saying something unseemly to a countess. And she knew, from being close to births, that the "practice" was much gentler than the real thing. "You must be very near your time," she said carefully. She did remember that some women had spoken of the practice pains very soon before the birth happened. "One thing I learned is that no one can ever guess when a birth will happen. It can be much sooner than one suspects—"

"But I cannot go home!" Breathing hard, Lady Cavendish launched to her feet. "When I'm there, all I can do is wonder where my husband is and whether he is with that woman—"

"Please. You shouldn't work yourself up." Anne put a quelling hand on her arm. "So you want to seduce him," she began. Her cheeks must be scarlet already. But she hoped this discussion would distract Lady Cavendish.

"Yes. After I've had the baby, of course. I want to know all the tricks a courtesan would know. I must know what things I can do to please him. To keep him from straying."

It was on the tip of Anne's tongue to point out that the countess was a lady. Well-bred ladies were not supposed to know a courtesan's tricks. Perhaps this was the very reason proper ladies were supposed to avoid courtesans and fallen women—in case they were tempted to ask questions and learn about seduction. She remembered some of the naughty things the prostitutes at Madame's had taught her. *Take a man's cockstand between your lips and he's yours. Or let him have you from behind, and you'll thrill him no end. They don't get that from the fine ladies.*

She had tried everything she could think of to entice Devon into keeping her, but how did she explain this to a lady? But, really, why should ladies not know about sex? Why should women be proper and lonely while men went to brothels for carnal things they couldn't get elsewhere?

Lady Cavendish began to breathe hard and look frightened.

"All right," Anne whispered. She must be mad, but Lady Cavendish instantly stopped rubbing her belly and paid attention. "We will begin with the one your husband will love the most. You must . . ." Her courage almost failed as she faced the eager, inquisitive gaze. "You must take him into your mouth."

"Kiss him? We used to kiss passionately. Since our marriage, he seems to have lost interest in such frivolities."

"That is not . . . uncommon for men. I—I think kissing for men is a part of seduction. Once the lady becomes willing to bed them without kisses or other preliminary play, men dispense with it." Though she remembered the wonderful kiss she'd shared with Devon in the rain. The times he'd kissed her when he didn't expect sex at the end of it.

"Well, that is terribly discouraging," the countess said with a frank, gusty sigh. "Then how am I to convince him to do it?"

There was nothing for it but the truth. "I meant that men like women to kiss their private parts."

"*That* part?" The countess gaped at her, then frowned. "You are trying to frighten me away."

"No, Your Ladyship, I am not. You wished to know what courtesans do, and that truly is one of the things. It's something men enjoy a great deal, but they would never ask it of a gently bred wife."

A blush swept ivory cheeks. "You mean, I simply open my mouth and let him put it inside?"

Heavens. "Well, um . . . yes. Gentlemen like a lady to . . . suck on it. The friction and pressure pleases them. They like a woman to . . . move her head up and down." She could *not* do this.

There was a sudden rap upon the door—thank heaven

for an interruption. Anne could imagine any number of Madame's whores who would relish explaining a few things to a naïve lady, proud to display their abundant experience. She was not one. She swiftly called, "Come in."

It was a young maid, Hattie. She bobbed a curtsy and began to announce, "His Grace—" But the duke passed her, lightly sweeping his walking stick.

"Not necessary, my dear," he said in his cool, controlled way that warned of a storm inside. "Both of these ladies know who I am."

His sister had come to Cerise for instruction in carnal arts.

Devon could not quite believe it. It was a good thing he had his walking stick to rest on, or he would have been knocked to the ground by Caro's astounding and grudging admission. He spun on his heel toward his sister—he knew exactly where she was, because her soprano voice was protesting loudly about interfering brothers.

"What were you thinking?" he demanded. "You cannot come here and speak with Cerise. It is not acceptable. It is not done. Do you realize there were a gaggle of maids in the corridor, straining to hear every word passing between you two?"

His mistress did not say a word—wisely, he thought, even in his exasperation—but he had to guess his sister would not be cowed. "I had no other choice!" Caro cried, and he could picture her the way she used to be before she had married. A wild hoyden who liked to ride and fish and shoot with the men. He should have known the supposed change to demure and happy bride wasn't real. The memory of what she used to look like, her eyes snapping, braids bouncing as she argued with him over something—usually his refusal to take her along with him and his friends—gave his heart a severe punch.

Cerise had helped him cope with his blindness, but nothing would make it easier to accept. Not when he knew he would probably never see his sister again or see his little niece or nephew at all. Until he'd fallen in love with Rosalind, babies had been something he hoped to avoid. Now the knowledge that he'd never see an infant's smile, not even his own baby's toothless giggle, if he had a baby—hell, it leveled him.

"Are you listening, Devon?" Caro said. "I said the person to blame for all of this is Phillip! If my husband had not fallen in love with someone else, I would not be here, trying to learn how to win him back. If he did not have a roving eye—"

"You loved him," he pointed out.

"I still do. But one-sided love is not enough. It's even *worse*."

Cerise's voice, lush, lovely, infused with gentle firmness, fell into his blue-gray void. "You must calm yourself, Lady Cavendish. It is true the fault is your husband's, but it would be best if you were to go home with your brother."

"I'm not going anywhere with my annoying brother. Even if I do, I will come back—"

"You will not!" he barked. "Do you have any idea of the shock to find that you had left my house and no one knew exactly where you were? In your condition? I managed to trace you to here, no easy task when I'm blind. Then I discover you are learning things you have no right to know, from my mistress, and the entire *taproom* is discussing it."

"Well, then, stop *shouting*," Caroline snapped. "Every taproom in England must be able to hear you. I don't see that I've done anything so very shocking. I am a married woman. I was expected to go to balls and watch that ferret of a woman, Lady Pomroy, throw herself all over my husband. And the worst I was allowed to do, according to Society, was give her the cut direct, when *she* is the most awful little whore—"

"Caroline!" Hades, his temple throbbed.

"Your Grace." The cool voice belonged to Cerise. She sounded oddly distant and icy. And rather condescending, though she and Caroline were the ones at fault here. Cerise had told *him* she should not be anywhere near his sister. Hades, because of *propriety,* his mistress had been forced to leave his house, condemning him to sleepless nights filled with nightmares. And thanks to propriety, he had been left missing her intensely, aching for the sound of her voice, wanting her touch, hungering for her.

"I do not think it is very wise to shout at Lady Cavendish," Cerise went on, making him feel like a disobedient schoolboy. "The person to blame in this is me."

He turned to her. Or at least to where he thought she was. She did not sound contrite. She sounded . . . furious. "That's not true," he groaned. "But you should have sent her home at once."

"Perhaps. Though was it really so wrong to offer some help and advice? While there may be rumors that I am your mistress, everyone at this inn was supposed to believe I am a widow and friend of your family. Unfortunately, your visits, and your reaction now, will have caused the gossip."

"So *I'm* in the wrong?" He could not believe this. How did his sister and his *mistress* manage to make him feel like the villain? "You were the one to insist on leaving my house to avoid gossip and protect my sister. You should have considered that today." He did sound like an idiot. She was correct: His visits, his need to be with her, had done the damage to his story. He had best keep his mouth shut and just get his sister home.

But Caro cried, "She did! Of course she did, you great lummox! *I* insisted on staying. I—"

His sister stopped shouting. A weak, girlish voice whispered, "Oh, dear." Who in blazes was that? Had one of the maids come in? That little timid squeak sounded like neither of the two women he was now arguing with.

"What is wrong, Your Ladyship?" Cerise was the one to speak, her beautiful voice filled with concern. Footsteps hastened past him, and he heard a low feminine cry of distress. What had happened? Damn the blindness. He tried to follow the frantic female voices.

"I'm all . . . wet. What—what does it mean? Could it be . . . blood?"

"I'm sure it is not," Cerise said, but he was stunned by the word. *Blood.*

"I haven't had any pain since before, yet now my skirts are soaked. . . ." The horror in Caro's voice pierced his heart. "Have I done something wrong? Am I going to lose my baby?"

"Shh," Cerise soothed, while his heart slammed against his chest with the force of a cannon blast. "Come, stand up with me. That should stop the flow—does it?"

"What is it?" he said into the void. "What's wrong?"

"You are right." Caro sounded relieved. "It did stop."

His heart was so tight with fear it was amazing it could still pump blood. "*What* stopped?"

"What I suspect has happened, Your Ladyship," Cerise said to his sister, as though he wasn't even in the room, "is that your water has broken."

Christ. No wonder she was ignoring him. Devon knew almost nothing about the business of birth, but he'd been at war, and there had been babies born in the camps, among the camp followers and officers' wives. Water breaking meant a child was on the way. What exactly had to be done? Should he get Caro home? Get a midwife? He felt like his head was going to blow off.

Then Caro gave an anguished cry that rooted him to the floor. "Goodness! Oh!"

"What is it?" he barked, panicked. He had to help her, but he felt . . . damned helpless.

"It is all right, Your Grace. It's simply a labor pain." Cerise's answer had him flushing scarlet and seeing red—a strange thing for a blind man. How could she be so blasted calm? Then he got over his frustration at feeling lost and useless. Thank heaven she was calm. Snapping back to his senses, he realized she was giving precise instructions to Caro. She briskly told his sister to bend over, hold the arm of the chair, and arch her back like a cat.

"Is this child coming now?" he asked.

"Oh, heavens," Caro moaned.

"Normally a first child does not come quickly," Cerise said. Then she urged, "Keep breathing in a rhythm."

Devon breathed like that, too, until Cerise said, "When I press against your back, does it help?"

"Oh, yes," Caro whispered, and it was obvious how grateful she was.

He stopped taking measured breaths, but his chest seemed to clamp around his heart as Cerise said, "There are times when a first child does come with haste. I have seen that before—where everyone assumed it would take hours and then the baby was born in mere minutes. Once Lady Cavendish's pains begin to come more quickly, that will mean labor is advancing. Now, Your Ladyship, each time the pain begins, arch against my hands and I will press. Remember to breathe slowly."

"Can I get her home?"

"Possibly," Cerise answered, but Caro gasped, "No! I don't want to move."

"I think we need a midwife or a physician, Your Grace."

Where was the local midwife? He turned, unsure where the door was, furious that he had to fumble clumsily for it in the midst of an emergency. But once he got out into the hall, he bellowed until one of the maids hurried forth. "Lady Cavendish is laboring with her child. Fetch a midwife at once."

Behind him, he heard Caro moan through a contraction, then tell Cerise, "If I don't survive the birth, I've written a letter so my baby will know who I was and how much I loved him or her."

His stomach turned upside down. Why would she plan for her death? What did she know?

"You are going to be fine," Cerise said, her voice quiet, firm, and calm. "Soon you are going to have a lovely baby. Then you can read that letter to your child yourself. It's going to be hard work—I won't lie to you about that, Your Ladyship. But you are strong and determined, and everything is going to go well."

It was amazing: She couldn't know that, but all she had to do was say it and he believed it. Cerise was a remarkable woman. She could push away fear, she could fight nightmares, she could make a battle-hardened man listen to the soft sounds of the rain and a panicked, laboring woman relax enough to giggle.

Vaguely, he wondered how she knew so much about birthing, but then she gave him orders. "Request blankets and water, Your Grace. Some sweet tea for Her Ladyship, if you please."

"Immediately," he called back, and he shouted until another maid came to do his bidding.

He had been sent to the taproom, and his sister had been laboring for eight hours.

But even when the midwife had arrived, Caro insisted Cerise stay at her side. Devon understood why. After just a few days, he had grown to rely upon Cerise.

He had bought so many rounds for the room, every man in the place spoke with a slurred voice. He'd been tempted to join them, to drown his worries in multiple tankards of ale, but Cerise's warnings about drink had welled up and stopped him. So he was as stone-cold sober as a statue, with no idea what was happening. He was a duke yet considered useless in a birthing room.

The truth was, he would be useless. If Cerise had not been there to take charge, he likely would have done more harm than good. On the battlefield, he had held men's guts in place to try to save lives. In the makeshift hospital tents, he had been an assistant while limbs were cut off. But he was thankful he wasn't in the parlor, witness to his sister's pain.

He'd heard muffled cries of agony. He'd overheard the midwife's bustling and Cerise's voice soothing his sister. Why did this business take so long? Cerise had said laboring could last days. If he didn't think he could survive days and nights of this, how would Caro?

"Your Grace." It was Cerise's rich voice, and it tumbled on him like sunlight after a long, cold night spent huddled on a battlefield. He'd been too lost in worry to hear her. The entire tap was silent, as though every man waited for the news.

"Lady Cavendish has had her baby. A perfect, very healthy, and remarkably strong little . . ."

He groaned as she drew out the suspense.

"Boy!" she exclaimed, and her voice glowed with happiness and delight.

Cheers resounded. Male voices shouted congratulations. Devon knew his duty: Though he felt almost wobbly with relief, he stood and raised his untouched tankard. "To the good health of my sister, Lady Cavendish, and her newborn son." As the shouts of joy resumed he ordered another round and let Cerise lead him out of the tap. "Is my sister all right? What can I do for her? It took so long."

"It wasn't long at all, and both your sister and your nephew are doing fine."

He felt his brows jerk to the ceiling. Not *long*? But with his throat aching, he murmured, "Thank you, Cerise. If you hadn't been here to help . . ."

"The labor went very well. And Lady Cavendish is so delighted with her beautiful son, she has almost forgotten the pain, I promise you." She laughed, and the lovely sound entranced him. "It seems to be nature's way. It's terribly painful, but when the baby gives that first cry, the mother is crying and laughing with happiness."

She moved to tug him to go, but he pulled her close to him. So close he could hear her quick breaths and notice she smelled sweaty. "To hell with propriety, angel. Come home with Caro and me. Come back and be with me. I need you. It's where you belong."

A note by express messenger could mean only one thing: That thug Taylor had finally found Anne. Sebastian leapt up from his chair in his library and snatched the letter from his footman's hand as the servant stammered, "L-Lady Julia de Mournay is awaiting you in the drawing room."

"Tell her I will be down shortly," he snapped. He swiftly unfolded the note and read:

I've found her, My Lord. Annie hid for a few days with an old friend of hers, a courtesan by the name of Kat Tate. Had to get my hands a bit dirty, but I got some information from the whore. Annie went off to a duke's hunting house to act as his private tart. I'm on my way to get her. Should return with her in a few days. Have my money ready, My Lord. You'll have her in your hands soon. Mick Taylor.

His hands shook. Shook so hard, Sebastian crumpled the note. Anne would rather be a duke's whore than his wife. The thought filled him with white-hot fury. And a duke . . . hell and damnation, a duke held power. Was it possible this man could keep Anne from him?

No, Sebastian would get her. Taylor was instructed to haul Anne back to him. With a special license, he would marry her at once and then begin to punish her. Already he had envisioned many ways to teach her obedience. Some of the painful discipline would take place in their bedroom. Soon he would break her rebellious spirit and make her obey.

But he did not want to make love to her. He did not desire that any longer. He'd thought he could endure bedding her for the money. But he was so filled with hate now, he yearned to wrap his hands around her throat and throttle her. However, he could not do that—not when he needed the money Anne would one day inherit from Lady Julia.

He would have to content himself with her punishment.

Sebastian folded the letter and thrust it into a pocket of his coat. He hastened to the drawing room and found Lady Julia pacing in front of the window. She stopped and gazed at him with haggard pain. "Has there been any word?"

He did not want the woman to know that Anne was ruined. What if Lady Julia changed her mind and refused to leave her money to the tart? Sebastian forced his lips to curve in a kindly smile. "Indeed there has. It appears Anne left London and has taken refuge with a friend in the country. I have a man on the way to retrieve her."

Lady Julia smiled in relief. "You have been so very good, Norbrook. So very devoted in our search for Anne."

"I am determined to find her." Since it was the truth, it came out with complete earnestness. "She will be home soon."

"Thank you," Lady Julia whispered. "You are closer to me than either of my sons-in-law. You are a good and noble gentleman. If Anne was gone, I would make you my heir, Norbrook, for you have become like family to me."

Sebastian clasped both Lady Julia's hands, then lifted one to his lips and kissed the gloved fingers. "You have become like family to me as well, dearer to me than any lady has ever been." Excitement shot through him. He must slather on the flattery and convince the old crone to make him her heir. If he could encourage her to do it, he would not even have to marry Anne.

If he were an heir, he could hurt Anne in whatever way he wished and still get the money. He could wrap his hands around Anne's pretty neck and know the delight of squeezing the life out of her. Or he could think of a different way to kill her—a torturous, painful one. A way that would ensure he could bestow the ultimate punishment upon her, yet not get caught.

Chapter Fourteen

IT PROVED SIMPLE to find the nursery—Devon just followed the warbling sound of the baby's cry. It had been three days since Caro gave birth, and in that time Cerise had transformed his bachelor house. She had employed nursemaids, and had overseen the preparation of the nursery for its tiny inhabitant. It had to be because she was once a governess, but mistresses were usually more interested in gowns and pleasures, not in taking charge of wailing babies.

He could hear her shushing his crying nephew, no doubt because Caro was sleeping downstairs. By all accounts the birth had been astonishingly fast for a first child—a mere eight hours. *Easy,* the midwife had called the process. But eight hours of pushing, laboring, grunting, crying with pain didn't sound easy.

The loveliest sound reached him, and he stopped and listened. In the same lush, gentle voice Cerise used to read to him, she sang a lullaby for his nephew.

But when he reached the door, she stopped. "Oh! Your Grace! Here, let me bring your nephew to you."

With his sister here, Cerise called him Your Grace again or used his title. He sighed. "I didn't mean to make you stop singing. I hate to deprive the wee thing of the pleasure." Indeed, the little lad began to squawk again.

"He has an enormous belly at the moment, from his feeding. I don't think he will settle until he gets rid of the air inside him."

He knew his sister had eschewed a wet nurse, instead feeding the baby herself. "How do you know so much about this, Cerise? Do you have children?"

"Oh, no. None of my own, but I lived in rooms surrounded by women, and my mother helped on several births. The whole thing was both fascinating and terrifying to me, so I watched and learned. I was always afraid of hurting a newborn, and it amazed me how confident women would be with tiny babies after they'd had several children. They would even keep a baby at the breast while they cooked a meal or tended chores."

He heard the awe in her voice, and the regret. "Do you imagine children of your own someday?"

"I—I don't know. Before, I never wanted it to happen and I learned precautions. Ways to avoid getting with child. But I . . ."

It occurred to him that he hadn't thought of it either, though in their contract, when he'd instructed her what to write, he'd given the standard provisions for a child, the ones he used in agreements with his previous mistresses. Was she using any of those precautions? Her hesitation made him suspect she hadn't. "If you were to become pregnant with my child, I would take care of you, Cerise. As I promised."

"Do you have children?" she asked curiously.

"No. I was always careful." His grandfather, the libertine duke, had taught him it proved a man's prowess to get his mistresses pregnant. As long as a gentleman ensured his bastards were cared for, Grandfather had advised him, it didn't matter how many he begot and it proved his manhood. His father had believed a man should be responsible and should not father children with any woman other than his wife. After listening to hours of lectures by his father, even though he never would have admitted his father was right, he'd taken care not to get his lovers pregnant.

But he hadn't taken care with Cerise, had he? The blindness, the nightmares, had made him forget. As she came to him and warned she was about to put the baby in his arms, Devon realized she could be already enceinte.

Her soft hands brushed his palms as she placed the infant's swaddled bottom in his hand, then she pressed her bundle to his chest and arranged his other hand to cradle the head. The lingering scent of curdled milk hit his nose. But no matter how stinky the little one got, the women didn't seem to mind.

He'd held his nephew only twice before, and he felt as though he was juggling a priceless vase, but he knew what Cerise meant. Gingerly, he cupped the back of the baby's head and held the warm body to his shoulder.

"Move him for a moment. Let me drape a cloth over your shirt."

He lifted the baby and felt Cerise lay something on his shoulder. This time he cradled his nephew so he could rest his cheek against the small, oddly shaped head.

"I wish I could see him." He winced at the raw yearning in his voice. He bloody well couldn't, and he had to learn to accept it. But this miracle in his hands felt so strange, and touch and smell weren't enough. They would never be enough.

"The shape of his head is changing," she said.

He felt the top of the head, still tender and delicate. "Not quite so much like a cone, is it?"

"Not anymore. He's very tiny, but not the tiniest I've

ever seen. He's strong and healthy, and he loves his food."

Devon laughed at that. It was hard to speak with his heart so tight. He ruffled the fine, silky strands of hair that seemed to make a circlet around the baby's head. Cerise's fingers stroked there, too, gently touching his. He liked the contact. This felt strangely, inexplicably natural, exploring his burbling nephew with his mistress at his side. "It's so hard to tell what he looks like by touching his face," he said. "I can tell he has a tiny button of an upturned nose and Cupid's-bow lips." He stroked the upper lip, felt a new, puffy place, and frowned.

"A sucking blister," Cerise told him. "Very common."

Then a cry vibrated next to his ear. Cerise's hand covered his on the baby's back, and she guided him to rub and pat. "I think a belch is coming," she warned. And it did—an amazing belch for such a small thing. Afterward, Devon's back felt unusually warm.

"His lunch came with it," she said lightly. "Fortunately, the blanket on your back caught it all. Now he may settle down to sleep. He's enjoying the way you're stroking him. His lids are closing. . . . He has lovely long eyelashes, just like yours."

He felt the rise and fall of the tiny baby's steady breaths pushing against him in a gentle rhythm. It was so soothing, it was putting Devon to sleep.

"Perhaps you should sit down, Your—Devon." Cerise led him to the chair. And as he sat, listening to the little one sleeping, he knew what he hungered to do. Nestle his nephew into the cradle and make love to Cerise. With his sister in the house, he hadn't done it for days.

But he wasn't certain if he would disturb the warm bundle slumped on his chest if he got up. He heard footsteps moving away from him. "Don't go," he said abruptly. "I need you."

"I've given the maids a break to go for tea, so I thought I would change the baby's bed."

He'd never imagined sitting in a nursery, holding a child. And right now, as much as he wanted to make love to Cerise, he knew he had to wait while she changed the bed. It was so astoundingly domestic for him that he laughed. "The truth: I don't know what I would have done without you, love. That's what I learned when you left for the Black Swan. I need you. Come here."

He could sense her at his side. "Bend down, angel." He kissed her, tasting her full lips. "You, love, are like no mistress I've had before."

"Oh, dear," she whispered. "I know I don't behave as a proper mistress should. I shouldn't be changing blankets—"

"I think it's charming, the way you tend to everything." Her anxious tones had touched his heart. She definitely was like no lover he'd ever had. Most of them were concerned only about what he could give them. "And you are taking care of my little nephew the way you took care of me. You are more special to me than any mistress I've ever had before."

She stood, utterly silent. The sounds of crunching gravel and churning hooves broke the quiet.

"A carriage," Cerise said swiftly.

He wasn't mistaking the trace of fear he heard behind her crisp tones. Cradling his nephew to his shoulder, he rose. He began to feel his way, taking slow steps to cross the room, but Cerise stopped him. "I will look." And within a moment she described the carriage below, the four black horses, and the tall golden-haired gentleman who jumped down from the vehicle.

"That must be Cavendish," Devon said. "My sister's husband."

A hand gripped his forearm. "You are not planning to

fight with him, are you? Not after your sister has just had the baby. You wouldn't dare call him out."

"That, angel, is not for you to decide." But what in hell was he going to do? Cavendish had broken his sister's heart. How did he forgive that?

His voice had been sharp, hard, and enough to disturb the baby's sleep. His nephew strained off his shoulder, away from the fresh blanket Cerise had laid on it, and cried. The plaintive sound was like nails driven into his nerves. He had to control his instinctive tension, the tightening of his hands, his urge to fight. He was holding a baby.

"You must not fight," Cerise declared. She could command his servants and rearrange his house, but she had no right to dictate how he should protect his sister. Then she plucked his nephew from his arms, startling him. Making him understand she feared his rage. "What are you going to do?"

He tried to stop his bristling anger. She was right: It wouldn't make Caro happy if he shot her husband, or even if he beat the bastard to a pulp. It wouldn't endear his nephew to him in the future. But he itched to take action, to make Cavendish pay. To teach him he had better behave himself with Caro. "I don't know," he admitted.

"Where in the blue blazes is my wife?"

From the shadowed foyer, through the open doors of the house, Anne saw the Earl of Cavendish storm toward Devon, who strode out to greet his brother-in-law, with his walking stick and a footman for a guide.

Tall, powerfully built, with thick golden hair, the earl glowered with fury, looking exactly like an avenging angel. Anne rocked the baby, keeping him quiet, amazed at the cool, controlled way Devon stepped forward and warned, "You will not see her unless you calm down. Caro has just had the baby, and she is recovering—"

"The baby! She's had my child and I didn't know."

Anne could see the earl's shock and anguish; Devon must have heard it. He moved to his brother-in-law, slung his arm across the man's shoulders. She was startled by the forgiveness in the gesture, and she sagged in relief. But the earl pushed his arm away. "March, why didn't you send her home the instant she got here?"

"Why didn't you pursue her at once?"

The blond earl yanked off his beaver hat and raked his hand through his hair. "Damnation, I tried. I assumed she had gone to March House. But there I learned she'd left without telling anyone where she was going. We assumed she went to a friend. No one thought she would come to you. I wouldn't have known but for receiving a letter. I was sick with worry about her. And having wasted time chasing her, I've missed the birth of my child."

"You would have spent the birth process in the taproom with me, drinking away worries—"

The earl went white. "Worries? Did something go wrong? Is that why she's in her bed?"

"No. I was told the birth was swift and relatively easy. Caro was marvelous and strong. Cavendish, come and see your son."

Anne retreated from the door, then hurried upstairs with the earl's son. She found Lady Cavendish just waking and struggling to sit up. She gave a beaming smile at the sight of her son.

"Here he is," Anne said. "Still sleeping, but I expect he will wake soon and want his dinner." She tucked the lad in his mother's arms while a maid placed pillows behind the countess's back. Even rising from very little sleep, the countess looked lovely, her dark hair tumbling over one shoulder, her violet eyes gleaming with delight as she stroked her sleeping child.

Anne got down onto one knee at her side. "Your Ladyship—"

"After all we've shared now, Cerise, I think you must call me Caro. You've seen me perspiring, grunting, and shouting in labor."

The gesture of acceptance touched Anne. "Your husband has come. Devon is bringing him."

"Oh, no." Color drained. The violet eyes went huge. "Oh! Oh, my God. What am I to do? I don't want to see him! He'll be furious."

"I don't think so. I think he will be delighted to see you."

A shaky hand fumbled to push back a wayward curl. "I look a fright—"

"You look beautiful," Anne said firmly. She faced her new friend. "You must see him and you must speak to him. You both have a newborn son, a child who deserves a happy family and will feel much safer if he senses his parents are in love. Devon told me you made a love match. Surely you can talk to each other and make things right."

She knew she had just overstepped the bounds of a new friendship. To Anne's surprise, Caro nodded as she cradled her son to her breasts. Little fists waved with hope. "All right. I will speak to him. He can come and see his son."

Anne planned to leave after she gave Caro's message to Devon. This was a family matter, after all. But he insisted she come with him and Cavendish to his sister's room. Once there, the earl and countess stared blankly at each other. The earl said, "That's our son?" His wife answered only, "Yes." They looked as awkward as young lovers pretending not to be nervous over a first kiss.

The baby must have sensed the tension, for he kept coming off the breast—Caro wore a lacy blanket for modesty in the feeding. He cried, and the countess could not coax him to stay on.

Finally Anne risked everything—Devon's anger, losing the countess's friendship, being tossed out. "Lord Cavendish, Caro came here because she is unhappy. She believes you have fallen out of love with her. I don't know what you have done, but you have given her reason to believe you've strayed. You two must talk to each other! You are brand-new parents. And, as you can see, your son senses unhappiness." She hoped that was a trump card, but she felt regret when Cavendish stared in shock at his baby and Caro clapped her hand to her mouth.

"Is this true?" the earl asked slowly. "You are unhappy? You . . . left me?"

"You didn't want me," Caro answered, a blush washing over her cheeks.

"How could you think that?"

"How could I not? Harriet made it very clear how intimate you had become with her. She told Lady Fenwick about your bed play with her when she knew I was in earshot."

Cavendish blinked. "I've never touched her, Caro. Whatever she said, it was lies."

They spoke swiftly back and forth, Cavendish refuting and Caro looking increasingly upset and embarrassed. He dropped to both knees by her bedside. "Why didn't you speak to me, Caro? Yes, Harriet pursued me. I told her to stop, I made it plain I wasn't interested, but the woman would not listen. She was driving me mad. The more she chased me, the more irritated I became."

"I'm so sorry," Caro cried. "I think I must have gone mad. I believed I'd lost your love—"

"Never. I admit, I've been afraid to touch you for fear of hurting the baby. I admit the idea of fatherhood overwhelmed me. My own father was a coldhearted brute. I know I've been withdrawn, worrying about what kind of father I would be."

The little one had finally settled to feed. Anne impetuously handed a cloth to the earl, advising, "You will need a cloth, my lord."

Devon grinned. "Put it over your shoulder," he advised. "For when your son is finished."

Then Anne and Devon retreated and quietly pulled the door closed.

"Do you think my sister has learned not to leap to conclusions?" Devon asked.

"I imagine so," she whispered. "They are obviously very much in love." Anne could not understand how Caro could not have seen the obvious—how much her husband loved her.

Caro's nervous voice sounded muffled through the door. "Do you forgive me? If I hadn't run away, you would have been there for the birth—"

"Devon tells me men are not allowed in the birthing room anyway. They stay by a brandy bottle and get drunk. Of course I've forgiven you. But I don't intend to let you out of my sight from now on, my lovely wife. Have you named our son, my dear?"

"I haven't given him a name yet! Cerise and I spoke of it, and she urged me to wait until you came. She was quite certain you would come for me."

"That was Cerise? I suppose she was certain. She must have been the one who sent the letter, telling me where you were."

"I take it you were responsible for the letter sent to my brother-in-law?"

As soon as Cavendish had uttered those words, Anne knew that Devon would confront her. She knew she had taken a great risk. Fortunately, it had worked. Had Cavendish not raced to his wife's side, would there have been a happy ending for them? "Yes," she said simply.

Devon pushed open the library door. He wore no expression, and she had no idea what to expect. Was she to be punished? Every instinct warned her to expect his anger. A mistress did not meddle with her protector's family. Anne was certain of that. Perhaps she'd finally pushed him far enough and he would let her go.

With his walking stick, he made his way to the long table. He leaned on it, turning to her footsteps. "You didn't tell me about it."

"I know. I've overstepped my bounds. Do you plan to punish me?"

"An intriguing idea." A slow grin lifted his lips. "But for what should I punish you, angel? Your plan worked. Apparently there is nothing like a baby to bring a man and wife together and make them have an honest discussion. I didn't bring you here to punish you. I hoped you would read to me while my family is . . . busy." He looked so boyishly hopeful, her heart fractured.

"Of course I will!" And she would do it magnificently.

"I have a special book in mind. It's called *The Mayfair Mansion*. It's up on the top shelf, at the end of the south wall, by the windows."

A brass ladder ran along a rail around the shelves, and Anne pushed it to the last column. Devon had followed the noise of the ladder, and he gripped the base as she climbed to the top. Running her finger along the books, she searched for the right one.

Suddenly her skirts flew up from behind. "Devon—"

He let her hems drop, but he held her hips. "Turn around to face me, angel. Carefully."

Heart pounding hard, she did. He looked so deliciously handsome with his head tipped up to her, his dark hair falling across his brow.

"I don't think I've thanked you properly for taking care of my sister while she was giving birth," he said softly. "I have to thank you for helping set things right between her and Cavendish, for healing her broken heart, for helping them find their love again."

"You don't need to—"

"Save that thought. When I've finished thanking you, you can tell me if you thought it wasn't necessary."

He lifted her skirts again, bunching them at her hips. She gasped as she saw her legs bared, her nether curls exposed. But Devon had locked the library door. There was nothing to fear. Except losing her balance as he embraced her thighs and gently kissed her curls. The ladder brought her quim to the level of his mouth.

"Wh-what are you going to do?" she whispered.

He flicked his tongue over her clit, and she trembled on the step. Then he moved back, looking, with his tousled hair and flashing eyes, like a pirate intent on ravishing her. "Guess."

His mouth touched her cunny once more, and he held her bottom to keep her pressed against his face. He devoured her, lavishly stroking his tongue over her most sensitive place. On the rung of the ladder, her feet tingled and her legs quivered.

Thank heaven he held her firmly. She trusted him. He wouldn't let her fall.

She ran her fingers through his hair as he nuzzled her nether lips. His tongue surged inside her, filling her with heat. "Devon, I might fall off the ladder when I come," Anne said.

Devon had to stop licking her to promise, "You won't." She was adorable. He'd never felt such intimacy with any lover before. Cerise was unique. All she had done was give to him, and, in truth, she'd asked for nothing in return but a safe haven. She touched his heart as no woman had done, except Rosalind. And he'd thought he would never let a woman into his heart again.

But, hell, a man did not fall in love with his mistress. It was too damned awkward. He had to remember that. This was about sex. He couldn't let it become more than that.

He licked her, savoring her every moan. He felt safe in this, the trade of pleasure. She began arching to him, and he held her tight, determined to keep her safe on the ladder but let her go mad with ecstasy. He had to admit he loved tasting her, making her come.

"I want you inside," she begged huskily.

But he intended to make her come first. He wanted to treasure her orgasm without being distracted by his own. So he nuzzled, nibbled, and drenched her plump, hard clit with his tongue. She tasted of sin and passion, more intoxicating than brandy could ever be. She rocked against him. Her hands tightened in his hair.

Then she came with a deep, hoarse growl. Her quim ground against his mouth, her cries echoed off the shelves, and he held her tight to keep her from falling. He knew when she finished by her gulping breaths. He lifted her off the ladder. "Grab the book now, love. I want to make love to you, but I would very much like you to read to me first."

As Cerise settled on a tall chair at his side, Devon heard pages flip and then her abrupt gasp of shock. "This isn't a book I can read. It's filled with erotic pictures!"

"You sound so embarrassed, angel," he said mildly. "What I want you to do is find one you like, then describe it to me."

"I don't know . . . I don't think I could do such a thing," she whispered shyly.

Devon begged her to give in. Finally she sighed. "All right, Devon. I will find one I like and then I'll describe it to you."

A dozen images flitted through his head. Which would she choose? She had admitted she'd never had an orgasm before, but she must have had fantasies. Tapping into them would make this a delicious session of lovemaking for her. He wanted to find out what they were.

Would it be a man performing cunnilingus on a woman? He knew she had not enjoyed that at first, but she seemed to like it now. Would it be an orgy? A woman commanding two men to pleasure her? Lovemaking in an exotic location—like the back of a horse, an open carriage in the middle of Hyde Park, or a bathtub filled with steamy water?

Any of his other mistresses would have picked something they thought he'd like. But he suspected Cerise would do as he asked and reveal what she found intensely erotic.

"This one."

His heart was hammering. "Which is it?"

"You know, I had no idea what gentlemen truly fantasize about. This book is very educational. But *this* picture is my favorite so far."

Educational. Dear God. "Angel, tell me which one." His voice sounded like a hoarse rasp.

"Of course, I am cheating—"

"Angel." He didn't care if she was. This was supposed to be playful. He'd never imagined he would be on the brink of going up in flames, hungering to know what she would say.

"I'm cheating because this picture is actually made up of four vignettes. I think it is a series about the adventures of an earl's son and the redheaded courtesan who has turned him into a quivering mass of desire."

That made him smile. "What man wouldn't want to be turned into a quivering mass of lust?"

"Of course, it appears he takes his revenge," she went on blithely. "He turns her over his knee and spanks her bare bottom."

Those words, in her sensual voice, had his erection bucking, his heart thundering. "They sound like us. Should I punish you now, as you suggested earlier? Turning you over my knee?"

"I don't know. Wouldn't it hurt . . . to be spanked?"

"Not if done playfully. There will never be fear or pain between us, I promise. Now tell me about the pictures."

"Mmm. In the first one, her ardent admirer is lying beneath her on the carpet of the . . . oh, the library. He can see up her skirt. Her dress is far too small—her bosom is spilling over the top. In the next picture—"

Devon never heard what took place in the next drawing. He drew Cerise with him to the floor, onto his carpet. He rolled her onto her back. Something thudded to the floor—it had to be the book. He rained kisses on her hot lips and the swells of her warm breasts. And he slid deep inside her, into her welcoming heat. Then he flipped them over, so he was the one on the floor.

He thrust upward and she drove down to meet him. Her arms wrapped around his neck. Her moans mixed with his grunts, growing louder and louder. And finally she gripped his shoulder hard, bounced madly on him, and cried, "I'm coming."

Those two words in her breathy voice finished him. His climax roared through him. He'd never known anything so intense. He shouted his ecstasy, which a man did only when he'd been pleasured beyond control. When his body finally stopped pulsing from his climax, he flopped back in exhaustion.

"Goodness," she murmured. "That was even better than the pictures."

Anne was quivering on top of Devon, so weak from pleasure she was ready to collapse. She slid to the carpet to lie at his side. She wanted to laugh, dance, spin circles. But she was too weak. And now she knew why Devon had rolled onto his back and insisted she ride him. Carpets were scratchy. It had been a sweet and gentlemanly thing to do.

"We should move," he said, low-voiced, "before we fall asleep here."

"I wouldn't mind that. It would mean I would be sleeping at your side."

He swiftly sat up, then got to his feet. She had pushed too hard; now she regretted it. "If you need me to read to you tonight, Devon, I will be happy to do it. Or happy to describe any erotic picture you desire instead."

His laugh was gruff. "Angel, you are indeed an angel. I am so tempted to never let you go."

Her heart gave a tug. What if—No, gentlemen eventually tired of their mistresses. She swallowed hard. Foolishly, her eyes had teared at his sweet words. But as he helped her to her feet and she blinked, a stack of papers caught her eye. The size of the paper looked familiar. . . .

Heavens, she knew what it was. A pile of news sheets. They would be from London.

Her blood went cold—so cold, her motions were awkward and stiff. But as Devon did up his trousers, she raced over to the pile of papers as quickly as she dared, as quietly as she could.

The top issue was only two days old, and there had to be a fortnight's worth in the pile. She had never noticed them, for this part of the room was generally shadowy. The servants must have placed them here, and since

Treadwell and the footmen couldn't read them to Devon, the pages had been forgotten. On the front page of the top one, she spotted a small article that spoke of a madam's murder and the hunt for the prostitute who had killed her.

Anne's heart stuttered in her chest. She had to destroy these. She would sneak down here later, when the duke was in his study and the servants were not about. Then she would have to think of a reasonable explanation for why all these papers had disappeared.

She glanced back to Devon. Over the last three days she had been so busy with Caro and the baby, so delighted to be with Devon, she'd forgotten who she really was. A fugitive.

Chapter Fifteen

LATE IN THE night, Anne dropped to her knees before the fireplace in the library and fed six of the newspapers into the flames, grinding each page into ash with the poker. A kind of desperate fury governed her motions. Her heart leapt at every pop and hiss in the grate, as if they were footsteps behind her. She was certain someone would burst in before she was done. Someone would catch her. Then her fear, her guilt, her panic would give her away.

But no one came in. As the last page was reduced to charred scraps and dust, she sank back on her heels. Now every issue containing an article about Madame's murder or the hunt for the missing prostitute—*her*—was gone. She should feel relief. But she didn't. Perhaps she was learning she would never feel completely safe again.

Grimly, she waited until the fire had died down, then she left the library, closing the door behind her. She went to the stairs. The house was thankfully quiet, but her nerves were drawn so tight that even the reassuring stillness made her shoulders tremble. Devon had given a lovely guest bedroom to Caro and her husband, and their son was slumbering up in the nursery. Devon slept on a cot in the small dressing room that adjoined the master's bedchamber. This way, she could be in the comfortable bed but be close by to soothe him when he had a nightmare. He still refused to try sleeping in the same bed.

She crept into the room, took off her robe, and slid under the crisp covers. Hours seemed to tick by. Twice she heard Devon moaning through the open door. She went to him, stroked him. To her surprise, he didn't wake up. Her touch lulled him right back into slumber. But she couldn't sleep. Her instincts kept telling her she must run. If she stayed any longer, she was going to get caught. The fear was irrational. In her heart, she knew she was willing, like an utter fool, to wait and wait, so she could stay with the duke. She would likely end up arrested as a result.

In the morning, she woke before he did. She was groggy, but there was no point in lying in bed for any more sleepless hours. She went to check on the baby. The nursemaid informed her that Lord Cavendish had already scooped up his son. He had carried the baby downstairs for his breakfast, then he and his wife were taking their leave.

"They're going?" Anne echoed to the maid.

"They decided last night, miss. Rather hastily."

A shiver of apprehension rippled down Anne's back. Lord Cavendish had come from London; could he have realized she was the woman hunted by Bow Street? No—Lord and Lady Cavendish *couldn't* know. If they had learned the truth, they would have told Devon immediately. Anne squared her shoulders and went to Caro's room, to say goodbye to the woman who had, in defiance of all of Society's rules, become her friend.

Sunlight streamed into the bedchamber. Three trunks sat open on the floor with fragile lace-trimmed undergarments spilling out of them. A bevy of gowns were strewn across the bed. Anne cleared her throat. Caro saw her and gave her a glowing smile.

There, she must be safe. Caro could not know she was a murderess and still smile.

She hurried in to help Caro and the two maids pack the trunks. Keeping herself busy worked wonders, she thought. She was convinced she was behaving quite naturally. But after a half hour or so, Caro paused and stared pointedly at her. "What is wrong? You are so jumpy and nervous. When the maid accidentally dropped the trunk lid closed, you almost leapt out of your skin." Caro's eyes widened. "Is something wrong with Devon?"

"No. I—I didn't sleep well. I will miss you, Caro. Very much."

Caro waved the maids out, then clasped Anne's hands. She looked so serious that Anne felt her stomach drop. "There *is* something, Cerise," she said, "but perhaps I shouldn't say it."

It couldn't be about the murder—what could it be? "Please do."

"We all hope Devon marries. I know he has said he doesn't want to take a wife, because he is blind, but the whole family has been absolutely *praying* he will change his mind."

"Yes. He should marry. He deserves to find a wonderful wife and to fall in love again." Anne blushed. "He told me about his fiancée, Lady Rosalind."

"He adored her! It thoroughly broke his heart when she died. Our mother is convinced that a happy marriage is the key to healing his heart and bringing him happiness. But Devon . . ." She squeezed Anne's hands. "Devon said he would never keep a mistress after he was wed. He vowed he would not even have one while he was courting a bride."

"Oh. You mean he will let me go."

"No. It is obvious he cares for you very much. I wonder if he will be *willing* to let you go."

"If he plans to marry, of course he will."

Caro bit her lip. "If he knows he will have to give you up, Cerise, perhaps that will give him one more reason to avoid doing his duty."

Anne had no idea what to say. Surely he would not let a mistress stand in the way of a hunt for a wife, if he was ready.

"He insists he must stay away from Society," Caro said. "When I told him he seemed to be quite fine, he said his improvement is all because of you. He told me he may never be able to marry, because he may never feel he could be with a wife without hurting her."

"I know he feels that way, but I think he can be," Anne said.

"This will seem an odd request, especially given what it will mean to you, but could you help him realize that himself? Would you do that for us—for his mother and his sisters?"

Anne's heart wobbled. How could she deny his family, who only wanted him to be happy? "I promise I will encourage him to go home, to go out in Society, and to begin courting. I will do everything I can to make him believe it's possible."

She spoke to Devon about it that night, when they were alone again. "You see," she said crisply. "Nothing bad happened during your sister's visit. You could go home."

"No, I'm not yet ready." It was all he said. All he would say for the next two days.

Finally, as they sat in his study two evenings later, Anne brought out *The Mayfair Mansion* and, in as throaty and sultry a voice as she could adopt, described a very sensual scene involving one gentleman and two bounteous courtesans. Then she snapped the book firmly shut.

"I will not describe another picture to you unless you cease to be so obstinate. You were afraid your nightmares would frighten your sister, but they didn't. She was sympathetic, not horrified. As was Lord Cavendish."

"Angel, you're so determined to do this. Have you thought of what will happen to you? I thought you wanted to avoid London."

"I do." She shivered, relieved he could not see it. For her, it would be the best if he stayed in this house forever. But he had rescued her, and he deserved to be happy. "I— It's just that I promised your sister I would try to convince you to go to your family."

"You promised that?"

She waited for him to coolly point out she had no right to make promises, but he cocked his head. "If you're so determined to get me back into Society, you must help me relearn some skills."

"Skills? Which ones?"

He quirked a brow. "I was thinking of dice."

"Dice!" she squawked. She was about to launch into all the protests she could think of, when she saw the twitch of his beautiful mouth. "All right. Do you wish to practice making wagers?"

"Exactly. Our wagers would be articles of clothing. Whoever loses has to remove a piece."

"Indeed. And when would we stop?"

"When one of us is naked."

Devon carefully explained the principles of hazard to her, but it seemed to be a game of complete chance to Anne. How could gentlemen wager such large amounts on something that depended on sheer luck and not skill? But she proved to possess a good amount of beginner's luck. She had Devon stripped down to only his trousers when Treadwell suddenly pushed the study door wide.

Devon turned to the door. "What is it? I'm busy gambling away the clothes on my back."

Treadwell bowed. He looked warily to her, and Anne shrank back on her seat. Why did he glare at her like that? Dear heaven, was the magistrate at the door?

"Begging yer pardon, Yer Grace, but Lord Ashton has arrived. He's brought a woman he claims is the courtesan he hired for you in London."

Devon heard Cerise give a strangled cry. An obvious sign of distress, but over what exactly? "What in Hades are you talking about, Treadwell?" he asked coolly. "The courtesan Ashton sent is sitting right here with me."

"Not according to Lord Ashton, Yer Grace. I took him and the lady to the drawing room."

"Has he brought me another woman? A second one for my collection?" That would be like Tristan. He never kept the same lover for more than a fortnight. Tris would assume two ladybirds would be more entertaining than one.

"No, Yer Grace. According to His Lordship, he hadn't sent ye a woman yet. Just the one he brought. His Lordship said he couldn't find the right woman at first. Said he had to sample the ladybirds on offer to ensure he brought ye one ye'd like."

Tris had not sent Cerise. Damn, he wanted to see. He wanted to know what expression was on her face. "Can you explain this, Cerise?" Tension crackled through him, his muscles instinctively tightening as they did when he sensed danger.

"I . . . All right, I admit I lied to you."

"Why?" Her voice had come from the right but farther away than it should have. She must have left the seat beside him. Was she backing away? Preparing to escape? "Come back here," he growled. "Come and sit beside me, so I know where you are."

Her skirts whispered as she returned. He could hear her fast, terrified breaths. "For the very reason I told you, Devon. I wanted to become a duke's mistress. Your mistress, so I could escape London and the stews and the horrible life I knew at . . . at the brothel."

"Still, I do not understand the necessity of the lie."

"It was the only thing that got me through the door. It was only when I insisted Lord Ashton had sent me that Treadwell let me come in. I did it because I had nowhere else to go."

"I made a mistake, Yer Grace," Treadwell began, but Devon lifted a quelling hand.

"There was no reason to believe the story wasn't true. You knew Ashton intended to send a woman. Right now I wish to speak to Cerise in private. Ask Ashton and his prostitute to wait, if they will."

"Very good, Yer Grace."

As soon as the door clicked shut, Devon rubbed his temples, where a headache throbbed with a piercing rhythm. "Did Ashton go to you? Were you one he 'sampled'?"

"No!" she cried. The settee creaked as she sat, but he barely felt the cushion dip. She must have perched on it, far away from him.

"Then how did you know to use his name to get through my door?"

"I did not mean any harm by it, I promise you, Devon. Lord Ashton came to a woman I know and asked her to be your lover. My friend has a protector, so she turned down his offer, but I was staying in her house and I overheard her conversation with Lord Ashton. I saw what a perfect chance it would be for me. I came to you without anyone knowing of it. Yes, I used his name so Treadwell would let me in, but everything I've told you since then is true."

It made sense. She had been desperate to leave Town and she had wanted to be more than a whore in a brothel. She'd wanted to move up in the world and find safety. She would want that whether she'd been a gentleman's daughter, a governess, or a poor girl born in the stews. Why were his instincts on the alert, nagging him there was more? "Come." He knew where she was by her voice. He grabbed what he hoped was her arm. "Ashton came all this way with a courtesan. I might as well show him I no longer have need of his gift."

A burst of masculine laughter came from a doorway ahead, followed by a woman's high-pitched giggles. Anne tensed. She knew Ashton and the courtesan he'd brought were only sharing a joke, but the raucous sound reminded her that people laughed and cheered around the gallows.

Devon stopped. "You're afraid. I can feel your entire body stiffen."

He felt that just through the touch of her hand on his arm? He had remarkable senses. "I told a lie involving this gentleman's name. I fear his anger. I fear yours."

His hand reached out, awkwardly found her cheek, and his thumb brushed her lips. Even in the grip of terror, she felt the answering tingle of her skin. She had thought he would throw her out as soon as she admitted she'd lied. Yet it appeared he would let her stay.

Delicately, his fingers touched her chin. He had found the tip of it readily and lifted it so she could look into his violet eyes. "I understand why you lied. You have nothing to fear from me if you are now telling me the truth."

Oh, dear heaven, she felt how tense he was. He couldn't look into her eyes and see guilt, but she was certain he was listening for it. *If you are now telling me the truth*. He didn't believe her story. He knew she'd lied once, and he must suspect she was doing so again. And she was.

"After all that you've done for me," he said softly, "I would not send you away."

Yes. Yes, you will, and you'll hear of my hanging without a bit of remorse because I had to kill a woman, because I was a murderess, even though I didn't mean to do it. But Anne managed a quaking "Thank you" and prayed that didn't give her away.

A flowery smell tickled her nose as they got near the door. Devon grimaced. "Scent. Ashton's gift apparently applies it pretty thickly. Maybe she assumed it would help me find her."

Anne looked at him quickly, astonished to see a grim smile. It felt like a mere heartbeat later that she was standing in the middle of the drawing room, while Devon explained to Lord Ashton the story she had told him. She had seen Lord Ashton at Kat's—he was an angelic-looking man with white-blond hair and dark-blue eyes. The courtesan, Miss Lacy, was a very voluptuous, bold brunette.

"I am so sorry I used your name falsely, Lord Ashton. But I ran away—"

Devon held up his hand. "Miss Lacy, my dear, you must be tired after your travel. My butler, Treadwell, will escort you to one of the bedchambers, where you can rest."

Miss Lacy perked up at the word *bedchamber*. She flashed coquettish smiles at both men, then followed Treadwell out.

Devon waved his hand. "Continue, Cerise."

Anne took a deep breath. She hadn't been able to fool Devon with her faked climaxes. Could she be convincing now? "I ran away from a brothel. You see, I had disobeyed my madam and I—I feared she would hunt me down and hurt me, or kill me, for my disobedience. I went to a friend, and she took me in. But my very presence in her house put her in grave danger. My madam employed brutish men to keep her girls in line. They would not think twice about killing an innocent woman because she was in their way or she knew too much."

"Who is your friend, love?" the Earl of Ashton asked, drawing her gaze from Devon.

She couldn't lie—Ashton would probably remember the courtesans he'd talked to. In this, she had to tell the truth. "My friend is Katherine Tate."

"Kat?" Ashton echoed in surprise. "Kat took you in and protected you? Kat is an exotic beauty and highly skilled in the bedroom, but I never would have guessed she would help a damsel in distress. She is also a friend of March's, which was why I approached her."

"We knew each other . . . a long time ago," Anne said. "Kat was very good to me. She explained to me the details of being a mistress. And she told me a great deal about His Grace. About how wonderful he was reputed to be as a protector."

A low, dangerous laugh rumbled from Devon. "Wonderful? When I once told her I wasn't interested in becoming her protector, she chucked a china shepherdess at me." He sighed. "Angel, I want the complete truth from you. What did you do to this madam of yours?"

Her heart froze. What could she say? "I—I helped . . ." Oh, God, she couldn't think of anything to say but the truth. Some of it, at least. "I helped three of her newest girls escape. The girls were innocents and Ma—my madam had hoped to auction their virginity."

"Very noble and brave," Lord Ashton commended.

Devon lifted a brow. He was listening intently, and she felt as if he could hear her very thoughts. "Indeed," he said softly. "Not surprising. But I doubt she would kill you over that. She might beat you and force you to—" He stopped. Raked his hand through his hair. "I want you to go up to bed, Cerise. I'll join you soon."

She had to leave. But what would Devon and Ashton say once she'd gone?

Devon smelled the smoke of a cheroot. "Intriguing," Tris remarked. "She told you I had sent her so she could have the chance to become your mistress."

Her story was entirely believable and highly sympathetic, so why had his gut clenched the way it would before the first cannon blast of a battle? Hell, he'd practically smelled her fear, and he knew the distinct aroma of it from the war.

"Who is she, Dev? She spoke of living in a brothel, but she's no dockyard tart. She speaks like a lady."

"She claims to be a housekeeper's daughter, one who lived on a country estate but ended up in London's stews. I'm beginning to wonder if that's a lie also. I intend to find out."

"I find her fascinating," Tris said.

"She's mine," Devon asserted.

Tristan's swift, knowing laugh raked over him. "You answered that one quickly. Don't worry. I'm a guest in your house. I would never dream of poaching on your preserve." With the groan of a man relaxing in a chair, Tris asked, "So, is it any different to make love to a woman when you're blind? Is it worse or is it actually better?"

Trust his friend to speak directly of his blindness without care or caution.

"Is it any different from having sex in the dark?"

"It's different," he replied, his voice curt and abrupt.

"How—" Tris began, but Devon glowered and his friend shut his mouth.

Devon snapped grumpily, "Of course it isn't the same. A man can always strike a light in the dark."

"Ah, there are times a man doesn't want to."

"Maybe you aren't so discriminating, but I am. I don't even know exactly what she looks like, and I never will."

"She? Ah, Cerise. She is lovely, by the way. I assume you've thoroughly explored her with your hands and mouth?"

"Yes. But there's a lot about her that I can't assess by touch, taste, or smell. There's no one in this house I can ask to describe her. How do you ask another man to describe your mistress?"

"I'd be happy to describe her in detail for you."

"I'm sure you would be," Devon growled. "I'd likely end up punching you in the nose."

"Whoever she is," Tristan said, "she's managed to make a remarkable change in you. You were an unkempt, hairy mess the last time I came, stinking of spilled brandy and refusing to leave your gloomy study. Now you look like the man I remember from our days in London before the war and before—"

"Before Rosalind's death. I may look different, but I don't think I feel any different. And now my mistress has joined in my mother's campaign to convince me to return to Town and start courting a bride."

He heard the clink of glass. It had to be Tristan setting down the brandy bottle after refilling his tumbler. Devon had to clamp his hands into fists to fight the urge to reach for a glass. He yearned to take just one drink. But if he began with one, he feared he wouldn't stop until he was unconscious on the floor.

Cerise's story sounded like the truth. Should it matter that she'd lied to him when she first arrived? It was obvious she wasn't here to con him or steal from him—she would have done that already. She had done nothing but take care of him. She had been wonderful in the way she had helped his sister and taken charge after the baby's birth.

Why was he plagued with this damned pervasive sense of doubt? Was it simply the uneasiness he now carried with him? The constant wait for a disaster to fall, the way he would wait for the command of *Charge* or the first explosion of a cannon before a battle?

But as much sense as her story made, if he attacked it from a different direction, he could pull it to pieces. If she had a friend in London, she had a safe place to stay, and Kat was a famed London incognita who had the wherewithal to introduce Cerise to the wealthiest of England's peers. Wouldn't it make more sense to stay with Kat and find a protector in London, rather than travel north on the faint hope of seducing a blind and reluctant duke?

"You're lost in thought," Tris observed.

Devon hesitated, then told his friend his concerns. "I don't know what to believe. If I take her tale at face value—that she was anxious to leave London and saw me as the perfect chance for escape—then I can understand why she made up the story. But . . ." He tried to put his doubts into words. "Her motives don't appear strong enough to justify a mad flight up here. Under Kat's tutelage, she would have had the opportunity to find a lover in Town. Once she was a peer's mistress, she would have been safe from her madam's vengeance."

"Your arguments are sound, Dev. But the only one who knows the truth is Cerise."

A faint knock came on the door. Devon lurched around, expecting Cerise to walk into the room. He expected to hear the firm tread of her steps, to smell her soft, natural scent, and hear her lush voice ask him if he required a nighttime story.

Instead, the heavy smell of perfume hit him, almost

making him gag. Miss Lacy said, in an exaggerated purr, "Your Grace, My Lord, how delicious to find you both together."

Devon groaned. He remembered Cerise playing the saucy courtesan, but there had been a sweet awkwardness in her performance. She hadn't sounded jaded and hard like this woman.

"Sorry, love, but His Grace is committed to his pretty mistress," Tristan said.

"How disappointing." Miss Lacy's skirts swished slowly. No doubt she was trying to seductively cross the room. "But the reason I came searching for you wasn't just to suggest some naughty fun between the three of us. After I had repaired myself in the bedchamber, I came downstairs and overheard the last things your mistress said, Your Grace. I apologize, but I must warn you. She claimed she helped innocents escape her madam. There have been stories all over London about a madam who was murdered in her brothel by one of her whores. The tart—whose name was Annalise, I think—helped young girls escape and then struck her madam with a fireplace poker. Annalise ran away. Bow Street has been searching all over London for her but can't find her."

Devon could hear the triumph in Miss Lacy's sultry voice. "When did this happen?"

"The woman was murdered about three weeks ago, Your Grace."

Devon suddenly couldn't find his voice. *Christ.*

"Dev, have you got newspapers in the house?"

"Hades, I don't know. They might have been delivered, but I can't read them."

"Treadwell," Tris called. Boots struck the floor harshly, and almost instantly Devon heard his butler's distinctive walk. "Treadwell, have you got news sheets for the last few weeks?"

"Aye, me lord," his butler answered. "I kept them after the valet left. I put them in a pile in the library, so ye could have them read to ye. Sorry, Yer Grace. I forgot to tell ye."

Anne shrank back into the shadows of the corridor, her heart jumping madly in her chest.

Though Devon had sent her to bed while he spoke with Lord Ashton, she'd been unable to stay in her room. Instead of undressing, she had padded back downstairs, planning to see if Devon wished to have her read to him later.

But when she'd reached the mouth of the hallway that led to the drawing room, she glimpsed a group of retreating figures. Silently, she'd hurried forward. She'd crept close enough to see Devon and Lord Ashton striding at the front, with Treadwell and the voluptuous Miss Lacy hurrying behind. She followed them all to the library.

Anne quickly realized someone had remembered the news sheets. She heard Lord Ashton say, "There are no stories in these about a madam's death or a missing whore. However, there are about a half dozen issues missing."

"God," Devon muttered. "No wonder she ran from London. She killed her madam."

"Cold-bloodedly too," Miss Lacy added. "You must have her *arrested*."

They knew. Somehow they— Oh, dear heaven, Miss Lacy wore a self-satisfied smirk. The courtesan must have read the stories, or heard gossip in London, and guessed the truth. And told Devon at once, so she could eliminate her competition.

Oh, God. How long did she have before Devon came for her?

Probably only moments. It wasn't long enough to go

back to the bedroom and take anything—not any of her other clothes, not even a bonnet.

Anne backed away. Then she turned and bolted. When she reached the drawing room, her lungs were already heaving. She raced across the room to the glass-paned doors that led outside. With shaky hands, she turned one handle, praying Treadwell had not bothered yet to lock it.

Her prayers were answered. The door swung wide. She'd shoved so hard that she lost her balance and stumbled out onto the flagstone terrace. Hauling up her skirts, she raced across the gray stones toward the dark lawn. What was she going to do? Where could she go?

It didn't matter. All she could do was run.

Chapter Sixteen

ANNE CROSSED THE lawns by staying crouched—at least, as low as she could manage in a wretched corset. Clouds shrouded the moon and the velvety dark hid her perfectly, but it made the lawn a treacherous sea of rolling blue-black waves, uneven and ridged, peppered with unexpected holes. Twice she put her foot in a void and went flying to her knees. Each time, she scrambled back up and raced desperately onward.

Deep in her heart, she wanted to believe that if she told Devon the truth, he would forgive what she'd done because it had been an accident, because she'd struck Madame in desperation to protect a young girl, because she had never intended to kill. She wanted to imagine he would shield her, protect her, help her. But would Devon knowingly harbor a murderess? Even though she'd acted to defend those girls, she had committed a crime, and she feared that was how he would see it. Her heart clenched. It wouldn't matter that they'd been intimate. It wouldn't matter that she'd helped him cope with his blindness. Heavens, he'd risked his life and given his sight for king and country. He wouldn't help her escape the law. How could he?

She raced around a clump of lilac bushes and made a mad dash for the woods. She hazarded a glance behind her. Lights now blazed in many of the rooms on the second floor. Devon must be looking for her. Any moment he would guess—

Bobbing lights appeared on the terrace. Lanterns, carried by the footmen. Devon had *already* guessed, and he'd sent his servants to find her. The lights suddenly parted, streaming in different directions.

Letting out a whimper of fear, Anne sprinted on burning, shaky legs. When she was young, she could run as fast as a boy, but years spent trapped in the brothel had sapped her strength.

When she'd fled from Madame's brothel, she had bolted through the twisting streets off the London docks, dragging the three young girls with her. She gripped the wrists of Violet and Mary so tightly they were sobbing. She carried Lottie, the smallest, on her back, with the child's arms clamped around her neck.

But rescuing the frightened girls had given her more strength than her body could dredge up to save herself. Either she was going to throw up or her lungs would burst into flame. She sobbed with relief as she finally reached the woods. Her momentum carried her in a wild, zigzag course among the trees. She stumbled over every possible root, smacked her toes against stones, and wrenched her ankles a dozen times. Twigs snapped beneath her feet, the sounds as loud as gunshots fired in warning. Every servant chasing her must have heard them.

She plunged forward, stumbling over the treacherous ground, falling against dark trees, then finally she had to stop. Not because she felt safe, but because her legs were shaking so hard she was certain they would break off at her knees.

It was no good. She couldn't push herself any more. Chest heaving, she sucked in as much air as she could. It was dark here—the canopy of dense leaves blotted out the moonlight, and if she stayed still and kept quiet, no one would spot her. Though it also meant she couldn't see anything. The woods contained dozens of sounds—shivering leaves, the bubbling stream, branches that clacked like bones—but she was sure she heard men shouting in the distance behind her. Anne forced her quivering muscles to move again, and she ran.

The splashing of the stream grew louder. She had described these woods to Devon, but now she had no idea where she was. Slipping through a grove of tightly spaced trees, she emerged to find she had reached the water. A stone bridge lay ahead of her. A *collapsed* bridge—the center had fallen into the stream. The only way across was to pick her way over the remaining stones and jump the chasm in the middle. Could she make it? She wasn't sure. But it was also unlikely anyone else would. It might be her best chance of escape.

Wishing she'd worn anything other than a gown, she put her foot on one of the stones. Of course, her boot slid crazily. She clutched the remaining piece of the wooden railing and took wobbly steps over the stones, which jutted up from the water in a jumbled mass.

Heavens, she was shaky, but panic gave her the courage to blindly throw her weight. Poised on the last stable stone on her side, Anne jumped. Her feet landed on a stone on the other side, but it was slimy, and her right foot skidded wildly. She fell, her left leg splashing into the water. But she managed to grasp the railing and pull herself out.

Her skirts hung around her, wet and heavy. Her left knee throbbed with pain. *Keep moving. Imagine the pain of hanging*. She struck ahead, leaving the bridge behind her, but she was limping and moving far too slowly. Devon's servants must be in the woods by now, and someone had probably heard the splash—

Behind her, footsteps crunched on fallen leaves.

Her heart plunged so fast, it sucked all her air with it. For some foolish, instinctive reason, she slowed down. The footsteps quickened, and a low, hard masculine laugh sounded a few yards behind her. The evil delight in it made her blood turn to icy slush.

She *knew* that laugh. It was a sound she would never forget. But it *couldn't* be real. She must have conjured it out of her fear-fogged brain.

She couldn't turn. For some reason, her body refused to twist so she could see. Her heart hammered and her jumbled thoughts coalesced into one command: *Run. You must run!*

Despite a throat so dry she couldn't draw in air, Anne yanked up her skirts and ran like the wind. It had to be her imagination haunting her. It had to be one of Devon's servants—

No. A servant wouldn't *laugh*.

She needed a weapon. Anything. A fallen branch. A rock—but she couldn't see one she could lift. The heavy footsteps behind her drew closer.

She gave a surge of desperate speed, but it wasn't enough. A black shape swept in front of her eyes. She tried to dart away, but her feet tangled in her hems, and her momentum carried her headlong into a leather-clad hand. Her attacker clamped his palm over her mouth. She was dragged off her feet, hauled through the air, and slammed back against a tree. Her breath flew out as her spine banged against unyielding bark. Pain shot from her head to her toes.

She screamed, but the gloved hand turned her shriek into a muffled squawk.

A hulking body loomed over her. "Hello, Annie love," the voice said cheerfully. "You caused me a lot of bother."

She gazed up at a familiar leering grin. She saw a bald head, a beak of a nose, a huge body. It *couldn't* be possible. By some nightmare, it was. Shaking, she met the narrow black eyes of Mick Taylor, Madame Sin's bodyguard.

"Don't you think you now have the truth?" Tristan demanded. "She's wanted for murder and she's bolted. It must mean she's guilty."

Devon scrubbed his hand over his jaw. He was carrying his damned cane, and he chucked it to the floor. His gut instincts told him Cerise was the murderess—it would explain her fear, her reluctance to speak of her past, her lies, her flight out into the night. And her story of the rescued innocents matched the motive for the madam's murder, according to Miss Lacy. "I think she did kill the woman, but I suspect she did it in self-defense." He could not picture Cerise, who had been so careful cutting his hair, so sweet when she read to him, so gentle with his nephew, as a cold-blooded murderess.

"You're smitten with her, aren't you?" Tris asked, his tone filled with astonishment. Tris handed him the cane.

Smitten. He was not smitten. Smitten was for virgin lads and aging codgers, not for angry dukes and their runaway mistresses. He was trying to be logical. "If the woman was a desperate criminal, she could have stolen from me the first night she was here and gotten enough money to flee the country." He swung his stick and began walking. "Take me to the stables."

"The stables?" The shocked voice belonged to Treadwell.

"I'm not going to stay here like a bloody invalid, waiting for her to be brought back to me. I want the truth out of her."

Anne was amazed she hadn't fractured into a thousand pieces—she felt as cold and brittle as ice. Mick shifted his hand, freeing her mouth, but he gripped her by the throat, pressing hard enough to keep her pinned without blocking all her air.

"It took me a bleeding long time to find you, Annie," he remarked lightly. She had spent five years living in fear of this man. She had seen exactly what kind of brutality he could commit. When Mick spoke in such a cheerful voice, it meant he planned to inflict pain.

He had pulled her into the middle of a grove of trees. The thick trunks surrounded them. He could do anything to her he wanted here. He could leave her body beneath a pile of leaves and no one might know for days.

"How—how did you find me?" Her voice came as a raw whisper. But a grin spread across Mick's face, and understanding came so swiftly, she sagged in despair. The pressure of his hand was the only thing holding her up. *"Kat."*

"That's right." His lips curled. "Eventually I convinced your whore friend to tell me."

Tears stung in her eyes. Nausea threatened to crawl up her throat. "What did you do to her?"

"Not much, love. Your friend crumbled quickly. Just a few slaps to her pretty face and she told me everything."

"I don't believe it. Kat wouldn't have done that. You must have hurt her badly."

"I intended to, duchess," he said mockingly. "But she's a cowardly little fool, so afraid of having her face and her tits carved up, she broke down after the first time I hit her."

Perhaps Kat did. Anne prayed it was the truth, that Kat had surrendered quickly rather than suffer a brutal beating. This was all her fault. She had brought danger to a friend who had given her nothing but kindness.

"I imagine she thought I'd back away once she revealed you were a duke's tart. But I'm not afraid of some fop."

Anne thought of Devon—the rough-hewn muscle, the strength, and the aura of rigidly controlled power that surrounded him. Mick might be brawny, but she did not doubt Devon would have been able to defeat him in a fight—if he could see. "The duke is a war hero," she spat out. "Hardly a fop." The insanity of it struck her. Devon had locked himself away here because he thought he was mad. He had refused to go home, because he feared he could be a danger to his family. And here was a truly deadly madman, who would never have such scruples.

"He ain't here, Annie. It's just you and me. I watched the house for a couple of days, waiting to nab you. Damned uncomfortable it was. I thank you for delivering yourself into my hands, but you're going to have to do more to make up for my irritation." Mick released her throat, wrenched her arms over her head, and pinned them to the trunk with one hand. His other paw clamped on her bosom.

She struggled beneath him, but he was too strong. He squeezed her breast, smirking with cruel pleasure.

"Stop! *Please.*" It was foolish to beg Mick Taylor. It would make him worse. "What do you want?" Even as she asked, she feared she knew. Revenge. For Madame's death.

His hand dropped from her breast. "I could haul you back to Bow Street. Watch you get locked up in Newgate Prison, where you'll rot away until they decide to hang you." His bulk leaned heavily against her. He pressed his thigh between her legs, trapping her skirts. The weight of him made her whimper. Somewhere in the woods, far away, she heard a faint crunching—it must be Devon's men, looking for her.

Oh, God. She could barely speak for the pressure of his chest against her breasts. "I *had* to hit her. I had no choice—she was going to shoot Violet." Without even a flicker of conscience, Madame Sin had been ready to shoot a girl of fourteen to frighten the others into submission. "I hit her *once* to stop her. I meant to hit her in the arm, to knock the pistol out of her hands. I never meant to strike her in the head. I did it to protect an innocent girl." The blow had been strong, far more than she'd thought it would be. But she'd been driven by desperation. The crunch of the poker hitting Madame's skull had been sickening. "You know what happened. You were *there*—in the room."

"Aye," Mick said around a chuckle. "Which makes me a grand witness. I remember you hit the bitch on the side of the head with the fireplace poker. I also know you didn't kill her, Annie. She woke up after you'd hopped it out the window."

"I didn't—" Wild thoughts collided in her head. "But she's *dead*. In the news sheets, it said she was—but . . . if I didn't kill her, who did?"

"That, love, I don't know."

She was innocent. Oh, thank heaven. Madame had been horrible, but Anne had felt so much guilt over the woman's death. This meant . . . it meant she was suspected of a crime she hadn't committed. She could be arrested for it. She could hang even though she was innocent. "Mick, you could stop this by telling the truth—"

"You're a stupid git, Annie. Do you really think I'm

going to go to Bow Street and tell them you're innocent and say, *By the way, I was in the room at the time, with the murder weapon*?"

She was so numb with fear it took seconds to understand what he was saying. "You—" She almost said, *You did it*. "You're afraid the magistrate will think you did it." There, she could say it without directly accusing him. But the mocking glare in his feral eyes made her doubt her suspicion. Madame had paid Mick a fortune to protect her. He had no reason to want her dead.

"I didn't do it, you stupid whore. But I believe I know who did, and that's how you're going to help me, you little tart."

She flinched at the names he called her, the venom with which he spat them in her face. Suddenly he lifted his fist. She hopelessly tried to wrench away, but his meaty hand slammed down, smashing into her temple. Searing pain streaked through her head; spots exploded in front of her eyes. She sagged forward in a fuzzy gray void. Mick lifted her into the air, tossing her over his shoulder. She almost threw up as her stomach hit hard muscle.

"The duke's bloody servants are getting too close. I've got a horse tethered—" He broke off and started to lope through the woods with her. She bounced on his shoulder. She was dizzy, confused, as though she'd drunk a whole bottle of brandy. His blow had knocked her almost senseless, and she was fighting to regain her wits.

They seemed to run for an eternity, and the pain was beginning to ebb when Mick stopped and let her drop to the ground. She was too scrambled and jostled to get her balance, and she fell heavily. Mick scooped her up and pushed her against something warm and soft, something that shied from her. A horse whinnied in protest. Mick gripped her shoulder. He leapt up on the horse, and once he was seated he dragged her up with his hands under her arms. Clamping her to his chest with one hand, he grasped the reins with the other.

Her dazed wits finally understood what was happening. She struggled in terror. But Mick was a brawler. Across her chest, his arm was like a cage, and she couldn't break free.

"I didn't hunt you down to take you back to Bow Street," he snarled by her ear as his horse cantered. The impact was jarring. "There's no advantage in that for me. I was paid by a titled fop to find you. I'm here to protect you from the law, because this gent wants you alive."

"*Protect* me!" she gasped. "I'm innocent."

"Ah, Bow Street won't believe it without my word, Annie. And I've discovered you're worth a hell of a lot to this man. You're going to be my ticket to a life of luxury."

Her mind began to grasp what he was saying. "What man?"

"Lord Norbrook. He's been scouring the stews for you. But the fine gentleman didn't like to get dirty, so he couldn't find you. He paid me to track you down."

Sebastian? Looking for her? "Does—does he know about the brothel, about Madame?" Of course he must, if he'd found Mick. But why would Sebastian have hired Mick to find her? He had to know what she'd become—a prostitute—and what she was accused of doing. She would have thought Sebastian would want nothing more than to wash his hands of her.

Mick leaned forward and licked her cheek. It was revolting, a parody of a caress that turned her stomach. "Apparently he still wants you. He thinks you would be willing to be his whore, in exchange for your life."

She understood. She was going to have to do whatever Sebastian asked, whatever he desired, or he would hand her over to Bow Street to be charged with murder. She had been afraid of her cousin years ago when she was naïve and innocent. After everything she'd had to do to survive, the thought of now becoming Sebastian's whore made her sick with disgust and horror.

Mick gave his horse a kick, urging it faster along the path, which Anne could barely see. He gave a low laugh by her ear. "Thinking about your fancy Lord Norbrook, are you? Thinking how you can stay alive by fucking him? There's something you'd better understand, angel—"

Angel. Devon had called her that. But when Mick said it, in his gloating, sadistic voice, the name that had sounded sensual on Devon's lips curdled in her stomach.

"You live and die at my pleasure now, Annie," Mick snarled. "Do as I say and I'll let you survive. I'll let you go to Norbrook. We've got a couple of days to travel together, and you're going to have to keep me happy. I want to see what a whore does for a duke while she's fucking him. Madame never let me have a crack at you. She wanted to keep you 'innocent,' as she put it, for her richest clients. Now's my chance to sample your slice."

Anne wanted to gag. But the most horrible thought came into her head. She was a whore—she was supposed to let men touch her when she didn't want them. If her life was at stake, she could bed Mick, then do the same with Norbrook. She would have to do it.

Then, wildly, she thought of the contract she'd signed with Devon. Why would she think about it now, that piece of signed paper that set out the terms of a love affair? She remembered how it had hurt her feelings. What a fool she had been. He had written it to protect her. He had not used his power to make her feel weak and defenseless. If she hadn't been suspected of murder, that contract would have given her the dream of a future, of independence.

She wouldn't have any future at all, hanging from a rope. She had no choice. She must do whatever Mick demanded, then she would please Sebastian, and she would live.

God, she *couldn't* do it. Mick's touch made her feel as though a dozen spiders were crawling over her skin. She now knew what it was like to want a man's touch—*Devon's* touch. She couldn't face the thought of letting Mick or her cousin near her.

"The duke gave me jewels," she lied.

Mick gave a kick to his animal's flanks, urging the horse faster. "Good, then, Annie. That will do nicely to cover the expense and trouble of me taking you to Norbrook."

"You don't understand," she said desperately. "The duke found out about Madame's death from the news sheets. He learned I'm suspected of murder, and I had to run away. I didn't have time to take anything with me. The jewels are worth a fortune, Mick. Far more than Norbrook would pay you. If you help me go back for them, I'll give them to you. I can get into the house while his servants are rushing around looking for me. If you let me go free, a king's ransom of diamonds and rubies is yours."

She had no plan. Just the knowledge that she would rather be caught by Devon and dragged to the magistrate than be a whore for Mick and her cousin Sebastian. She'd done so many sinful things to simply survive. She couldn't do it anymore. She couldn't face doing one more thing that made her heart sick and her stomach roil, one more thing she would desperately fight to forget. You couldn't really forget things like that. They haunted you forever. Just as Devon's memories of death and battle haunted him.

She prayed greed would drive Mick. Prayed he would turn his horse and take her back to the house. She didn't know what she'd do after that. Throw herself on Devon's mercy? She now knew she was innocent, after weeks of fearing she'd killed a woman. But would he believe her?

Mick slowed, obviously thinking it over. Then he began to wheel the horse around—

A new sound broke through the woods. It was the faint but steady beat of hooves. She hadn't heard it over the noise of Mick's horse, the hammer of her heart. It rapidly grew louder.

"Shit," Mick muttered. Now, between the dark columns of the trees, she could see flashes of motion. The sounds of pounding horses and shouting men washed over her like a wave. It was too late for Mick to run.

"Keep your mouth shut," Mick snapped. "Remember, the duke believes you're a murderess and will want to see you hang. Don't think he's going to save you, Annie." His horse snorted as he forcefully turned it again to face the oncoming riders.

The mass of horses and riders came completely into view. Her nervous wits distinguished six mounted men. Four were Devon's grooms and, in the center of the pack, on his black mount, was Devon. He was hatless; he appeared to have thrown a greatcoat over a shirt and trousers. At his side, dressed far more elegantly, rode the Earl of Ashton. At a word from Ashton, all the riders halted a few feet from Mick and her. Two of the grooms and the earl lifted pistols. Anne's heart stuttered: Three round black muzzles pointed at her.

Something brushed against her back, then stopped beside her head. It was the barrel of Mick's weapon, and he held it pointed at Ashton. Her heart thrummed in fear. Devon should not have come—he was on his horse, completely reliant upon his hearing and direction from his men and Ashton. Was he so angry with her over her lies, so sickened by her supposed crime, he had come to ensure she was arrested? She wanted to tell him the truth at once. "Your—" she began, but Ashton shouted to Mick, "Identify yourself, sir."

As Ashton waited for the response, he leaned toward Devon. In the gloom, Anne could not see his lips move, but guessed that he spoke. Devon's expression grew hard in response.

"Christ Jesus," he snapped, and his deep, commanding voice froze everyone on the spot. "Ashton, put down your damned pistol!" he roared. "The rest of you, do it also."

The grooms hesitated. Even though Devon could not see, he barked, "Do it, damn you. I will not have you pointing weapons at Cerise. Now, you on the horse, I don't know who you are, but I am the Duke of March. You will release the woman and you will send her here to me."

Mick did not lower his gun. Anne almost choked as his grip tightened around her chest. "My name is Mick Taylor, Your Grace. This woman is suspected of the murder of a woman in London. I've been sent to collect Miss Anne Beddington and bring her back to face justice."

Anne Beddington. She saw Devon flinch at Mick's use of her real name. At the sudden jerk of the duke's body, Abednigo shifted uneasily underneath him and pawed at the ground. Anne's heart caught in her throat as Devon swayed on the horse, then regained his balance. "The woman is Anne Beddington, you say? I know her by a different name." Suspicion kept his face brutally cold and his eyes so narrow they were shadowed wells.

Oh, God. Now that she had been caught in yet another lie, he would never believe her real story. But she was desperate. She had nothing to lose. "He's lying!" she cried to Devon. But she had seen his face look so ice cold and hard only after one of his nightmares. "Mick Taylor worked for my madam. He's not a Bow Street

Runner. He is not going to take me to the magistrate. He's been paid—" She broke off. She hadn't said the most important thing. "I didn't kill anyone, Your Grace." She dared not call him by his Christian name. "Mick can prove my innocence. He *knows* I didn't kill Mrs. Meadows, who was known as Madame Sin."

"That's to be determined by the courts, Miss Beddington," Mick said behind her. "I'm not a Runner, but I have an interest in seeing the murderess of my employer swing."

"Assuming she is guilty," Devon coldly pointed out.

Anne didn't know whether to despair or grasp at faint hope. At least Devon spoke as though he was willing to doubt her guilt. "I am innocent," she cried. "I had to rescue three young girls from Madame—virgins she was going to *sell*. She threatened to *shoot* one of them. To get away, I had to hit her. I meant to hit her arm, so she wouldn't kill the girl, but I struck her head. Yes, she collapsed, but Mick has told me she was *alive*." Her story sounded like a jumbled mess, but she was so desperate to spill it out. It was as though she had only seconds to convince him. "It's the truth. I did not kill her. Someone *else* did." But the more she gasped out protests, the more she feared she sounded guilty.

For an instant there was a stunned silence. Then Ashton began to speak, but Devon held up his hand. At that, all his men steadied their mounts. It was as though they were waiting for him to shout, *Charge*.

"I don't give a damn who you are." How calmly he spoke. But each word vibrated, like a slicing rapier. "You will turn over Cerise—or Miss Beddington, or whatever her name is—*now*."

She felt Mick tense behind her. "With all due respect, Your Grace," Mick protested, "I don't feel comfortable giving her over to you. How do I know you will hand her over to the magistrate? Seeing as how she's your mistress—"

"I'm the Duke of March, Taylor. I have no intention of letting you leave with her. Do you understand? Surrendering her now will make this go easier on you."

Mick's laugh was harsh and snide. "Considering I'm holding both her and a pistol, Your Grace, I don't see how you plan to do that."

Anne felt the end of the weapon slide along her cheek, and she quivered with shock. She knew exactly what Mick was going to do, even before he gave an evil chuckle. "Admittedly, I've got only one shot. Not enough to stop your men, but one shot is all that's needed to mete out justice to a wanted criminal. Back off with your men, Your Grace. I'm not letting this whore get away. She's mine. If there's a reward for her capture, I'm getting it."

Reward? There couldn't be a reward. She understood what Mick was doing. He had to give a plausible reason for his determination to take her—one that did not involve her cousin Sebastian.

"You are a bloody idiot, Taylor." This time Ashton snapped at Mick. "Release her."

Gazing helplessly out at Devon and the other men, Anne gritted her teeth. Would Mick shoot her? She didn't think he would—if she was dead, what good would she be to Sebastian? Why was her cousin willing to go to such lengths to have her?

This was madness. She couldn't just sit here, like a sack of potatoes balanced on a horse, her body acting as a shield for Mick. Devon had demanded that his men lower their weapons rather than put her at risk. What was Devon going to do? What *could* he do?

Devon dismounted with easy grace. That, she hadn't expected. Resting his hand on his horse's flank, he shouted, "Taylor, last chance. Let her go."

Mick's horse shifted, hooves smacking against the dirt of the track. Devon began to walk toward the sound. Anne's heart leapt into her throat. She wanted to shout at him to go back, but she couldn't yell orders at Devon in front of his men and Mick. She should tell him to walk away, keep himself safe, leave her to her fate. But her foolish heart, her fear, wouldn't let her.

"Stay back, Your Grace," Mick warned, but his voice rose with nervous uncertainty. He wouldn't want to shoot her. Dear heaven, he wouldn't be mad enough to shoot a duke, would he?

For almost five years, she'd kept herself safe by trying to understand Madame and her lackeys, by trying to learn what they would do so she could anticipate rage and violence and avoid it. Would Mick fire a shot at the duke, something to frighten him? He was aiming at Devon, who had now moved out from the line of his servants. But Devon couldn't see him. He didn't know the danger. He would not do as Mick expected—

"Your Grace, please don't come closer," she cried out. She knew Mick was vicious when thwarted. Once, he had tried to rape one of the girls, and the young woman had scratched him to stop the attack. He had bided his time—then the poor girl was found outside the house, beaten to a pulp. Mick had insisted it was done by a footpad. But all Madame's girls had guessed the truth.

Devon possessed a calm and confidence that astounded her. But then, he'd run into battle, toward hundreds of men who were firing rifles and cannons at him with the intent to kill.

Mick would not shoot her. She had to break free of this numbing terror and *do* something. Mick had her body clamped to him, but she had two free hands. She hit out, slamming her right hand into his wrist, trying to jostle the pistol free. With her left hand, she jabbed wildly behind her, praying she could stick her fingers in his eye.

"Bitch," he barked. He swung his free arm at her flailing hand.

Devon was moving across the black ground for her—his steps fast but uncertain. He had never looked harder or more ruthless. "Taylor!" he shouted.

"The wench is mine, Your Grace, and I'm taking her back to London," Mick retorted.

Devon's arm suddenly arced toward them, and he lifted a pistol and trained it on Mick's head—he must have followed Mick's voice.

"You wouldn't dare shoot!" Mick sneered. "You're blind—you'd hit her by mistake."

Through the buzzing in her ears, Anne heard Devon issue a curt command, and she felt Mick twist around in panic. Black shapes seemed to ooze from the trees. She saw fists flying—more of Devon's men. One grabbed for her, pulling hard at her arm, but Mick held her tight. Another came at Mick from the right side, swinging a stick at him like a club. Mick had to let her go to defend himself. He had the pistol but, she realized, he didn't want to waste the shot.

"Bloody hell," Mick snapped. "All right, Your Grace, you win this round."

She was pushed from behind. She slid off the horse, cried out, and fell into a man's arms—one of Devon's grooms. The man jerked her quickly away from the horse, away from Mick.

"Where is she?" Devon barked.

"I've got her," the groom answered, though she struggled in his arms like a beached eel. A moment later, Devon's strong arms plucked her from his groom, hauling her to his chest. From the corner of her eye, she saw Mick's horse rear up on its hind legs. Long powerful forelegs pawed through the air, and she was frozen, watching disaster begin to slowly drop, as though magical strings guided the animal's movement. She would be crushed beneath those hard hooves, and Devon would be too.

She was too stunned to warn him, but a man yelled, "Look out, Your Grace!"

Devon jumped to the right, pulling her with him. He landed on his back, she fell on top of him, and his breath flew over her in a *whoosh*.

His men were shouting. Devon lifted her off him and leapt to his feet, amazing her. She knew she'd knocked his wind out, yet he seemed unfazed. She had to struggle to get up—until Devon's hand clamped around her wrist and she was jerked swiftly to her feet.

"Damn it," spat one of the men. "I'm sorry, Your Grace, but he's run. Once the horse reared, we couldn't get near him. He must have jerked that animal around in midair."

"Two of you, go after that man. He threatened me, and I want the truth of what is going on here."

"I'll take up the chase," yelled Lord Ashton. He and a servant spurred their mounts and took off along the track in fierce pursuit of Mick.

"They're riding too fast," Anne gasped. "They'll kill themselves." Unless Mick fell first. She hoped he did and broke his neck—death was something she would never wish on anyone, but Mick was thoroughly evil.

"They won't. Ashton is a brilliant rider," Devon said coolly. "I hope I didn't frighten you with that pistol. Taylor was right: I wouldn't have taken the shot, but I needed to distract him while my other men got in position to attack."

"It worked!" Her voice shimmered with gratitude, but his face remained hard. "Thank you," she said breathlessly. "You rescued me."

All he said in response was, "Your dress is wet."

She hadn't realized her dress was like a cold vise clamped to her body. Obviously she was more soaked than she'd suspected. But when she shivered, it was because of the frostiness she sensed in Devon, not because of her wet clothes. "I fell, trying to cross the stream."

"You're shaking like a leaf. We need to get you home, dried, warmed."

Those words flooded her head. Would he get her dried and warmed to hand her over to the magistrate? Perhaps he would. He had rescued her, yet he sounded so cold.

"Then, I want the truth, Cer—I mean Anne Beddington. Assuming that is your real name."

"It is," she answered numbly. *The truth.* She would give him every single piece of it. But would he believe her?

Chapter Seventeen

CUPPING A BRANDY balloon, Anne huddled in Devon's warm greatcoat, surrounded by the familiar scent of him. They were alone in his study—he had sent his servants away. He had carefully poured the liquor, held it out without a word. When she'd taken it, he sat across from her. She noticed he hadn't poured any for himself. At least there she'd done some good.

Lifting the glass to her lips, she took a sip. The spirits set a fire in her belly but didn't ease the icy feeling in her heart—a cold that had nothing to do with her wet dress or the fact that a cool rain was now falling. It reminded her of their first walk outside together, and her chilled heart ached.

Devon must have been listening to the sounds of her swallows and her gasps, for when she stopped, he lifted his head. "You knew the man who captured you?"

Of course his tone would be as cold and foreboding as his expression. "Yes." She tried to keep her voice steady. She knew Lord Ashton had returned empty-handed. Mick had gotten away. "His name is indeed Mick Taylor. He acted as a kind of bodyguard to my madam, protecting her from irate clients, thieves, and other unsavory characters. Madame was *horrible*. She was willing to hurt anyone for money, even a young and terrified innocent. She was going to shoot a fourteen-year-old girl. That was why I had to hit her—"

"Shhh. Let's go about this in order." Devon leaned back in his chair, his face terribly blank and emotionless. She had told him over and over that she wasn't a murderess—she was so giddy with relief over it, she couldn't stop saying it. "Tell me what happened, Cer—" He stopped. "Miss Beddington."

Finally he revealed an expression. He looked . . . hurt. She wanted to fall through his floor, ashamed. She felt wretched for lying to him, but she'd had no choice before; she had thought she was guilty. And he *was* being kind to her: He was listening. "I always planned to escape from the brothel, but I was too much of a coward to do it. I truly did fear what Madame or Mick would do to me if they caught me in the attempt. And Madame did keep us locked up. Like prisoners. Like slaves."

Devon looked so pained. She knew she was flushing with shame. But he said softly, "I'm sorry you went through that, angel," and her heart gave a tremendous lurch.

"You were very strong to survive it," he said. "You told me you had rescued a young girl. I suspect that was what prompted you to finally attack the woman."

She breathed deeply. "Yes. I overheard Madame—her real name is Mrs. Meadows, but she called herself Madame Sin—instruct Mick Taylor to acquire innocent girls for her. She wanted three and he was to kidnap them. She planned to auction the girls' virginity. On the night of the kidnappings, I witnessed one being brought into the house. From my window, I saw a black carriage stop in the street by the door. Mick got out carrying a sack—a burlap sack that wriggled. At least, it did until he struck it with his fist." It still hurt to think of that moment—when she'd realized there had to be a young girl held captive in the sack and that Mick had hit a small defenseless person because he was annoyed by the struggles. She saw, in Devon's face, answering horror.

"I searched the whole house to try to find the girls. There were rooms in the attic that Madame always kept locked, so I guessed that was their prison."

"What happened then? Did you confront the woman?"

His voice was now so gentle it eased her nerves. "I didn't intend to. I knew there was no point. Madame had no conscience at all. My *plan* was to help the girls escape. I worked with my hairpins for two nights before I figured out how to spring the lock."

"Bravo," he said quietly.

"Then I slipped inside the room—" As soon as she had seen the three pairs of frightened eyes, as soon as she'd realized the girls were too frightened to even scream, her thoughts toward Madame had been murderous. But she'd known the best revenge was escape.

"Tell me everything, love."

His voice was gentle and tempting—it sounded like the voice of a man who would believe her.

"I thought all I would have to do was lead the girls out of the house. But they were so scared they could barely move. The poor things had been beaten to the point that they were almost frozen with fright. I forced them to come with me, but we moved too slowly and Mick caught us before we got out. He dragged us to Madame's private office."

Suddenly Devon asked for her glass. She surrendered it and watched as he poured more brandy, using his finger to know when he'd given enough. It gave her time to slow her pounding heart—had he known she needed a few moments?

"Madame was furious. She wanted to terrify the girls and punish me. I was . . . half mad with rage and fear.

There were only the girls and Mick and me in the room with her. I was desperate."

He held out the glass and she took it. She jumped as her fingers touched his. He let his linger—a gesture of support she savored. She didn't drink, just cradled the glass. "I insisted she let me take the girls and leave. Madame laughed, and she took a pistol out of a drawer in her desk. She pointed it at one of the girls. She threatened to shoot the child to show the others what would happen if they disobeyed. Her finger went to the trigger, so I—I snatched up her fireplace poker."

"You hit her to stop her from shooting a child."

"Yes, I tried to hit her arm so her shot would miss. I put all my strength behind the blow. At the last second she moved toward me and I hit her in the *head*. It was an accident. It wasn't what I meant to do at *all*—"

"Love, you did it to protect a child."

Love. "I thought Madame was dead. I thought I'd killed her, and I felt . . . sick. But I had to rescue the girls—I was afraid of what Mick would do. I grabbed the pistol before Mick could get to it. I kept it pointed at him, and I made the girls jump out the window. There was a low roof below us, and they landed there, then slid to the ground. As I pushed the last one outside, Mick lunged at me, but I managed to escape."

"Did you hurt yourself?"

"I landed in a heap on the roof. Bruised my knees and jarred my elbows."

"What did you do then?" He leaned forward. "I have to admit, at this moment, you have my every sympathy."

Did she? But what did that really mean? That he would help her? Or that it would hurt him when he turned her over to the law? "I stuffed the pistol down my bodice, and I grabbed the girls and ran with them.

Mick and some of Madame's male servants chased us, but we lost them in the stews." Her voice rose. "But I hadn't killed Madame. Mick told me that when he caught me in your woods. He told me she was still alive. And he hit Kat badly to learn where I was."

He stayed silent for a long time, while her heart roared in her ears.

"You got the three girls to safety?"

She blinked. "Yes. I finally made the smallest, Lottie, climb on my back, and I held the other two by their wrists. I got to Kat's house, then the next day I took the girls to friends of Kat. Friends who ensured the girls were returned to their home in the country. To pay their way, I gave the girls almost all the money I had saved."

"Leaving you with almost nothing, which was why you came to me."

"Yes. When Lord Ashton tried to tempt Kat to 'heal' you, as he put it, I could not resist. It meant escape from London. I knew I was suspected of Madame's murder. I thought I was guilty. Coming to you meant . . . a roof over my head and safety. But I put Kat at risk."

"And you say Taylor told you the woman was not killed by your blow."

"Yes. After weeks of thinking I'd killed her, I really hadn't!"

He frowned. Of course, she had no proof. Only Mick's word, and he was gone. And Devon's next words made her fear he thought she was lying. "Miss Beddington, if you did not kill her, how did your madam end up dead?"

"Someone must have hit her again after I escaped with the girls. Perhaps it was one of the other women in the brothel. It might have been one of the clients. I thought of Mick, but he wouldn't have any reason to want Madame dead."

"Are there any men you suspect?"

She desperately tried to think. "I don't know. When I

overheard her talking with Mick, she said she had already told certain gentlemen about her innocents. Maybe one of those men was driven to fury by thwarted lust."

"I doubt it," Devon countered gently. "He could have found other young women at another brothel. However, if your madam had already taken money for the girls, that might have enraged a man enough to kill her." But he frowned, as though he doubted the theory.

Her stomach roiled. Her story sounded implausible: Who would believe she had left the madam alive, then, coincidentally, someone had killed her? Even she found it hard to imagine she was reprieved from the horror of being a murderess.

"Come here, angel."

She stood, surprised. Why did he want her close? Did he want to grab her, then give her to the magistrate? Her heart stuttered. If he did, she supposed they would keep her in jail here, then eventually transport her to London.

As she came near to him, he settled his hands on her waist. He moved her between his open legs. "Who are you, Anne Beddington?"

She almost lost her balance. "What do you mean?"

"I mean where do you come from? Where were you born? How did you end up in the stews? In the brothel?" One last tug of his hands brought her against him, so his chin pressed to her belly. "I don't know if anything you told me before is the truth, angel."

"I didn't lie exactly," she admitted numbly. "I tried to hide everything I could. It was because I feared I had killed Madame. In truth, I was a gentleman's daughter, but my father died and my mother and I were forced to leave our house." She swallowed hard. "What are you going to do to me? Do you believe I'm innocent?"

He didn't answer that question. Thoughtfully, he said, "Since Taylor knew you were innocent, he had no reason to bring you to justice. Why did he really want you?"

To her surprise, he pulled her down, depositing her on his right leg. His thigh was tensed and rock-hard beneath her bottom. "No secrets, love. If you want help."

Help. Goodness, he was going to help her. But there was something harsh in his face—and suddenly she understood. "Oh, God, you don't think Mick and I . . . I *despised* Mick Taylor. He did *not* come after me for revenge. He hunted me down because my cousin paid him to find me."

Devon's hand tightened on her waist. "All right. Who is your cousin?"

"His name is Sebastian Beddington. When my father died, he became Viscount Norbrook."

His brows arched. "A viscount's daughter? It explains why you speak and behave like a lady." He frowned. "Your cousin forced you out of your home? I don't understand. Your mother would have dower rights."

His voice was so cool and logical. Did it mean he didn't believe her? She told him of her father's sudden death when she was fifteen and the arrival of his heir, her cousin Sebastian. "Sebastian promised we would always have a home, that my mother need not move into the dower house. Within a month he had explained we could stay only if he was allowed to . . . to marry me. He gloated—he was certain we were in his power. And when Mama refused, he spread vicious lies about her character. He made up stories of love affairs, intrigues, and scandalous orgies. Sebastian could appear to be the most charming gentleman, and he turned my father's family against her."

"What of your mother's family?"

She shook her head. "I never knew them. My mother's father had married against his parents' wishes. He was disowned, and my mother never met her grandparents or her aunts."

"Your cousin was desperate to marry you—at any cost?"

"Yes. It seems mad, doesn't it? I'm sure he doesn't want to marry me now. Though Mick said he still . . . wants me." She shuddered.

His mouth tugged down at the corners. "He sounds like a blackguard, but you couldn't have known that when you first refused his proposal. Why did you?"

She took a huge gulp of brandy, despite all her warnings to him about drink. She'd promised the truth, but she didn't want to speak of this. "I didn't . . . like him. When my mother continued to refuse, he finally became furious and he . . . he tried to force a marriage between us. Physically."

Devon's arms tightened around her and a vein in his temple twitched. "He raped you?"

"No. I threw my chamber pot at him and got his immaculate shirt and trousers wet. And my scream brought my mother and servants running."

"You saved yourself with a chamber pot." He tried to pull her closer, but she was tense and rigid, remembering. "That night, my mother decided we must leave. We ran away. We went to London. Mama found work as a seamstress, and she toiled there until she became ill. Then she wasted away."

How inadequately words expressed her pain and sorrow. How could she describe the way she'd ached with pain, watching her mother massage her cramped hands? Her rage when her mother's eyesight had failed from sewing by meager candlelight? The guilt she'd felt when her mother had tried to protect her from grueling work, or thievery, or prostitution.

"And the brothel—how did you end up there?"

"A gentleman took me there and gave me to the madam as payment of his outstanding bills."

"Who?" he growled. "What was his name?"

"It doesn't matter. I—I thought he wanted to be my protector, but I was naïve and foolish. He did look after me for a few weeks. With that money, I helped my mother as best I could."

"How old were you?"

"Old enough that I should not have trusted him."

"Your age," he demanded.

"I was seventeen."

"I have four sisters, and I know how naïve and sweet a girl is at that age. Give me his name, angel. Never in my life have I wanted to beat a man and destroy him."

"It doesn't matter. He's *dead*. He died years ago, of an illness." She added impetuously, to defuse his anger, "I met you, five years ago."

"When? At a ball? In Society?"

"Heavens, no. The first night I decided to become a prostitute. You were the first man I approached."

He jerked his head down. "Are you saying I was your first? Did I take your virginity, without knowing it?"

"No. *You* told me not to sell my body. You gave me two gold sovereigns for nothing, told me I was pretty, and sent me away."

His heart thudded by her ear. "I'm pleased to know I didn't . . . hurt you, love."

"You—you were a hero to me. In the end, I had to go back to the Drury Lane theatre."

"Was that when you met this other man? I don't sound as though I was much of a savior."

"But in the end—" It was hard to speak. "You did save me. I understand if you can't now."

"Enough, Cerise. You've been through hell, and I understand how that feels."

"Are you going to turn me in?" For she would have to

go to trial and attempt to prove her innocence, wouldn't she? Bow Street wouldn't believe her unless Mick told the truth.

"I'm not sending you anywhere tonight."

You can spend the night. He said that on the first night she'd come here. She had temporary safety again, her life was in his hands, and she had no idea what he planned to do with her.

Devon paced his study. The scent of brandy was a hellish temptation. But he resisted.

In so many ways, Cerise—no, *Anne*—had given him the ability to cope with his blindness. She'd opened up senses he had believed could never be enough.

He had deposited her in his bedchamber and left two footmen guarding the door. He didn't know if she would try to run again. And what was he going to do with her? Did he keep her hidden here, harbor her, or take her to the magistrate so they could argue her innocence? She would still be arrested and held until a trial.

Was she innocent? She admitted to hitting the madam. How plausible was it that someone else came on the same night and murdered the woman? She claimed Mick Taylor had told her Mrs. Meadows survived her attack. If she was lying, why would she not simply deny she had hit the woman?

But without Taylor's evidence, would Bow Street believe her story? Would a jury?

He didn't blame her for hitting the woman. He understood why she had to do it. He knew what it was like to have to make brutal decisions. Just as when he was at Waterloo and had suddenly realized, in the middle of battle, he was aiming his rifle at a young French boy. And if he didn't pull the trigger, one of his men would die. . . .

One thought hammered in his head: He couldn't keep her as his mistress anymore, could he? She'd been forced into this life. She had been born a lady, taken to the brothel against her will. The truth was that a life as his mistress was better than any alternative she had now. But he felt too guilty.

A fist rapped at the door. "Yer Grace," called Treadwell. "A bloke named Taylor is here."

Bloody hell. Taylor had the audacity to come to his house? "What does he want?" If it was Anne Beddington, Taylor wasn't going to get her.

"To speak to ye about the murderess, he said."

He sorely wanted to slam his fists into Taylor. But what he needed was the man's evidence to help Anne.

Again he was thankful for the way Anne had helped him learn to stride with confidence through his house. Devon stalked into his study to confront Mick Taylor. He couldn't see the man, but he'd had Treadwell give him a description: bald, hooked nose, sharp eyes, and thickset, muscled body. A typical bruiser who roughed up men and women alike.

Devon heard clothing rustle near the fireplace. He made his way to his desk, counting paces in his head. In his walking stick, he carried a blade. He should be able to fight Taylor by sound if necessary. But he had to play this carefully. "If you came for Anne Beddington, Taylor, I will not surrender her. As you are aware, she is innocent."

"Your Grace, this is madness. The gel is a killer. She should be hauled to Bow Street in chains." Taylor's gravelly voice held a sneering note of disrespect.

"That will not happen. Miss Beddington told me her story, including the fact that you admitted to her the madam was alive. She didn't kill the woman."

Mick Taylor snorted. "Madame Sin was dead. I saw Annie slam that poker into Madame's head. I checked her pulse before I went in pursuit of Annie. There wasn't one. She was dead. I was a witness and I'd swear to it."

"And the story you told Miss Beddington? That her blow had not killed the woman?"

"An outright lie. I never said that to her. And I would tell Bow Street Annie did it."

Devon understood. No doubt Taylor had given Anne the truth to coerce her into going with him. Now he was denying it. Taylor was giving him a warning: There was no point in taking him captive or threatening him, as Taylor would tell a story that would ensure Anne was hanged.

Damn. He really wanted to pound Mick Taylor, but he needed information from the blackguard. "I believe you came to retrieve Miss Beddington for her cousin Viscount Norbrook."

"For Norbrook? She said that? Hell, no." The denial came swift and loud. Too quickly.

"I know for a fact Norbrook is involved," Devon bluffed calmly.

"L-Lord Norbrook came looking for Annie at the brothel. She'd run away from home. When he found out she's a whore and a killer, he left in disgust."

The implication was clear: He was a misguided fool if he harbored Anne Beddington, a ruined woman. Devon's anger snapped. "Get the hell out, Taylor. Now. Before I pull the sword from my stick and gore you so I don't have to listen to your filthy mouth anymore."

"But—"

He drew the sword with a swish and brought it down to rest on his desk. "I can take you to the magistrate and have you arrested for kidnapping Miss Beddington. I doubt questions would be asked about what condition you arrived in. And if I catch you on my grounds again, I will beat you to a pulp and drag your arse to jail."

He heard the scramble of Taylor's boots over his floor as the man backed away. "Remember, Your Grace," Taylor spat, "if I were to tell Bow Street what I was witness to, Annie would hang."

In a sharp bark, Devon demanded his footmen come in to drag Taylor out.

"I'll leave. But you're mad, Your Grace, if you keep a murderess in your house. She'll try to kill you to save her arse! You should hand her over to me for your own sake."

"Oh, my goodness! Mick Taylor came back? What did he want?"

The sheer terror in Miss Beddington's voice touched his heart, though Devon knew she would also be afraid if she was guilty, if what Taylor said he witnessed was true. "You, my dear."

"Wh-what did he say?"

Following her panicked tones, he crossed the room. He found the bed by using his walking stick, then sat down on it at her side.

"He said he witnessed you hit your madam, that he checked for the woman's pulse and found none before pursuing you."

"That can't be true. He told me she was alive!"

"I won't surrender you to him." War had honed his senses—he'd had to learn to know when an enemy was bluffing. That instinct told him she was telling the truth. How could he not trust Anne, who had helped him, helped his sister, because of the word of a brute like Taylor?

"How can I prove I'm innocent? I have no proof. No witnesses except Mick, who will lie."

He slid his arms around her, but she didn't fall into his embrace. She stiffened, just as she had earlier. He dropped his arms. After all, he now knew she'd never been a willing whore.

She would be arrested and charged. As a duke, he had power and influence. But would it be enough to save her? "You did have witnesses. You had the girls."

"They wouldn't know whether Madame was still alive. They were already out the window."

"At least they could prove you struck the woman to defend one of them."

"I can't bring them back to London to tell their stories. It would ruin them."

"You'd risk hanging to protect them?"

There was a pause. Then she whispered, "Yes."

In that moment, Devon admired her more than he had any other woman. "The way to prove your innocence is to find the real murderer. Cerise—" He stopped. "Which name do you prefer? Cerise or Anne?"

"I don't know. I made up the name Cerise. Anne is who I have always been." Cerise was to have been a new name for a new life. She'd been a fool to think she could escape her old one.

"Anne, then. I'll have to get used to that."

Anne wished he would put his arms around her again. She had tensed before because she was thinking of Mick . . . and Sebastian. Now the need for his embrace was overwhelming.

His hand cupped her cheek. He turned her face and she saw his mouth come to hers. For a moment, he waited and they traded fierce breaths. Then he drew back. "Now that I know your story, I know you came to me out of desperation. I've never forced or coerced a woman."

She blinked. He leaned against the bedpost, put his hands above his head, and gripped the solid column.

He'd told her he had been to brothels. Had he really thought those women were *happy* to trade their favors for money? But then, faced with the choice of bedding a handsome young peer like Devon or an aging roué with odd tastes, they probably were.

"It wouldn't be forcing me. You never forced me. I always *wanted* you." It hadn't been quite true at the beginning. She hadn't wanted *any* man. She'd seen Devon merely as an escape, not as desirable. Panic hit her. If he didn't want to be intimate with her anymore, he would no longer be her protector and he would have no reason at all to help her.

She moved to him and splayed her hands on his chest. "I always wanted you. From the very first moment I saw you," she whispered. She skimmed her hands up to his shoulders. Her heart pounded fiercely. As she ran her fingers up and cradled the firm muscles of his neck, she knew she did truly want this. She wanted to feel close to him again. Her heart ached for it.

She didn't want to feel completely alone, as she had in Madame's brothel.

Gently, she kissed his chest. He wore only his linen shirt and trousers. No cravat, and the throat of his shirt lay open. Her lips touched his warm skin. She stroked her mouth over him. Tingling leapt from her lips to flood her body. This was the way it was with Devon. She couldn't make herself not feel anymore.

His neck tasted salty with sweat, from the exertion of hunting her down and rescuing her.

He drew back. "Love, I can't stand to think of you being so desperate that you sold your body. I hate to think of what it must have been like. You must hate men like me."

"I don't," she whispered desperately. "Ever since that first time I went to Drury Lane and you told me I deserved better, I—I liked you. I had no idea who you were, but I held your words in my heart, along with my parents' love for me, and it helped me survive."

What she said was the truth. She had replayed that moment over and over in the brothel—when the dazzlingly handsome black-haired gentleman had tipped up her chin and told her she was pretty. When he had told her she was worth more. Eventually, she'd seen his likeness drawn in news sheets because he was a hero of battles, and she'd discovered he was the Duke of March.

She moved onto his lap, straddling him. With her legs spread wide, she settled on his erection. Relief struck her. He still *wanted* her, just as she wanted him.

He had been holding back, barely responding to her. Now he tangled his hand in her hair and he held her to his mouth. His lips parted wide and his kiss ravished her. He growled hungrily as he did. There was none of his usual melting skill—it was dizzying and stunning and wonderful. This was raw desire, and it left her reeling on his lap.

With his right hand, he gave a ruthless tug of her bodice. Enough to pull seams open, ruining the poor seamstress's work. His mouth went to her breast, covered only by her shift. If his wild, hungry kisses had made her light-headed, his mouth on her nipple made her soar. He suckled deep and hard, until she was a limp puddle of whimpers and moans.

He caught her around the waist and lifted her with astonishing ease. Then he tossed her onto the bed, and before she'd finished bouncing, he climbed on top.

She was going to burst with desire. He was fully dressed and so was she, and she fumbled with the falls of his trousers. He tried to push her skirts up, but the fabric was trapped between them. She managed to get her hand into his linens, then wrapped her fingers around his hot, rigid shaft. She moaned with need; he groaned in delight.

Freeing her skirts, he bunched them at her waist. He stroked between her thighs, teasing her, as she swept her palm up and down his cock. It swelled larger and larger, until her fingers could barely reach around it. "Goodness," she whispered. "You're huge."

"It's you. Needing you is making me harder than I've ever been. If you don't let me make love to you right now, I'm going to explode."

"So am I." For it was true. His caresses on her sensitive nub made her moan and squirm. She thrust up to rub against his beautiful fingers, and she was close to a climax too.

Together, they led his cock to her passage, their fingers tangling. He slid deep, pressing his groin to her, and she wrapped her arms and legs tightly around him. They were completely joined. The very first thrust made her scream, for his shaft drew mercilessly along her sensitive clit. He gave a raw laugh, and then they moved together. Anne couldn't think about trying to please him. All she could do was savor every amazing thrust.

They rocked together wildly. She wanted to make him cry out in pure ecstasy and agony when he came.

"I want this to be good for you," he murmured between pants. "I want you to melt with delight when you come."

She almost laughed. She embraced him as snugly as she could. They both wanted the same thing—they were both working madly to give each other pleasure. Then his hips arched, his shaft gave one sweet stroke to her throbbing nub, and the head touched somewhere amazing inside her. Pleasure burst. She screamed and sobbed her orgasm, and then he cried out harsh and loud. He cried out her name. *Anne. Angel.*

After his body stopped its wild jerking, he rolled over and held her tight to his chest. She lay there, aware of tears trickling. And she knew something she had not known before. Or perhaps it had been in her heart for a long time, but she'd known it was a dangerous thing to feel.

She loved him. It had to be love—it was crushing her heart; it was tearing her soul apart.

He stroked her. "I'm going to do everything I can to help you, love. Unfortunately, even as a duke I can't circumvent the law, but I believe you are innocent and I'm going to prove it. First, we are going to have to go to London. I can hide you. Not in the ducal house, though. My mother is staying there, with two of my sisters. Somehow, angel, we are going to save you."

She couldn't let him try to save her.

Anne slid open one of Devon's drawers, careful not to make a sound. He had gone to the bed he always did, in the adjoining room. Even after all this, he was afraid he would awake in a nightmare and hurt her. What did it mean that he still cared that much about her?

It wouldn't mean anything when he woke up and discovered what she had done.

When he had spoken of his family, she realized she *couldn't* ask him to help her. It would cause a scandal for him and hurt his family. How could she bring pain to Caro, who had been her friend? He had four sisters, and the two with his mother were unwed. It would ruin their chances of a good marriage if their brother was harboring a suspected murderess. It would break his mother's heart. It would devastate his family to have him risk so much for the sake of . . . of a whore. She'd hoped he could protect her. But she had to protect *him*. She had to leave.

Quickly, Anne dressed—in one of Devon's shirts and a pair of his breeches. She had dreamed of building a life where she could be independent, but after tonight she knew she didn't want to be alone. But she had no choice.

She had to take one last look at him, this wonderful man she could never see again.

She crept to the doorway and watched him sleep. She didn't dare touch him. He was too sensitive, too aware—he would likely wake. It felt like thievery to take his clothes, and she had vowed she would never stoop to that. Yet here she was, doing it.

"I love you," she whispered. He was asleep. He couldn't hear. It was safe to say it. She darted away, crossed to the door of the master bedchamber. Of course it was locked. He had put guards outside, and she'd almost forgotten that.

First she shrugged on his dark-blue tailcoat—it would cover the white shirt. Then she swiftly pinned up her hair and found a hat in his wardrobe. She clutched that in one hand, raced to the window, and awkwardly pulled it open. She crept up onto the sill and swallowed hard. There was still a light mist of rain, and it was foggy now. It was a long way to the ground, but there was a garden below, with soft earth to break her fall.

Before she could lose her nerve, Anne jumped.

Chapter Eighteen

ANNE WAS RUNNING again, with her lungs heaving and her chest tight. At least Devon's clothes made it much easier to move, but every quick breath she took flooded her nose, her conscience, and her heart with his rich scent. It was truly agony. She vowed she would return everything to him.

Dawn lightened the sky, but the rain had brought out a thick morning mist. Layers of fog billowed over the lawns and twined among the trees. She was running as blindly as she had in the dark.

This time she hoped she had a better plan. She raced to the woods and took the opposite direction to the one she had before. This way, she should be able to reach the road to the village, and she could travel more quickly along a road than on the paths in the woods. In dark masculine clothing, she would not attract attention.

Behind her, in the gray mist, twigs snapped. Her heart jerked wildly in her chest.

What if it was Mick again? Surely he would have given up on watching the house. She prayed that he had, that he thought she was well and truly in the duke's possession now.

Crunching sounds pursued her, and she risked one glance back. She couldn't see anything but mist and the trees close to her; their black trunks seemed to dance crazily as she swept her gaze back and forth. She left the path, just as she'd done last night, and she ran through the woods. If it was Mick, he wouldn't let her get away this time. If it was Devon—

Her right foot didn't land on the ground—it dropped away beneath her. She was too shocked to scream. Her boots slid, her bottom slammed down, and she went flying along a slope into thick fog. Then she cried out in shock, damning the sound as it echoed everywhere.

Splash! Her feet hit water. Cool water instantly poured in through the lacing of her boots. Her spine felt as though it had been smacked with a hammer, and her hands had been scratched and torn up by small rocks. She quickly jerked her feet out of the water, but it hurt to move. She had nearly fallen into the wretched stream.

"Anne? Where are you?"

It was Devon. Not Mick. Relief left her light-headed, but she stayed silent. She had to get away. The only way he could help her was to throw himself into a scandal that would hurt him.

His footsteps grew closer, muffled by the mist. "Anne?" Then a pause. "Taylor? Taylor, are you out here? If you have Anne, hand her over to me right now. I swear I will shoot you."

Devon didn't sound angry. His voice was strained with panic.

Heavens, he was running now, his footsteps hard through the fog. It sounded as though he was racing over her head, but that was impossible. . . . No, he was running along the path she'd taken. Running, even though he couldn't see. The path would bring him to the edge of the ravine—

"Don't!" she shouted. "Stop! You'll fall down the hill!"

But her cry was too late. She heard a startled male shout, a horrible thud, and a terrible amount of crashing, as if Devon was tumbling over and over as he fell down the steep side of the ravine. Then there was a huge splash, several yards behind her.

Sheer panic forced her pained body to move. She turned and limped as fast as she could toward Devon. Fog had pooled in the ravine, and she couldn't see anything through it. Not trees until branches smacked her in the head. Not rocks until she collided with them. Heavens, this was what it was like for Devon. No wonder he hated it. How strong he had been to learn to cope.

Through the veil of gray mist, she saw a ghostly white outline. Her wits clicked into place, and she understood what she was looking at. Devon's shirt was white. It was rippling on the water of the stream. He hadn't slid in, as she had. His entire body had tumbled in, and he was facedown in the water.

Anne ran into the stream, forcing her legs to push through flowing water. An eternity raced by as she fought her way to him. The current tugged at him, but he wasn't moving. Now she could see that his arms and legs were outstretched, the water slapping at him, flowing around him.

Finally she was at his side. He had landed chest-first in the water. His head had struck a large flat rock. He lay on it, his cheek resting on the slippery surface. Water lapped at his lips.

His face wasn't submerged. That gave her hope. But his skin was ashen and waxy in his unconsciousness. *Please don't be hurt. Not badly hurt.*

Anne had known horror when she'd found the virgins in Madame's house, when she'd watched Madame crumple after the blow to her head, when Mick had caught her. But this was the worst terror she'd known.

She touched his cheek. Even though his skin was sheet-white, it wasn't as cold as she expected. She had to get him out of the water. She grasped his heavy right arm and tried to lift him. All she succeeded in doing was unbalancing herself, and she fell on a rock.

Sore and soaked, she clumsily got to her feet. He weighed a ton. She gave another tug, desperate now, for the water was splashing at his slack mouth.

He moved. His cheek slid along the slippery rock, then he was free of the stone support, but she still couldn't lift him. Damn and blast, his head was starting to sink. . . .

His head ached like the blazes. He tasted dirt against his lips. Bits of rock jabbed into his side. Why was he soaking wet?

Devon kept his eyes shut and lifted his hands to his aching head. It felt as if a sword had pierced his skull. Or a bayonet. Where was he? In battle? No, he was in England. Wasn't he?

Visions flashed through his head. A bayonet slicing through the ash- and scream-filled air, coming right for his eyes—

"Devon!" A tremulous, fear-filled feminine voice flowed over him. Anne Beddington's frantic voice brought him back from the battle in his head. As she always did. Gentle as a feather, her hand caressed his shoulder. He heard her stifle a sob, and warmth brushed over his cheek. Her breath, he guessed. "Thank heaven," she whispered.

He intended to agree—thank heaven he'd caught her. Instead, he started to cough. He was lying on his side, and he sputtered, spitting out water. His mouth tasted like the stream, his lips felt slimy. He could hear the water burbling close by. With his eyes still shut, he asked, "What happened?"

"You were running after me through the fog. You did the very same thing I did—you slid down the side of a ravine and landed in the stream. I managed to pull you out."

It all hurtled back. The smell of cool night air wafting through the open window in the bedroom. Driven by panic and frustration, he hadn't bothered to gather up servants, and he'd made it to the woods. Once in there, he'd heard her. She moved quietly, but he was used to listening for every sound. Then he'd heard her scream. "Thank you. Are you all right, Cer—Anne?" There was no point in opening his eyes—he couldn't see her to know.

"Yes, I'm fine. I slid down on my bottom."

"So first you try to heal me, now you're trying to kill me. Angel, why did you try to run again? Don't you believe I will help you?"

"I fear you *will* try to help me. I cannot ask that of you. I caused Kat to be hurt. I don't want to hurt you."

At her confusing words, he instinctively lifted his eyelids. And his vision was flooded with bright gray light. It was so intense, pain shot through his skull. He felt . . . blinded. Stunned. He shut his eyes again.

Devon's heart thundered. Maybe he was in shock. Or he *had* drowned after all, and for him purgatory consisted of a burning gray light and Anne's voice to haunt him for eternity.

"What's wrong? Are you in pain?"

Pain. In his *head*. "Where did I land?" he asked hoarsely, with his eyelids clamped shut.

"On a rock."

Doctors—the ones at the London Dispensary for Curing Diseases of the Eye and Ear—had told him his sight could come back if the fragment of bone or knot of blood in his skull was to move. "Did I hit my head?" he demanded. Why didn't he open his eyes again? It was as if he was afraid—afraid to find he'd hit his head and still couldn't see. At least the blow hadn't dislodged the thing from his optic nerve and killed him.

"I think so. I found you lying in the water, with the side of your head on a rock. When you landed, you must have hit it."

She pressed a place on his left temple, and he let out a growl of pain. At once, her hand withdrew. "There's no blood but definitely a bump."

He caught hold of her wrist so she couldn't run. He pulled her down on top of him and wrapped his arms around her. Then he cursed himself for cowardice here, in front of Anne, and he opened his eyes.

A canopy of dark-green leaves loomed over him, and a soft fog rolled among the trunks of trees. He could see faded browns, ebony blacks, and some splashes of yellow leaves. He could see the stream out of the corner of his eye, frothing white where it bubbled over rocks. The sun was rising, burning away the fog. He could see leaves rippling and shimmering where the light struck them. He was assaulted by the detail, by all the color and form around him. He was soaking wet, his head throbbed with pain, but he'd never seen anything so . . . miraculous.

The most wonderful miracle of all waited in his arms. Anne. More abruptly than he intended, he pushed her up so her face hovered over his. For the very first time, he saw her, and he felt his eyes go wide as though he was trying to draw in every detail.

Her huge eyes peered down at him. Eyes of an exotic green, dark and shiny as ivy leaves. Eyes filled with worry—for him. He saw her wet, disordered hair—half was pinned up, the rest tumbled down her back in a curtain of reddish-blond silk. She had an oval face with a stubborn, firm chin to anchor it. A wide, lush mouth so sensual he wanted to haul her down and kiss her—

No, look at her first.

She looked . . . nothing like he had imagined. He'd never pictured she would look so young, so innocent. She possessed a straight nose with a bump at the end and a trail of freckles across the ridge. Long lashes of amber. Her skin was like pearl, and perfect. She looked like a lady. No wonder she'd been prized at the brothel. *Hell.*

He reached for her cheek. The ability to direct his hand, to touch what he saw, was like a miracle. Something a child took for granted, but it filled him with awe. He felt the grin explode on his mouth.

"Why are you looking at me like—" Her eyes went wide as saucers. Her hands flew to her mouth. Pretty hands with long, graceful fingers. Wild images shot through him. Of what it must have looked like when she stroked his chest or wrapped her hands around his erection.

"You are beautiful," he said, even as his head ached from the onslaught of newly found sight. It was so much, too much, hurtling at him. But he fought the instinct to close his eyes.

"You can see," she whispered.

Devon saw the shock in her eyes dissolve and happiness flare to life in her face. "I can," he murmured. He let his gaze flow over her. Like a drunk man draining the last drops, he wanted to take in everything. This was the woman he'd made love to, the woman who had healed him. A heartbeat later he observed, "You're wearing my clothes." And in a faster heartbeat, "The shirt is soaking wet, love."

Anne looked down, dizzy from the knowledge that Devon could see. Water had turned the linen translucent. Between the sides of the tailcoat, the shirt stuck to the curves of her breasts and to her erect nipples. She might as well not have been wearing anything at all. "I'm sorry I took your clothes. I couldn't run in skirts. And I planned to return them to you. Somehow—" Then Devon grimaced and rubbed his temple, and she gasped, "Is your head all right?"

"The doctors told me this could happen—a blow to the head could bring my sight back."

"You can see everything? Perfectly well?"

"I think so. It's overwhelming right now." Groaning, he finally tried to push up from the muddy ground. He still held her hand. "We need to get home. Get you out of your wet clothes. Again."

She tugged her hand free of his grip. "I'm so sorry. But I must go."

She backed away from him. Through sheer force of will, she had dragged him out of the water, onto the bank. She had rolled him onto his side, in case he'd swallowed water. She had prayed he would open his eyes. But she couldn't go with him.

Another two frantic steps back. He was watching her. He was trying to stand, but his fall down the hill had obviously hurt him, and he was blinking as daylight glowed through the mist. She should *help* him, but he would never let her go then.

"Thank you for believing me, Devon, but I can't ask you to hide me and hunt for the real killer. There'd be scandal. Or worse. You could be arrested. For hiding me. I'm sorry." She was babbling wildly and, before she could lose her nerve, she ran.

He wasn't badly hurt . . . he could see now . . . he would be all right. She tried to make herself believe it, repeating those words as she raced through the woods. Now that he could see, he would be safe and happy. He could find a wife. He could find love. He could have everything he deserved.

Every fiber of Anne's being wanted her to turn and go back and ensure he was safe. *Devon, please be all right.*

She heard a roar of fury behind her. Then crashing. Dear God, he must be running after her. Relief and fear clashed inside her. If he could run, he must not be badly hurt. He could see now. He should be able to catch her. But somehow he didn't.

She ran like wild through the woods. Just when her legs wobbled beneath her like rubber and she was ready to collapse, she heard crowing, barking, shouting—all the sounds of a village waking with dawn.

Then she saw it. There was a small farmhouse ahead, and in the lane beside it stood a cart filled with baskets of apples. There was no one around. She ran to the cart and squeezed between the baskets, slithering her way to the back. She was cramped, and rough wood scratched her, but she was hidden.

Minutes later, the cart jiggled as a man leapt up to the driving box, then he called out a command to his pony. With a lurch, they set off.

How had she managed to vanish into thin air?

Devon stood on the muddy road. The breeze had whisked away the rest of the mist, so he could see up and down the road and across fields. He could see so much it made his head hurt.

But he couldn't see Anne.

What had possessed the foolish woman to run from him? He knew exactly what he was getting into. He had faced cannons and rifles, but Anne Beddington thought she should protect him.

He had to squint as sunlight filtered through the sky and landed on the wide strip of road. It was searing for eyes that hadn't seen for three months.

How had she escaped him? Admittedly, he'd been unsteady on his feet, disoriented because he could now see. At first when he was running, he'd tripped over every blasted root in the forest. He'd been worse than when he was blind. But he should have been able to catch her.

He swung around in a circle. Instinct warned him he was in the open and vulnerable. He shook his head—that was a remnant of battle. Now he was hunting a damsel in distress, one determined to evade his help. Leaves rippled around him. Sheep dotted a hillside to the right, behind a quiet stone farmhouse. Every detail of the farm loomed at him—the time-mellowed edges of the stone, the golden thatch on the roof, the pink of late roses rambling up a wall. On the other side, the woods stretched to a meadow, following the hill downward toward the village.

The one detail he couldn't see was a slim woman in a wet shirt and breeches running down the road, through the meadow, or across the fields.

The farm would be filled with hiding places. More than he could effectively search. He needed to return home. Bring out a band of his servants and scour the farm, the woods, and the fields from top to bottom. He had to send a man to the village inn. If Anne made it that far, if she could find another hat to disguise her head—she'd dropped his at the stream—and made herself look convincingly male, she might try to get on a stage. But she would need money to buy a ticket. . . .

Devon's heart gave a strange, hard kick in his chest. Anne had worked in a brothel. He now knew how lovely she was. Any man she approached would want her—certainly with her wearing that wet, almost transparent shirt.

God, the thought left him reeling more than the onslaught of color and images that came from regaining his sight.

* * *

Two days later, Devon strode down the steps toward his waiting mount. His groom held the reins of his fastest horse.

"Are you certain you should ride alone so soon after taking a serious blow to your head?"

He jerked around to see Tristan coming down the steps, his courtesan following on his heels, the plumes of her extravagant bonnet waving in the wind. "Dev, why not ride with us?"

"A horse will travel faster than a carriage. I feel perfectly fine." Fine, but impatient.

Two days of searching and he still had not tracked Anne down. In hours, she had fashioned an escape plan of her own, one worthy of a general. Worthy of Wellington. He could imagine the praise the Iron Duke would have heaped on her for this clever plot.

"So she didn't vanish into thin air after all? Treadwell told me you had reason to think she'd gone to London. I thought she'd want to avoid Town at all costs."

"It's a long story."

Tristan grinned. "Give me a summary. I want to hear how she outwitted you."

Devon scowled. He'd found a young boy who had seen a "gentleman" sneak out from the back of an apple cart. But after that, the "gentleman" had disappeared. However, Devon had discovered his clothes neatly bundled up behind the stables of the Black Swan. Like Tris, he'd been certain she wouldn't take a stage to London.

He'd been wrong.

He briefly explained that to his friend. "It was a chance comment by a maid at the Swan that finally made me realize what Anne did. One of the girl's dresses was missing from her wardrobe, along with an old straw hat. I questioned the innkeeper, and, indeed, a woman in plain servant's style of dress had bought a ticket on the London stage two days ago." He also had his men searching for Mick Taylor, who had effectively disappeared.

"She bought a ticket? How did she get the money?"

That question haunted him.

"So you're going in pursuit?"

"Of course."

Tristan crossed his arms over his chest and grinned. His expression implied he knew something Devon did not. "Why are you going to chase her down, Dev?"

"Obviously, I—" He paused. It seemed . . . natural for him to pursue her. "She could be in danger. I can't abandon her."

He mounted Abednigo and took the reins. Barely aware of his servants or Tris and Miss Lacy watching, he set his horse trotting. Anne had gone to London. Why? Had she done it because she guessed it would be the last place he—or anyone—would look for her? Or was it because of Kat? She had been terrified that Mick Taylor had badly hurt her friend.

That would be his Cerise. She would risk her own neck to ensure Kat was safe.

As he rode out onto the road, he urged his horse to a gallop. He was two days behind Anne, with no hope of overtaking her now. But some instinct made him want to move quickly.

This morning, he'd realized that, even though he could now see, he hadn't actually taken a look at himself. He'd finally faced the mirror in his bedchamber. And discovered he wasn't at all like the man who had gone to battle. He had been mourning Rosalind then, and he'd looked grim, empty, ravaged.

Now he wore every mark of mourning, loss, and fighting on his face. A bayonet scar gouged his temple. His nose had been broken in a fall from his cavalry horse—it was no longer perfectly straight. Various scars from blades had left a trail of white lines over his jaw and his forehead. He hadn't shaved in days, and black stubble shadowed his face. He looked . . . like hell.

Anne Beddington had lived through a hell of her own. She had lost her home. Lost her father and mother. She'd ended up in a brothel that should have claimed her soul.

But she had not looked like a haunted woman. She had still looked pure and lovely, every inch a lady, no matter what she had seen, what she'd been forced to do. To do that after what she'd endured . . . it showed how strong she was. Was she strong enough, clever enough, to evade him in London?

No, she wasn't. He hadn't commanded a regiment of men for nothing.

Just as she'd done more than a fortnight ago, Anne crept up the mews behind Kat's house and used a tree to help her scramble over the back wall. She stole to the kitchen at the rear and slowly pushed open the door. Kat's plump cook, Mrs. Brown, turned quickly from the stove. "Miss Beddington? Let's get you upstairs to the mistress. She has been worried about you!"

Anne's heart lodged in her throat as she followed the cook to Kat's sitting room. She was so afraid of what she would see. Mrs. Brown cried, "It is Miss Beddington. She's returned safe."

Kat rose slowly from her chair and turned. Fury toward Mick Taylor burned in Anne's heart. "Oh, my goodness, Kat!" Bruises blossomed on Kat's cheeks and jaw. A scab had formed on her lip, where Mick had obviously split it. But, despite that, Kat held out her arms in welcome.

Anne embraced her dear friend. "Oh, Kat, were you badly hurt?"

"Nothing worse than I've endured before. But I'm so sorry, Anne. I couldn't hold out, though I tried. I told Taylor you'd gone to the Duke of March, to his hunting box. I sent you a letter to warn you, but I feared it would arrive too late. Did he find you?"

"Yes." Her stomach gave a fierce growl.

Kat's brow arched. "You can tell me everything that happened while you eat."

Anne did, speaking swiftly between mouthfuls of delicious steak and kidney pie. Kat's large brown eyes widened at every twist and turn of Anne's tale, including her revelation that she hadn't killed Madame after all. "The Duke of March rescued you from Mick?"

Anne nodded. "He wanted to help me. It was his plan to hide me while we searched for Madame Sin's true killer, but I couldn't let him take such a risk for me."

"He must have cared for you very much to offer such a thing."

"I'd helped him before he regained his sight. I assume he felt obligated to help me."

"If you went to Bow Street, could you convince them you're innocent?" Kat asked.

"I don't know. Without Mick's story, how could I? I'll be arrested. And Mick Taylor could withhold the truth and give evidence *against* me. I'd hang for certain then."

Kat set down her wineglass, frowning. "Anne, you are a viscount's daughter! You can't believe your cousin would let you hang. Surely he will help you. He's gone to a lot of trouble to find you—he must want you back very much."

"That's what frightens me. Oh, Kat, he was always horrible." Anne felt her lip wobble. She gathered her strength. "I have to leave England. I'll get money somehow. Enough to buy passage on a ship."

Kat swept to her feet, hurried over, and embraced her. "I have money, Anne."

"Kat, I can't—"

"You can. What good is money if you cannot use it to help a dear friend? This doesn't begin to repay the debt I have to your mother."

Kat had once lived in the stews beside them, in a small, dingy room like theirs. Without funds and desperate, Kat had finally got employment on the Drury Lane stage. One night she was returning home after a performance and a man attacked her. Mama heard the screams, ran outside, and rescued Kat by fighting off the man with a frying pan.

"It does, Kat," Anne said softly. "For you would be saving my life."

Chapter Nineteen

"How much for these?" Anne asked, drawing a small velvet pouch from a pocket in her cloak. Grime coated the windows of the cramped shop, situated on a narrow street off Petticoat Lane—a place where money was handed over for all kinds of goods, whether obtained legally or not. She spilled out two necklaces: a modest one with small rubies and a second with a pear-shaped sapphire. Kat had given her these. Somehow, in some way, she would repay her friend.

She watched the door nervously, as if by magic Bow Street would catch her here.

The slender man behind the counter, Mr. Timble, picked up the rubies first, his face carefully impassive. He studied them, grunting. Then he gave his assessment and she gasped in disappointment. "They're worth far more," she protested.

"It's all I'm willing to pay for them, my dear."

"What about the other?"

Timble named a second figure, also depressingly low, but it was enough for her to buy passage and start a new, frugal life in a different country.

"All right." She pushed the jewels across the counter.

He put a small stack of notes in front of her. Five-pound notes—large and colorful, something she had not seen in years. She pushed the money into her bag and slipped out of the shop. In a fog-laden lane, she found a hackney and instructed the driver to take her to the London docks.

Katherine Tate gracefully arranged her curvaceous form on a Grecian chaise. "Your Grace, how wonderful to see you, and how unexpected. Unfortunately, I had no time to dress. I am wearing nothing but my silk robe."

Devon rolled his eyes. He knew exactly what Kat's game was. He knew her from the time he attended Cyprian balls, when he used to keep mistresses, before he met Rosalind. He knew that her seductive play was intended to buy her time and distract him. She was staring at him curiously. He had ridden straight to London, stopping only at the inns along the Kings Highway for fresh horses, and had come directly to Kat's without even bothering to stop at his London house. He was aware that his clothes were disheveled and coated in road dust.

"I can see you, Kat," he said. "Miss Beddington helped me regain my sight."

Kat's kohl-darkened eyes opened wide in surprise that he didn't believe. She laughed in silvery delight. "How wonderful! Impetuous Anne did heal you, after all. But where is she? I thought she hoped to make this affair with you into one of a longer duration."

He could tell she was putting on an act. "I don't know, Kat. I came here so you could tell me where she is."

"I have no idea, Your Grace. I have not seen her since she went running off to your hunting box, determined to seduce you."

"You're lying, love."

"I am not," she said, her voice a seductive caress. "I have not seen her since she left." Graceful fingers stroked the edge of her robe, tracing the red silk—*cerise* silk—from her pale throat to the shadowed valley between her large breasts. Her attempt at distraction wasn't working. All he could think of was Anne. He had never been so obsessed with a woman before.

Courtesans like Kat were his past. And what he wanted, what had driven him here, finally struck him. He wanted Anne to be in his future. He wanted her back. He could see, but he still wanted her to read to him, he still wanted to walk in the rain with her, ride with her, be with her. This wasn't about rescuing her. It was about taking her, keeping her, having her. And that scared him. He wanted to possess Anne with the same driving need that had made him steal Rosalind away from Gerald, his former best friend.

"Is something wrong, Your Grace?"

He pulled his thoughts in line. "You've made yourself up well, but I can see the damage from Mick Taylor's attack. Did it take long for him to force you to betray Anne?"

Pain flashed in Kat's exquisitely made-up brown eyes. "I did not want to betray her. I tried to endure it, but that man is a monster."

"Why shelter her, Kat? Taking risks for another woman, a competitor, isn't like you."

Kat waved an elegant hand. "Her mother saved my life once."

He leveled his gaze at her, drinking in the nervous tics of her jaw. "Kat, if you didn't know for a fact that Anne was safe, you'd be upset, given Taylor is after her. You wouldn't be so calm."

She stiffened on the chaise. "I didn't think she was in danger from Taylor—he was working for her cousin. Surely, her cousin would not want to hurt her."

"So why would you not tell Taylor where she was? Why make him beat it out of you?"

Kat's eyes widened and flicked nervously around the room, as though she was seeking escape. He reached out and clasped her wrist to remind her there was none.

"All right." She sighed. "I knew she was in danger from Mick Taylor and her lunatic cousin."

Devon tightened his grip, hating having to be rough. "Why do you call her cousin a lunatic?"

"What would you call a man who set his young cousin on his lap and touched her in ways that made her feel ill? That is the sort of man he was. He began fondling her when she was only eight years of age and he was twenty. He is a perverted madman who is obsessed with her. But I am telling you the truth, Your Grace. She did *not* come back here."

"She did. Kat, I expect you to trust me with the truth—we have known each other for a long time. You know I would not hurt Anne. She has nothing to fear from me." But his gut was churning at what he now knew about Anne's cousin.

"Of course I know that! But she does not want you to help her. She only wants to escape. She has fallen in love with you, of course."

He frowned. "That's not true."

She wagged her finger. "You must listen, Your Grace. Anne does not want to hurt you or your family by putting you in a scandal. She is leaving you to protect you. It is better if you let her go."

It was not. He could not let her run with no money or protection. After all she had done for him, he owed her so much. "How does Anne plan to escape?"

"She would not want me to tell you. Why are you so determined to catch her, Your Grace?"

He didn't want to threaten Kat, after what she'd been

through at the hands of Mick Taylor. "I need to find her because she is accused of murder—"

"You aren't looking for her to turn her over to Bow Street and the law, are you?" Kat cried. "She does not deserve to hang! Her madam was a cruel witch, and if Anne killed her with a fireplace poker, I can promise you *that* woman deserved her fate."

"She claims to be innocent." He watched her eyes. Did Kat believe it?

"Of course she is." But Kat didn't sound convincing.

"Either way, I can help her," he pointed out. "But unless I know where she is, there's nothing I can do for her. I rode directly from my hunting box to Town in pursuit of her. I am hungry, exhausted, sore, and my head is pounding. You will tell me the truth, Kat. I have no intention of leaving until you do."

"She is just your mistress. Why not let her go?"

"Kat, if you care about Anne, you'll let me help her. Trust me with your friend's life."

Her teeth tore at her lip.

"Unless you want Taylor or Bow Street to find her first."

"She is planning to escape England by ship," Kat admitted. "I gave her two necklaces so she could buy her passage. How could I not help her? She came back to London, risking capture, to ensure I was all right."

"Where is she planning to go?"

"I don't know. I don't think she knows yet. All she is thinking about is running. Remember, her heart is most likely breaking—no woman thinks clearly through that."

Was he too late? Had she already gone?

The docks stank of dead fish, muck, rotting wood, and unwashed sailors. Devon realized he probably didn't smell much better. Sweat, from hard riding, made a filmy layer between his shirt and his back. It soaked his hair beneath his beaver hat.

At a public house on Wapping High Street, he tied up his horse. A lad hurried out with a tankard of ale. Devon tossed it back to quench his thirst, threw the lad some coins, and strode to the hubbub of the port.

Where was she? Dozens of ships bobbed on the water, hundreds of sailors teemed on the docks. There were women too. Wives in dull dresses, whores in garish garb. Was Anne still wearing the servant's dress and hat? Or she could be disguised as one of the women in plain brown wool or one of the tarts in scarlet silk.

Suddenly he wondered: Would he know her?

He would. He had seen her face for only minutes, but the wide eyes, lush mouth, and delicate oval face were burned on his brain. At every posting inn on the way here, he'd given her description. Two miles outside London he finally found a man who had seen her. A groom had witnessed her fighting off the advances of a drunken gentleman. Devon's heart had gone ice cold, until the groom told him she had driven her knee between her would-be attacker's legs. The man had dropped to the ground, and Anne had escaped.

Devon found one of the shipping offices, gave Anne's description, and asked if such a woman had bought a ticket. The young clerk shook his head.

He tried several more, with no success. He stood on one of the docks, watching sailors carry barrels up the gangplank to the hold. Perhaps she had bought her passage privately. After all, what captain would refuse her?

Where would Anne want to go—where would she flee to spend the rest of her life? He had no idea. That was the problem. He knew very little about Cerise, the courtesan who had been his mistress, and he knew nothing about Anne Beddington. How much of Cerise had been an act? He believed her strength, her determination, the stories she told about her past—about walking in the rain with her grandfather and reading him books—those were part of the *real* Anne.

Still, he knew nothing that gave him a clue to what kind of escape she would seek. The warm breezes of the West Indies? Exotic India? Opportunity in America?

Grimly, he began to search the taverns. In a low-ceilinged place called the Anchor, he found a captain of a ship scheduled to leave on the tide the next day. The captain was blond and grizzled, with the hard eyes of a man who drank to quell devils. "A female passenger?" he mused. "I might have taken payment from a fetching lass in exchange for passage to Bombay. But my memory's foggy. I need a drink to clear it."

Hell, Devon could imagine why this man would have sold a passage to Anne. One look and the captain would have been salivating.

A bosomy barmaid gave a sarcastic laugh. "Aye, that'll help you, Rogers."

Devon bought the man a tankard of ale, but he gripped the man's wrist before he could take a drink. "Answer my question and you can have your drink in peace. The woman I'm looking for is slender, with red hair and green eyes. She is about two-and-twenty years of age."

The captain frowned at his captured arm. "My lass meets the description. Except her hair was dark—black ringlets. She wore a hooded cloak, but I caught a glimpse of her hair. I'm looking forward to getting a peek at the rest of her—"

Devon's blow connected with the man's jaw. The captain jerked back for one brief instant, then slumped sideways and slithered from the taproom bench to the sticky floor. Devon set down the tankard he'd rescued.

Anne had red hair. But then, the color of a woman's hair could be changed. Easily done with a wig or dye.

This had to be Anne. Good thing he had found out when the ship was sailing before he'd questioned the man about her, because it would be a while before Rogers came to.

First he had to go home. Then he would hunt again for Anne. He would either track her down tonight or catch her here tomorrow before she got on the ship.

"Mother, come here! Devon is riding up the drive. He's home!"

The feminine shout sent Devon hurtling back to the days when he would arrive home and his four sisters' arguments could be heard before his carriage stopped.

His heart lurched, and he reined in his horse on the strip of gravel that swept in front of March House. As he dismounted, footmen cheered around him. He hadn't been here since he left for war—the greeting was in celebration of his reputation as a war hero, a title he didn't want and didn't deserve.

"Devon! Devon! Thank heaven you're home! Why didn't you tell us you were coming!"

In an explosion of shouting and squealing, two of his sisters rushed down the steps toward him. It was Lizzie and Win, both unmarried and still at home. Tears spilled to their cheeks, tears that wrapped around his heart and tried to crush it. Lizzie, dark curls bouncing, rocketed into him as Caro had just days before. Lizzie had been even more of a hoyden than Caro was. She never would have worn such an elegant—and low-cut—gown.

Win danced around him, her blue eyes shining. The last time he'd seen Win, her hair was in braids—not pinned up in this gleaming golden design of curls.

"You look . . . exactly like you always did, Devon!" Lizzie cried.

Win wiped at her eyes. "We were afraid. So afraid you'd never come home," she whispered.

He had to admit his own eyes burned. "I'm sorry it took me so long." Lizzie moved back and Win hugged him. Her arms slid around his neck. She smelled of violets. She had been sickly when young and had always been delicate. "Win, you shouldn't be running full tilt at me," he admonished, his heart aching. "And, Lizzie—you've grown so much."

Lizzie let out a high-pitched squeal. "You can see! You can, can't you?"

"It's true, Lizard," he said teasingly. "My sight came back to me."

Win embraced him tightly. "Thank heaven," she breathed. "Of course, that means Mama will be ensuring you are hastily wed, Devon. She will refuse to wait any longer for you to give her grandchildren."

"Regaining my eyesight was a miracle," he said lightly. "But I can't produce a baby for her instantaneously, I'm afraid."

Lizzie's eyes, bright as lilacs, flashed wickedly. "She believes she can find a wife for you instantaneously. The *ton* is here for the end of parliament, before leaving for hunting. You are to be dragged to all the balls, musicales, and fashionable parades through Hyde Park. The matchmaking is about to begin."

The young maid bobbed a swift, respectful curtsy. "Her Grace is in the nursery, Your Grace. Lord and Lady Cavendish have come and brought wee Lord Peregrine."

Devon gave the servant a nod. Then he took the stairs two at time. After three years, it was time to see his mother and face the consequences for not coming home. If she despised him, he deserved it. Anne had been correct, of course. He should have come home.

His mother's perfume, along with the strong scents of a nursery in use, reached him at the top of the attic stairs. When he was young, he had been in awe of his mother. To him, she shone like the sun; she'd been as dazzling, as warming, as blinding. With her lovely voice, her tempered and controlled emotions, her famous wit, she had always been every inch a duchess. She and his father had been a love match.

He stood in the doorway. His mother held a bundle of white blankets in her arms. She sat on a window seat, her sky-blue silk skirts spreading around her like a pool. Sunlight touched her blond hair, revealing a large amount of gray. He drank in all the color surrounding her. Pain, regret, hit him like a blow to the chest. She looked so content, so quiet, he was tempted to turn and leave her alone.

"Devon, I know you are there," she said, softly but firmly. "You cannot sneak away."

He stepped into the room, cheeks hot, certain he looked sheepish.

Deep lines crossed his mother's forehead and framed her mouth. Three years had gone by, but he'd apparently aged her by ten. In her arms, his cherub of a nephew, Peregrine, slept.

Anne had told him his mother's last letter was stained with tears. Given that he had gone to war despite his family's disapproval, he hadn't been sure whether he'd be welcomed back. Blindness had given him an excuse not to find out. He moved to his mother's side, dropped to one knee, and gently stroked his nephew's little arms through the blanket. His mother's blue eyes glowed with delight as she smiled down at her grandson.

"Is it true, Devon? Obviously it is. You've regained your sight."

He focused acutely on her voice—on its melodious rhythm, on the slight hesitation, the sadness. He heard things beyond the words that he never would have before. Anne had been right. His mother was trying to hide a great deal of fear and pain, and he now knew it. "I'm sorry—"

"For what?"

"A boatload of things," he admitted. "Sorry for not coming home. For making you worry. For putting myself in harm's way in battle. I'm sorry for putting you and Father through fear and pain. I'm sorry I pursued Rosalind and caused a scandal when Father told me to let her go."

"Are you sorry you went to war?"

At that, he had to shake his head. Which seemed insane. Why wouldn't he have preferred to stay in England, to never know what it was like to watch thousands of men die in mere hours, never lose his sight, never make choices that led to men's deaths and left women widowed and children fatherless? "It was my duty, as much as it was the duty of any man who was there, to fight for my country. I've got so much grief and so many regrets about war, I can't even begin to untangle them. But I had to go."

His mother stood, cradling the baby's head to her shoulder. Her eyes were red-rimmed. "I am so glad to have you back s-safe." Two tears leapt from her eyes and ran down her cheeks.

He'd never seen his mother cry. Duchesses were always strong, his mother used to say. If a duchess let herself cry, a whole family could unravel.

Devon wrapped his arms around her, careful not to disturb his slumbering nephew. For the first time in Devon's life, his mother pressed her forehead to his chest and cried. His hands stroked her back awkwardly, but he soothed her and promised he was going to be safe now.

Except that was a lie—because, to save Anne, he was

going to have to hunt down a killer and risk another scandal.

His mother lifted her head. A smile lifted her lips. “Now *I* am sorry. You have come home, and you should be greeted with smiles, not weeping. You’ve been through so much.”

“So have you. I left and then you lost Father.” He wasn’t certain if he should speak of it now but it had been more than a year. “If it’s not too difficult for you to talk about,” he said softly, “I’d like to know how he died.”

She lifted her chin. “I don’t really know, Devon. William was found in his study, by one of the footmen. At first, the poor servant thought your father was sleeping in his chair. Finally he summoned the courage to shake William, but your father did not awaken. It appears his heart gave out. I like to think he simply closed his eyes for a nap and did not wake up.”

She wore a sad smile, but she appeared to be strong. Stronger now than when she’d cried over him.

“How did you cope with it?” he asked. “You loved him so much. When Rosalind died, I thought I would go out of my mind. I couldn’t see how I would ever stop grieving.” He looked around the nursery. Five small beds were arranged in neat lines along the walls. He remembered playing with his father up here. His father had seemed so huge but had sat down in a child’s chair and helped him build castles from blocks. Impossible to think the man who had shaped so much of his life—with kindness, lectures, and battles involving shouting and stomping on his part—could now be gone.

“It hurts. I suspect it always will, Devon. That’s why it is so important to seek out love, to celebrate happiness, to find joy.” She smiled down at the baby.

“Blissful thing,” he said quietly. “Tearful only when he isn’t fed right away.” The lad’s mouth worked, as though the little one had heard him and was now dreaming of his milk.

"The birth of Caroline's baby has been such a wonderfully happy event," his mother said. "It has brightened all our lives and done much to push aside sorrow and worry."

Sorrow and worry he had caused.

"I want our family to know more happiness." She sounded decisive. "There are many blessed events to come. Charlotte will have her baby before Christmas—perhaps she might even have twins again. I am determined to see Win and Elizabeth married next season. And as for you—"

He held up his hands, but she went on. "You deserve the happiness of marriage, Devon, and the joy of having a family. This will be my campaign—to find you a bride, to watch you fall in love. I want to see you happy."

He hadn't been happy for a long time, until Anne had come into his life. Would he have been as happy to see Caroline, to see his brand-new nephew, if Anne had not worked so hard to help him cope, if she hadn't lightened his heart? He owed her so much. And the only way he could repay her was to make her safe.

His mother's voice cut through his thoughts. ". . . very eligible ladies," she was saying. "After we celebrated peace in June, once it was known that you would be coming home, there were several young ladies who decided not to accept offers of marriage."

"Even though I was blind?" he asked wryly.

She hesitated. "That was not known at first. And now, of course, it is not an issue."

He shook his head. "I've changed, Mother. I don't know if I can marry a delicate young lady. I have nightmares and fight and shout in my sleep. I'm not as bad as I was, but I would terrify a gently bred girl. Besides, I thought you wanted us all to marry for love, not duty."

"Of course I do. I firmly believe in love! I believe you shall find it without any difficulty. And I know exactly the place to begin. The Duchess of Richmond is holding a ball—"

A ball. Three years ago he had looked across a crowded ballroom and seen Rosalind, and after that it was as if the rest of the room had vanished into darkness. All sound had turned into a roar, and he'd stalked across the dance floor toward her, not even noticing who had collided with him and who had stepped hastily out of his way. "I'm not going to fall in love across a ballroom floor again," he murmured.

His mother lifted a brow and he tried to explain. "Father described falling in love as the moment when a man is standing there, minding his own business, and suddenly she—the woman who is going to be the most important person in his life—smiles at him and changes his world forever. It's not going to happen again."

"Of course not. I might believe in love, but not at first sight."

Devon felt himself rock back on his heels. "What about Father?"

"I didn't fall in love with your father the first time I saw him. In fact, he did not impress me at all. But he was persistent, and I soon came to appreciate how he was different from any other gentleman I'd met. He fascinated me and, little by little, I fell in love."

Little by little. "If it wasn't a consuming passion, how did you recognize it for love?"

A small smile curved her lips, as though memories of her love with his father had instantly summoned happiness. "In many ways. Ones that creep up on you until one day you realize you smile each time you see your beloved, until you cannot imagine waking up without him, until you cannot imagine a life without him."

"I don't know if I would be ready to fall in love again.

It hurt like the blazes the first time." But even as he said it, Devon knew it was a stupid thing to say to his mother. She had lost the grand love of her life, yet she'd survived the pain, the grief. What was it about women that made them so strong?

"That does not mean it also will the second time."

"Maybe. But I'm not going to a ball. I have a list of people to find now that I'm in London. Now that I can see."

"People to find?" His mother echoed. "What do you mean?"

He told her. Of the missing wife and child of Captain Tanner, the man he had not been able to save. "I hired an investigator to find them. I haven't had a report for two weeks. I need to know what is happening. Also, I need to search for my mistress."

"*Mistress?*" With a cautious eye on her grandson, his mother swept across the room to a cradle. She laid down the baby and tucked a blanket around him.

Then she surprised him, fiddling with the lace-trimmed neckline of her gown like an awkward girl. Finally she took a deep breath, as though gathering courage. "Caroline told me about the rather unorthodox circumstances of my grandson's birth. She told me your mistress helped her before and during the labor. She also admitted she asked your courtesan for advice on how to entice her husband. . . ." His mother blushed crimson.

Devon took a step back. Caro had told their mother about that? God, had she given details of what Anne said? No, he didn't want to know. He did not want to have that discussion.

He had the suspicion his mother felt the same way. She walked to the window that looked out over the rear garden. "Caro spoke very warmly of your ladybird, Devon. She claimed the woman is her *friend* and that this was the woman who wrote a letter to me. Your mistress wrote to me because you would not do it! I have to admit I was scandalized."

He planned to apologize, but different words came out of his mouth. "Don't be. My mistress was once a lady—a viscount's daughter. She is the most remarkable, courageous woman I have ever met. Now I need to leave and find her. She has been wrongfully accused of murder."

Being able to read again—it was glorious. In the library, Devon drew out a large, leather-bound book: *Debrett's Peerage*. He flipped the pages to find the entry on Anne Beddington's family. Damn, it was good to be able to do this with his own eyes. But he had to admit: If Anne read the *Peerage* in her lovely voice, she could make even these dry facts sound erotic.

He ran his finger down until he saw it. The title of Viscount Norbrook had been created in the early 1700s, and he traced the list until he got to Anne's father. *Fourth Viscount Norbrook, b. 1768, d. 1808, m. Millicent Mariah de Mournay, 1789. Children—Anne Mariah, b. 1793.*

At Anne's name, his hand stilled but his heart leapt into action, beating hard. When had his heart slammed into his chest like this, other than when there was danger and risk? The only times he could remember involved Rosalind. The first time Lady Rosalind had shyly caught his eye and smiled at him. The first time he had touched her hand. Their first kiss. He had been sexually experienced since the age of fifteen, but Rosalind's very smile had made his heart pound harder than any other woman ever had. Now just seeing Anne's name had his heart thundering.

He stared again at the entry. De Mournay was the family name of the Marquis of Wrothshire. Had Anne's mother been related to a marquis? Anne should never have ended up in the slums. The address given for the current viscount, Anne's blackguard cousin, was Brook Street.

But when Devon arrived at Viscount Norbrook's house in the ducal carriage and sent a footman to rap on the door, he learned that Anne's cousin was not at home. The viscount was having a private training session in fencing at Henry Angelo's school.

Devon commanded his coachman to take him to Angelo's. He had a membership there. It would feel good to pick up a sword again.

Chapter Twenty

One look at Anne's cousin, and Devon knew he was staring at a bully. And he sorely wanted to break the bastard's nose with his fist.

Instead, he stripped to his shirt and waistcoat, grasped a foil, and stalked over to Viscount Norbrook, who was grunting, sweating, and trying to defeat William McTurk, successor to Henry Angelo and now the master. Throughout the large practice room, gentlemen stared, nudged one another. Apparently all of London was now learning that the Duke of March had regained his sight. Even McTurk, in the middle of clashing foils with Norbrook, glanced to him in surprise.

The viscount drove the tip against the elder swordsman's padded tunic. "First blood," he crowed triumphantly. Anne's cousin had blond hair, carefully styled in tousled waves, and the typical "fair-haired boy" good looks that hid a black heart.

"The student has defeated the master," Norbrook shouted. Frowning, the viscount finally realized his opponent was staring over his shoulder. Anne's cousin turned, obviously angered to have his victory diluted, then took a fast step back. "Your Grace." Norbrook swept a bow. "I am surprised to encounter you here. I heard you had been left blinded in battle—"

"You heard correctly. I was fortunate enough to regain my sight."

With an exclamation of congratulations, McTurk came forward, his foil tucked beneath his arm. "Your Grace, it is good to see you."

"Thank you, McTurk. I thought I would have a bout with Norbrook." He stared down his nose at Anne's cousin. "I have matters to discuss with you, sir, concerning one of your female relatives."

Norbrook's throat moved as he swallowed. "Indeed. I wouldn't mind engaging swords while we discuss my wayward cousin." Norbrook dropped his voice to a harsh growl, one only Devon could hear. "I assume you speak of the fallen woman of our family, Anne Beddington? I had come to Town to rescue her, only to discover she had become a prostitute and to learn that you, Your Grace, were enjoying her favors at your hunting box. It appears my cousin is no longer respectable. She has become a disgusting whore."

Devon snapped the foil up instantly, pressing the tip to Norbrook's throat. Norbrook was the blackguard here, but *he* felt in the wrong over this and it angered him. "Speak that way about the lady again, and we'll meet at dawn."

Norbrook's eyes blazed with fury as he was forced to retreat from the rapier's point—fury he was too cowardly to pursue, Devon suspected. "I speak the truth, Your Grace. Surely you know of your mistress's past. She serviced countless men in that foul Wapping Street brothel."

"The fault for that lies with you. You forced her out of her home."

"I did not. Her mother did not want her daughter to enter into a marriage with me. She took her daughter away. Her mother's behavior was scandalous—affairs, orgies, lewd house parties. The family turned their backs on them both. I did not. I searched for Anne. Alas, I found her too late." Blade swishing, Norbrook lunged.

"An interesting story." Devon parried, riposted. In a quiet, deadly voice, he said, "I was told you'd been touching your cousin in perverse ways that frightened her since she was eight."

Norbrook pressed again, driving the foil toward Devon's heart. An easy blow to deflect. The viscount winced as Devon pushed his blade sharply to the left, twisting the man's wrist.

Bouncing on his toes, Norbrook retreated. "That, Your Grace, is an outright lie. Where in blazes did you hear such a thing?" He launched forward, as if expressing rage at a slander.

Devon deflected the waving foil with relaxed moves of his own. He glared down at Norbrook—who was shorter and pudgy—as though he had noticed a pile of horse dung in the path of his boot. "From someone who knows the truth," he said coldly.

"Who? Do you mean my cousin, the woman you've taken on as your *whore*?"

Pure venom spat out with the quiet word. Devon felt his body flinch with guilt. "No. I demanded the truth after I had to rescue her from the grip of the violent brute you sent to retrieve her. However, she kept this information from me. I assure you I had no idea who Miss Beddington truly was. Unlike you—who forced her into ruination." Hades, what was he doing? Why was he explaining himself to this piece of garbage? True, he hadn't known she was a viscount's daughter, but he had suspected she came from a lady's background. Yet that hadn't stopped him from bedding her, from treating her like a courtesan.

It was what *she* had wanted him to do. But that was still no excuse.

Norbrook clashed his sword against Devon's with a triumphant smirk on his face. "*You* were the one to help in her ruination, Your Grace."

"You attacked her." He wanted to toss aside these blunted foils so he could use his fists and do some real damage. But was it Norbrook he was so furious at, or himself? Anne could never go back to the world in which she belonged. Not after being ruined at a brothel. Not after being his courtesan. "Mick Taylor told her you still intended to bed her," Devon growled. "A generous-hearted man, aren't you, to your destitute cousin after the way you abused her?"

"That man was the lackey of a whore. His word cannot be believed. I will admit I hired him to search for Anne. My intent was only to help her." The pale eyes were watchful. Norbrook flicked his tongue nervously over his lips.

With foils colliding, Devon drove him back. "You frightened her. She sensed that your interest was sick and wrong." She hadn't said that, but he remembered the way she had shivered when she talked about her cousin.

Norbrook's flush of anger deepened. Spittle flecked his lips. "What right do you have to look down on me?" Like a typical bully, he lashed out with rage, though he kept his voice low. He was slashing madly with his weapon, but Devon had taken command of the fight. "*You* soiled her, Your Grace. I would provide her with a home. With a chance to live quietly and respectably."

The barb hit home more than he would ever admit. But he struggled to keep control, even as guilt slammed into him. If he wasn't careful, guilt could make him seriously injure this man. "As your mistress?" he snarled.

"Better mine than yours." The man was shaking. "Are

you going to keep her as your tart even though she's a murderess? Did you know *that*? She killed her madam, smashed the woman's head in with a fireplace poker. Do you still want her now?"

"Yes!" He shouted the answer with such fury that silence hit the room. Foils stopped clacking. Heads turned. "I know she's innocent," he said quietly. He gave two swift blows with his foil. Norbrook cried out as his rapier was knocked free of his hand and clattered to the floor, leaving him unarmed.

The man's eyes showed a blend of fear and pure hatred. "I want to see her," Norbrook gasped. "Regardless of the sins she has committed, she is my cousin. Where is she, Your Grace? I must know. Perhaps there is some way I can help her."

Devon lifted an icy ducal brow. "She has no desire to see you. And I will make it my work to crush you like the insect you are."

Bright spots of red bloomed on Norbrook's cheeks. His hand shook as he swept up his fallen sword. "I can offer her the dignity of a quiet life, away from vicious rumors, away from gentlemen who will assault her because they know her to be a whore. What sort of life will she have with you? She'll likely end up hanging for her crime. Or are you planning to buy her freedom, using your wealth and power? Then what will become of her? Someday you will discard her. If the little fool remains with you, she'll end up abandoned on the street, a clapped-out old jade."

He spoke loudly enough for others to hear. Devon's heart roared in his ears. He took a menacing step toward the viscount, who scuttled away but tried to do it with his head high.

Out of the corner of his eye, Devon saw William McTurk walking toward him. Norbrook's reactions and behavior did not make sense. The man had spat venom at first over Anne's ruination, and now was playing the noble relative who would offer help and rescue.

McTurk bowed. Devon gave his tutor a nod. "Before I leave, I should thank you. Thank you for the skills you taught me over the years. They saved my life many times in battle."

The master bowed once more. His gaze slid to the direction in which Norbrook had skulked. "You have always been my prize pupil, Your Grace, the student who did indeed surpass his master. However, I must remind you of the rules—this place is not for you to exorcise personal battles and grudges."

"It won't happen again." No, next time he worked on his private grudge with Norbrook, he'd do it someplace where he could give the bully a good pounding. But what in hell was he going to do about the viscount? Would the man cease his pursuit of Anne?

What he had to do first was find Anne and ensure she wasn't arrested. The best way to do that was to find the actual murderer. After that, what would he do with her? He wanted her. But he couldn't keep her as his mistress now that he knew who she really was.

Number 10 Bow Street, Magistrates' Court. Devon walked past the court entrance to the door that would take him to the offices. In mere minutes, he was seated across from Sir John Lawrence, the current magistrate. Sir John was an old friend of his father's and, despite age and graying hair, the man was alert and astute.

Sir John poured a small amount of brandy in two glasses and held one out. Devon took it, stared at it, turning it in his hand. He hadn't touched the drink since Anne had commanded his servants not to bring it to him. Wryly, he recognized how much she had changed his world. He had to wonder: If it had not been for

Anne, would he have stayed alone in his hunting box, drinking himself into a stupor for the rest of his life?

"To the return of the prodigal son." Sir John lifted his glass. "One of England's famous heroes of battle."

"To my father," Devon returned, lifting his glass. He took only a small sip to toast his father and felt the clamp of grief around his heart. To Sir John, he admitted, "I regret the fact that my father and I fought on the last night I saw him."

The wooden chair creaked as Sir John leaned back. "March, I can tell you your father was deeply proud of you. You were a responsible, intelligent, and beloved officer. I was told by your commanding officer, and by gentlemen who served as officers under you, that you were well respected by your men."

"You might be mistaken about my father's feelings. He didn't approve of me going to war. Since I was his heir, he accused me of being both selfish and irresponsible for doing it."

Sir John shook his head. "Your father loved you dearly, and he respected you."

Devon wished it was as easy for him to believe as it was for Sir John to say.

The magistrate lifted his glass once more. "Another toast—this one to a medical miracle, I think. Did you regain your sight through the work of doctors here? I believe you had visited the London Dispensary for Curing Diseases of the Eye and Ear?"

"I did, but it wasn't the work of the doctors." No, it was the work of a stubborn woman. "I fell and hit my head on a rock. The physicians had told me my sight could come back after a blow to the head." It was time to get to the point. "Sir John, I came here about a woman you are searching for. I believe Bow Street thinks she is responsible for the murder of her madam."

The magistrate set down his glass. "What is your interest in this case, Your Grace?"

"Devon. I believe the woman is innocent," he said carefully. "What evidence do you have of her guilt?"

Sir John lifted a brow but said, "Several witnesses claim she argued with the madam, a thoroughly despicable woman by the name of Mrs. Clara Meadows."

Devon's lips twisted. "I believe Mrs. Meadows called herself Madame Sin. Were there witnesses to the confrontation? Anyone who will say Anne Beddington struck a killing blow?"

Now both of Sir John's brows were raised. "Anne Beddington? The name I was given by Mick Taylor was Annalise Black. You seem to know a great deal about what happened, Devon."

She hadn't used her real name, even in the brothel. Had that been to protect her family—the family that had done nothing to protect her? Or had she done it in the hope that she could return to her old life, without anyone knowing what she'd been forced to do? "Do you have a witness or any real proof that Miss Beddington killed the woman? It's my understanding Mrs. Meadows was struck unconscious but was not dead. Someone else killed her later that night."

"I didn't assume instantly the woman was guilty. My Runners spoke with all the whores and servants, but each had an alibi."

"All of them?" Devon countered. "The girls would have been in bedrooms with men during the night. Easy enough for one to slip away and kill the madam. The servants would have had the same opportunity. Any of the clients at the brothel could have done it as well."

Sir John grimaced. "Had to tread carefully while interviewing them. All were gentlemen, and half were members of the peerage. Devon, the women gave their clients alibis, and of course the men insisted they had spent all their time in view of at least one of the whores."

"What whore wouldn't give an alibi for money? Someone is lying."

"No doubt. The problem is trying to prove it. Devon, given the amount of information you have, I must ask you: Do you know where Miss Anne Beddington is?"

"No. At this moment, no idea." It was the truth.

"Devon, you almost sacrificed your life in war to protect king and country. Do not take the law into your own hands here. If you have this girl, bring her to me. It's better that we find the truth than that you harbor a fugitive. Your father was like a brother to me, but I cannot allow either your position or my feelings for your family to stay my hand if I have to prosecute Anne Beddington for murder and you for abetting the flight of a criminal."

"Kat, what are you doing here? How did you even know where to find me?" Anne firmly pushed the door closed after her friend came into her small, gloomy room. She slid the bolt across. It was so good to see Kat, but . . . "I told you I couldn't see you ever again, for your safety! Mick hasn't come back, has he? I'm so afraid he will think you know where I am now, and he'll hurt you again."

"Anne, you must calm down. I am fine. As for finding you . . ." Kat sat down on the one wooden chair. "I thought you would return here. After all, it's a place we both know very well." Her friend swept her gaze around. "You have money now, Anne. You do not have to stay here."

"It's only until tomorrow morning." Compared to some of the foul lodging houses she and her mother had been forced to stay in, this was almost luxury.

"The Duke of March came to see me today. He pursued you to Town. He rode straight here, rode like the devil. Anne, he wants to help you. Perhaps he can. Why won't you let him try?"

"I can't—" She was ready to list every reason she had already given why she would not put Devon at risk of harm or scandal, but Kat lifted her hand.

"Anne, are you running away from the charge of murder or from your heart?"

"From my heart? What do you mean?" But she knew, didn't she? Kat had guessed she had fallen in love with Devon. "If it was just because I'd foolishly fallen in love, I wouldn't sail halfway across the world, Kat. I would simply recover from a broken heart."

"You recover only when you stop loving hopelessly. Perhaps you fear you can't do that."

"I have to go, Kat." She snatched up a page from the table. "I've written a letter to my cousin. I'm going to post it tomorrow morning, when I go to the docks. When it's delivered to Sebastian, I'll be safely at sea, where he can't touch me. It tells him I've gone to Boston. I want him to know I've gone, so he will leave you alone."

"The duke wants to find the truth of who murdered your madam. He wants to set you free."

"I won't ever be free. Not as long as my cousin wants me."

"I told the duke a little about what your cousin did to you."

Anne felt her eyes grow huge with horror. "You shouldn't have! I don't want him to know—"

"Why not? It made him understand what kind of perverse beast Norbrook is."

"I—I'm ashamed of it. I should not have let it happen. I—"

Kat firmly shook her head. "It was not your fault. You

were a child and you did as you were told. Believe me, I understand what you endured."

"He didn't do anything really . . . very bad. Not until the night he came into my room, and I was older then. Before that, it was just sitting on his lap, touches, kisses. He did want to marry me—"

"Anne, stop! It was wrong of him to touch you when you did not want it. He was wrong; you were not." Kat smiled. "And I do not believe March will break your heart—I don't think he will ever let you go. However, I suspect you are breaking his."

After Bow Street, Devon had gone to the office of his investigator, Wynter. He received a report on the search for Captain Tanner's missing wife and child. He gave Wynter a description of Anne and asked him to take some men to the docks in the morning. Then he headed to the Wapping Street brothel where Anne Beddington had been a prisoner for five years.

Sex and opium scented the place. The walls were hung with crimson, and once he stepped out of the foyer, he was confronted with an enormous oil painting of a nude. Life-size painted breasts pointed right at his eyes.

At least he'd never been to this place before. He would have hated to think he'd come here when Anne was a prisoner only a few feet away.

But he'd been to brothels like this. He'd gone for pleasure, while for Anne this had been hell. He had come to places like this because he'd been raised by his libertine grandfather to believe he should. To prove his manhood. Now he saw what an idiot he'd been. His father had told him once that any idiot could sate his lust. It took a clever man, his father had said, to fall in love and delight in having a wife as a partner, in bed and out.

He walked into the salon, trying to look like a rich

lord with nothing on his mind but the pursuit of pleasure. Strange, he had no idea how to look the part now.

Men lounged on the sofas in the large salon. Most had a glass of liquor in hand and an attentive half-naked woman draped over them.

Anne. His heart hadn't ached like this since he'd lost Rosalind.

Something touched his waist, startling him. He looked down to see two hands sliding around his body. "Aren't you a handsome one?" a woman cooed. One hand dove down and clamped on his crotch. "Want to go up to me bed?"

He hauled her hand away and turned. She was so close, he smacked into her breasts. The urge to curtly send her away was overwhelming. He forced a lazy drawl. "Perhaps later. I was interested in a particular lady tonight. I believe her name is Anne?"

The woman drew back. "Annie? Oh, sir, you see . . ." She floundered a bit, and he watched her. "Annie isn't here anymore."

"I didn't think she would be." He drew out a note—five pounds. A fortune for a woman who likely never saw any of the money she earned for her madam. "Since she is wanted for a murder she didn't commit. I would like information about that."

The woman glanced around with swift, fearful eyes. "How . . . how did you know? At Bow Street, do they know?"

"Not yet. But soon they will. Can you tell me exactly what happened here that night? If you can, my dear, I promise to give you enough money to leave this place. To start again, do whatever you want. My offer stands for any of the other women here. Anyone who can help me find the real killer of Mrs. Meadows will be amply rewarded."

Her deep breath pushed her breasts almost over her low neckline. "Are you a Runner?"

"No, my dear. I'm a duke."

She gasped. "Then come with me to my bedchamber, Your Grace. There's another girl who knows what happened. She *saw* it. If you'll give us that reward, I'll get her to tell you the truth."

The bosomy prostitute propelled a slender girl into the bedroom, glanced behind her, then shut the door. "Your Grace, this is my daughter, Sukey."

Dear God, the girl quivering in front of him looked barely sixteen years of age. "Why is your daughter here?"

"What else is she to do? She's been working here since she was thirteen years old."

Devon shuddered. No wonder Anne had been driven to save those young innocents. No wonder she had risked everything to do it. Anne Beddington humbled him. To Sukey, he smiled gently. "Your mother tells me you saw Madame Sin's murder."

"Go on, Sukey," her mother urged. "You can tell His Grace everything. He's going to take care of us. There's a reward—enough for us to leave here and do anything we wish."

He took the girl's hand and guided her to sit on the side of the bed. She clambered onto its edge and perched. She wore only a shift. "I heard someone shouting in Madame Sin's rooms, so I peeked in. I saw Annie hit Madame with the poker. Then she pushed three little girls out the window and jumped out herself. Mick came toward the door after that, so I got scared and I ran away." The girl paused. "You just want me to talk? You don't want me to play with you?"

"No." God, no. He launched up, pulled the counterpane off the bed, and draped it around her. "Cover yourself, my dear child. You'll catch your death of cold." Without hope, he asked, "Did you see anything else, Sukey?"

She nodded vigorously. "Mick went out to chase after Annie. I went back to Madame's room, to see if she was dead, but Madame was moving on the floor, moaning. Then her eyes opened, and she saw me."

"What did you do?" he asked softly. Inside, he was soaring with relief.

"I thought if I helped her, Madame might be kind to me. She gave rewards to the girls who served her well."

Devon saw that the poor creature had thought there might be no other life than this one. Neither she nor her mother would have escaped. Not like his courageous Anne.

"I tried to help her, but she got up and slapped me. She was in a rage. First she wanted me to help her tidy her hair and put ice to her bruise, because she had a client coming, but instead she shoved me out of the room. I went downstairs and I passed a man in the hallway. I didn't see his face. I was going to try to entice him, but he went to Madame's room."

"Do you know who he was?"

Vehemently, the girl shook her head. "No, Your Grace. I heard Madame call him 'My Lord.' He was angry at her. Then I heard Madame say my name, so I crept to the door again."

"Did you see his face?"

She nodded. "He turned around. He scared me! I thought he was a monster, then I saw he had on a mask. One of those ones like in Venice, and it was all white."

"Why did Mrs. Meadows use your name, my dear?"

"She wanted to sell me to him. She was trying to tell him I was a virgin. That made him even angrier. He said he had paid for Anne and he expected Madame to give him what he'd paid for. Madame had to admit Anne had run away. He didn't believe her. He picked up the poker and threatened to kill her if she didn't give him Anne. Madame started to cry. Then he hit her. He hit her so hard, there was an awful crack. She fell down. This time, she didn't move at all."

"Thank you, Sukey." Impetuously, Devon made a decision. "You aren't to stay here anymore. This is no place for a young woman like you."

"Do you mean . . ." She gaped at him, slack jawed. "Do you want me to be your mistress?"

He remembered Anne, so determined to rescue herself by doing that very thing. To think that becoming his mistress represented survival and salvation. "No, not my mistress." He looked to her mother. "Sukey is a witness to a crime, and I would like to ensure she is safe. Will you come with me now? I will find a place for you to stay—perhaps a small town house?"

"A town house." The mother appeared stunned. "Yes, of course, Your Grace."

Sukey glanced from him to her mother, confused. "Is this what you meant, Mama, when you said that someday a gentleman would come and want me and would take us away to a life of luxury?"

Chapter Twenty-one

SHE WAS ONLY a few feet from freedom. Why did her legs no longer wish to move?

Her ship, the *Saucy Wench,* bobbed on the waves, tugging at its mooring ropes. Anne took a deep breath. The ship smelled the way she imagined India would—as if the aromas of exotic spices were sunk into the timbers.

Here was the escape she'd yearned for, ever since she and her mother had been forced to live in squalor. Here was the ship that would take her away from imprisonment and give her the freedom she'd dreamed of for years. Yet she was not running toward it when she knew she must.

Why was it so hard to leave England, leave Devon, when she knew it was the only thing she could do? She turned away from the ship for one last look at England, at the crowded, noisy world that didn't feel like home. The stews had never been a home. The brothel hadn't. Longsworth was so far in the past, she could only think of it like a remembered dream. India would have to become her home. Or perhaps she would never have a place again that would have all the special elements of home. Love, safety, family—

Then she saw him. A gentleman in a blue superfine coat, black trousers, and towering beaver hat strode through the crowd. People retreated. Anyone would know, at once, he was a duke.

"Anne!" He began to run, his strides swallowing up the pier as he came toward her.

She snatched up her bag and ran with stumbling haste toward the end of the dock, where a rowboat would take her to the ship. No—Devon would catch her before she reached Captain Rogers's boatman. Whirling around, she raced like a chased fox over the uneven boards of the dock. She careened around barrels and coils of rope, stumbled past sailors and women. Everything was jiggling up and down as she ran; she could barely see.

She had to lure him away from the ship, get him lost on the teeming piers. Once she had him tangled up in the maze that was the London docks, she could come back.

She prayed the ship wouldn't have left by then.

He was not going to lose her. As desperate as she was, Anne was encumbered by skirts and a valise, and he was tearing across the crowded dock as if his life depended on catching her.

Devon shoved his way through a throng of smoking sailors. He vaulted over a pile of crates. Danced around a line of men carrying barrels. He lengthened his strides, his boots pounding the deck. Then a group of burly men turned and made a human wall, blocking his way. *Hell.* What had she said as she ran past to coax them to help? Or did sailors always come to the rescue of beautiful, fleeing women?

She had outwitted him in the woods outside his hunting box. He refused to be bested again.

He ran at full speed toward the men, who rushed him. Accustomed to grappling on a battlefield, he clasped one of the beefy sailors' shoulders, shoved the man to his knees, and hurdled over him. For seconds, the group of them stood stock-still, letting him put a few yards between them. Then they took up the chase. Every sailor on this dock could come at him—nothing would stop him from catching Anne.

Ahead by fifty yards, Anne ran toward a row of wooden barrels. He raced for her. As he thundered nearer, he saw her steps grow more panicked and clumsy. Her hat flew off. Her red waves tumbled down. In seconds, she was so close he could reach out and touch her flying hair. He sprinted full out toward her, grasped her by the waist.

"No," she cried. She tried to wrench out of his grip.

He was watching her, not the deck, and at the same moment that she jerked away from him, he tripped on an uneven board. His momentum sent him flying forward, and he dragged her with him. Instinct screamed to protect her. With his arms wrapped around Anne's struggling body, he twisted as they both fell. His back slammed against the unyielding planks of the dock. She landed on his chest, where her elbows jabbed mercilessly into his muscles and her bottom whacked his groin. Her head hit his chin hard enough to knock him cold.

But he was too damned angry to be felled so easily. He gritted his teeth and discovered he still had his arms clamped around her.

"Let me go!" She squirmed on him, her delectable derrière bouncing. It was madness, given he was bruised and exhausted, but arousal shot through him.

"Give it up," he growled by her ear. "This time you are caught." Keeping her captive in his embrace, Devon sat up with her on top of him, then he turned her to face him, and he kissed the tempestuous, frustrating woman.

For the first time, he saw her as he kissed her. Saw her ivy-green eyes widen, her pink lips part as his mouth slanted over hers. He kissed her, savoring the sight of her. His head ached from the impact, and for one moment he wondered if he could go blind again. He pulled back from the kiss, cupped her cheeks, and stared up at her pale face.

"Wh-what?" she gasped. "Why are you looking at me like that?"

"Because I can," he murmured. God, she was lovely. Maddening, but beautiful.

In his peripheral vision, he saw bodies massing in on the sides. Sailors, apparently ready to rescue Anne. He glared at the group with ducal hauteur. "My mistress," he said in a low, dangerous voice. "And therefore none of your concern." Keeping one arm locked around Anne's waist, he drew his tailcoat open to reveal the pistol tucked into his waistband.

The men retreated, disappearing into the crowd. A throng had stopped to stare. Now they slowly returned to their work, leaving Anne and him alone in the middle of the busy dock. "You might as well have shouted, 'My property,'" she snapped. "Will you let me go?"

"I chased you all the way from London without stopping for food, with a bruised body and aching head. I spent the night scouring the stews for you. And, after all that, I still had to throw my body onto the dock to get you. Nothing will induce me to release you now."

"I did not ask you to pursue me! I didn't want you to suffer. You should not have been riding across the country after you struck your head." She let out a fierce breath. "Don't you understand, My Lord Duke, that I am doing this to protect you? What are you going to do with me now—take me to Bow Street?"

"Of course not, and don't call me 'My Lord Duke.' After the trouble you've put me through, you will do as I ask. And I ask you to call me Devon."

Her shoulders quaked. In fear? Or fury? "But you must take me to the magistrate. Anything else will get you in trouble. Dear God, it enrages and sickens and terrifies me to think I might hang for something I didn't do. But I couldn't face watching you be charged for helping me. I would admit to the crime before I'd let that happen."

She was willing to sacrifice herself for him. When he'd been in battle, he was known as the Mad Lord Major, for the wild ways he'd fought to save others. To be willing to admit to a crime she hadn't committed, to save him—that was true madness. He got to his feet, hauling her with him.

"You might have signed a contract with me," she said fiercely, "but you didn't buy my soul."

"Indeed I didn't," he retorted, but the fear in her eyes twisted his gut. It brought other nerve-racking thoughts to mind.

"What were you going to do in Bombay?" He tried to sound cool and calm, when his molars wanted to grind until he was left with stumps in the back of his jaw. "Were you planning to be a courtesan to some British officer? Or to a rich nabob involved in the East India Company?" He scruffed his hand over his jaw. "What did you have to do to get the money for the stage?"

All around them, the business of the port carried on—loud, raucous, industrious. But even though he could see it all, he felt locked in a void, waiting for her answer.

Why did the thought of her being a courtesan to another man make him so angry? Why did he feel so possessive of her? She wanted to leave, he was supposed to marry, and she had just reminded him she was not his possession. He'd vowed he wouldn't keep a mistress after he wed. . . .

"I got my ticket for the stage by assisting an elderly woman—she had no maid and I acted as one for her. In exchange, she paid my way to London," she finally said. "As for Bombay, I have enough money to begin a new life. An independent life. That's what I want. What I *dream* of having."

Which meant he was dashing her dreams. Damnation, how did she do this? How did she manage to make him feel the villain in this? "My carriage is waiting. You are not sailing away from me today, Anne. I have no intention of letting you go."

He was furious with her.

Anne knew it. Devon's expression was cold and hard, and he had looked away, out his windows, as though he might be driven to violence if he looked at her. His coach, a plain black one, rattled down Wapping High Street, making slow progress amid the crush of carts and teams, giving Anne far too long to be trapped with an angry man. Then she realized he was carefully checking behind them.

"You're afraid someone is following us?"

"I went to Bow Street's magistrate yesterday. To tell him I believed you innocent, to find out what evidence he has against you, find out if he has other suspects. He was a friend of my father."

Oh, goodness. "You are betraying a family friend for me?"

Coolly, he said, "I assume he would have assigned Runners to watch me. I took care to ensure I wasn't followed. I brought the plain carriage. We left before dawn and took a circuitous route to the docks. But I know not to be overconfident."

She had forced him to be disloyal to a family friend who was also a magistrate. She'd abandoned him in the woods after he had been hurt. She hated thinking of what she'd done to him. And she hated the icy frost in the carriage.

What would an angry duke do to her? He had told her he would not hand her over to Bow Street. Years in the stews had taught her to expect the very worst. What if he had another punishment in mind? No, this was *Devon*. He would not hurt her. All the time she'd lived in his house, he had been afraid he would hurt her by mistake. "What are you going to do with me?"

"Help you," he muttered. "Apparently, even if it kills me."

She had to break through this stubborn determination to help her. She had to make him see that the only thing she could do was run. The irony was laughable. She had to seduce him into letting her go. And, to start, she had to chip through the ice.

She let her shaky fingers brush along the edge of his thigh. Her fingers grazed rock-hard muscle. What would he do? Flinch? Pull away?

He didn't move his leg, but he turned and watched her, his lids half lowered. His long lashes seemed to stand out for inches, sumptuously curved at the ends. She stroked him more deliberately. She skimmed her hand up his inner thigh, coasting over his snug trousers, her throat so tight she could hardly breathe.

Lightly, she tickled the juncture of his legs. He wasn't stopping her, but he didn't look aroused either. His face was impassive.

She wasn't going to seduce him by barely grazing him with her fingers. She had to take the risk. She had been willing to sail to Bombay and leave him forever. But here, now, she was afraid she would do something wrong, she would make him angrier, she would lose him forever.

Gathering courage, she caressed his left thigh. She wriggled her hand beneath his hard derrière and the velvet seat and squeezed. Audaciously, she found the soft ridge of his cock and stroked it through the fine wool of his trousers. His breath hitched. His lids lowered again, and he didn't push her away.

She should feel victorious. Instead, she felt empty.

The last time they had made love, it was wonderful. Precious. Spectacular. She had come for him, really and truly. Now she felt as she had when she'd first gone to seduce him—as if there was a void inside her, as if she was incapable of feeling anything.

She wrapped her hand around his shaft. Relief hit her as it pulsed, then hardened under her touch. Despite his carved-from-marble expression, his body revealed how much he did like this.

She wished she could go back in time and they were still at his hunting box, when lovemaking had become more exhilarating, more sweet and wild each time they did it.

She unfastened his trousers. His erection lifted his silky drawers. He was aroused, but he still exuded frost. She had to do something. Something that he couldn't resist. Slowly, she licked her lips and leaned toward his lap.

"Stop."

He stood, looming over her. He braced his hands on either side of her shoulders. His erection stuck out from the open placket of his trousers, thick, rigid, pointing at her. "Do you want this?" he asked hoarsely. "Or are you doing this to manipulate and distract me?"

"I'm sorry . . ." She couldn't bear the raw confusion on his face. "Even though we are in the same carriage, it feels like there is a wall of ice between us. I'm a whore.

I don't know how else to make you stop being angry with me."

"Angel, you were never afraid of my anger before. You provoked it many times, when you were battering away at my stubborn idiocy." He lifted her hand. He leaned down and kissed her index finger. "You aren't a whore, love. Don't call yourself that. You are so much more. You are the woman who tried to stop my nightmares."

He sucked on her middle finger. "The woman who taught me to listen to the rain."

He used the tip of her ring finger to trace his lips. "The woman who helped my sister. The woman who tried to heal me, no matter how damned stupidly I behaved."

His touch made her tremble. The softness of his tone gave her hope. Perhaps her seduction was working. Daringly, she leaned forward and planted a kiss to his swaying cock. He tasted earthy, slightly sour, delectable. Parting her lips wider, she took him inside. Her eyes shut, and she focused only on pleasing him.

His moans were hard, filled with desire. "It's been only five days since you ran away from my bed, angel, but it feels like a lifetime. Erotic thoughts about you, along with unbearable worry, haunted me as I rode to London. Do you know how difficult it is to ride with an erection?"

Still using her mouth to embrace his shaft, which kept swelling larger, she shook her head.

His cock pulsed with every harsh breath he took. "Anne, I was so afraid something had happened to you. That Mick Taylor or your cousin had caught you. Or someone had clapped you in jail. I felt like a blackguard, thinking about all the ways I was going to make love to you when I had you safe, while you could be in danger. I've realized there is only one way to keep you under control. I have to keep you with me and make love to you as much as humanly possible."

A jerk of his hips drew him out of her mouth. "I don't want this to be a job, a duty for you. I want to drive my cock into you until you forget everything but me. Until you are weak with delight, wild with lust. Just as I feel right now. You're making me lose my mind, Anne Beddington, and I want to return the favor. But first I want to take you to your house."

"My house?" she echoed.

"I rented a house for you. You will need somewhere to stay. It's on the fringes of Mayfair." He smiled gently. "A short carriage ride from my home."

He had rented a house. This is the life she *could* have had, as his mistress. "I cannot stay in a house near Mayfair. Not when there are stories about me in the news sheets."

"The house has been rented for a Mrs. Osbourne. A widow. I believe we can easily change your appearance again."

The moment Anne saw the town house Devon had acquired for her, she almost cried. Symmetrical white fronts marched down the street; windows glittered like diamonds. Black railings neatly framed each little property, and steps led up to glossy doors.

It was a lovely street. However, it screamed of respectability. "What if my neighbors find out I'm a courtesan? They will be *scandalized*."

"You are worried about shocking neighbors?" He shook his head, as if in disbelief. "After we've cleared your name, the house is yours. Whether you choose to remain with me or not."

Whether she chose . . . What would she do if she was safe? She'd thought only about escape.

He jumped down from the carriage, then helped her negotiate the steps to the sidewalk. Devon had hastily purchased some veiling and they'd wrapped it around her hat. She could barely see through the lacy shield. He had pulled his hat low to hide his face. At the front door he stood behind her, so his broad back blocked her from the view of anyone on the street, and handed her the key.

She unlocked the door and hurried inside. His true generosity struck her as she stood frozen in the foyer. She could barely take everything in. Gleaming marble tile. A massive chandelier pirouetting in a breeze. Dainty Queen Anne benches. Heart wedged in her throat, Anne went from room to room, discovering that each one was more sumptuous and lovely than the last. In a parlor she spied an enormous pianoforte. She ran to it, giddy with excitement. "This is for me?"

He smiled. "Do you play?"

"I did. It's been so long."

"Do you like the house?"

Like the house? "I'm . . . I'm thunderstruck. Overwhelmed. It is beautiful. I wish . . ." She wished she could have brought her mother here. Wished desperately they could have fled from Longsworth to a home like this. Mama would still be alive, and she . . .

How could she have had such a house without being a courtesan with a protector? She wished, perhaps, she hadn't clung to her decency for so long. But her mother had insisted Anne must never become a light-skirts, even for their survival. It was a vow she couldn't keep.

"It is what you deserve, Anne. Soon, I hope, you will be able to live here without fear. I went to Mrs. Meadows's brothel last night—"

"You went *there*?"

"Looking for clues."

It also meant he had seen the life she once lived. A

blush of embarrassment swept across her face. She didn't know why this seemed so terrible. Devon had been to brothels. As soon as she'd told him she was once trapped in one, he must have been able to guess everything she'd done. Then his words sank in. "What kind of clues?"

"To the identity of the real killer of your madam."

Hope soared, then crashed. "You didn't find out anything. You would have told me."

"I was rather busy chasing you across the London docks. I did find a witness—one of the girls—who saw a man arrive, apparently a client who wanted you." He told her everything the girl had seen: a lord disguised with a Venetian mask. This man had murdered Madame in anger because he had paid for Anne, and Madame had lost her.

"Do you know who he is, Anne?"

"No. Who would want me so—"

"Your cousin?"

"No! I can't believe he would kill someone over me . . . would he? How could he do such terrible things to have me?" She shivered in fear.

"I don't know, love. It may not be Norbrook, but I will talk with Bow Street. We will find out the truth. The best way to keep you safe is to find out who the man is."

"What of the girl who spoke to you? She will be in danger!"

"Her name is Sukey. I took her and her mother away from the brothel. They are well hidden and protected."

Sukey. That sweet, simple girl. Thank heaven, Sukey was now safe. It was so good of Devon. "Without proof of who that man was, the magistrate won't believe in my innocence," Anne said grimly. "He will probably think you bribed Sukey to lie for me—"

"I'll deal with those problems if they arise. For now

you should explore your house. And before I go, I'd like to see the bedroom."

"The bedroom?" she echoed. "Oh, yes, of course." Not an hour ago, she'd wanted to seduce Devon to coax him to leave her alone. Now she was quivering in shock over the possibility that Sebastian had been willing to kill for her, and she wanted to embrace Devon and never let him go.

She should please him well to thank him for this generous gift, but for her this was so much more than payment, more than the business of being a mistress. She needed him.

This time, this precious time, he would see her come. The thought had Devon's desire surging even more. It would be like their very first time, all over again. No—not like the first time. He had been unwilling and angry when she'd first come to him. This time, nothing was going to stop him from enjoying every inch of her. Certainly not her clothes: He dispatched her gown and corset quickly, loving the way her round breasts jiggled as he freed the laces.

He shouldn't be doing this. She was a viscount's daughter. She was born to be a lady. But he couldn't stop. "I am going to protect you, too, Anne," he murmured. "I will dress you in luxurious silks. Wrap diamonds around you. Here—" He lifted her thick hair and kissed her damp neck. "And here." Her wrists next. He laved his tongue over them, and she moaned.

"Especially here." He pushed up her shift as he dropped to his knees. He kissed the insides of her thighs. Silky and lovely, her creamy nether lips, half shielded by gold nether curls, were pure temptation.

"You can't put diamonds there," she admonished.

"I'm a duke. I can decorate my lover in any way I

wish." He gently parted her thighs. He should stop. *She deserves to be more than a mistress, and you are expected to marry some proper young lady.* He shoved the damned thought away. He needed Anne. Needed her so much. He cupped her bottom and pulled her sweet quim to his mouth, then licked and suckled, and watched Anne squirm and arch in erotic abandon.

Anne grasped Devon's shoulders. Slowly, his tongue swept all over her. Oh, this was devilishly wonderful. She loved the sight of his dark head framed by her thighs, his large tanned hands on her skin, the muscles flexing in his broad back. Now he could see everything too.

He moved away from her and his hand strayed down. He opened his trousers, drew out his erection, then stroked his thick shaft. Watching him excited her to her core. He touched himself so differently than she had. With years of experience, obviously. She drew her shift back up, aware of his hot gaze following the hem's journey up her legs. Her heart pounded as she touched the damp curls at the apex of her thighs, as her fingers slid between her slick folds, and she—

Giggled. With nerves. With shyness. He winked at her and fondled his ballocks with one hand, as he caressed the taut head of his erection with the other. "Perfect, love."

She watched him as she stroked herself, as he kept all his attention on her. Nerves melted. They shared a smile, then moaned together. His hand wrapped around his shaft, and he pumped hard into his fist. "Angel, it's the most arousing thing I've ever seen. I want to watch you come. Night after night, I imagined what you would look like. Make yourself come, angel, so I get to see you. You're on the brink, aren't you?"

Between gasps, she thought, *How does he know?* Then her stroking fingers ignited her, and the climax broke upon her like a sudden summer lightning storm. Pure pleasure washed over her. Before her eyes, Devon gave a deep groan, then clutched his shaft. His head fell back, and his semen shot out, spilling onto his hand.

She fell against his chest. "Oh, dear, it is messier for you, isn't it?"

His rich laugh filled the room. "Only you, angel, would think of that." He kissed the top of her head. "Watching you was delicious, Anne."

He drew out a handkerchief, cleaned his hand. Then pointed toward the bed. This was the master bed—one of dark wood and gold hangings. There was a lovely white-and-gilt bed in the adjoining room, which was to be her private bedroom. "Shall we try it out?" he asked.

"Already?" A glance down revealed he was growing aroused again. "Of course."

He tipped up her chin. "Are you going to stay, Anne? You can run, and live in fear for the rest of your life, or you can trust me, and we can work together to find out the truth."

If they found the killer, she could stay in England. She could stay with Devon—no, she couldn't. She'd promised his sister she would encourage him to find a bride, knowing he could never keep her once he did. She couldn't go back on her word. "I'll stay," she whispered.

But eventually she would have to go. How could she stay in London and hear of his marriage to someone else?

He swept her up into his arms. Startled, giggling, she was carried to the bed.

He left Anne and went to his investigator, Wynter, and then to Bow Street. After an interview with Sir John,

Devon headed to White's. He had not been to his club since before he had argued with his father and left for battle. There, he encountered Tris, who urged him to go to a gaming hell on Curzon Street. He went but found he had no interest in deep play. Eventually, he and Tristan ended up in a tavern near the London docks, only yards from where he'd caught Anne.

"What's bothering you, Dev?" Tris asked. "You've turned that whiskey around in your hand for an hour. You haven't drunk a drop."

"I'm thinking." Of how close he had come to losing Anne. Of how Wynter, his investigator, had found Captain Tanner's missing wife, but not his son, in the stews. He needed to talk about at least one of his problems or he would explode like a jammed rifle. He chose Anne, giving Tristan a summary of what he'd learned from the brothel. "The man wore a Venetian mask, beaver hat, and a cape with the collar turned up. The witness couldn't give me any detail with which I can identify him."

"Nothing?" Tris drained his drink. "Not a limp, a wooden leg, or maybe the tendency to drag his right leg behind him when he walked? What about a distinctive coat or cane? It's not fair if the bugger didn't give us any clue at all."

Devon shot him a sour look. "I believe the murderer was Anne's cousin, Viscount Norbrook, or a thwarted client. If it was a client—"

"Your mistress is cousin to a viscount?"

He gave a curt nod.

"So she was a lady at one time. Interesting."

It burned on Devon's tongue to point out that Anne was still a lady—at least in every sense of the word that should matter. "I've been trying to figure out the motive if it was a client. Would anger at not getting Anne be enough to drive a man to murder?"

Tristan gave a wry grin. "You tell me. You rode straight to London like a madman and chased her down on the docks. Clearly you're obsessed with her."

"I'm not obsessed," he snapped. "I was protecting her."

"You weren't willing to lose her, Dev. Why not let her do as she wants—give her a good settlement and put her on a ship? You know, as do I, that obsessing over a woman is a fool's game."

"I can't just hand her a wad of notes and send her on her way. I wouldn't know for certain whether she was safe. If her cousin is willing to kill for her—"

"You don't know whether that is the truth."

"Who else?" Norbrook hungered for Anne, obviously, but was it enough to commit murder for her? Something about this bothered him. "Bow Street will not arrest a viscount without evidence," he growled. "They were even reluctant to assign men to watch him, so I hired my own investigator to do it. But I need to confront Norbrook over this."

"You aren't going alone."

"He's not going to confess if I show up with you, Tristan. Of course I need to go alone."

It was almost midnight when he returned to the house he had rented for Anne. A maid let him in, but Anne hurried into the foyer. She dismissed the young servant and took his hat and coat.

"Devon, you look exhausted. For heaven's sake, it is late. You took a terrible blow to the head only days ago." Her hands stroked along his shoulders, lightly massaging. Her touch felt so incredibly good.

He had to grin. He adored her like this—clucking over him like a mother hen. With her hand tight around his wrist, she towed him to the parlor and led him to a chaise. She poured him a small amount of brandy, then held the glass over a candle flame.

He watched, bemused. "What are you doing?"

"What mistresses are supposed to do. I've also summoned a dinner for you. All this comfort is not only for me, after all—it is supposed to be for you to enjoy when you see me." She frowned. "You look so tired your skin is literally gray."

He was tired. Tired, dragged down by guilt. "I spoke with Bow Street today, but they will do nothing to your cousin until I have proof. I went to Norbrook's home to confront him, but he ran for the country last night. His servants won't reveal where he went."

"Oh, no," she whispered.

"Don't worry, angel. I will find him."

She caressed his shoulders again. He groaned in pleasure. "You've done everything you can."

"I have not," he said curtly. Suddenly he needed to talk to someone, just as he'd felt earlier today with Tristan. "I went to see Wynter, the former Runner I hired to investigate for me—"

"Yes. You told me about him."

"There's a great deal I didn't tell you. There was a man, Captain Tanner. He was killed in battle and left behind a wife and a child. They had been thrown out of their home because they could no longer pay the rent. I hired Wynter to find them and help them. He has found the wife, but the boy, Thomas, is missing. Apparently Thomas was kidnapped off the streets of the stews. Wynter believes he might have been taken to a brothel. The boy is only twelve years old."

"Heavens! Did your investigator search the brothels? Did he go to the one in Blackbird Lane?"

"No, angel, he hasn't gone to any yet. I thought that street contained only opium dens."

"It's known for that," she said, "but I heard, from the

gossip at Madame's, that one of the houses also specializes in prostitutes—young male ones. The boys are chained to their cots so they can't escape." She blinked quickly, tears glinting in her eyes. "I used to think that if I could become a wealthy courtesan like Kat, I would help children like that. I would fight to close down such evil houses and I would stop the trade in children."

She amazed him. She had gone through so much, but she had not lost her good heart. Any other woman might have ended up hard and cynical, but not Anne. Both Bow Street and her mad cousin hunted her, yet it was the plight of children caught up in brothels that made her cry. She had strength and courage that put generals to shame.

Her arms slid around his neck. "You do not have to do this alone, Devon. I know the stews. We could search together. I could help you. It would give me something to do rather than worry about whether a Bow Street Runner will knock on my door."

Chapter Twenty-two

WITHIN AN HOUR, he had helped Anne disguise herself with a dark wig and a hooded cloak, and they were in his carriage, slowly rattling through the twisting maze of narrow, cobbled lanes off Whitechapel High Street. Anne had her face pressed to the window, and as they wound deeper into the stews, her breathing became swift and uneven.

"What's wrong, love?" Devon asked gently.

She spun away from the window, her lips trembling, her hands fisted. He'd never seen her like this, not even when he'd chased her down on the docks. She looked ready to break down. He lifted her and planted her on his lap.

"Hundreds of children are kidnapped off the street and forced to work in brothels. I would like to tear down such places with my bare hands. I would like to kill the horrible villains who steal children—" She put her hands to her mouth. "I suppose, if I were to say that on the dock, no one would believe my innocence."

"Angel, feeling rage at pimps and whoremongers is natural."

She bit her lip. "The truth is, when I hit Madame with

the fireplace poker, I was so furious I wanted to hurt her. I didn't want to kill her, but I wanted *her* to feel pain. It was pure luck that kept me from being a murderess in truth."

"You feel guilty because you had murderous thoughts."

Anguish showed in her dark-green eyes. "Yes. It makes me no better than she was."

His sardonic laugh escaped before he could stop it. "You are as different from that witch as an angel is from a demon. As for what you felt when you swung the poker, Anne . . ." He sighed. In this he had a lot of experience. "Don't think about it. That's one thing I learned in war. You take action without doubt or regret and move on afterward."

"*You* didn't learn how to do that. *You* have nightmares."

"It's what a man with sense does. That's why many men survived war without turning into mad, haunted wrecks."

"You're not a mad, haunted wreck." Her feisty determination was fixed on him. Then her lips parted in shock. "Even though you have your sight back, you are still having nightmares."

Devon shrugged. "I doubt they will go away. I doubt I'll ever forget things I saw. Take my advice, love, and don't torture yourself. You didn't kill her—likely your good soul took charge and ensured you didn't hit her that hard."

Anne wanted to believe him. She was innocent, she hadn't killed Madame, yet she felt guilty because she'd been *willing* to kill. She saw how haunted Devon was. Why had she assumed all the horrible memories of war had gone away simply because he had his sight back? "You don't have nightmares about men shooting at you, do you? You have nightmares about the ways you had to kill other men." She wasn't expressing it well, but she understood. "You cannot forget the things you were forced to do, just as I can't. But, Devon, those soldiers were the enemy. You were expected to shoot at them. You had to—to save the lives of your men, to save England."

His laugh was harsh, so full of self-recrimination it froze her blood.

"Devon, you would have been shot if you hadn't fought in battle. For cowardice."

"Anne, my angel, what bravery is there in shooting a boy who was probably no older than fifteen?"

She stared helplessly, unsure of what to do. What to say. What to *feel*. "What do you mean? You had to shoot a child?"

"He was a soldier, Anne. As the French lost troops in battle, they became desperate to replenish the ranks. They began to press younger lads into service. Our forces are not much different—boys of twelve go off to serve in the navy—but that knowledge doesn't change the horror of pointing your weapon at a child's face, knowing you are supposed to pull the trigger."

She touched his forearm. It was tense, inflexible as iron. "Is this what has haunted you? That you had to shoot a boy—"

"I didn't shoot him. And while I hesitated, he shot Captain Tanner. Too late, I tried to tackle the lad, to stop the shot. But someone shot me, hitting my shoulder, and I fell in the mêlée. The boy then tried to drive his bayonet into my skull. I shifted, but he slammed it hard into my head, knocking me out. That's what blinded me, but I don't care about that. If I'd taken my shot, Thomas's father might still be alive."

It was horrible. He blamed himself for not killing the young soldier, for not saving Thomas Tanner's father. Yet he knew he would have hated himself for a lifetime if he'd shot the boy.

"I need to save Thomas," he said quietly.

Now she understood why he was here. To make things right in his soul, he was trying to save the family of the man he hadn't been able to save. He was trying to forgive himself for having been given a devil of a choice, where every solution left him damned. Impulsively, she kissed his cool, hard lips. They didn't soften, but she wanted him to know she did not blame him.

"We *will* save Thomas." She looked to the window, as a brick wall passed perilously close to the glass. A street flare illuminated a sign on the wall. *Blackbird Lane.* "It's here."

From the outside, the brothel looked like so many of the other buildings—quiet and still. Shutters covered the windows. A single lamp burned, but it was situated away from the door, so anyone who entered did so in shadow. It was disgusting: No one cared what terror the young ones had to endure, but great care was taken so the *gentlemen's* reputations would not be tainted.

As though he knew she wanted to rush out of the carriage and batter down the door, Devon put a hand on her arm. "We have to plan this carefully," he said. "We can't barge in and demand the child. I need to get in without raising suspicion. You are to stay here."

"I am going with you."

"Angel, I can see, so there's no need. And gentlemen don't escort ladies to brothels like this."

He had called her a lady, this time without even thinking. "Please let me help you."

He frowned, then sighed. "I think it best if we don't go through the front door. We'll break in the back."

From the shadows of a smelly alley, Anne watched Devon approach the rear door, walking with ease through the dark. A man leaned against the wall. He must be a guard, to provide a warning if Bow Street Runners raided the place. Devon made no sound as he closed in on the man, and she realized now that Devon was dressed entirely in black—black shirt and trousers and coat, with no cravat. He almost dissolved into the shadows.

Breathless, she watched him slip into the gloom near the brothel, then toss something past the man's head. It clattered on the ground in the dark.

The man twisted at once in that direction, away from Devon. "Who's there?" he shouted.

Devon moved with such speed, the guard was slumped unconscious in his arms before Anne could really understand what he'd done. He lowered the limp body to the ground with surprising care, and she hurried to him on the rear step. The back door proved to be unlocked. "For the gentlemen to escape swiftly, in case of a raid by the law," Devon explained quietly.

He clasped her hand and led her through dimly lit corridors. "How will we find Thomas?" she asked. Would it have been better to have gone to the front door and played the part of a couple looking for a sexual diversion?

"We'll have to search." He opened a door in the paneling at the end of the hall. It opened to a dim, narrow stair—the servants' stairwell. Fortunately, there was no one in it, and they used it to climb to the second floor, where the bedrooms must be. Anne wanted to hurry out before someone entered the stair below and they were caught, but Devon took the time to survey the corridor.

He drew her across the gloomy hall to a room with an open door. It was an unused bedroom. They waited until another door swung open. A man slipped out and hurried down the hall.

"You wait here," Devon whispered, "but take this." He drew a pistol from his pocket.

"Is it loaded?"

"It wouldn't protect you if it wasn't." On that, he left

her, moving stealthily across the corridor. She heard a faint cry, then silence, and a door was shut. A moment later, Devon returned. "I questioned the young boy in there. There is a lad in the house who matches Thomas's description. He's locked up in an upstairs bedroom—the one farthest from the stair."

Anne's heart dropped to her stomach. Thomas was a prisoner, just as she once had been, but he was so much younger. The poor child.

Devon's fury burned hotter with every stair he climbed. Anne followed. The upper floor was lit only by slanting moonlight that fell in through half-covered windows, but he felt at home in the dark. Just as that thought raced through his head, he heard a boyish howl of terror, followed by a sharp curse spat by an older man.

Blindly driven by rage, by the desperate need to take action, he charged forward. Anne's hand fell away from his forearm. He ran down the corridor and drew out his second pistol. One kick smashed in the door.

A large man jumped back from a bed. Recognition clicked: Orston, a fat, half-naked earl. A thin young boy was tied hand and foot to a disordered bed.

This was the right bedroom, and the lad must be Thomas. It was as though Devon went blind again—all he could see was a red haze. He had been forced to watch this child's father die because he had been unable to shoot a boy soldier. Orston was going to violate the lad for a fleeting moment of pleasure.

Devon was going to kill Orston. Grab him by his shoulders, pound his head into the floorboards until he was senseless, then rip his heart out of his chest.

He rushed in. Orston gave a girlish shriek of fear, scrambled off the bed, and ran like a frightened hare toward the door in the other wall. Devon lunged toward the bound boy, but Anne was already there. "Are you Thomas Tanner?" she whispered. The boy did not answer, but he jerked back in surprised recognition at the name. Anne drew a dagger from a sheath in her bodice and began to saw at the ropes, telling Thomas he was now safe.

Devon jumped over the bed. He grasped Orston by the shoulder and shoved him chest-first into the wall. The earl cried out in pain, but this was nothing compared to what Devon intended to do.

He spun Orston around and drove his fist into the flabby stomach. Then sent an uppercut to the man's jaw that slammed his head against the wall, denting plaster. Orston began to slide down, but Devon propped him up. "You bastard," he growled. "He's a child. And unwilling."

"Didn't know . . . unwilling . . ."

"You didn't know? Christ Jesus, didn't the white face, the tears on the cheeks, the ropes, give you a bloody clue?"

"Not your business, March."

He wrapped his hands around Orston's throat and pressed his thumbs into the man's windpipe. In war, he'd had to kill. He hungered to do it now. So easy . . . just a bit more pressure . . .

"Devon, don't!" Anne cried. "Don't kill him!" She tried to pull him away.

"Get back," he barked. "Let me do this."

But she pushed her way between Orston and him, her eyes enormous with horror. "You must stop! You could hang for this, even though you're a duke. You would hate yourself. Meet him at dawn. Drag him to Bow Street. Anything but this."

Panting, he bowed his head. He had to force his hands to loosen their grip. The bulky earl slid down the wall, whimpering, blubbering.

Devon stepped back. Anne murmured soothing things, as though he was a mad, wounded animal she was trying to tame.

She had stilled Devon's fists; now she must go back to Thomas. The poor lad was bound hand and foot to the bedposts. Anne had already cut through the ropes that tied his right hand. Thomas had watched her, his gaze darting like an animal seeking escape. As she'd freed his hand, she told him in gentle tones that he would be safe, that they were going to take him away. Her words hadn't seemed to ease his fear one bit. Once, when her hand had strayed near his mouth, he'd snapped at her with his teeth.

She hurried back to him to finish. She wanted to be quick, so she did not bother to speak. She set down the pistol, drew out the dagger she'd brought in her bodice, and got to work. Thomas was a beautiful boy, small for twelve years of age, with golden curls. He shied away as she cut his left hand free. Then she set to work on his feet. She was aware of his small chest rising and falling as she sawed at the last rope.

Across the room, the client was spilling his tale to Devon in the hopes of striking a bargain. Devon was watching her with Thomas. He was trying, as quickly as he could, to learn from the man the identity of the blackguards who had taken Thomas. His eyes still gleamed with murderous intent, which made her nervous.

From the corner of her eye Anne saw something move, and she jerked away from the rope as it broke. A pillow slammed into the side of her face, knocking her over. She heard Devon shout, but something grasped her wrist and wrenched it hard.

Thomas. She shoved the pillow from her face. The lad was crouched at her side, his hand gripped around the knife. He held it to her throat. Anne winced as sharp steel bit into her flesh. "Thomas, don't," she whispered. "We want . . . to . . . help."

Devon's heart pounded wildly. The lad was so terrified, he was lashing out at anyone. Devon had seen men do it in battle—lose their wits in fright and shoot at anyone near them. Thomas held the dagger at Anne's throat. One slice and he could kill her.

Devon had to stop the boy, get the knife from him. He tried to assess every move, every approach, but his brain fixed on one horrific image: Thomas's fear-driven hand moving the knife, then Anne's slow slump to the floor. Raw panic gripped him, and he couldn't fight it. If he waited, as he'd done in battle, Anne would die. He began to move toward the boy.

"Keep back," Thomas cried. "Keep away from me."

"Thomas." Despite having a knife at her throat, Anne's voice was soft, melodic, sweet. "This is the Duke of March. You can trust him."

"Anne, don't speak," Devon warned. The knife made a small cut in her skin. Blood welled.

She ignored him. "Thomas, the duke fought with your father in battle. At Waterloo."

Of course, she said that to Thomas hoping to win his trust. But though the boy didn't know it, it was the reason for Thomas to hate him. Warily, Thomas flicked his gaze from Anne to Devon, and the distraction caused his hand to move. Fortunately, he didn't cut her, but her eyes were huge, and Devon could see her fighting for calm.

"Thomas, let her go. We've come to help you." Devon took another step forward.

"That's what *they* said. They were going to give me

money to help me mum. When I said I wouldn't go, they told me I had to or they'd hurt her."

Footsteps pounded across the floor, and Orston ran out, face white, gasping for breath. The sudden movement startled Thomas and sent his hand slicing in front of Anne's neck. Devon's knees almost collapsed under him. Anne closed her eyes, but she didn't scream. She had managed to jerk so the knife had not cut her. But Thomas pressed it against her flesh again.

"Thomas," Devon pleaded. "Let her go. I'll let you hold the knife to my throat in her place. You have nothing to fear from me." He had a second pistol in his back waistband, but he didn't dare take it out and threaten Thomas into panic. Hell, would he have to use it on a child?

"The duke was your father's commanding officer," Anne whispered. "He saw how brave your father was. He came to help you, because he respected your father so much."

No, Anne, don't speak of it.

"Me da died at Waterloo." Tears welled in the boy's eyes. His hand shook.

Yet Anne still found the strength to say calmly, "He did, Thomas. He died bravely in action and saved many men's lives."

What if the boy asked exactly what had happened? What would he do if he learned Devon had not saved his father when he had the chance?

"Me dad's death broke me mum's heart. The men said I had to come or she would be hurt."

"Your mother is safe," Devon said. "I have my men watching over her now, to protect her. Put down the knife and I'll take you to her."

"I can't go." The boy's voice shook.

"You did nothing wrong, Thomas," Anne said, so firmly no one would ever doubt her word. "If any of those men touched you, it was not your fault. Your mother will not be angry. Nor would your father. Your parents would only be happy you were safe. They would want you to let me go and let the duke help you."

As though mesmerized by her voice, Thomas let the knife fall a few inches from her throat. In an instant, Devon had the boy by the arms, the knife lay on the carpet, and Anne was safe.

"You have nothing to fear, Thomas," he said gruffly. "We are going to take you home to your mother. I will help her. Your father was a noble soldier—your mother deserves far better than to live in poverty. I will take care of both of you."

Thomas stared at him, fear and suspicion in his young eyes. What had the boy experienced to make him afraid of everyone, including those who would help him? Devon looked to Anne. If she had not known the boy needed reassurance, he might have had to make the choice again between saving a life and hurting a child.

"What in 'ell is going on in 'ere?"

Devon leveled his second pistol at the well-dressed man who stalked into the doorway. Thin, about thirty, with a ferret's eyes, the man held a cane, lifted as though ready to use it in a beating. At the sight of the pistol, he stood still. "Stop or I'll put a ball in you," Devon roared. "Drop your weapon and get down on your knees."

"That's one of them," Thomas cried. "One of the men who kidnapped me."

The man dropped the cane and immediately went to his knees, his gaze locked on the gun's muzzle. "Don't shoot me! It weren't me. I had to do it! It was Semple. I only work for him." The man spilled information so quickly, Devon had to fight to keep track of it. His name was Arthur Bevis, and the man who stole boys and ran the brothel was named Semple.

"If you want to escape the noose, Bevis," Devon snapped, "give me Semple."

"All right." Bevis led them through a hidden passageway to a large office. At the sight of the pistol, Semple pulled out one of his own. Devon shot it out of his hand. Within minutes, he had both men captured and bound—just as they had done to poor Thomas.

Anne was draping a blanket around a trembling Thomas. Quietly, Devon told her, "I'm going to leave my footmen to guard these two. I'm going to Bow Street and will have them send Runners to make the arrest and get the boys out. I will take Thomas with me, then bring him to his mother. I'm going to take you to your house, and I want you to stay there, in hiding."

She looked nervously from Thomas to him. "I want to look after him."

Did she fear he was capable of hurting a defenseless boy because his head was so tormented with guilt and battle memories? "I would never hurt him," he said bitterly. "Not even over what he could have done to you."

Her green eyes went wide. "I did not think you would! But I understand a little of the experience Thomas has been through. I was taken prisoner, as he was." Suddenly she touched his arm. "Devon, are you all right?"

His hands were shaking, and she said softly, "I know you went through hell. You were confronted with the same horrible choice you faced in battle."

He couldn't stop the bloody trembling. "I didn't know what to do. I prayed only that I could save you both. If I'd had to make the choice . . . I wouldn't have let you die. Even if it haunted me forever, I couldn't have let that happen."

"Devon, Thomas is safe; I'm safe. This time it ended happily."

Her words went to his soul, but he knew she wasn't yet safe.

"Devon, I would like to go directly to the boy's mother and let her know Thomas is safe and that you will bring him from Bow Street. I can take a hackney."

"A hackney?" he exploded. "You would be unprotected."

"Devon, I lived here for years without protection. I know how to survive."

It was a stark reminder of what she'd been through. He looked at Thomas, who was terrified beyond belief, and he realized how very strong Anne had been.

It was so wonderful to be able to introduce Devon to Mrs. Tanner when he arrived with Thomas. Anne's heart swelled with joy as Thomas's mother gave a sobbing cry of joy, rushed to her son, and fell to her knees in front of him. Anne looked to Devon and smiled. This had been worth a few small nicks to her neck. Devon had fussed over her, but she was quite all right.

But she noticed how stiffly Thomas stood in his mother's hug. He didn't wrap his arms around her neck, press to her bosom, or cuddle against her. Perhaps it was only because, at twelve, he felt he should behave in a more grown-up way, but it worried Anne.

Through tear-blurred eyes, Mrs. Tanner gazed up at Devon. As she had embraced her child, the woman seemed to grow years younger. She had been pale, but now color bloomed in her cheeks. "Your Grace . . . I don't know how . . . how can I ever thank you?" Mrs. Tanner bent to press her cheek to her son's curls. Poor Thomas kept his head bent as though he did not want to look at his mother. She whispered, "I feared I had lost my boy as I lost my husband."

Devon ran his finger around his collar as if it choked him. "Mrs. Tanner, there is something I must tell you," he said gruffly. "Once you know of this, you may not feel such gratitude."

Confusion passed over the woman's face. Anne whispered, "No. There's no point in this."

"I have to," he whispered back. "If I'm to be condemned, I'd rather face it honestly."

"There's nothing to be gained," she persisted. "It will only hurt you both."

He leaned close to her, as Mrs. Tanner stared down at her son, and murmured, "Perhaps, for Mrs. Tanner, having a villain to hate will help."

Anne was about to protest—this *was* madness—but Devon bent to Thomas and ruffled his hair. "This lad should go to his bed. After he is settled, madam, we must speak."

Anne argued desperately as Mrs. Tanner led her son to his bed. "You saved Thomas. You have given her happiness. Haven't you eased your guilt? Don't—" She had to stop. Mrs. Tanner stood in the doorway, wringing her hands.

"Your Grace, what did you want to tell me?"

"Mrs. Tanner, please sit down." Devon waited until the woman lowered shakily. Then he told his tale: of Tanner's bravery and nobility in battle, of what an admired soldier Tanner had been, then finally of his horrible choice. He paced, his face anguished. "I hesitated. There is no way I can explain that to you, but I paused, unable to shoot down a young lad. In that moment, the boy took his shot on Tanner."

"Your Grace, I don't understand—"

"Allow me to speak bluntly, madam. Captain Tanner was shot because I could not kill the French boy, though it was my duty to do so."

Mrs. Tanner simply dropped her face into her hands and sobbed.

Anne saw Devon's face go gray and his expression

harden into one of cold self-recrimination. It was as if he were turning to stone in front of her.

"You must forgive His Grace," she said. "He would have saved your husband if he could. He had a terrible choice. Your husband's death was the fault of the French, not of His Grace."

Mrs. Tanner wiped her tears. "I understand that my husband went through the most horrible of experiences. I can understand why you couldn't shoot. I have a son. How could a man be asked to shoot any woman's son? I believe . . . I believe I would have done the same, if I were you."

Devon looked as he had when he'd first regained consciousness after falling in the stream—stunned. Thank heaven the woman was obviously one with great sense and a good heart.

"You are a very gracious woman, Mrs. Tanner," he said slowly. "Allow me to help you and your family. I owe your husband a great debt, and it is my duty to support you all."

Mrs. Tanner straightened her shoulders. "I do not need charity, Your Grace. I thank you with all my heart for rescuing Thomas, but now that he is home, we will be fine."

Devon tried to insist, but even a duke was no match for a proud and stubborn woman. Anne knew she must act. Devon needed this. Grasping Mrs. Tanner's hands, Anne faced her squarely. "I have been in the same position as you—my mother was forced to leave our home and we ended up living in lodging houses. My mother refused charity out of pride and worked herself to death. Your health and security, and Thomas's, are far more important than your pride. His Grace believes it is his duty to make amends for your husband's death. This is not charity—it is to repay Captain Tanner for his sacrifice."

"We have always worked for what we've gotten," Mrs. Tanner insisted.

She would not be swayed. Anne left the house with Devon, worried about Thomas's withdrawn behavior and the family's future. She was staring back at their simple home when Devon slipped his arm around her waist. "Thank you," he said softly, "for coming to my defense, for helping me to find Thomas. Can you tell me if there is any way I can help them?"

"I don't know. But I am determined to think of something."

He lifted her hand and gave a melting kiss to her palm. "Thank you," he said. "As Mrs. Tanner said to me, I don't know how to begin to thank you."

"What of Orston?" she asked. "What will become of him?"

"I will ensure he is too afraid to make use of young boys again."

She did not doubt Orston would be terrified by the hard determination in Devon's eyes. Then he took her home in the carriage, and she invited him inside. She stood at the front door, shyly asking, "Would you care to . . . to spend the rest of the night with me?" Why, when she was behaving as his mistress, did her tongue suddenly get tied? She pushed open the door. "Would you care for a bit of brandy in the parlor? I shall warm some, and then . . . then, of course, you will have whatever you desire."

He gave a rumbling laugh. "Forget brandy. What I need now is to make love to you. I keep thinking of what could have happened to Thomas, if you had not known the place to look for him. Rescuing the boy, rescuing the family, should have brought peace, but I don't feel that way. All I feel is a lot more regret and a lot emptier. I need your touch, love." He frowned and touched her neck. "But you were wounded—"

"No—it doesn't hurt, truly. And I want you to come inside."

Carriages rolled by, but he bent and kissed her. Anyone who saw would know just what she was now. It didn't matter. Helping Devon mattered. Her heart ached for him. "Come inside. Come inside me," she whispered. "I want you in my bed."

Anne woke. She was alone in bed, and guilt crashed in. She'd slept so soundly she hadn't noticed when Devon left. She pulled on a robe, but she didn't find him in the adjoining room. He wasn't in the house. Questioning servants, she discovered he'd left just after dawn.

She returned to her bedroom and summoned maids to dress her. She stared at the disordered bed, two questions hammering through her head. Had he spent the rest of the night with her? And had he slept peacefully, with his demons slain, or had reliving the awful choice he'd faced in battle made his nightmares worse? She wouldn't know until he returned. To keep her fretting mind busy, she would go to Thomas and his mother.

The boy had been so reticent with his mother, so embarrassed and stiff and awkward, that it worried Anne. It was risky, but she would wear a disguise—one of her maid's day dresses, her black cloak, and her dark wig. And she wouldn't go without protection. She didn't want to carry a bulky pistol, so she tucked her dagger in its sheath, then slid it into her bodice.

But once she reached the Tanners' home and sat with Thomas alone in the parlor, Anne realized she had no idea where to begin with the boy. He stared blankly ahead. He wore a tattered shirt and trousers. Anne knew why his mother had refused charity—her mother had done the same. But the future of this young boy was at stake. How could pride be worth more than Thomas's safety and well-being?

"Are you still frightened by what happened to you?" she asked softly.

"I'm not afraid," he said sullenly.

"You also have no reason to be ashamed of it. None of it was your fault."

That made him jerk up his head. "I weren't raped, if that's what you mean, miss." He stared defiantly into her eyes. Obviously he planned to shock her, scare her into leaving him alone. But she could not be shocked. At least, not over things that happened in the stews.

"Good. But perhaps other things happened. Things you did not like." She hoped she was not botching this. Thomas's chest rose and fell fiercely, but he *was* listening. "Perhaps the men who took you to the brothel touched you in ways that felt wrong. That is their sin, not yours. You were the victim in this, Thomas."

A flush washed over his cheeks. "The men said they would hurt me mum if I didn't go with them, so I was too afraid to run. One of them gave me arse a squeeze. Told me I'd learn to like it. I should've fought him. I should've kicked him. I should've been able to escape—"

Anne wrapped her arm around Thomas's thin shoulders. He tried to jerk away, but she whispered reassuringly, "You are not to blame. You must not be angry with yourself because you couldn't escape." Finally she admitted, "It happened to me. I was taken to work in a brothel against my will. My mother had just died, and I had no money. I was kept like a prisoner. I was seventeen, much older than you, but I couldn't escape, I couldn't fight hard enough to rescue myself. For a long time, I was very angry that I couldn't get away, but then I realized I had to forgive myself. You only wanted to protect your mother, which was a noble thing. From now on, the Duke of March will ensure no one can hurt her. I promise you." She stroked his hair. "You have nothing to blame yourself for, and I am so proud of you for being so strong."

"Proud of me?" he echoed.

"Of course I am. Your mother is too."

Thomas looked so hopeful. Anne rose, clasped his hand, and took him to the room where his mother worked at the small stove. Very quietly, Anne explained the boy's fears, while Thomas ate a biscuit at a rickety table. "You must tell him you are proud of him," Anne whispered. "I think then he will put this behind him."

Mrs. Tanner nodded, her face pale. "He's been so surly with me. I thought he blamed me."

"He blames himself. He needs your love and reassurance." Anne added, "For Thomas's sake, you must take help from the Duke of March. What future will he have if you do not?"

The woman blanched more, and Anne felt a tremble rise up her spine. She was shaking, as she used to when she worried about her mother's health. Why were women so stubborn? What was wrong with a little charity? She had taken coins from the Duke of March years ago, when he'd given them to her so she would not have to sell her body. That had hardly been wrong.

On an impulse, thinking of her mother, Anne asked, "Do you sew well?"

When Mrs. Tanner smiled proudly, Anne asked to see her work and quickly satisfied herself that the woman was an excellent seamstress. The employment was grueling and poorly paid . . . but did it have to be? What if women such as Mrs. Tanner could own their own shops? They could share ownership and, instead of getting pennies a day, earn enough to survive. Heavens, she could sell the carriage Devon had given her and set up a dozen women in their own shops!

She had her solution for how to help Mrs. Tanner.

Instead of giving charity, she would give opportunity. She explained her idea to Mrs. Tanner. "I would invest in your business and earn a profit from it. It would *not* be charity."

The woman bit her lip, pushed strands of disheveled curly blond hair from her face, and finally smiled. "I would be very grateful, miss."

Brimming with relief and hope, Anne left. Filled with purpose, she hurried down the stairs.

A heavy footfall sounded on the steps behind her.

She turned and froze for a precious second, while her eyes took in what she could not believe she was seeing. A bald head. A beak of a nose. Triumphant eyes. *Mick*.

Anne spun and ran down the stairs. Her feet slid on the steps, and she had to grip the banister to keep from falling. Mick pounded down the stairs behind her. She screamed for help.

But these were the slums, and no one came. No one would come to the aid of a shrieking woman, fearing they would end up in danger.

One more flight of stairs and she could race out the door, run for her carriage. Her feet thundered on the creaking steps. How had Mick found her? He must have followed her. But if he'd found her house, why not attack her there?

Idiot. She'd come here alone, of course, so she wouldn't frighten Thomas. Mick must have been waiting for her to make such a stupid mistake—

Something slammed into her back. She slid off the step, but a hand grabbed her clothing. Mick wrenched her so hard she fell against his chest. His arm locked around her.

Her dagger. She could slip it out. She had to. It was the only way to save herself. But threatening Mick with it wouldn't be enough. She would have to stab him. She clutched the neck of her pelisse, praying he would think it was a gesture of fear. She worked her fingers inside and touched the handle of the knife. Once she stabbed at him, she would have to kill him. . . .

Oh, dear God, she couldn't do it. She couldn't take a life. Not even Mick's.

"Get moving, Annie," Mick snarled. "The viscount's waiting."

He dragged her toward an open door. Her heart sank. He was going to take her out a different way—not through the front door. Her servants would not know she was gone, at least not for several minutes. Long enough for Mick to make her vanish.

She had to at least threaten him.

One hard tug pulled out the dagger. Wincing in horror at what she was going to do, she thrust it at his arm. But she was clumsy. The blade didn't go in; it slid along his biceps.

Mick roared. "Going to make trouble, are you, Annie? Stupid whore."

The word bit into her soul as Mick ruthlessly jerked her wrist. She tried to cling to the handle, but her fingers opened against their will. The knife clattered to the floor. Mick shook her with such force that her brain seemed to slosh in her skull. Something white swooped at her face. She tried to rear back, but she only banged into Mick. Wet fabric was slapped to her mouth, and a sugar-sweet, cloying scent twisted her stomach. Anne struggled, aware of her limbs growing numb. Blackness rushed in. From miles away, a laugh of triumph brushed against her ear, then the floor dropped away from her and she fell dizzily into the dark.

Chapter Twenty-three

ABRUPT SHAKING WOKE her. Anne felt her brain bang around in her aching head again. "No . . ." she croaked. Desperately, she tried to reach up to stop the person—it must be Mick—from hurting her, but her hands wouldn't move. No matter how hard she strained, her arms wouldn't budge. Awareness trickled into her confused mind. Her hands were bound behind her back.

She couldn't see Mick, but he must have set a candle down, for a large circle of light spilled around her. She lay on the floor, arms and legs bound, and a shadow loomed over her from behind.

"Let me . . . go." Her lips felt swollen, and she could barely move them. "Mick—"

"It's not Mick Taylor, my dear."

She recoiled at the voice but could not pull away. "Seb . . . astian." She tried to turn, to see him. Her head pounded with pain. She swallowed over and over, fighting the urge to be sick.

"That idiot Taylor bruised you quite badly." Fingers stroked along her cheek, and she shuddered. Her cousin prodded a tender place on her face, and she gasped.

"Painful, is it? What hell you've endured because you

rejected me, because your mother refused to make you my bride." Her cousin's fingers were as elegant as Devon's, but the way he touched her—it was awful. It was as if he enjoyed the bruise on her cheek.

"I—I was fifteen when we left," she croaked. "You—you frightened me." Whatever Mick had given her to knock her senseless still fogged her thoughts. She sounded like the girl who had cried helplessly after her cousin forced her to sit on his lap and touched her in a way that made her skin crawl. The girl who had frozen in shock after she threw her chamber pot at him and knew he would take his revenge. The old sense of being afraid and trapped washed over her.

It was a feeling that stole her strength. It paralyzed her. She remembered it from when she had first been in Madame's brothel. She'd never before equated it with how she'd reacted to Sebastian's attentions. Was this why she hadn't been able to find the courage to escape Madame—because the old emotions she'd felt with Sebastian had taken control?

Memories she had pushed far back suddenly rushed out as if a dam had burst. Threats. When she was very little, Sebastian had threatened her. He'd destroyed her favorite doll to make her let him kiss her. He'd threatened to break another toy if she told. When Father died and Sebastian ruled their house, he'd threatened to hurt her mother, to send her mother away, if she didn't let him touch her breasts. She had given in—to protect her mother. It happened only once, but after that he had come into her bedroom and climbed on top of her, and she'd felt . . . as if she'd given him encouragement by letting him touch her. Then Mama had taken her from the house.

Images swamped her like rushing water, threatening to drag her down into dark depths, into madness, just as Devon had feared his memories could do to him.

She understood what Devon had to endure when the battle memories took control of him. He'd confronted his worst nightmare when they'd rescued Thomas: the choice of having to hurt a child to save a life. If he could face that, she could face her fears now.

She forced courage into her voice. "What do you want?" Mick had said Sebastian wanted her to be his mistress, but to tie her up like this, he must have accepted she would never willingly let him into her bed. "Are—are you going to rape me?"

As though strolling in a park, Sebastian walked slowly around her. As his boots moved, she craned her head and tried to see. Her head felt less dazed, her eyes accustomed to the shadows. Where was she? Not in his house. The floor was rough plank, the walls had broken plaster, and a musty smell filled her lungs. This looked like an empty warehouse, but a moth-eaten mattress lay in one corner.

"Rape you?" His voice was harsh, mocking. The mere sound made her freeze—then she squirmed on the floor, so she wouldn't become paralyzed. Something stabbed into her thumb. A splinter. The sharp prick of pain made her think . . . and gave her a spurt of hope. Sebastian couldn't see what she did behind her back. She began to slowly stroke the twine binding her wrists against the splintered floorboard.

His boots came close to her face and she had to stop moving. She looked up, meeting her cousin's cold blue eyes as he glared down at her. This was the first time in seven years that she'd seen Sebastian. Once he'd been handsome, with his muscular form, golden hair, bright blue eyes, charming smile. After she had seen the monster in him, though, that was all she could see.

Over the years, the monster appeared to be getting out. Muscle was turning to fat. His coat strained at his waist. Lines creased his forehead, framed his mouth. His jaw had gone soft.

He crouched near her. A sneer distorted his face. "After all those men had you in that brothel? March may be willing to plow another man's leavings, but I am not. How could you still be so lovely, Anne, after what you've become?"

He hated her. He had been the one to try to attack her, yet *he* hated her. It was . . . mad. Utterly mad.

Why had he brought her here and tied her up? For what purpose if he didn't want her? She tried for reason. "You don't want me, so let me go. You'll never have to see me again."

"I am sorry, Anne, but I cannot do that." He turned and began to stride away.

"What are you doing? Let me go!"

But he picked up the candle, and his boots slapped against creaking boards. She forced her body to roll so she could see him. Was he leaving her here to starve slowly? "Sebastian! This is madness. I've done nothing to you."

"Nothing? You put me through hell, Anne Beddington—or should I say Annie Black, as they called you in that filthy brothel. *Annie.*" He shuddered with distaste over her name, for heaven's sake. "I went to a great deal of trouble to find you. I had to search for years, combing through these disgusting slums. I had to negotiate with a whoring madam for you. I had to dirty my hands over you in so many ways, you little tart. Why would I let you go now, when I am so close to having exactly what I want?"

Dear God, he had admitted to her that he was going to buy her from Madame. But if he had killed Madame for her, why was he leaving her like this now? Was there no appeal she could make to a complete madman? "You could let me go because you are human."

No response came, only the sound of his boots moving farther away. A door groaned on its hinges and the glow of light grew fainter. If he had killed a woman over her, he was *not* human. She should let him go. She would rely on herself.

The door slammed and she was plunged into blackness. Immediately, fears sprang to life. Buildings in the stews were filled with rats. She hated this, hated being blind. But Devon had survived being blind. He had learned to cope with it, and she had helped him do it. Surely she could keep her wits in her head and help herself now.

Groping with her fingers, Anne found the broken board again. This time, she sawed her bonds ferociously against it.

Faintly, over her panting breath, she heard glass break. She strained to listen, but as seconds ticked by she wondered if it had been her imagination. Then she did detect a sound—a strange roar. An acrid smell floated to her, one that seeped into her lungs and made her cough.

She'd lived in the country. She knew what happened in dry summers when lightning struck or a cooking fire got out of hand. She knew the smell, the sound. The building was on fire.

How? Why? She let her head fall back to the floor. For some mad reason, her breaths came even faster, as though she was eager to suck in smoke. She had to calm down. She couldn't panic, but that was easy to say and very difficult to do.

Once, the stables at a nearby house to Longsworth had gone up on a hot August night. Flames had reached so high they seemed to lick at the moon. She would never forget how fast the fire had moved, how unstoppable it seemed, how viciously it consumed everything in its path.

It couldn't be a coincidence. Sebastian had done this.

He didn't want to make her his mistress anymore; he wanted to burn her alive. Could he hate her so much? For the chamber pot and refusing to marry him? For ending up in a *brothel*?

Hysterical laughter bubbled up. Was her cousin really going to punish her—*murder* her—as retribution for her ending up in the place that had ruined her life and her future, that had almost stolen away all her hope and her strength? Her wits were all tangled up, but one emotion pounded above all others: She was *furious*. Did Sebastian think she'd happily chosen to go to Madame? Did he think she'd done it because she was wanton?

Who was he to pass judgment on her? She was *not* going to die in his trap. She was going to get out—then find him, denounce him to Bow Street, and watch him pay for every wicked thing he'd done.

Fury renewed strength, and she dragged the rope along the board. Her gloves shredded to pieces, and splinters ripped into her skin. Her shoulders screamed in pain. She pulled so hard along the board, she cut the back of her hand. Pain stung, but the rope broke. Thank heaven . . . but her wrists were so sore, her hands so numb, it took precious moments to unwind the rope.

The smell of smoke was growing stronger. There was a strange sound, like water rushing, but it must be flames eating up the wooden building. She tore at the knot binding her ankles. It was infuriatingly tight. She twisted a large splinter until it broke from the board, then she sawed frantically until the cord finally frayed and snapped.

Her legs wobbled as she stood. Her feet were numb from being bound. It was so dark, she couldn't quite tell which way was up, and she almost lost her balance. She sucked in smoky air, coughing. The smell was so strong, the sounds so loud, the fire must be close.

Sebastian would have wanted to set it near her if he

wanted to kill her. The hallway beyond the door could be filled with flame. Oh, God. Was there another way out of the room? Windows? What had she seen in this room when there was light? There had been boards on the wall across from her—they *must* be boarded-up windows.

Which way were they now? She tentatively moved forward. She had to go faster, but it was so hard when she couldn't see. How did Devon ever get used to this? His courage amazed her.

She ran forward blindly. She slammed into the wall and felt along until she reached the jagged edge of a board. Curling her fingers around it, she pulled, but the board was nailed in place. Feeling along the wall, she tried all the windows. Hope vanished. Each board held fast.

A dark void separated her from the door, but she thought of how confidently Devon had learned to move. She ran across the floor, made it safely to the other wall, and groped. At least Sebastian hadn't locked the door. The knob wasn't hot—that had to be a good sign. She tore it open and rushed out to a long corridor. Light spilled in at the end of the hall—it must mean there was an uncovered window. She ran in that direction.

Suddenly there was a roar at the end of the hall, and a rush of hot air pushed her back. She dropped to the ground as smoke billowed over her. She kept her cheek pressed to the floor. Dear God. Slowly, she looked up.

Ahead, down the corridor, flames licked at exposed boards on the ceiling and the floor. The plaster walls rippled eerily. She got to her feet, yanked up her hems, and tore down the hallway away from the fire, but as she turned a corner, she stopped. More flames rushed up the walls ahead. Sebastian must have set two fires, trapping her between.

Sebastian was not going to win! There *had* to be a way out—

A black shape came running through the fire, wings flapping at its sides. She must be losing her mind, or the smoke was stealing her wits. No, it truly was a man running toward her, and he held a blanket over his head. The fire behind him illuminated him, but she couldn't see his face. Sebastian? He wouldn't come back. Mick?

The blanket swept down and she drank in dark hair, a handsome face streaked with soot, a face she loved but couldn't believe she was seeing. Perhaps she'd fainted and was dreaming—

"Anne!" His voice was hoarse, and he coughed. It was Devon. It really was. He ran to her and wrapped the blanket around her. Wet wool slapped against her. He had soaked the blanket to keep the flames off them. He cupped her cheeks and gave her one mad kiss. Then he grasped her by the wrist and began to drag her with him. "I got in through a window. Hopefully the fire hasn't blocked our way back."

She was weak with relief and whispered, "How did you find me?"

"Yesterday I instructed my investigator to go to the house party Norbrook was attending. But your cousin left this morning—"

"He came back to kill me," she croaked. "But how did you—" She coughed helplessly. How had Devon known to find her here?

He held her tighter. "Wynter followed Norbrook here, then sent his lad with a message for me. I'd just learned you hadn't returned home. When I got here, Norbrook had already escaped in his carriage. Wynter rode off to pursue him—we thought he had you with him. But then I spotted a prostitute on the street corner. She said she saw a red-haired woman—you—sneak into the warehouse this morning. So I came in."

"I—I *didn't*. Mick caught me, knocked me out. I woke up here—"

"Shh. I know. Norbrook paid her to lie and say you came alone. Right now we have to get out of here. Then I will deal with your cousin."

Smoke billowed in the corridor, and Anne's eyes were stinging so badly, she couldn't see. She held on to Devon and let him lead her. She trusted him completely. In her life, she'd known only three men she could believe in: her father, her grandfather, and Devon.

A thundering crash behind them made her scream.

"Part of the roof must have collapsed," Devon growled.

The entire building would come down at any minute. They would be trapped and fire would consume them. "You're going to die because of me. I'm so—"

He shook her gently, then grasped her wrist tightly and tugged her to start her running. "No, angel, I'm going to get us out of this alive. I didn't survive war to let both of us die here."

He had to move—this end of the building was creaking and shuddering above them, and Devon was getting dizzy from lack of air. Anne couldn't speak anymore, and she stumbled as he pulled her along. He was blind in the smoke and dark, but he'd lived like this for weeks. He didn't need his sight to find his way back through the winding corridors. He would not let Anne die. He'd lost his sight, almost lost his life, lost his soul—he believed—in battle. He'd lost Rosalind and his father. But losing Anne was the one thing he knew he couldn't face. The one thing he couldn't survive.

After he'd talked to the prostitute, he knew Anne was still inside—the woman had seen only Norbrook come out. Devon had sprinted around the building and found a window that wasn't boarded. He broke it and climbed in. He had to reach it now. He'd never been so hot in his life. The flames, the explosions, the blinding ash and smoke were like a battlefield. He'd thought charging into combat was like running into hell. He'd been wrong. He'd never run into cannon fire and flaying bayonets while dragging an innocent woman with him. This, here, now—*this* was hell.

Above them, the building gave another deadly shudder. Anne fell, her legs collapsing beneath her, and he caught her. She was limp, so he tossed her over his shoulder, clamped his hand to her rump. She had to be all right.

Crash!

An enormous piece of the ceiling thundered down behind him. The heat of the flames was scorching. He knew he was only a few yards from the window, and the licking fire threw light ahead of him. He had no air left in his lungs, but he sprinted forward. *There*. The window. He had to get Anne out. Saving her was all that mattered.

Gently, he set Anne on the sill. Her eyes were open and she struggled to speak but coughed instead. Then her eyes widened with horror at the exact instant he heard a groan behind him. He twisted to look. The fire illuminated a man in the doorway, dragging himself along the floor, clutching his gut. The eerie red light gleamed on his bald head.

Anne was trying to move off the sill, and he knew she intended to risk her life to help Mick Taylor.

"You first," he breathed against her ear. "I'll get him, and bring him out. I want you to run away from the building, love. I'll come after you. But just in case I can't get out, you have to get away before the building collapses."

"No—" she began, but he lowered her out the window, then gave her a push so she had to stumble away from the warehouse. The structure gave a long, agonized creak. "Run, Anne," he shouted. She did, moving clumsily. He hurried to Taylor, who had collapsed. Dark liquid covered the man's hand—blood. It was leaking from his stomach onto the floorboards. Taylor had been shot. He must have seen them and pulled himself after them, hoping for rescue.

As swiftly as he could, Devon turned the man over. He saw the eyes—wide open and blank. Without hope, he searched for a pulse to make certain. There was none. Taylor was dead and there was no point in dragging him out. Devon raced to the window and grasped the frame to jump out, when the building made a sound like a scream. Flame and wood rained down on him, and a great weight slammed him hard between his shoulders, knocking him to the floor.

Chapter Twenty-four

DEVON. ANNE HAD turned back, had seen him in the window, then there was an awful roar and the wall of the building fell in. Dust and smoke flew at her face, blinding her. It billowed up, hiding everything. Was he buried? Crushed? She could barely breathe through her scorched throat, but she didn't care. Dizziness swamped her, from lack of air, from fear, but she stumbled back toward the pile of ash and flames. She had to get Devon *out*. People surrounded her—a fire in the stews attracted hordes. She pushed through the crowd to get closer to the building, then someone grasped her shoulders and pulled her away.

"Keep back, miss," barked a male voice.

It was a stranger. She fought his grip. "No. Devon . . . I must get him—"

"Look!" shouted someone else. "A man's coming out of the smoke! How'd he survive *that*?"

Tears streamed down her face. They hurt her cheeks—her skin must have been singed. She broke free of the hands restraining her and ran forward. Her legs wobbled, but then Devon was there. His strong arms hauled her against his chest, and she breathed in the scents of him and smoke and sweat. Her tears of relief swiftly soaked his shirt. "I thought you were dead. I thought I'd lost you."

"Never." Devon scooped her up and carried her away from the raging fire. Bells clanged. Now that she knew Devon was safe, she really saw everything around her. Men raced with buckets, working to put out the blaze. A man rushed out of a neighboring building, and he was propelling a terrified woman who held a baby. Anne shuddered in horror. This is what her cousin had caused. She'd always known he could be cruel, but she'd never imagined he was so evil. "Sebastian," she croaked. "I have to stop him."

"Shh." Devon had every intention of destroying her damned cousin. First, he wanted to ensure Anne was safe. He carried her to his carriage and laid her down on a seat.

He caressed her, his intent to make certain she had no cuts, no broken bones, no injuries. Her wrists were raw and chafed.

"The building came down . . ." she croaked, "on top of you. . . . How did you escape?"

"I managed to move quicker than the collapsing wall," he said simply. He turned and gave an instruction to one of his footmen, then he shouted to his coachman, "Make haste to Dr. Milton, on Harley Street. And keep her safe. Do not let her out of your sight."

"Can we just go?" she whispered. "Should we not wait, tell someone . . . about Sebastian?"

"I want to have you examined by a doctor. I'm going to stay and ensure that everyone has escaped from the surrounding buildings." He stroked her cheek, brushing away soot. "Rest, Anne," he urged. "I'll come after you as soon as I can. You'll be safe with my servants."

He jumped down from the carriage, and as it rolled down the street, he headed back toward the fire. Out of the corner of his eye, he noted his footman had found the prostitute who had given him the information.

Suspicious of her story from the start, Devon had coaxed her to reveal the truth: A blond man who matched Norbrook's description had paid her to say that a red-haired woman had gone into the warehouse alone. At first, Devon assumed Anne's cousin had done it to deflect suspicion from himself. But he couldn't understand why Norbrook had specifically paid this woman to say she had seen Anne. After the fire, though, the woman's story would have been evidence that Anne had died—

Hell. In the fire, a body would have been burned beyond recognition. The prostitute's story would have given proof of Anne's death. Why would Norbrook want that? Was it because he thought Bow Street would stop investigating the madam's murder if Anne was dead?

Fury raged, roaring through Devon's heart and soul like devouring flames. What in hell did the motives matter? He wanted to kill Anne's cousin. First, he was going to stay until people were safe and the fire was under control, then he would go to Anne. After that, he would get Norbrook.

What was he going to do when he found Anne's cousin? Stay cool and logical and ensure that the man trapped himself so that he could be locked up in prison? Or give in to the hatred that was coursing through him and publicly tear the viscount apart?

"Sebastian is here?" Anne stared in horror at the elegant front of the Boodle's Gentlemen's Club, situated on St. James's Street. Blinding anger welled up. "How could he? He murdered Mick Taylor, he left me in a burning building, and he came to his *club* to play the gentleman?"

Devon drew her instantly into a soothing embrace. "Apparently he's confident no one would suspect him of setting that fire. He's a fiend, love, but in a few minutes he's going to get a very unpleasant surprise."

He spoke softly, but his tone was lethal. Devon looked over to Sir John Lawrence, the Bow Street magistrate. Devon had come to her at Dr. Milton's, exhausted, sooty, but smiling with delight as Milton assured him she was healthy. The fire had been extinguished and everyone from the surrounding buildings rescued. She had been deeply relieved to know her cousin had not hurt anyone innocent. But then Devon had told her he must take her to Bow Street. . . .

Anne would never forget how afraid she'd been, even at Devon's side, to face gray-haired, obviously astute Sir John in his offices. Nor would she forget how intensely Devon defended her, convincing Sir John of her innocence and her cousin's guilt.

Then Devon had wanted to take her home before he searched for her cousin. He'd argued she should rest—Dr. Milton had warned that she'd breathed in a great deal of smoke and must be suffering from shock. But she'd insisted on coming with him. She wouldn't cower from Sebastian now. By not letting her old fears paralyze her, she had survived his attempt to kill her.

Well, actually she had survived because Devon came to her rescue. He had rushed into a burning building to save her. At first she had wondered if gentlemen normally did such things for mistresses. But she knew Devon would have risked his life to rescue anyone. He didn't believe he was a war hero, but he was wrong. He was a hero in every way.

He gently stroked her neck, trying to soothe her, as the footman opened the door. He planned to confront

Sebastian, who was a true madman, yet he was worried about *her*.

She had known for a long time she was in love with the Duke of March. Now she knew she could never love him in a halfhearted way that wouldn't ultimately break her heart.

Devon lifted her hand and bestowed a gentlemanly kiss. "You will have to wait here."

"No! I'm not afraid of him. I want to be there with you, to ensure he doesn't hurt you."

"Angel, I promise you have nothing to worry about. If the French army couldn't kill me, your bully of a cousin won't succeed. But the reason you can't come is that you are a lady. Ladies are not allowed in gentlemen's clubs."

"I'm not a—"

"You are," he said intensely. "I'm afraid even a duke could not get you across the threshold." He glanced to Sir John. "I will lure Norbrook outside, so have your men hiding on the street and ready. I'm going to destroy him for what he's done to Anne."

As Devon pushed open the door, Sir John warned, "March, you cannot take the law into your hands. If you kill Norbrook in the middle of St. James's Street, I will be forced to arrest you."

Ten minutes of nerve-racked waiting later, Anne saw the enormous door of the club burst open. Devon stalked out. He was hauling Viscount Norbrook by the scruff of his neck. Elegant gentlemen were everywhere—strolling down the sidewalk, alighting from carriages. Each and every one came to a halt and stared as Devon slammed his fist into her cousin's nose. Norbrook screamed in pain, blood spurted, the shoulders of Devon's burned coat tore with a *rrrrip,* and her cousin fell on his back in the street.

Anne jumped out of the carriage. Devon was not going to be arrested over her. She lifted her skirts to run for him, dimly aware of raucous male laughter surrounding her. She didn't care—she couldn't. "Dev—" She stopped, then quickly corrected, "Your Grace, no, you can't!"

Ignoring her entreaty, Devon jumped into the street, grasped Sebastian by his shoulder, and pulled him to his feet. She cried out as Sebastian punched Devon's jaw. As Devon reeled back, Sebastian drew out a blade from his sleeve.

She ran at her cousin. "Don't you dare hurt him, you monster!"

Sebastian whipped to face her, and she knew, in that instant, he hadn't noticed her before. He gaped at her, all color slipping away. "Anne . . . it's not possible. You can't be. You're—" He seemed to regain control of his wits. "You are safe. Thank heaven. I've been searching for you, trying to find you—"

"Oh, stubble it!" she cried, heedless of the blade he held. "You tried to kill me. You killed Mrs. Meadows and you shot Mick Taylor. I've told Sir John of Bow Street everything."

Sebastian launched at her, his blade raised, but before she could move, Devon tackled him, slamming him to the sidewalk. He wrenched Sebastian's arm behind his back, and the knife fell free. Then he hauled her cousin to his feet. "We can do this here, or we can go to Bow Street and you can answer the magistrate's questions in private. But make any attempt to escape and I'll kill you. I've spent the last three years in battle, and I learned how to kill men in ways you couldn't even begin to imagine."

Sebastian, who had smirked in front of Anne only hours before, shook in Devon's grip. "These accusations are madness," he hissed. His eyes widened in desperation as the Runners stepped out—five ruthless-looking men in scarlet waistcoats. Sir John moved forward and Norbrook appealed to him. "How can you listen to this insanity, Sir John? This woman is a prostitute—"

Devon's fist knocked her cousin to his bottom in the street. He landed in a pile of ripe-smelling mud. Crossing his arms menacingly over his chest, Devon glared down at Sebastian, his violet eyes like ice. "You made a lot of mistakes, Norbrook. Should I list them all? Sir John is listening, so I think I will, and you will keep your mouth shut."

He was mocking Sebastian. Anne had never seen her cousin turn such a deep red with rage. He tried to scramble out of the mud, tried to salvage his pride. But Devon pushed him back with a boot to his chest. "First, you admitted to your cousin, just before you left her to burn to death in a warehouse, that you had been to the brothel before the madam's murder. After you left London, I spoke with your banker. He is normally the soul of discretion, but once I warned him I would remove my money from his institution, the poor fellow had no choice but to tell me the truth. You withdrew several large sums of money from your accounts."

"Gaming debts," her cousin whispered. Their conversation was so quiet, onlookers couldn't hear, even though they strained forward. The Runners kept them back.

"You don't play. I had Mrs. Meadows's accounts investigated. She deposited the same amounts of money in her bank within days of your withdrawals."

Sebastian flashed a fearful glance toward Sir John. "I will admit I used her services."

"I think when Bow Street questions Mrs. Meadows's girls, they will find you were never a client. You were searching for your cousin. You discovered that Mrs. Meadows was holding her captive and would not let her go without a generous payment. What happened on the night of her murder? Your cousin escaped. Did you go to the brothel with your last installment, intending to finally take her with you? Then, after you paid, you discovered the madam had lied—your cousin was no longer there. There was a witness to your meeting with Mrs. Meadows, a girl who saw you hit her with the—"

"Stop. Enough. I don't want everyone to hear this. I am willing to go to Bow Street."

Devon snarled at Sebastian. "Tell me why you wanted to kill your cousin. You went through so much to find her. Why would you want her dead?"

Anne shivered, waiting for the answer. She wanted to run away now—she didn't want to hear what Sebastian would say about her. All these gentlemen were watching her, assessing her. She was wearing a cloak over her sooty clothes and she had the hood up to shroud her face, but all these men must know she was Sebastian's cousin. Some might know her from Madame's.

Devon jerked Sebastian to his feet. Her cousin was shaking with rage but impotent. "I did not want to hurt her. I certainly did not set that fire. It was a tragic accident."

"Like hell." Devon shoved Sebastian ahead of him, and two of the Runners came forward, obviously to arrest the viscount and take him to Bow Street. How could Sebastian have come to this? How could he have done so much evil? For her?

She was watching her cousin so closely, she saw his hand go to a pocket in his coat. Silver flashed. "Devon," she cried, "he has a knife—"

It wasn't a knife. It was a tiny pistol. Devon commanded him to put the weapon down and lunged, but Sebastian put the gun to the side of his head and, in a heartbeat, pulled the trigger. A small explosion rent the air, smoke puffed, then Sebastian fell to the ground with blood running down the side of his head.

Anne wobbled. Devon rushed to her, held her, while Sir John and the Runners went to her cousin. She twisted in Devon's arms as he hurried her to the carriage. Sebastian's face was turned toward her, but his eyes were sightless. He was gone, gone to his own hell.

What would happen now?

Anne snuggled to Devon beneath the warm covers of the bed in her town house. His long, muscular body lay beside hers, his arm resting possessively over her chest. Her cousin was dead, and Sir John had accepted Sebastian's guilt in Madame's death. Her name was cleared. Devon had made her safe, and now, in his arms, she felt it. She loved him deeply. She would not think about the future, when he would leave her bed and never come back.

"Would you stay?" she whispered. "Tonight, in my bed?"

He kissed her forehead. "I shouldn't, love. I still have the dreams about battle. I still cry out in the night and might lash out—"

"I'm not afraid of your nightmares, Devon," Anne said softly. "I'm afraid of mine."

Her words touched Devon deeply. Why had he not thought of that? He had been planning to leave her to sleep, as he always did. But her fingers were gripping him tightly. She needed him, and he couldn't run away from her. If he had to stay awake for the entire night to keep her safe, to be there if she woke up afraid, he would do it.

He cradled her. "I won't leave you, Anne. Don't fear that. I'll keep you safe. Always." He stroked her hair. The bath had washed away all but the lightest hint of smoke.

"Thank you," she murmured sleepily.

"You have nothing to fear now, Anne. You are free." He turned and kissed her. He didn't want to think of the future. Having to marry. He didn't want to let Anne go. He remembered thinking she was a lady in every sense of the word that mattered.

His family had always insisted he marry for love. Right now, as he cradled Anne close, he couldn't imagine marrying for anything less.

Nestling his cheek to her hair, Devon closed his eyes. . . .

Hours later, he blearily opened them again. He remembered cradling Anne, then nothing but warmth and the sense of being completely relaxed. He'd fallen asleep.

He jerked up in the bed. Anne muttered something but settled back into sleep.

He hadn't had a dream. How was that possible? He'd been plagued by nightmares every night, yet not tonight.

Last night, while he'd bathed Anne and helped her dress for bed, she told him of her plan to help Thomas and Mrs. Tanner. Due to Anne, he had been able to pay his debt to Captain Tanner. Was that why the nightmares hadn't come? Or was it because he had saved Anne? Had he finally found peace at night because he now knew Anne was safe? Or because he'd decided he was never going to let her go?

He'd fallen in love with Rosalind in a heartbeat. Love had slammed into him like a runaway carriage. So hard, it had figuratively knocked him off his feet. It hadn't been like that with Anne. True, every few seconds he thought about her and hungered to be with her. And the thought of losing her had been more terrifying than facing cannons, swords, and rifles in battle.

Anne had never knocked him over, but she had done something more powerful: She had become the one thing he believed he needed to keep standing. She hadn't unbalanced his world; she had become his world. He'd fallen in love exactly the way his mother had described it.

Anne woke, aware of wetness and warmth swirling around her breasts.

Startled, she opened her eyes. Devon was gently suckling her left nipple. Beneath his lazily twirling tongue, her heart pounded. He'd spent the night with her in her bed. "Did you sleep?" she asked quietly, though, given his tousled hair and bright eyes, she suspected he had.

He lifted his head and gave her a brilliant smile. "I did, angel. Because of you, I believe."

Her heart soared. And arousal soared even higher as the nudge of his cock against her stomach told her exactly what he wanted to do. But he stopped. "I shouldn't do this after what you've been through—"

"You must. That's why I want it." She closed her eyes and thought of nothing but the pleasure of his touch, his mouth, his beautiful body against hers.

He brought her to a climax with his fingers, then his mouth, then he drove deeply into her while she was still sobbing with pleasure, and he made her truly explode. She was so dizzy with ecstasy, it felt as if the room were spinning.

Then he simply kissed her, for what seemed like priceless, delicious hours.

Finally, he groaned reluctantly. "I have to leave you for a while. I should go to Bow Street and ensure all is in order with Sir John. I should go home and see my family. No doubt they've heard rumors of what has happened."

Guilt surged. "Of course. They may think you were hurt! They must be—"

"I sent a note of reassurance to my mother. They won't be worried, but they will be bursting with curiosity." He cocked his head. "It's a beautiful day. You can do anything you wish. You could take a drive in your carriage and shop as much as you want."

"I would like to take a walk in the sun. I always dreamed of walking through Hyde Park."

"You've never done that?"

"No." She didn't want to say more and spoil the moment—didn't want to remind him that she could not go because she'd been a prisoner in the brothel and, before that, she'd been far too poor to walk among fashionable people in the park.

Devon gave her another long kiss. His eyes, filled with regret, held hers. Was he sorry for her past? He talked lightly with her as he dressed. He made plans—to take her to the theatre where he kept a private box, to the museum, boating on the Thames. It was as if he was organizing a campaign to give her all the pleasures of London, the way he would plan for battle. She laughed, hugged her knees. "Your list has me breathless."

"It will be my pleasure to treat you as I should have all along." He smiled. "After all, I promised you quite a bit in our contract. It's time I delivered." He gave her a formal bow that made her heart ache. Then he left her.

The bed felt decidedly empty without his broad shoulders and long legs filling it. She swung her feet over the edge and jumped out. She gave the bellpull a tug.

It took an hour to be dressed by her maid. Since she still possessed very few clothes, Anne spent the morning shopping on Bond Street. It was her duty to dress fashionably, to be a credit to Devon. In truth, she rather liked having lovely things of her own. It had been so long since she could dream of pretty gowns.

Shopping meant she did not have to think about Sebastian, how close she had come to dying and to losing Devon. She had an ice at Gunter's, again something she'd fantasized of doing when she had been poor in the stews. It was a bittersweet pleasure—she wished she could have treated her mother to one. She took her carriage to Hyde Park. She wanted time to herself, without her maid trailing after her. Although Society would frown on her walking alone, she sent her servants home and she went through the gate into the park.

The sun slanted low, glinting on the rippling surface of the Serpentine. It was as lovely as she'd always dreamed. Devon's London home, March House, was close by. It was one of the enormous mansions overlooking the park. Of course, she dared not go there. She couldn't *call*. It might be only several feet from where she stood, but it was a world away.

She shook off the heaviness around her heart. She was *free*. Almost four weeks ago she had traveled to Devon's house, determined to become his mistress. Determined to escape. To build an independent life. She had done all those things.

She did feel relief and happiness and joy. For the first time, she could look toward the future with hope. But she felt a strange sadness she could not shake.

Behind her, men laughed and hooves thudded in the sand of Rotten Row, the track used by the *ton* for riding. Anne turned. Sunlight limned the two riders and blinded her. The gentlemen stopped and one challenged the other to a race. Then the man's gaze settled on her. "Moreton, take a look. It's lovely Annalise. She used to work at Madame Sin's. Tasty morsel, isn't she? Read in the news sheets this morning that she was cleared of the madam's murder. Apparently Viscount Norbrook clubbed the woman's head in. He took his own life in the middle of St. James's Street."

"Shocking affair," said the second man. He lifted his hat to her, the gesture exaggerated. He gave a low, suggestive laugh. Anne felt her cheeks prickle. She knew him. He used to come to her at Madame's. He had done so regularly on Wednesday nights for two months.

Should she acknowledge him? Did politeness dictate it? The thought immobilized her on the spot. What were the rules in polite Society about meeting a former brothel client?

She didn't want to say a word. She wanted to pretend none of it had ever happened. Her stomach churned. Anne whirled away from the two riders, but she heard the first man say, "Rumors are flying that she's now the Duke of March's mistress."

"Lucky man," the second drawled. It surprised her he didn't give a hint of what he and she had done at Madame's. Some madness made her look back at them. The second man smiled. His gaze lingered audaciously on her bosom. He gave a suggestive wink.

A blush scalded Anne's cheeks. With desperate strides, she hurried back toward the entrance gate. A walk in the park on a sunny day no longer seemed like a pleasure.

She would always be what she was in Madame's brothel. She would always be considered a courtesan. Men would gape lasciviously at her breasts, assess her with undisguised lust, and think about how much they were willing to pay for her.

Never again. After Devon decided on his future wife and ended their relationship, she would never take another protector. She couldn't face the thought of touching another man, of being with any man but Devon. And now that Devon had slept a night without a nightmare, he was healing, he was putting war memories behind him. He could marry now. It was his duty.

But, more than that, he deserved to find love and happiness. She had seen how gentle he was with Thomas. She remembered how lovingly he had cradled his sister's newborn child. He deserved to be a father.

A mad thought popped into her head. Was it possible for a duke to marry his mistress?

Oh, God, what was she thinking? It was *impossible*. Even if she hadn't been ruined by her time at Madame's, she still couldn't dream of becoming Devon's wife. Dukes also did not marry daughters of viscounts. They aspired much higher.

Anyway, Devon had never spoken of marriage. This morning he'd told her he was pleased to have the chance to do the things he'd promised in their *contract*. He planned to give her all sorts of pleasures but to treat her like a mistress.

Now she knew the reason for the painful tug around her heart. She wasn't free at all. She might never be. It wasn't only a matter of having her heart broken. She didn't think she would ever stop loving Devon. Hopelessly. Just as Kat had said.

Chapter Twenty-five

His mother assessed him with a shrewd gaze that traveled over him from head to toe. "You certainly look sound. And you are telling me the stories I heard were exaggerated—that you were not almost killed in a fire while rescuing your mistress?" She spoke in a low voice, for they were in the nursery and little Peregrine was sleeping in his cradle, but she was pale.

"Isn't gossip always exaggerated?" Devon said lightly. He had told her most of what had happened when he and Anne escaped the fire, though he did omit the part about the building collapsing just as he got out.

"Perhaps. But knowing you, I wonder . . ." His mother tickled Peregrine's stomach through the covers. A little smile curved the baby's lips, though Cavendish had told Devon that such smiles were likely gas. "Anyway, now that you have found your missing people, as you put it, you will be ready to court a potential bride."

There was no point in trying to ease gently into this. "You believe I should marry for love, Mother, but what if I've fallen in love with someone inappropriate, someone Society will say I shouldn't marry? What if I plan to ask for her hand?"

His mother blinked. He'd thrown a lot at her, but she asked with admirable calm, "How inappropriate is she?"

"She's my mistress." He took his mother's hand and kissed it, then led her away from the sleeping baby. He told her everything: Anne's flight from her home into the slums, the time she had approached him outside the Drury Lane theatre, and how he'd turned her away. Her imprisonment in a brothel. The way she had seduced her way into his life. The way she had coaxed him to heal. "I don't want any other woman as my wife. I love Anne Beddington."

His mother was pale. "Surely you can find another who captivates you as much—"

"No, there will never be anyone else."

"You thought no one could replace Rosalind, yet you have found this girl. You will find someone else, Devon."

His mother had championed love, but he'd suspected it would not be stronger than scandal. He shook his head. "I love Anne more than I loved Rosalind."

His mother's eyes widened in shock. "You pursued Lady Rosalind with single-minded determination and caused scandal to possess her. I presume nothing I say will change your mind."

Three years of regrets and pain crashed into him. His last argument with his father washed over him. "I don't want to do that again. I don't want to hurt you."

"*I* am willing to weather scandal. There was a great deal of gossip when you stole Rosalind from your friend. I worked very hard to quell it, Devon, for Rosalind's sake. The cruel things that were said, the pointed fingers—it hurt her. If you marry your mistress . . . It does not matter if it hurts me, Devon; I'm certainly strong enough to cope. What I cannot do is let you hurt your sisters. That would materially hurt Win's and Elizabeth's chances of making good matches."

Anger surged, along with icy pain, at the stupidity of Society for punishing his sisters for a choice *he* would make, but he knew his mother spoke the truth. And after putting his sisters through three years of pain and worry, he could not hurt them again. "You've always ranked love so highly, but, in truth, love doesn't conquer all."

Deep lines bracketed his mother's mouth. In that instant, she looked old. "You will fall in love again, Devon," she whispered. "I am sure of it."

He shook his head. "I very much doubt it. If I marry—"

"Devon, you must. It is your duty to wed and have an heir. And you are far too young to spend the rest of your life alone, without a wife, without a family of your own."

He thought of Anne cradling Thomas in a swift embrace to make him feel safe, how she spoke to him as if he were a man to soothe his pride and help ease his shame. For all Devon was male, he hadn't understood that a twelve-year-old boy would have his sense of manhood hurt by what had happened to him. Anne would make a wonderful mother. What in Hades should he do? He couldn't bring pain to his family by marrying Anne. And he didn't want to marry for duty alone.

"If you had been killed in battle . . ." His mother stopped and took a shaky breath. "What do you think your last regret would have been?"

"That the last words I said to Father were in anger, I believe. That I put you through pain—"

"I think you would have regretted the loss of your future and the fact that you would not have another chance at love. You came home, Devon. Take that chance. Please." His mother rested a shaky hand on his wrist. He hated hurting her.

But how could he marry for duty when he was deeply, intensely in love with Anne?

Hyde Park. The fashionable hour. Even in September, the *ton* came to see and be seen in the late afternoon. Walking alongside Tristan, Devon cast a jaded eye over the ladies and grimaced. They all looked the same to him. Each girl wore much the same dress, twirled a lace-trimmed parasol, and each wore an identical placid expression on her face.

Before he'd left his hunting box in pursuit of Anne, he found her scarlet gown in the wardrobe in his bedchamber—the gown she wore to come and seduce him. She would have looked like a delicious treat in it. In gowns, in breeches, in nothing at all, she was breathtakingly lovely. Anne was intriguing in a way no other woman was.

"Christ, I just realized why you wanted to come here." Tristan's exclamation of surprise made Devon jerk toward his friend. "You're looking for a wife."

"Last week I promised my mother I would consider courting." He glanced toward his mother, who was chatting with several *ton* matrons while Lizzie and Win giggled with the women's daughters. It hadn't taken long to realize his mother had barely been out in Society since he'd left.

His mother had not been going out; Win and Lizzie hadn't married. It was as if they'd stopped their lives for the three years he'd been at war. At least Caro and Charlotte had not done so; their babies were evidence of that. How did he make up for three years he'd taken from their lives?

He turned and walked with Tris, aware of a dozen *ton* mamas peering at him through lorgnettes. For his mother's sake, he was here, making an attempt to do his duty.

To not do it would break his mother's heart. But his own heart was not in it.

"Dev? You don't seem to be paying attention to the eligible misses."

He groaned. With his sight back, he could see all these pretty English ladies, but he wasn't looking at them. They were part of the background, a blur of fluttering dresses and parasols. All he could see were Anne's large green eyes, her fierce determination, her beautiful smile.

He had no interest in spending interminable hours in inane banter with any of these giggling debutantes, knowing he could never ask the most important questions.

Would you be willing to charge into a brothel to rescue a boy? Would you have forced me to shave my face and give up brandy, when I was blind? Would you have walked in the rain to teach me I could listen to the sound of it on the trees?

He walked away from the chattering crowd, toward the Serpentine, Tristan following. He was almost at the lake when a hand clapped on his shoulder, and a deep, mocking voice said, "So, how is the murderess in bed? Has she tried to hit you with a poker the way she did to her madam? Can't understand why you would take a dockyard whore as your mistress."

Devon spun around. The words were like flame to a cannon's fuse. Inside, he was sizzling. The man goading him was the Earl of Duncairn—they had been enemies at school. Duncairn had also been Gerald's friend and had hated Devon for breaking Gerald's heart over Rosalind.

"Let it go, Duncairn," Devon growled between gritted teeth.

"I'd like to know if she's any good, March. Madame Sin whipped her girls well if they didn't perform as they should."

"I said be quiet," he warned.

"Or what? You'll call me out? Over a whore?"

"Yes," he snarled, but in that instant Duncairn's fist came at Devon's face and slammed into his nose. He'd pulled back, saving his nose from a break, but blood spurted. His battle instincts surged and he drove his right fist into Duncairn's gut, his left into the man's jaw. War had made him stronger. It had also made his blows a lot more lethal. Duncairn thudded to the ground.

Women screamed and men exclaimed in protest. Devon saw his mother shake her head grimly and restrain his sisters from running to him. After all, a gentleman did not knock another man senseless in the middle of the fashionable hour.

"What the hell were you thinking?" Tristan shoved a white monogrammed handkerchief at his face. Devon pressed it to his bleeding nose. He crouched beside Duncairn, pushing aside the man's friends. He wanted to make sure he hadn't killed the earl. Fortunately, Duncairn was still breathing and Devon had restrained his anger enough to avoid breaking the earl's jaw.

"You do realize you were fighting over your mistress's *honor,* Dev?" Tristan snapped.

Devon dabbed the handkerchief to his sore nose again. He lifted it away. It was soaked with bright red blood—red coats didn't show blood, but white shirts did. How many white shirts had he watched soak completely with blood in a matter of seconds?

He thought of Anne, and the battle memories receded. "I know exactly what I was doing."

"Dev, it's a fool's game to fall in love with a mistress. Makes life damnably miserable. You wouldn't know that—your father and mother were notoriously besotted. My father had the sexual morals of an alley cat, and it made my mother's life miserable. Consequently she was always angry, unhappy, and brittle. Look at Prinny.

He fell for Maria Fitzherbert. Did it make him happy? By all accounts, he got dead drunk on the night of his duty wedding and heaved his guts in the fireplace. Dev, are you listening?"

He was. But mainly he was turning Tristan's words over in his head. He loved Anne, and he knew he could never settle for anything less than a marriage made for love. There had to be a way he could claim the woman he adored without hurting his family.

Nerves had Anne shredding her handkerchief. She glanced toward Devon, who sat beside her in his ducal carriage. For the third morning in a row, she had thrown up her breakfast. She'd kept it a secret from Devon, but she knew what it meant. She was carrying his child.

Should she tell him about the baby? Or wait for him to guess for himself? Surely he would do so soon. Her breasts were already tender and fuller, and while her belly was still flat, it wouldn't be long before it began to expand too.

A woman of courage would tell him. She was going to lose him anyway when he found a bride. He had a right to know about his child. Their contract stipulated he was to take charge of the baby. Perhaps he would decide to place the infant with a family. Often gentlemen did that with their bastards. Loving parents would raise the baby as their own, and the gentleman would provide funds for the child's care. She might never see the baby again. It would be for the best, of course, so the child would never bear the stigma of being a courtesan's child.

"We're here." He leaned toward her window.

Bewildered, Anne peered out too. The carriage had stopped in front of a house so enormous it appeared to encompass half the block. Window upon window reflected sunlight. Sweeping steps led to large doors. A gleaming wrought iron railing surrounded it all. Anne blinked. She remembered this house from a long time ago—she had walked past it with her mother when she was young, when her parents were alive. It had been one of the times her family had visited Town and stayed in their London home, the one Sebastian had inherited.

She whirled on Devon. "Why have you brought me here? This is my great-grandmother's home. I cannot go there! She disowned my grandfather and never acknowledged my mother!"

He leaned over and gave her the sort of slow, tingling kiss designed to whisk away a woman's wits. Over the last few days, she'd seen a whole new side of him. With his guilt eased, Devon's nightmares were coming less and less often. He no longer acted out battles in his sleep. And he was surprisingly playful—he enjoyed teasing her both in bed and out. Delicately, he held her chin, but his touch was firm enough that she couldn't escape his violet eyes. "I came here yesterday and coaxed your great-grandmother to speak to me," he said. "She wanted desperately to know where you are."

Anne didn't quite know why, but she wanted to demand they drive away. She had the unbearable urge to bang her fists against him. Why had he done this? She didn't want this. She asked, as though she was only curious and her stomach was not churning into knots, "Why would she want to find me? She disowned the family over my grandfather's marriage."

The carriage door opened, but Devon instructed his footman that they needed a minute before leaving. Anne had no intention of going into the house. What would be the point? "We couldn't go to her when Sebastian attacked me. My mother said we couldn't. She said my great-grandmother would let us starve in the street rather than help us."

She clasped her hands tightly, trying to control her anger. And her . . . fear. She did not want to see this woman. She did not want to be rejected. Devon caught her wrists and she struggled to break free. He had forced this on her—he was *not* going to quell her. She didn't care that she'd signed a contract promising to please him. "Did you tell her everything? Did you tell her what I've become?"

He lifted a brow, utterly, irritatingly calm. "Why did you not tell me you are a great-granddaughter to Lady Julia de Mournay? She is the last of one of the oldest and most important families in England, and one of the wealthiest women in the country."

"And for that reason she wanted nothing to do with my mother or me."

"That's not true, love."

"My mother explained why she could not go to her family when we had to leave our home. She knew they would not help. My great-grandmother had disowned her son—my mother's father—over his marriage. He had fallen in love with my grandmother while she was an opera dancer on the Drury Lane stage. They ran away to marry. I never met any members of my mother's family except my grandfather."

"He was the one who was blind?"

She nodded. She remembered how hurt her mother had been by her family's rejection. Her mother had spoken of it only once, but Anne would never forget Mama's deep pain and humiliation. Even when her grandfather lost his sight, Lady Julia would not speak to him. She had showed him no kindness or mercy.

"My mother was desperate when we were forced to leave Longsworth. But she knew all of her family would turn us away. All because this woman had taught them to hate my grandmother, my mother, and consequently me. All because my grandmother was not a lady."

"Your great-grandmother regrets what she did," he

said gently. "She had three children—a son and two daughters. She lost all of them, and her daughters died without producing children. By the time you—her only great-grandchild—were born, she was alone. She told me she realized how foolish it was to end up that way simply because one did not approve of a marriage. Two years ago, she went to Longsworth in the hopes of seeing your mother and you and making amends. She found out you were both gone. Your cousin offered to hunt for you."

"Why? In the warehouse . . . the way he spoke . . . it was obvious he hated me. Why would he search for us for the sake of my great-grandmother?"

Devon coaxed one of her hands free. Gazing into her eyes, he kissed it, and it was enough to make her forget the horrible things Sebastian had said. "He wanted her money. As Lady Julia's only living relative, you are her heir. Norbrook thought this time you would agree to marriage, and he would gain control of the wealth."

It stunned her. "Then why would he want to kill me?"

"While searching for you, your cousin wormed his way into Lady Julia's good graces. Norbrook was so kind and gentlemanly to her that she grew to admire him. She feared you had died in the stews and, just a few weeks ago, she told him he would become her heir if you were found to be dead."

Devon gently cupped her face. "I told Lady Julia how you helped your grandfather with his blindness. Her heart was touched. Now she would like to meet you."

"No! How could I? She doesn't know what I am. She would hardly accept me, hardly see me if she knew I was your mistress, knew what I had to do."

"Anne, I told her about your mother's illness, how you were desperate for money, and how you were forced into a brothel."

Her heart slammed against her ribs. "Why did you tell her?"

"I wanted her to know what you had been through. I wanted her to understand what pain her actions caused your mother and you. She knows it all, and she wants to see you."

How could that be true? "I don't know. I'm afraid—"

Devon lifted her hand to his lips, the way a knight would bestow a respectful kiss to a lady high above his station. "Angel, you are the most fearless person I've ever known."

She was hardly fearless. He had found her family. He had convinced her cold, aristocratic great-grandmother to see her. Anne was certain Devon was responsible in some way for Lady Julia's change of heart. But Lady Julia had rejected so many people out of pride—how could she open her heart to the most ruined type of woman of all? Fear froze Anne's hand on the carriage handle. She didn't know whether to push the door open or hold it closed. "Why does this matter to you, Devon?"

"My family means so much to me. I didn't like thinking that you had no one."

I have you. But Devon was reminding her he would not be in her life forever. "I do not need a family. It was always my plan to eventually have an independent life. I've recognized that is what I must do. That's exactly what I intend to do when . . . our contract ends."

"Come and meet her first, love, before you decide."

What would her great-grandmother be like, this mysterious woman she had never seen? Anne could not tamp down the fury in her heart. How could this woman have disapproved of her grandmother and mother? Both women had been the loveliest and kindest Anne had ever known.

A liveried footman had admitted them. He now returned. "Her Ladyship will see you in the drawing room." He bowed and led the way.

Devon's hand rested at her low back, and he urged her to follow. Why did he want this so much? Did protectors normally take such an interest in their mistresses?

They reached a room that was entirely white. Astonishingly white. The floor was marble tile, white silk covered the walls, and the moldings that looped and swirled like confectioner's icing were white plaster. All the furnishings were white and gilt.

Anne glanced at Devon. She wasn't quite sure what to make of the intensely bright room, and she realized . . . she was looking at him for support. As though they were more than courtesan and protector. She was looking to him as she had seen her mother look to her father and, even more often, her father look to her mother.

Heels tapped on the marble. Between two white screens, blue silk moved. Anne swallowed hard. Then the most elegant lady she had ever seen appeared before her. Lady Julia leaned on a walking stick, but she held herself tall. Silver hair was piled on her head, hair as pale as the room, carefully styled and shimmering. The austere brilliance of the white and silver made her gown all the more startling—it was an exquisite creation of sapphire silk that clung to a slender form. Her great-grandmother had ivy-green eyes, exactly like her own.

Suddenly Lady Julia rushed forward and embraced Anne. "My dear, what you have been through. What a fool I have been. An absolute fool!"

Anne found herself seated at a small round table in a bay window at the end of the drawing room. Her great-grandmother poured tea with a shaky hand. "I am so sorry I disowned your grandfather. So very sorry your mother believed she could not come to me for help." Great pain crossed the lined face.

"I had wanted so much for my children," Lady Julia said sadly. "Then your grandfather ran off and married an opera dancer. I decided that mistake must not happen again, so I pushed my daughters into grand marriages for duty. One married a duke's son, the other wed a marquess. Both men were scoundrels. My eldest daughter died of a broken heart because of her husband's infidelities. The other died of illness while her husband spent all his time in gaming hells. Gradually I realized what I had done. The lives I had controlled, I ruined. I saw I would eventually be quite alone. The only relative I had left was your mother. I wanted to make amends for my foolishness, so I tried to find her, but she had died. So I tried to find *you*."

"My mother believed you would not even speak to us," Anne said. "When we left Longsworth with no money, she would not come to you. She thought it would be pointless."

Lady Julia let out a long breath. She hung her head. "Your grandfather brought his child—your mother—to me, when she was about twelve years of age. I was still angry with him for defying my wishes. I sent him and your mother from my house and told them never to return." Her Ladyship looked up, tears glittering in her dark-green eyes. "His Grace told me about everything that had happened to you. What has befallen you was *my* fault. I should never have turned my back on your grandfather and his wife. I would have taken you and your mother in, yet your mother believed I would not because of what I said in anger when she was a child. She thought me so heartless that I would turn her and you away. And I had been heartless."

Anne knew she could agree, she could hurt this woman in revenge, but perhaps she must put pride and anger behind her too. "You have learned. That's the most important thing."

"March told me everything about Sebastian. What must you think of me? How could I not have seen what a despicable madman he truly was?" Her great-grandmother put a hand over hers. At first Anne tensed, then she relaxed, determined to move toward the future, away from the sorrow of the past.

"I have finally found you," Lady Julia said softly. "Or, rather, March has brought you to me. I cannot ask you to forgive me, Anne. But please, *please*, give me another chance. I wish to make it known that you are my great-granddaughter. I have eschewed the *ton* for years now, but I will have to return. There is much work for us to do!"

"Work?" She stared blankly as her great-grandmother smiled at Devon, who returned it with a grin. Both of them seemed to know something she did not. "What sort of work?"

"Your reintroduction into Society, of course."

Anne pulled her hand back. "Impossible. You know what I had to do, what I had to become, because of poverty."

"Yes." Lady Julia winced. "I am determined to change your life, Anne."

"No."

Devon leaned to her. "It can be done."

"It can't. I was a whore. I can't put that behind me." She remembered the men in Hyde Park. Their bold looks and leering smiles. "It's too late. I'm not a lady anymore. I never can be again."

"You still are," Devon said fiercely. "That's never changed, Anne."

"It has. I want to go forward, not back. I want to be *independent*. I know that is all I can have, and I am happy with it." She was trembling as though she would fly apart. Devon had called her fearless, but she didn't have the courage to believe in the impossible. She leapt up, knocking over her dainty chair. Spinning on her heel, she ran blindly.

He caught her at the foyer. In front of Lady Julia's servants, Devon grasped her around the waist and scooped her into his arms. "This time," he growled, "I'm not letting you go."

The marble tiles and domed ceiling whirled as he turned her fast enough to leave her dizzy, then carried her through a large doorway. Anne heard gasps of shock and snickers—apparently, the impassive servants were not immune to such displays of male possessiveness.

"What are you doing?" she demanded. "Put me on my feet. This is my decision to make."

To her surprise, he lowered her gently, and as her feet touched the ground he said, "I don't believe you are ruined forever. With powerful allies, you can return to Society. Your great-grandmother is ready to help you. My mother is adored in the *ton*. Both those women wield a great deal of influence. If they accept you, no one of the *ton* would dare dismiss you."

"Your mother? How could you ask your mother to do such a thing?"

"I believe Caro would help too. And I am sure I can enlist the help of my other married sister, Charlotte. Her husband is the Duke of Crewe, one of the Prince Regent's good friends."

How did he do this to her? How did he make her yearn to hope? But she shook her head. She wrapped her arms around her chest, as though shielding her heart from the determination in his eyes. "It's impossible. How could I go out in Society? Young ladies are warned to never associate with fallen women. It is as though I have a disease—I'm to be avoided at all costs, in case ruination is contagious."

His blazing eyes narrowed. "You deserve so much more than that."

"Perhaps, but that is how people will behave." She told him of her encounter with the two gentlemen in the park. Finally, though she hated to do it, she revealed that one of the men had been a client. She expected him to leave her once he knew that. Instead, he took a step toward her.

"No one will bother you in Hyde Park. I defended your honor there a few days ago, and no gentleman would risk making me angry again, I promise."

"What—what did you do?"

"I knocked the Earl of Duncairn on his arse. Unfortunately he got in a good blow of his own." Devon touched his nose.

"So that explains the bruises and the swelling. You told me it was an accident."

"It was. It was an accident that I allowed one of his fists to land on my face." He grinned, then winced. "You saved me, angel, in so many ways. Now let me save you."

"Devon, it is impossible to change Society's views."

"I survived battle with the French. I'd like to believe I can survive battle with a lot of narrow-minded matrons and hypocritical peers."

"You can win victories like the fight in the park, but you can never win the true victory—which is to change their opinions."

His lower lip protruded, giving him a sulky boyish look. "So it is your plan to go off to the country, rent a cottage, and . . . and what, love? Take a lover from the country gentry?"

She was doing a terrible thing now, keeping the truth about his child a secret. But she might be wrong about the pregnancy, she might lose the baby—there was no point in speaking of it when it might not happen at all. "I will have some money, Devon. I should like to start schools so young girls do not have to end up as prostitutes. That should keep me tremendously busy. And I could also hire a companion." She saw his eyes roll and she squared her shoulders. "I think it is a very good plan. I like the country. I enjoy simple pleasures. Few people are fortunate enough to have everything they've always dreamed of. In being independent, I will."

"And you are saying you don't want to be my mistress anymore."

"I—" Being enceinte made it impossible for her to ever be part of Society. Even her great-grandmother and a duchess could not make the *ton* accept an obviously pregnant courtesan. And she could not hide her pregnancy for very long. Only a few more weeks. "It would be for the best," she said. She was going to have her heart broken eventually. If she truly had courage, she could face it now. "I know you must bring an end to our arrangement anyway when you are ready to propose. To the lady you choose to be your bride, I mean."

"You will be free to take a lover, angel."

"I will never take another protector. I will never love anyone else—" She broke off. What had she done? She'd said aloud that she loved him.

Would he be embarrassed? What should she do? How did a woman tell a man she loved him and then assure him she understood that their sexual encounters had been only business?

"I am planning to make a proposal of marriage," he said softly. "One that will bring an end to our relationship as tempting mistress and besotted protector."

"Besotted? You can't be. I think you've mainly been irritated with me." Despite the hurt tugging at her foolish heart, she managed a wobbly smile. "I am glad you have found a bride."

He gazed at her as though seeing her for the very first time. "Sometimes, I've been told, it takes a while to realize when someone is unlike anyone else you've ever known."

She supposed she was quite different from other mistresses he'd had. More stubborn, less obedient, more annoying . . .

He traced her lips, igniting tremors worthy of an earthquake. "I'll never forget the time you took me walking in the rain, Anne. At first I thought you were mad—"

"I'm not surprised," she whispered. "I feared you would think me crazy." Heavens, she didn't want to leave him. She didn't want to let him go.

"You opened my world for me, Anne. By showing me the sense of space that sound could give me, you changed me from hopeless to hopeful. You've done that for me in so many ways. Little by little, you helped me to open my heart again."

He was telling her he had fallen in love with someone. This was to be goodbye, just as she'd said it should be, and in his kindness he was making it as sweet as he could.

"You helped me come to grips with my guilt over Captain Tanner's death. You helped me sleep through a night without nightmares. Somehow, in some miraculous ways unique to you, you helped me find peace. I am going to miss having you for my mistress, Anne Beddington."

She swallowed hard. This was the true test of strength. She must give a gracious goodbye. No tears. She was going to wish him happiness. She loved him so much, all she could hope for him was joy.

"My family has always believed in marrying for love,"

he said. "To my mother and father, love was the most important thing. Caro was encouraged to marry the earl she loved, rather than the duke she didn't. When I realized I'd fallen in love with you, Anne, I thought I would have to make the choice between marriage and love."

He slanted his mouth over hers. She was only barely aware of his kiss. Her whole world had become five unbelievable words. *Fallen in love with you.*

He drew back. "I'd planned for something spectacular, love, at my house. A trio of violinists was supposed to play for us, and I intended to walk you to a bower festooned with roses to surprise you. But I'll have to do this now. Here." He fumbled in the pocket of his greatcoat. "Blast, I can't get the thing out."

She couldn't even give a nervous giggle. That would have required a breath.

He yanked out a velvet-covered box. He opened it, plucked something out, and threw the box aside. When he opened his hand, she saw a dark-red stone sitting in the center of his palm—a huge heart-shaped ruby with dozens of facets to capture the sun.

"I wanted something striking and red, for you will always be Cerise to me. Bold, seductive, brave Cerise." He dropped to one knee in front of her. Taking her left hand, he held the ring poised before her finger. His dark hair fell across his eyes as he gazed up, surprisingly uncertain.

"Marry me, Anne," he said.

Devon felt lost in the silence. As the quiet stretched, cold swept through him, slowly freezing its way through his veins, as though he'd been dunked in ice water. "Anne?" Why was it taking her so long to say yes?

"You found—" Her lovely voice quavered. He'd focused on her tones so carefully when he was blind, he knew she was shocked. "You found my great-grandmother, you plotted my return to Society, because you want to marry me?"

"Yes, angel."

She scrambled back, away from his hand and the ring. "You cannot seriously be asking me to marry you. There must be dozens of eligible ladies you can court—"

"I'm not interested in any of them. I am seriously asking you. *You.*"

"Devon, no. No, I can't marry you."

No? "You are telling me no?" It made no sense. What mistress did not want to be a wife?

"Yes. I mean, my answer must be no."

"It can't be no. I love you." Hades, he sounded like a petulant boy.

"I— It doesn't matter what we feel. It is impossible. I can't marry you. You wouldn't be happy. And, consequently, neither would I."

"Indeed. You know how I would feel?"

"Yes, I do, because our marriage would hurt your family. You adore your family, and I will not be responsible for causing them pain. You would eventually resent me for that. Your sister Lady Cavendish was so kind to me. She called me a friend. If we wed, it would cause a huge scandal, and it would break my heart to hurt her. Your mother does not need any more pain. And there are your unmarried sisters. The soot on my reputation would tarnish them."

It was exactly what his mother had said. "We can try to make it work," he growled stubbornly. "Once you are part of Society again—"

"My answer has to be no. Always no. Nothing you can say will change my mind."

"You said you loved me."

She winced. "You are a wonderful man, but I—I am not in love. I don't believe I could ever fall in love with anyone. I want to be independent, Devon. That is what I truly want."

Was she saying she had been so hurt by her past that she could never open her heart? "Anne, don't be afraid of falling in love. I was. You helped me see I couldn't hide in grief and fear forever."

"Oh, you don't understand!"

Devon watched her run to the door, her skirts swishing. He should follow, but he couldn't make his boots move. When he'd made his proposal of marriage, he'd imagined that now, five minutes later, he would be a betrothed man.

Not a confused one.

Chapter Twenty-six

May 1816

Expecting a baby forced one to change plans, even about an independent life.

Spring had brought the moors to life, and Anne smiled as she walked along the path to her cottage. This was one change: She could not stride swiftly back home from the nearby village of Princeton. Every few yards she had to stop and puff out a few breaths. She was now the size of a house, with a taut, rounded belly, swollen ankles, and hunger that seemed never to cease.

Still, she was achieving everything she'd wanted. She was content—except for the great pain in her heart. Her heart was not growing any protective scar tissue at all. It simply hurt.

At the post office, she had collected a letter from her great-grandmother, and it was tucked into her pocket. Lady Julia had agreed Anne must live quietly out of sight until she bore her baby, but they wrote regularly. In that, Devon had been right. Anne was so happy to have family. But she cradled her belly as she walked. "I hope, when you are old enough to understand, you can forgive me, little one. I fear you won't. I don't know if I could, if I were you. I do promise you will never want for anything." It was true. Devon had not understood her refusal, but he had been very generous. Even though she had simply . . . left him.

When she began her school in the Whitechapel stews, he'd sent her the settlement he'd promised in her contract. He'd also sent a generous donation. With it, she had been able to employ teachers and refurbish a large town house to use as both a school and a home for the girls.

Three months ago she'd come here and rented a small cottage on the moors. Even with high-waisted gowns and voluminous skirts, she feared her pregnancy was too obvious. She could not cause a scandal, which would hurt her school and her students.

And she couldn't return to active involvement. Not unless she gave up her baby, and she was not going to do that. Her fear was that someday her child would learn a duke had asked for her hand in marriage, that he or she could have been born a legitimate child to wealth and privilege, except that his—or her—mother had said no.

It was for the *best*. Devon's sister Elizabeth was now engaged to a handsome earl, and the London scandal sheets were abuzz with the latest rumor about the Duke of March. In five days a ball was to be held at March House. It was the *on-dit* that he would announce his engagement at the ball. While there had been weeks of speculation as to the lady's identity, it apparently remained a mystery. Still, in five days, Devon would belong to someone else.

The path began to descend, slowly winding between boulders and gorse bushes. Sheep darted across the path, searching for grasses to nibble. Anne took slow steps, punctuating each sensible word that she spoke aloud with deep, hard breaths. "It. Is. For. The. Best."

A black-faced sheep looked up, eyed her doubtfully, and bleated.

There were no trees on the sweeping hills of the moors. She had a clear view of her cottage. Given that she was pregnant and unmarried, she'd wanted to be isolated. In the winter, though, she'd been very, very alone. She'd kept busy during those long nights by sewing in preparation for the baby and by reading. Though reading made her think longingly of Devon—

A carriage was rumbling up the track to her cottage. Sunlight lit an insignia on the door. It stopped near and the door swung open. Anne forgot to draw a breath, even when the outriders assisted an elegant lady to her path. It was Lady Cavendish, and, behind her, two other young women spilled out of the coach.

The servants moved sharply forward again as a white-gloved hand gracefully extended from the shadowy doorway. Another elegant woman was helped down the steps, a rose-trimmed hat hiding her face. Could this be Devon's other sister? Why on earth were they here?

Lady Cavendish clasped Anne's hands, then hugged her. She waved toward the two young ladies. "My sisters Elizabeth and Winifred. And this is"—she turned toward the tall lady who stepped gracefully forward—"our mother, the Duchess of March."

His mother? Anne blinked as the duchess approached and took her hand. Devon's mother was beautiful, of course, with vivid blue eyes. A rueful smile lifted the duchess's lovely mouth. Then she asked, "You are expecting my son's child?"

Anne couldn't speak. She managed a nod, with her face burning, then tried to execute a curtsy. The duchess stopped her. "You did not tell him?"

She felt so guilty for . . . for being pregnant and for not telling Devon she was. "I did not want to make things more complicated. He proposed to me, but marriage between us was impossible, and I feared that telling him about the child would . . ." Her voice died away.

"You thought my son would insist on marriage."

Anne gaped at the duchess, who took her hand and led her toward the cottage. "Let us go inside and discuss this."

Panic hit Anne. "Oh, no, Your Grace. It is just a cottage. It's very simple."

A musical laugh danced on the air. "I am quite sure it will be fine, my dear."

Caro moved close to Anne and whispered by her ear, "Mama wanted us to bring her to you so she could meet you. Devon has done nothing but slouch in a chair and stare at the wall since you left. The only time he showed any pleasure was when he went to visit your school."

He had gone to her school? It did not surprise her, but it touched her heart. He must be the only duke who had gone to a school for destitute girls in Whitechapel.

Inside, Anne quickly lit the stove and set a kettle on top. She tried to pull out one of her chairs for the duchess, but Devon's mother took it from her hands. "You will use this." The duchess smiled as Anne slowly lowered to the chair. "You must know why we have come, Miss Beddington. It is to encourage you to change your mind and accept Devon's proposal."

Was she in a dream? Anne pinched her arm and smothered a yelp of pain. "You could not want me as a daughter-in-law. I am ruined—"

"My dear, you have behaved with exemplary discretion since you left my son. You have done a wonderful thing to help impoverished children. Devon glows when he speaks your name. It is pride and admiration but also because he loves you. I have always urged him to marry for love. He challenged me to accept his love for you. I am sorry to say I could not at the beginning. Now I can see how much it hurts him to be without you. Treadwell tells me he is exactly as he was when he first returned from battle. He is grieving and lost. You helped him once. You could do so again, if you love him. You must tell me. Did you reject him because you do *not* love him?"

The duchess's speech left Anne whirling. "No . . . I . . . I love him very much. I said no to protect him and all of you! I do not want him to be the way he was before." It truly couldn't be because of her, could it? How could it be, if he was supposed to be ready to announce his engagement? She pushed up from the chair. "I wish to help him at once."

"I know, dear, and that is why I believe you must marry him," the duchess said.

Dark-haired Lizzie leapt forward. "Protecting us doesn't matter anymore! Caro and Charlotte are safely married, and I am going to be wed in a month's time. We would rather see Devon happy than watch him suffer his way through a duty marriage. Mama has refused to let any girl of the *ton* marry him, you know, when he is obviously so deeply in love with you. It would be a recipe for disaster."

"But isn't Devon going to announce his engagement?" Anne asked.

The duchess nodded. "I fear he has decided to marry someone he does not love."

Winifred, obviously the youngest of Devon's sisters, hastened to the whistling kettle. "My plan is to marry the Earl of Ashton, although the earl doesn't know it yet. It wouldn't bother him at all if Devon married you, Miss Beddington."

"You are not going to marry the Earl of Ashton," the duchess said swiftly. But then she sighed. "He loves you, Miss Beddington, and you love him. I want only to make this work. Tell me, are you willing to marry my son?"

* * *

Devon shut his eyes. He was in his study at March House, and his sisters had just returned from a trip to see Anne. Through Lady Julia, they had learned that Anne had taken a cottage on the moors.

He kept his eyes closed—what an irony that he was trying not to see. But Caro did not go away. She strode to him, and he heard Peregrine give a squeaky giggle as her swift pace bounced him up and down.

"We went to convince her to come back and agree to marry you," Caro declared. "But once we saw her, we knew it was *impossible*."

"Impossible?" He opened his eyes, jerked up in his chair. "Why? Has she found someone else?" Tension sent him off the seat and into rapid pacing on the study carpet. "Caro, she refused to marry me because of all of you—"

"That was why we all went to her—Mother, Lizzie, Win, and I. Now that Lizzie is engaged and Win has set her heart on Ashton, there is no need to be worried about marriage prospects."

"Win is not going to marry Ashton. And there is your husband to think of, Caro, as well as Charlotte's."

"Oh, rubbish, Devon. You asked her once already! This didn't bother you then—"

"He's afraid!" He turned as Win rushed through the study door. "He is afraid to ask her again, in case she says no. Our brother is afraid she refused him because she doesn't love him."

Caro said softly, "She loves you, Devon. *That* was why she refused you in the first place."

He winced and turned away. "That makes no sense. And she said she wasn't in love."

"When a woman loves a man, she does not want to hurt him. Of course she said she doesn't love you. She believed she had to walk away. But she is enceinte, Devon."

He spun on his heel to see Caro glaring fiercely at him. "She is expecting *your* child. It was quite obvious she is very, very near her time. Peregrine arrived early. You might have very little time to marry her before the baby comes."

"Yes!" Lizzie popped her head around the door. "There is no other choice, Devon. You must go to her. And you must hurry!"

Caro waved his other sisters away. She opened her mouth, but Devon stopped her with a shake of his head. "She told me she wants independence, Caro, not marriage."

"Devon, she is going to have your child!"

"I should force her into marriage out of duty and responsibility?"

"If that gets her to the altar, I would use it. I know she *loves* you. Before we left, I asked her if she believed it was right to deny you the chance to be a father to your child."

He blinked. He'd never known Caro to be so blunt or so harsh. "What did she say?"

"What could she say? She tried to look stoic and determined. She tried to bluster through an excuse. But she knew, in her heart, nothing could justify denying both you and her the chance to have a loving family. Please go to her, Devon. If you don't, Lizzie, Win, and I have decided we will work together to make your life a nightmare."

He quirked a brow. "How so?"

"Do you remember all the ways you used to tease us? Salamanders in our beds. Flour in my face powder, and a noxious-scented liquid in Lizzie's first bottle of perfume. The things we can do to *you* will be worse. If you refuse to marry Anne, I will throw giggling young women at you until you go mad."

Go mad. Ten months ago he'd thought he was going mad. Anne had forced him out of his self-imposed darkness. Now she was the one hiding.

"Do you still love her, Devon?"

"I'll always love her, Caro."

"Then go! Go marry the woman you love, Devon. After all the pain you've endured, I want you to have a happy ending. We all do."

He knew she was right. But he asked, "An ending?"

"Of your bachelor life. The beginning of a much richer and more wonderful life, I promise."

"No need to promise, Caro. I believe you."

Devon ducked beneath the eave of the low roof and rapped on the cottage door. He waited but heard nothing moving inside. He pounded again. His fist slammed into the door so hard the leather of his gloves split over his knuckles. "Anne! Are you there?"

There was no sound except the mournful moans of the wind. It was a typical English spring day on the moors—rain pelted his greatcoat and wind whipped across the back of his neck. His blood felt icy for reasons that had nothing to do with the weather on the moors. Was he too late? Where was Anne?

Panic gripped him. The same fear and tension that had haunted him in battle. *Something is wrong*. It was almost crippling, but he fought through it and headed for the stone stable. A pony munched hay, and as he stalked around the building, he almost collided with a stableboy.

"Where is your mistress?" He prayed the lad wouldn't say she had gone into labor. What if something had gone wrong? "I am the Duke of March," he added awkwardly. "A friend."

"My mistress went walking along the path." The lad pointed to a narrow track that went along the hills. "Up to the tor."

Then he saw her. A small figure trudging up the path. She was walking. Alone. Even from here, he could tell she was very rounded. Caro had said she could go into labor at any minute.

Next thing he knew, he was running up the path, pursuing her as fast as he could. Before he'd left, Lizzie had admonished, *You gave up far too easily!* Win had added, *If you love her, you have to keep fighting for her heart and never give in.* They were two of the most romantic girls in England. But they were right. He should have fought for her. For seven months he'd been introduced to every eligible gently bred girl in England, which had proven his point. No other woman could capture his heart as Anne had. And because he hadn't pursued her, he'd missed all those months while she'd been enceinte. He'd missed the chance to see her glow and change as their baby grew. "Anne!" he yelled. "Stop!"

She did, turning slowly. Rain lashed her. "Devon?"

He ran to her and swept her up in his arms. But she gave a squeak as he pressed her belly to him, and he immediately put her down. "Angel, I'm sorry." He had been an idiot. In battle, would he have given up so easily? He had struggled for hours to take a few yards of land, but he'd been willing to let the love of his life go. He hadn't wanted to treat Anne like someone who should be conquered. He'd loved her and he'd wanted her to have what she wanted. Even if it was a life that didn't include him. That was what his sisters didn't understand.

When a man was in love, he couldn't throw a woman over his shoulder and drag her back to his bedroom. He had no right to pursue a woman at any cost, as he'd done with Rosalind. Love meant accepting her choice, even if it broke his heart.

He was going to fight for her, but if she refused him again, he had no choice but to let her go.

"Devon, why have you come here? In four days you are supposed to be getting engaged."

"That was an unfounded rumor. But I'm hoping to get engaged today. Here. Now. There is no one for me, Anne, but you."

Her face paled. She touched her belly suddenly. He gathered her into his arms and began to carry her down the path. "All right. Not here," Devon said. "You shouldn't be walking in your condition. Certainly not alone, up a rocky path, in a storm."

"And you should not be carrying me, Devon. I fear we'll both fall."

A tender look came to Devon's eyes. Anne swallowed hard. It was a look that could steal a woman's heart. She loved him. Seven months had done nothing to change that. She still loved him breathlessly. Endlessly. Hopelessly.

"I came in hopes of sweeping you off your feet. Instead, I have to put you back down." He did so but tucked her hand into the crook of his arm. "You're right, as always. I can't sweep you away and make you do what I want. I tried to do that before—when I hauled you to your great-grandmother and insisted you go into Society. I wanted you so much, I unfortunately became the soldier I'd been in battle and tried to win you as I would a military mission. I hope you will believe I've learned my lesson. Years ago I felt I had to capture the woman I wanted. Now I've realized that loving you means I have to give you the choice. I want you, but I can't come and take you by force. All I can do is give you my offer one more time and hope you will say yes."

When Devon, a duke, said, *I've learned my lesson,* Anne went weak in the knees.

"I love you, Anne. I have the blessing of every member of my family to pursue you." He grinned. "They did more than give me their approval. They demanded I come to you at once."

She wanted to believe it. Once upon a time, she'd been a gently bred young lady who could dream of romance and love. Survival had made her practical. She loved this man, too much to allow him to make a choice he would eventually regret. "Your sisters told me I won't hurt their marriage prospects, but the scandal of our marriage will still hurt them. I was a whore," she said flatly. "How can I marry a duke and become a duchess? I'll never be accepted. I have to think of our baby. My tarnished reputation will affect our child."

"Believe me, Anne, no one in Society will dare say a word against you—"

"Devon, you have not bludgeoned any more men in Hyde Park, have you?"

"No. They know better than to provoke me. When you are my wife, they will treat you with respect."

"Grudgingly. Venom will be behind the politeness, and that will find a way of coming out."

He stopped and turned her to face him. He was white-faced, the wind whipping his wet hair. "Anne, what does it matter what anyone thinks? I don't care about your past, and I don't give a damn what hypocritical society matrons think of it. I love you for who you are. For seven months I've watched in awe as you opened your school and worked to change the world. You are the most amazing woman I've ever known." He ducked his head. "Or do you keep saying no because you don't feel I'm good enough for you?"

"Devon!"

Hesitantly, he reached out. The bulge of her belly

stood between them, and he rested his palm on the crest of the curve. "I want our child to be legitimate. I want to raise our baby with you. Let me have that, Anne. I promise to be a good husband and father. I know you want independence, but would you be willing to trust me and let me try to make you and our child happy?"

Her heart broke. Of course she wanted to marry him, and he had come here in a mad dash and deserved honesty. "I want to say yes, but I'm so afraid—"

Her stomach tightened so intensely, she couldn't speak. She splayed her hand over her belly, just below his. She had to pant for breath. He held her elbow, keeping her up. A whoosh of water soaked her between her thighs. "Goodness! I was walking alone because . . . because the midwives in the stews always claimed that a baby might come if a woman was active. I was getting impatient! I think I did too good a job—my water just broke. The baby is coming!"

The pains were coming quickly. Devon prayed the parson hadn't left the sitting room.

He'd had his servants bring the midwife and parson here, but Anne's cottage was surprisingly rustic and sparse. Water had boiled earlier on the stove, and now he used the warm water to bathe her face. He stroked back her sweat-dampened hair. How could he ever have let her walk away from him?

"I know what Society is like," she whispered. "I hate it for the fact that it holds innocent victims to blame. I despise the *ton* for condemning girls who are 'ruined' simply because a man takes advantage of them. I know I will never fit in with Society. You are a duke. You need a wife who is clever, witty, admired by the *ton*—"

She broke off. The pains were coming again. He pressed on her back as the midwife had instructed. "I want a wife who dazzles me every moment of the day—with her brilliant mind, her good heart, her sensuality, and her strength. The only woman who dazzles me is you, Anne."

"I don't know if I have the strength to stare down gossip." She flinched as the pain intensified. She arched against his hand. "I'm afraid that if I go back into Society, I'll discover I don't have any courage at all."

"You are the most courageous woman I've ever known, and I promise I will always be at your side. I'm not leaving now or ever."

"It's true—you are at my side now." Another pain came and forced Anne to stay quiet. Her breaths came in fierce puffs, and he coaxed her through it. That one had come without any rest between. The midwife had told them there would be a period of very fast, very intense pains, and then the real business of pushing the baby out would begin.

Most peers would stay in the study and drink through their wife's labor. Yet Devon was with her, soothing her, giving her courage. How could she keep him from being a true father to his child, just because she was afraid? She had been afraid in the brothel but determined to survive. She had been afraid when she'd discovered those poor innocents were being held prisoner, but she had rescued them. How could she be more afraid of the *ton* than of people like Madame and Mick Taylor?

Was it because she truly was ashamed? Devon wasn't. He told her he didn't care. He knew all the worst things about her and loved her anyway. He had risked his life in battle. How could she not risk far less to give this wonderful man the family he wanted? How could she be so cowardly that she couldn't accept love from this perfect man? "Oh, my God," she cried. "I've been an idiot—"

Another pain. Oh, God. Through a haze, she heard Devon tell her forcefully, "You have not, Anne. I understand why you are afraid. I wouldn't go home or go out in public because I couldn't see. I was happier hiding. I do understand. And I would never let you be hurt."

"Yes. I want to . . . to marry you. Yes!" Her words came out in a breathless jumble, but fear turned her heart to ice. "I've left it too late. It's too late!"

"Never," he assured her. He pressed a kiss to her forehead. Her hair was stringy with sweat. Then Devon went to the bedroom door, pulled it open, and hauled a man inside. She goggled. It was Reverend White from the village. Shielding his eyes, the reverend let Devon drag him to the head of her bed.

"We're ready to say our vows," Devon said, as though it was utterly normal to be wed in the middle of childbirth. "But you'll understand, sir, we should make this hasty."

Blushing fiercely, Reverend White sputtered, "Indeed. Yes, Your Grace. Quite quickly." He lay a book over his hand and clumsily flipped pages. Words began to flow over Anne. "We are gathered here," the reverend began austerely. Anne couldn't help it—she dissolved in giggles. Which stopped abruptly as she panted through a labor pain. When it eased, she saw both men peering at her, looking awkward.

"Her full name is Anne Mariah Beddington," Devon said.

"Do you, Anne Mariah Beddington, take this man—"

The rest was lost to another spasm in her womb, and she cried, "Yes. I do. Yes."

"Could we do this faster?" Devon asked.

The poor man tried, though he stumbled hopelessly over Devon's extensive name: Devon William George Stephen Audley. Then he got to the moment where the question was done, and Devon had to give his answer. "I do," Devon said. "Nothing on heaven and earth will keep me from taking this woman as my wife."

"Then I now pronounce you man and wife," the reverend concluded. "Now, as swiftly as I can, I will complete the marriage lines, and you will sign them."

As the man took a seat at Anne's small writing desk, Devon brought the midwife back in. The woman hurried to her, lifted her skirts, and looked. "The head is beginning to crown."

Anne winced. "What a madwoman I was to leave this so dangerously close."

But Devon took her hand and kissed her. "It's done now. You are my wife. You aren't escaping me ever again."

The reverend returned with the marriage document. Devon signed it, then held it for her so she could. With a swift stroke of the pen, she became Devon's wife.

Anne had thought, with the head making an appearance, that the business would be swift. But apparently the head could recede again. The true work of labor had just begun. She pushed, breathed, screamed, and strained. She was dizzy with pain and exhaustion and worry. Surely it shouldn't take this long. Not when the baby was so close. But no matter how hard she pushed, she seemed to get nowhere. At one horrible moment, the midwife told her to *resist* the urge to push. She tried, her body rebelling. With Devon holding her hand, speaking firmly but lovingly, she managed to do it. She understood why men had gone into battle for him. He had a way of making her believe she could do this.

"All right, Miss—"

"Actually," Devon corrected the midwife in his elegant drawl, "Miss Beddington—I mean, Mrs. Audley—is my wife and is the Duchess of March."

"Duchess?" The woman blanched. "Goodness. Well, Your Grace, you must give a good push." The midwife clasped Anne's leg and pressed Anne's foot to her hip. Anne gave a huge push, but the midwife coaxed her for more and more.

Then Devon said, "Anne, there's a head."

She was too exhausted to say anything, but she laughed for joy.

"Another push for the shoulder, Your Grace," the midwife urged.

After that, she felt a slippery sort of motion, then a cry filled the room. "Good and healthy," the woman crooned in a triumphant tone.

Anne felt triumphant, too, in a wash of joy that left her giddy.

"A blanket, if you please, Your Grace," the midwife said to Devon. Then she brought the bundle-wrapped infant to Anne.

"Is he a boy or is she a girl?" Anne asked Devon, confused.

He blinked. "I forgot to look."

She laughed, delirious with relief and happiness. "I thought dukes were anxious for sons."

"I'd love a daughter too. Though if she's like her mother, I will have gray hair very soon." Gently, he parted the blanket and they both peeked.

"There, you are safe," Anne giggled. "A boy." Thank heaven, she'd found sense and courage and married Devon, so his son could be his heir. And, thank heaven, Devon had proved to be such a patient man, willing to wait for her. Willing to pursue her.

The midwife cut the baby's cord and tied it. Anne discovered the work was not quite done—she was ruthlessly massaged for many minutes until the afterbirth was dealt with. She had also forgotten the worry about bleeding, until the midwife gave a satisfied nod. "I think the bleeding is lessening. A very good sign. I believe all has gone well." The gray-haired woman bustled to the side of the bed and helped Anne put baby to breast.

"Oh, dear," Anne said to Devon as she finally managed to get the little mouth to latch on. "I thought this would come naturally and happen with ease."

"It's an adventure for us to explore together," he said. "My darling wife."

Their son sucked and stared up with surprisingly wise eyes. He looked like a wizened old gentleman with wrinkled skin, a squashed head, and huge violet eyes. Eyes like Devon's. A ring of dark hair ran around the back of his head. "What a journey you have had, little one," Anne said softly. She looked to Devon. "Would you like to hold him?"

"A dream come true," he answered, a glorious smile on his lips. "Just as you are to me."

The poor man did not get the chance of a wedding night for four weeks. It worried Anne, but Devon did not seem to mind. He insisted she rest and recover, and he spent almost all his time with their son, whom they named William, for that was the name of both her father and Devon's.

Finally the night came when she was ready. Dressed in a gold peignoir, with her hair loose, Anne stood in front of her cheval mirror. Her hair had returned to its natural color and fell to her waist. She had changed in other ways too. Having William had made her plumper. Her breasts were large and generous. Just looking at their reflection seemed to spur them to fill with milk, and she winced. She pulled the satin away, prayed they wouldn't leak.

She stared at the connecting door to Devon's room. They were staying at Eversleigh, one of his four estates. On a wedding night, did she go to his room or did he come to hers? She hadn't thought to ask. She had pursued him so fiercely at the beginning of their relationship. Then he had pursued her, chasing her to London, then the moors, forcing her to stop hiding and to find happiness. This time, who should pursue whom?

But one question worried her more: What did he want in a wife? She'd seduced him boldly to become his mistress, but should she now be demure in bed? Normally, dukes married untutored innocents. If she was wanton, would it remind him of her past?

He'd said he didn't care about her past. He'd told her he loved her. She knew he must. No man would go through all the hellish bother she'd put Devon through unless he loved her deeply. But she didn't know what to do for her wedding night. . . .

Gathering courage, she stalked to the connecting door, pulled it open. And walked right into Devon's solid, robe-covered chest. They had met halfway.

Grinning, he kissed her. But she was as stiff and awkward as she'd been at the beginning. He must have sensed it, for he drew back. Shivering, she admitted, "I don't know what to do. I don't know how to make love to you . . . as your wife."

He wrapped his arms around her and drew her into his bedroom. "I want you to be you."

"But wives should be . . . proper."

He laughed. She frowned. She was on tenterhooks, and he *chuckled*. "I love your wanton sensuality, Anne," he assured her. "There's nothing wrong with it. It doesn't prove you are sinful. There is no rule that states you must lie beneath me, stiff as a board and not enjoying yourself, because you are my wife."

She had to laugh too. He did make her fears sound . . . silly.

"I love you, Duchess Anne. You bewitch me. And this is a partnership—in bed and out."

As though to prove his words, he carried her to his enormous bed and laid her upon it. He gracefully moved over her so his mouth was at her quim, his thighs were on either side of her head, and his erection was wobbling, upside down, before her eyes. She arched up and took him in her mouth. She loved the rich, earthy tang of his skin, the sensation of the shaft swelling and pulsing. Devon had to stop kissing her quim to moan deeply. Then together, as partners, they licked, suckled, nibbled, and drove each other to wild ecstasy.

Anne wailed her climax and fell back to the bed, floating on a cloud of pleasure.

"The perfect wedding night," he murmured. He moved around so their mouths were in line and kissed her. She could taste her juices on his lips, knew he tasted his flavor on her mouth. He hardened almost instantly and slid inside her.

"Mine," he whispered against her lips. "Mine always."

"And you are mine," she answered.

He was every bit as naughty with her now as he was when she'd been his mistress. Gentlemen, it appeared, always liked their pleasures to be wicked. She climaxed over and over, until all she had to do was gasp when he was inside her and she came.

Finally he collapsed over her, braced on his forearms. "You've drained me, angel."

She wrapped her arms around him, and they fell to the bed together. He groaned. "We might not make love again for another month. It might take me that long to regain my strength."

She was worried—until he laughed. He nibbled her ear, his breath a warm caress. She was snuggled in his arms, sleepy and content.

He whispered, "Now that William is a month old, love, I want to take you to London. Before the *ton* leaves for the country for the summer, my mother is determined to hold a ball for us."

"London?" Panic gripped her. Suddenly she knew she still wanted to hide. But as Devon's duchess, she couldn't. She couldn't avoid London forever. "I don't want to disappoint your mother. Of course we will go."

He kissed her forehead. Then her nose, her lips, and each throbbing, aching nipple. "She always wanted me to marry for love, and she was right. I could never have been happy with anyone but you, Anne."

London meant facing scandal.

Anne had feared one—she was so terrified Devon and his family would be hurt. Of course, their marriage caused shock, horror, and a tremendous furor. At every ball, rout, and musicale, matrons traded gossip behind fluttering fans. Devon was determined to charge through all of the whispered talk. He glared down everyone with icy ducal hauteur. He threatened men who gave her even an appraising look. He took William for strolls in the parks in a perambulator, which dukes simply did not do. Society was calling him the "mad, besotted duke." He must be deeply hurt to be called mad, and it was all her fault.

Tonight was to be his mother's ball—the one that had been postponed when Devon came to the moors. The dowager duchess was hosting a grand event to introduce her daughter-in-law to Society. Anne felt as though she were about to face cannons and a charging army. She had accompanied Devon's mother and Caro to the most fashionable modiste in London, and she wore a gleaming dress of ivy-green silk. Small emeralds adorned her hair.

As she stepped out at the top of the stairs, Devon was waiting in the foyer. His eyes gleamed when he saw her.

"You are beautiful," he said softly. "And I made a good choice."

"In me?" she asked, confused.

"Yes, and in these." He drew a long, slim box from his pocket. Inside was a necklace of huge emeralds—a dozen of them, each the size of a robin's egg. Devon lifted it, dropped the box, and stepped behind her. The stones were cool, heavy, dazzling against her skin. He fastened the clasp, then kissed the nape of her neck. Instantly, she was hot with desire.

"Now, Anne, give me the chance to show the world what you mean to me."

She had no idea what he meant, but she tipped up her chin and walked with him to the ballroom. At his side, she greeted the two hundred guests. Then, with her hand in his, Devon led her out to dance. Couples whirled around in the waltz, which was considered a most scandalous dance. But Devon stopped. "I wanted to waltz with you. Unfortunately, that will have to wait."

"Wait?" she echoed. "For what?"

Instead of taking her in his arms, he dropped to one knee before her. Other couples had to weave around him. Many came to an abrupt halt. At the edge of the onlookers, Anne spotted the dowager, and she had a very delighted gleam in her eye.

Devon gazed up at her. "Anne, my love, will you do me the honor of becoming my wife?"

The music halted with a screech. Every head craned toward them, because her husband was proposing to her. *Again.* She gazed helplessly at him, but his smile only widened.

"Marry me all over again, my duchess. I love you, Anne. You are the most beautiful woman in the world. You have the kindest heart, the most generous nature, but more than that: You are my love. I asked you to marry me once before, but you refused me—"

Fierce whispers washed over the crowd at that.

"You asked me again and I said yes," she pointed out.

"Then say yes to me this time, love. I want the world to know I love you."

Everyone waited, straining to hear.

"Yes," she whispered through a very tight throat. "I love you, too, Devon."

He surged up, swept her into his arms, and kissed her. In front of two hundred stunned guests, she had just become engaged—to her husband. She could hear the talk buzzing. *A duke marrying a courtesan for* love? *How scandalous. How sordid.*

How perfect, Anne thought. And by proposing to her in public, Devon had made himself even more shocking than she was. She loved him. She wanted fervently to show him how much. "Can we escape?" she whispered. "Right now?"

"Eager for another wedding night?"

"I'd like to celebrate our . . . um . . . engagement by engaging in a little sin. But we can't run out on two hundred guests. We should be proper—"

"Anne, angel, neither of us is proper. At heart, we are both wild. So let us be wild." Devon grinned and set her down on her feet. Despite the shocked gasps they provoked, they darted across the ballroom hand in hand, toward the doors. Toward the future. A glorious future, Anne thought—one that had begun the very moment they had engaged in a bit of delicious sin.

Read on for a teaser chapter of
Sharon Page's THE CLUB...

Chapter One

London, May 1818

"How am I going to explain to a man I've paid that I do not actually want him to make love to me?"

Jane St. Giles, Lady Sherringham, asked the question of her image in the cheval mirror, but her reflection could provide no answers, obviously, that she could not think of herself.

So speaking aloud to it was quite pointless.

Groaning, Jane stalked around the brothel's bedchamber, biting her thumbnail, and dreading the knock that was soon to come.

She had come here searching for her best friend Delphina, Lady Treyworth. She had come for answers. She'd paid a veritable fortune for the services of one of the young men employed by Mrs. Brougham, the woman who ran this Georgian house on the fringe of Mayfair, known simply as the "The Club." But since it had been a ruse, she now had to convince the man to leave without touching her.

Would he be angry?

She shivered.

Would he come to her aroused? Fear coiled, tight and cold, around her heart. She knew—though she had never experienced it with her own late husband—a man could become belligerent when he was aroused and the woman refused to play.

With Sherringham, she'd never had the courage to refuse to play. She had always toed his line, terrified how brutal he would be if she pushed him too far. But he had now been dead for thirteen months, and she no longer had to endure the nights he came to her bedroom. She no longer had to fight to find the nerve to send him away, then despise herself when she couldn't.

Jane paced, hugging her chest.

Surely a large tip would soothe any ruffled . . . well, whatever might be ruffled on a randy young man. The man she'd hired had intimate relations for money, so wasn't money the most important thing? And there were dozens of society ladies in attendance. Any reasonably attractive, healthy, and erect young man wouldn't be frustrated for long.

Oh, dear God, she thought, and she took hold of one of the bedposts for support.

The ostentatious bed almost filled the entire room. Shackles of iron—lined with velvet—hung from the carved gilt bedposts. Jane's stomach roiled as she stared at the relief crafted on the posts: entwined serpents and something that might be a sword, or could be the male privy part.

She remembered the afternoon two months ago when her two dearest friends had told her their husbands brought them to this club. Despite the sun pouring into her morning room and the cheery promise of the early spring day, a shiver of dread had rippled down her spine. "But ladies do not join a gentleman's club," she had said slowly.

"This one, they do," Charlotte had breathed. Her

eyes had been wide and in their cornflower blue depths, Jane had read surprising horror and shame.

"That is the novelty of this club," Del had explained, her voice as demure as if she were speaking of a successful rout. "The gentlemen bring their wives—in costume. Every Friday evening, the ladies are required to dress as nuns." Then her voice had lowered and her lashes had dropped. "I still have the marks on my derriere from the spankings with the crop."

Jane had felt her mouth form a soundless O of horror. She'd endured Sherringham's punishments with the flat of his hand, but he'd never dared touch her with a crop.

Now, she shuddered as she gazed around the bedchamber. *Del, is this horrible club the reason that you've disappeared?*

A sharp rap echoed on the door and Jane jolted so abruptly she stubbed her toe on the post. "Madam? May I enter?"

Her hired man possessed a seductive voice—low-timbered, not entirely cultured, but with a growling note that sent a shiver of fear . . . it must be fear . . . down her spine. What did it signify that he spoke so politely? Would the sort of prostitute who had an educated voice be easier to manage or more difficult?

"Y—yes," she answered shakily.

She had not even removed her cloak and she had chosen to wear her widow's weeds, with the veil lowered to shroud her face. But still, as the door opened, she turned her face so no one would see her, and waited with rigid shoulders for the door to click, the signal her male prostitute had shut it behind him.

While her husband had generally smelled of sweat, drink, and other women's perfume, this man was preceded by a combination of citrusy bergamot and sultry sandalwood. She certainly couldn't smell his perspiration, and oddly, he didn't smell as though he had come to her from another woman.

But really, that didn't matter. All she had to do was get rid of him. There was no reason to feel so unnerved. She'd survived a whole half hour so far in this wretched club, after all.

But before she could force herself to face him, he asked, "Is—is there something wrong, love?"

Concern laced his gentle voice, and there was a surprising vulnerability in his hesitation. Obviously he wasn't accustomed to a woman who looked as though she wanted to hide from him.

Jane glanced to the cheval mirror to see what he looked like, but the glass only reflected part of his side. She saw a large hand clad in a black leather glove, and a long, long leg in well-tailored trousers. A lean line of hip that vanished into a tailcoat, a glimpse of a very broad shoulder, and that was all.

Big. He was big and male. Panic flared in her chest and she struggled to breathe. *He can't hurt you. Here you can scream. You can scream and bring help and he has no right to hurt you.*

She must search inside to find greater strength. She'd vowed to herself that this time—finally—she would take action. How many times had she made that promise before, then taken the easy path, and slipped back into being a coward? And because she had been a coward, Delphina had disappeared. Del was in trouble.

"Turn around, love."

Grasping for that courage, Jane did. "I am so sorry, but—"

Her words—her very thought—died abruptly. The man stood by the wall and leaned against it in a lazy, relaxed way, and though several feet separated them, she had the sudden sense of the room shrinking in on her.

Shoulders—he had shoulders that seemed as wide as her legs were long. His legs, crossed casually at the ankles, stretched endlessly in front of her, and when her gaze followed them upward from the tip of his gleaming boots, the moment lasted a lifetime.

A black leather mask left his eyes a mystery, but beneath she saw he had not shaved—dark stubble ringed his square jaw. A scar forked down beneath the mask, another cut deeply into his chin.

But his lips quirked up in a kindly, sympathetic smile and deep dimples showed in his cheeks. He held out his hand in a coaxing sort of way—as though offering food to a timid deer. "It's all right, love. I won't hurt you. I'm at your command, after all. Your slave, so to speak."

At her command. The exact words to remind her that, for once, she had power here.

But, faced with him, she didn't feel powerful.

"You are in mourning?" He took a slow, easy step away from the wall toward her.

"No, no!" she said hurriedly and she scrambled, back until her legs trapped her skirts against the bed. And as her heart pattered wildly, she saw the perfect escape.

"I—I mean, my mourning year has not quite passed." She fluttered her hands—it was no stretch to act like a nervous woman who had changed her mind. "And the truth is, I—I was . . . lonely. So I thought I could . . . but I can't. Not with you. Not now."

He was so near she could see his eyes in the oval holes of the mask. Indigo blue eyes surrounded by abundant black lashes. The bed pushed back on her as she tried to retreat.

Another slow step brought him terrifyingly closer. Her heart thundered. He had not understood.

"I can't . . . use you tonight. I—I've changed my mind. I'll pay you . . . extra, if you want. In case you are disappointed—"

His eyes lit up with understanding. "So that's why you did not give your name."

What on earth did he mean? She did give a name. A false one.

Goodness, the way he tilted his head, the thick black hair, the shape of his mouth, the straight, attractive nose—why was it all so suddenly familiar?

Ridiculous. When would she have ever encountered a male prostitute in her daily life?

But she couldn't tear her gaze away from his mouth—his sensual lips were wide and generous. His lower lip was much larger, much fuller than his upper. Again, she felt as though she had stared at this mouth before. His skin was the color of clover honey, a sign he had spent much time under a hot sun.

Surprising for a man who earned his living in a bedroom—though perhaps he hadn't been doing it for very long.

His lips smiled again, smugly. He knew she was staring and he must think it meant she desired him, this large man who stood between her and the door.

A dull roaring began in her ears. He wasn't going to take no for an answer.

"I hope I have not frightened you, madam."

"No, no, you've done nothing wrong. You've been . . ." What should she say here? "Lovely. Yes, you have been so very . . . wonderful, and I hope you are not upset. I *will* pay you. You won't have wasted your time—"

Then he was there—right in front of her, filling her vision with a black tailcoat and a white embroidered vest.

"Of course I'm not upset. But if you don't want me, I understand." He bowed over her hand and lifted it so slowly to his lips that she forgot to breathe and her legs swayed beneath her.

"No." She jerked her hand back from her prostitute's mouth.

"Do I not please you, Lady Sherringham?"

"Stop. Stop!" She dragged her hand away, aware of a louder rushing sound in her ears. She had not given her real name. Mere moments before he had even said that himself.

"How do you know who I am?" she cried.

His expression revealed him then. She knew exactly why he had looked familiar and she was so startled that she tumbled backward onto the soft, deep bed, grasping at air as she fell. Her skirts flew up, her legs parted as she tumbled back and she slammed her elbow against the bedpost in her fall.

Shooting pain and humiliation changed her shock to anger as she lay back on the bed in a tangled heap. "You aren't my hired man! I recognize you now. You are Delphina's brother. You are Lord Wickham."

Known, for very good reason, as *Lord Wicked.*

How could he be here, in this revolting club that had destroyed Del?

"I am surprised you recognize me, Lady Sherringham."

Jane scrambled up on her elbows. She saw it now—she saw the handsome young rake of twenty in the masked face of this older man. He had been Christian

Sutcliffe when she'd known him—his father had still been alive. Eight years had changed him. As well as the scars he now bore, his cheekbones were more prominent, his face more deeply lined. He was broader, tanned, and far more muscular.

"I suppose you would be surprised," she snapped, over the pounding of her heart. "After all, you've been away, on the Continent, in India, and the Far East. You have been everywhere but in England, where you could have helped your sister before she was forced to marry Lord Treyworth."

"And I remember you," he murmured, looking down on her. "The tartar."

Jane glared up at the dark blue eyes. But for the color, his eyes were just like Del's. "What are you doing here," she demanded, "in England *and* in this disgusting club?"

She dragged her legs closed as quicly as she could. Falling onto the bed. Of all the useless things for her to do.

She started as Wickham held out his black leather-clad hand to her. He didn't jump on her, as Sherringham would have done, and take advantage of the situation. He wore a bemused smile that barely reached his eyes as he helped her back on her feet. She had known Del's brother for three years before he'd left England and they'd never had a conversation that didn't include an argument.

A hundred questions raced through her mind, but oddly, she picked the most inconsequential to blurt out. "Where is the man I hired?"

Wickham's coal black eyebrows jerked up at that, above his mask. "Trussed up with his own selection of velvet ropes and stowed in a closet," he answered impatiently. "Now, Lady Sherringham, talk to me. What do you know of this club?"

His hand closed on hers, large, warm even through the supple leather.

"I'm not a member, if that's what you mean," she said. "And I asked you first—"

"Your husband did not bring you?" he continued, speaking over her indignation and cutting off her words.

"No, but I do know that Del's husband brought her. For over a year, Treyworth forced her to come here. She admitted to me that she was frightened of this place."

There—let him chew on that, the irresponsible wretch. He'd never once tried to help Del after he left England.

He lifted her with ease and Jane had to reach out and grasp his other arm to steady herself as he abruptly pulled her to her feet.

"If you believed Delphina was afraid of this place, Lady Sherringham, why did you come and hire a man for the night?"

"It wasn't for... for passion, if that's what you are thinking—which I am sure is all you've ever thought of." All her hopeless anger and fear was rushing to the surface now, making her tongue sharp and wicked. She jerked her hands from his and scurried around him, so she was the one closest to the door. "It was a ruse. I was stopped at the door and taken to Mrs. Brougham, so I told her I was a lonely and wealthy widow. She wouldn't let me enter unless I—I bought a man. Why did you tie him up in the closet?"

"To question you, Lady Sherringham."

"You were spying on me?"

"I'd gone to your house to talk to you about Del," he said. "You were leaving, obviously disguised, so I was intrigued enough to follow."

"Obviously disguised?"

"I know your husband has been dead for over a year. I heard he wasn't worth mourning."

"I assume, that if you were following me, you don't know where Del is?"

She saw the sharp flash of pain in his eyes, and he leaned heavily on the carved column of the bed. "No. Do you?"

"No!" Jane threw up her hands in exasperation. "That is why I am here. Her husband told me that she had gone to the Continent. But I know that is impossible. I was the one who talked about running away. Del and Charlotte didn't have the will—"

"Running away?"

In the end, she had not had the courage either to escape her husband. But she did not tell Wickham that. Instead a horrible thought began to take root. "Why are you in England?" she demanded. "Is it a coincidence?"

"Del wrote me to tell me she was afraid of her husband, that she had been debased by him, and she was afraid for her very life."

"So *finally,* you came home to help her."

Firelight glinted off his dark eyes. "Yes."

She felt the wild, foolish need to hurt him—to punish him. "Del *is* terrified of her husband, Treyworth. I know he beats her, but he does it in ways that do not leave marks."

"Christ," Lord Wickham muttered.

Jane jabbed her finger toward his broad chest. "She endured whippings at this club. She was forced to . . . to do things with multiple men at one time! She—"

He surged forward and clamped his hand over her mouth. She sucked in panic and the smell of fine leather. "Stop it," he growled. "This helps no one."

She couldn't breathe. Dizziness swamped her.

He bent close. "When you open your mouth, will it be to tell me something of use?"

Gritting her teeth, fighting fear, she nodded and his hand moved away. She pulled in a long breath. "What did Treyworth say?" she gasped out. "How did he explain Del's disappearance?"

"He told me, in a blind rage, that she had run off with a lover. Then he tried to force me out of his home at sword point—"

"Tried?"

"I got hold of his damned sword and snapped it in two." He raked his hand through his dark hair, leaving it in shiny black disarray.

He had snapped a sword in two? "I'm afraid he killed her." Jane was astonished she'd managed to get out the words without giving in to tears.

She should have tried harder. She should have forced Del to escape Treyworth. She should have had courage for once in her—

"So you think that." Wickham stalked away from her, over to the mantel, and braced his hands against it. His body gave a long shudder, then stilled. "I've found no evidence of it."

"Neither have I."

He turned in surprise, his face stark with anguish. It seemed . . . that he cared about Del, after all. But anger still boiled in her blood. Why could rakish Lord Wicked not have discovered that he possessed a heart a few months earlier? Or a few years earlier?

"And you came here, looking for her?"

Jane shook her head. "I did not think I would find her here. Because Charlotte still comes here, and Charlotte insisted that nothing had happened to Del here.

Charlotte—Lady Dartmore—is our other friend. She was very convincing, but I didn't believe her. You see, Charlotte has changed—I cannot define how, but I know she has. I cannot trust anything Charlotte says anymore, because she still loves her husband and always will."

Wickham was gaping at her, obviously lost somewhere in her rapid words.

"I came here looking for some . . . some sort of clue. Answers. I really do not know if this club has anything to do with Del's disappearance, but I know she was afraid of this place. And I know she was becoming more and more frightened."

"She told you that, too?"

"No, I know it because she began to refuse to talk to me. Only a woman who is very afraid would stop talking to her best friends."

"But she wrote to me," he muttered and he stared down at the flickering flames.

The mantel clock ticked away cheerfully and the fire crackled as it would in any drawing room, unaware that danger and sin lurked everywhere in this evil club.

"Obviously she felt you would help her," she said softly.

Could she really trust Del's brother? Had he finally accepted his responsibility, or was he here for a sinister reason? Could she tell if he was lying from his expression? She had always been able to tell when Sherringham had been lying, but she rather thought he made it deliberately easy for her. It was, for Sherringham, just another form of torture.

For two weeks, she had been writing desperate correspondence to Treyworth and making frantic visits to Charlotte in the hopes she would convince them that Del must be in danger. She hadn't expected Treyworth to agree with her—he was the most likely suspect, after all. But with Charlotte so adamantly certain that Del really had gone away, Jane had begun to think she was mad and delusional.

But if Del had written to her absent brother and begged him for help, she must have been truly afraid.

Which meant Jane had no time to waste. "You are perfect," she said to Wickham.

"I beg your pardon?" He jerked away from the fireplace to fully face her, so quickly that his thick dark hair flew across his brow.

"I have to search the club, but it is really for couples. Together we can get into rooms that I could not on my own, and—"

"No."

"What do you mean 'no'?"

"It's not a difficult concept, Jane Beau—Lady Sherringham," he corrected. He had almost used her maiden name. "You are going to leave this bedroom, and take your well-bred bottom out of this club. You are going to go home where you will be safe."

"I will not. And I'm not innocent—I might have a title, but I have never once been protected from the dark and dirty side of life, my lord."

A dark brow lifted. "Indeed. But you need me to partner you."

She felt her eyes narrow with suspicion. "I need a gentleman I can trust to help me get into the most secret parts of this club."

"But the problem is that you can't trust me."

Her stomach dropped away.

"Do you know what I originally planned to do, sweeting?"

The endearment raised the hair on the back of her neck. They were no longer speaking as equals with a common goal. He suddenly seemed larger, colder, and far more intimidating. Eight years ago they used to argue and spar whenever they met. Now he felt like a stranger to her.

"What did you plan to do?" Her words came slowly, hesitantly.

"I was intending to carry the ruse to its end, and ask you about Del while you were floating in the delicious aftermath of your many climaxes."

It took a moment for her wits to resume function after he had growled the word *climaxes.* "You were going to . . . to *sleep with me*?"

"Yes. For all I knew, you were involved in my sister's disappearance up to your pretty neck. I didn't plan to reveal that I knew you and that I was not your gigolo, until I realized you weren't going to invite me into bed."

"I would never hurt Del! You really are wicked. Wicked. Wicked. Wicked." She hated the childish sound of her words, but she couldn't think of any other to describe him.

"Which only proves, sweeting, that you don't belong here. You can't trust me, and if this place is what you say it is I doubt you could trust anyone else here. I believe Del is alive. I'm certain she's alive. And I'll find her. But you are going home."

"No, I—"

"I'm sure Mrs. Brougham already suspects your motives for coming here, since it appears this club is intended for gentlemen to bring their wives. She would have to wonder why you came alone, in widow's weeds, when your husband never brought you."

"She won't know who I am. I gave her a false name, asked her not to give it to you—I mean, to her employee."

"It doesn't matter who you are. She has to be wondering what it is that you really want."

Jane frowned. He could be right. Mrs. Brougham had insisted she hire one of the men, and she had played along to allay suspicion. What if Mrs. Brougham had been testing her and had hoped to use the prostitute to keep her busy and preoccupied?

But how could he think she could just go home? He had left Del. He had no understanding of what a person did for someone they cared for.

She could not waste anymore time with Lord *Wicked.* So she did what she would have done with Sherringham. She lowered her head obediently and mumbled. "All right. You must be right. I'll go home." She jerked up her head and met his blue eyes—it gave the convincing touch. "But you have to tell me what you find."

"Of course," he agreed, and she knew he was lying. "I will escort you to the front door."

"I am sure that you will," she muttered. But she knew from what Delphina had told her that there was a back door to the club. Brothels always had them—an escape route in case the law appeared.

She had prayed that Del had used that to escape the club, if she had met danger here. The problem was, she had no idea what Del might be running from, or where she would go. She wasn't anywhere where Jane had desperately hoped she would be—Del hadn't sought refuge with any friends or at any of Treyworth's country estates.

For Jane, tonight, that hidden door wouldn't be a way out of hell. It would be a way in.

Also available from *Rouge*:

TO SEDUCE A BRIDE

Nicole Jordan

The thrill of the chase…

Free-spirited Lilian Loring doesn't believe in love. For her, marriage is best avoided entirely, despite what her parents – and society – think.

So when the charismatic Marquess of Claybourne – a notorious rake – begins to show interest, she goes into hiding in a scandalous boarding house.

Never having had a woman discourage his advances before, Claybourne is set on winning Lilian's hand – even if he must besmirch his reputation…